Period
Pieces

Eleanore Hill

Beta Books 2014

Period Pieces © copyright 2014
Beta Books Eleanore Hill
ISBN 978-0-930012-16-8
Cover art Stanley Trent Bemis

www.eleanorehill.com

Books by Eleanore Hill

The Family Secret: A Personal Account of Molestation
The Last American Housewife: Pieces of a Marriage
Period Pieces (when Marty becomes her own man!)

How to Cook for Your Dog, by M. Bowser

(and more to come)
The Homed (a novel)
The Gingerbread Girl (short stories)
The Corduroy Leopard (collection of stories)
In the Aftermath of an Overdose
(an account of a death and funeral)
& more: The Landlady; Coffee Talk…

Beta Books is an imprint of Mudborn Press
www.betabooks.us limited editions, ARCs
also
www.bandannabooks.com college classics

Contents

JOHN

SAL

MARTY

FLYNN

FLYNN AT LAST

MARTY

ALEX AT LAST

MARTY

The Marty Series

Period Pieces is the third volume in the Marty Series, centering on the ordinary and yet remarkable life of one Marty. Eleanore Hill's prose takes you inside and outside the development and sexual matchups of Marty, from the 1940s hardscrabble life through marriage to mature selfhood and independence.

To catch you up, the first volume, *The Family Secret*, covers Marty's childhood (Mama's main helper in raising the other kids in the family), teens (being noticed by boys; even in a beauty pageant), and early adulthood, typical of many daughters—with the exception in her case of two decades of molestation.

The second in the series is titled *The Last American Housewife*, denoting Marty's marriage with Alex. By the beginning of the Sixties, however, the traditional roles of wife and husband were shifting. Even to succeed as a "housewife," and mother of three grown children, would not sustain their life together.

After the divorce (*Period Pieces*: periods through her 56th year), Marty's role changed dramatically. She retained the house (but Alex lived in a camper next door), and no one else but Marty was willing to offer space to her old, frail, failing father (yes, that one). And other men now entered her life, often for five years at a time. But Marty is no longer a "housewife," she is the landlady "with men underfoot."

The reader may notice a style shift within this book—one piece may be written in first person ("I"), and the next in third person ("She"). The ambiguous style in this series is indebted to the fashion of "New Journalism," in which the writer is often the major participant in the unfolding story.

Introduction

When I turn fifty my body chemistry turns on me. It gives me a clear eye with which to view men. And a sarcastic tongue. I am no longer a female, but rendered just a human being without the need for a male. I begin to wait out their deaths to free me. Surrounded by thge men I've had in my life all along, I calculate how long they'll live, and how old I'll be when my real life can begin. This clarity of viewing men for the first time without my female longings intact is baffling. How did I ever "believe" in one man after another as someone I needed, craved, desired, and couldn't live with or without. And as each one passed emotionally out of my life, they stayed around in body, taking up my time and space as before. I learned I could treat them like furniture, side-stepping them, move them around, be in control of them, as was with any other object underfoot. They seemed to need me after I stopped needing them. And so I took advantage, as they had, of using them to do jobs around the place. The Place being my house and property, which was my half of the divorce settlement. And when a woman owns a piece of property, there will be people hanging around to squat on it with her. If I'd lost everything in the settlement, rented a small room, and always scraped for a living, there wouldn't be a man in sight. Part of my appeal was ownership of something. Anything will do to attract a male when you are a female.

These men consisted of: my ex-husband who lived next-door due to the division of property. He got the half acre next to mine, which we had bought during the marriage because of my foresight. He never wanted to buy the lot because we'd have to pay taxes on it. That's a testament to his ability to invest in the future. Because of me, we bought the half acre next to our half acre because it was only twelve thousand dollars. During the divorce, it went up to sixty thousand without water, and with water, a hundred and twenty thousand. And now with a house it's worth a half million. After the divorce he developed the property in those steps, living in the family camper which wasn't declared as an asset, and began building his house according to County code, after practicing on our house for twenty-five years, doing everything wrong. I inherited a house and half acre that had every County inspector coming out making me comply. That's why I decided these men who were hanging around and had contributed to my problems, could be put to work to solve them. After all, before I lost my lust for men, what did I know? I believed they were intelligent, caring creatures. I didn't have the film plucked from my eye until my estrogen levels began to subside.

There was my father, aged and broken, who had molested me as a child, who was too pathetic to turn out into the cold. Like the grasshopper in winter, he came to my doorstep, and I discovered enough pity left in my heart for his condition and situation to let him in to stay. I figured he wouldn't live long. He'd smoked for sixty years, was seventy with a bad cough, weighed a hundred pounds of psoriasis-covered skin and bones, and was frail beyond belief. It was as if my eye refused to adjust to his visage. I gave him the front bedroom on the opposite side of the house from me, and avoided him most of the time. His social life was at the Carrow's coffee counter talking to the waitresses, or at Radio Shack where he played the video games, like Solitaire, appropriately. He wouldn't eat in my kitchen, saying he didn't like cat fur on everything. His stay would last ten years, and I would see him dwindle down to nothing and die, sorry for what he did to me and stoic, expecting just this kind of loneliness and rejection in the midst of my life.

There was my big brother whose name rhymes with Marine. Gene had been a sensitive boy growing up. The family had called him Einstein. Astronomy was his love. With fondness, we had nicknamed him The Absent Minded Professor. He lost everything from his paltry paychecks to his bus fare, glasses, and graduation watches. It was cute as a boy, but not endearing to me when he became a man and used my property as a place to park his van during the week, sixty miles from his own home over the hill, to work in town. That's when I learned what the Marines had done to him. He was like a bullfrog, bragging his presence, full of the toughness he'd endured, still losing his car keys, eye glasses, and when asked to fix something around the place in exchange for the use of my kitchen every night, didn't know how to wipe off a sinkboard, not to mention the stovetop. He would use logic rather than a County code book to make repairs of installations, and endanger my house and property with these innovations. And Einstein he still was, but Einstein knew better than to try to be a fix-it man. He kept his nose in a book until he wrote his own. Gene's best feature as a grown man and still my big brother was his bent for writing verse, Kipling and Robert Service style. He waylaid me anywhere and read me his latest. This was the only "reward" for having him.

The other men were my ex's. One was in Texas like the song. The other lived in town and I became akin to a whale watcher, straining to catch a glimpse of him on the main street of this one-street small town. Or a drive-by shooter, driving by his trailer and shooting glances at him through his open door with the new woman he'd taken up with.

Rhythms

The rhythms stand out almost cartoon blatant. Feeding Alex over the fence, asking Alex to fix something, Flynn repeating his feedings at the counter, Sal in bed, Sal dragging me to meetings about menopause, PMS, immunity, and to lectures about relationships, care-givers, and to macrobiotic dinners at the library with a gutted facilitator. No rush-of-the-blood being each of the group's goal. No excitement. Peace. Sal: his Yoga position on my new wicker furniture. Transcending, as I bet he can't, under The Real Test, until he gets mad and descends to earth and yells at me about walking the three-mile Foothill Road with Alex. The John memories flooding in. Remembering his insults and emotional neglect. I try to make sense of it. Flynn at the counter, Alex repairing things and eating. Sal proselytizing, pontificating, and prostrate. And the vague reflections of The Past with John.

Bold pieces stand out: Scenes of Flynn in his aging dilemma. His past of evoking pity, now home to roost and kill him. Where is the self pity. Under the gun, he's become a fighter. Alex, still typical of himself, mechanically competent and mentally frustrated, spewing his curses, while his inability to take care of himself without getting headaches gets our attention. Sal, plump, pompous, pedantic, and sometimes a pest pleasantly smiling, while piddling in spirituality and physical health. Visions of John: selfish, self-serving, self-obsessed, self-absorbed, as I remember him severely sizing up society to suit his self-image. Insufferable. And where do I fit? I'm at The Counter, In The Yard, In My Room, In The Gym pushing resistance, Along The Side Of The Road, running, Under Sal sometimes, On the Phone, running *up the bill* over mama, who is a telephone voice throughout, repetitively revealing The Rest of the Family members, and her past with Flynn. And my grown children: Also telephone phantoms...?

What is the point of each repetitive day, week, month, year? To show the holding power of each of us? How I am letting them shape my life? How I grew into this structure like a tree locked and linked to stone? Or that my life once again and continuously lends itself to these needs of men and children like Mama?

What could it mean? Flynn's attempt to eat? What is the point of that? This father figure so infant-like still trying to stay alive, and my assistance in the face of the Past already spent holding him together. (Therapists would throw down the book. I'd lose credibility.) Who wants a woman who can't see her way out of all this. The no-insight into her own dilemma would bore anyone. The no-guidance that she knows better than to keep an old once-abusive father (even though "lovingly" abusive) around. Her belief that he didn't mean to abuse her. Abusive by his deep-rooted fear? —which required her to "comfort" him? What is the point of understanding him at the counter getting progressively older, thinner, weaker until he dies? Unless *she*, herself, is learning something from it? Does she, in fact, get anything out of his still being in her life? Or why is she allowing it? No one else she has ever spoken to would. In the family there is the unspoken understanding to let Marty do it as always? And why does Marty still do it as always. Why hasn't she broken with that painful role? Is it still feeding her somehow and if so, does this come out, is it ever revealed if life were a *story*?

How is it shown. Is this point illustrated in any of the repetition? And, if so, isn't the therapist right? It's sick. Is that what this is about, being a victim? Someone still sick? Will anyone care if I am not aware of this as I live it, and talk it? How can I point something out that I don't feel. I feel "*heroic*," or simply practical, not sick, in letting Flynn finish his life off under my roof. It would be too easy to kick him out. He has no fight left. I could easily kill him with the rejection. He could die in disgrace. A father no one wanted... And everyone is willing to throw the first stone if I'd let them. Why do I protect him, Flynn? Is he only mine and no one else's because of what he did. My right to do what I want with him.

And what is the meaning of Alex next door, living in the old family camper. In his state of "transition," permanently, since the divorce, not able, either, to start a new life, but hangs around the old one sniffing its carcass and seeing if there's any life left, like an old mated elephant, the remains of what once was his mate. An ex-family man, ex-head of household, ex-husband, and dad, devolved to a vagabond in blue shirts, wet-combed hair, and still contorted face, declaring his love for me and pitching in and fixing *the house* if I pay him....

The House is the setting. It's components are: the tenants, my attempt at privacy, the sounds, smells, feels, and tastes of the place. The birds, cats, dogs, and various visitors to throw light. How do they see me. How would they see me if they knew about Flynn. Still a secret in my life. You don't just tell everyone. And all the while my body is turning older, still bleeding (*Period Pieces*, each month's cycle to 56 years), but twenty pounds lighter, crinkling, spotting with pigment, losing its attraction to the male, or to any eyes. And my age being an issue to me, if only in my mind and not in fact yet. The world still treats me good, as if I am strong, healthy, and a viable participant. And a potential partner to someone....

I need to decide what my *body* means in all this. Hormones, vitamins, mammograms and gynecologists I have avoided for ten years. The elements are: My house. My body. And both showing signs of wear and tear that exact real time to maintain. The *men* (past, present, future.) The *phone*, and those voices with information. The distant connections. And each element breaks down into settings. The house has The Kitchen Counter where everyone gathers to eat and talk. The couch is too formal. No one wants to sit down. They like to stand and lean and be on their way to somewhere else. My place on the stove side, theirs on the front room side, perched on rickety stools, The floor worn with my 120 pounds shows where I've *served* for 30 years. My body, always clad in tights and t-shirts revealing my effort to stay mobile (as Flynn and Mama go crippled). My wardrobe would be reduced down to second *skins*... and like the gingerbread girl, I rely on two strong legs, that carried me away from Flynn, Alex and John....

"Bad men" were always in the house, never outside. The only "good man," Sal, has taken me on as his project, his cause, to rehabilitate, instruct, guide and comfort into health, while I resist up to a point, knowing most of what he says already, and being healthier and stronger than he is by all practical application: physical function and mental accomplishment. He fits himself in as a kind of manager, mediator, moderator. He gets programs going to help Flynn, Mama, and in turn me. He slips information sheets in front of me about financial aid and registration deadlines, to help my *grown children*, and me, in turn. He is a Behind-The-Scenes man. I call him the Wizard of Oz, the small man at the switches behind the scenes.

And John: His reason to be in my thoughts? To know my past behavior, needs, folly, illusions, wanting my way, not getting it? And he, an archetype male in taking from a female and not giving? A large version of Flynn, richer, bigger, better educated, but still sex-obsessed, living for it, never not chasing it, using it for the impetus to get up in the morning. No interest outside how he looks to a woman. Even though Flynn had hobbies, he did them to show off to a woman too. Did them on cue. The same as John. John's rubber raft, He never took it out. There were no girls out on the ocean.

Flynn brought out his oil paints or charcoal and painted and sketched, or brought out his guitar and sang and played, or built a boat and raced, or built a car and raced.... while women admired. John brought out his electric keyboard and sat playing with himself (the keyboard had a memory that would record). He did this when a woman came over.

Or John would go out where women could see him with his lap computer, again, playing with himself, this time in public. Both men sought perversion in bed and had affairs all their lives, hoping to finally find that perfect female who would orgasm for hours just looking at them.... Both men could discard women after using them, as if they deserved it for not being what he wanted....

14

At Fifty: an Introduction

They never ask. They tell me. Everyone tells me what he did. What my father did to me. The molestation. I can't be angry, silent, sullen, quiet, hesitant, incompetent, fearful, shy, rigid without everyone knowing, "That is what he did to her. That is what molestation does to you" When I'm friendly, happy-faced, pretty, polite, courteous, kind, loving, compassionate, intelligent, successful, they say, "She's overcome what he did to her. She's strong enough to not have let it affect here. She's not letting it get her down." They think, "She should be ruined. If she were an alcoholic, nymphomaniac, drug addict, quivering neurotic, penniless or ignorant, and eventually a bag lady with broken capillaries, or ending up in a mental institution, we would certainly understand. It would be right for what he did to her. All those years. Her whole childhood and into adulthood...."

At fifty, I tell people, "You can't undo child molestation. You are what happened to you. You try to sort out the molesting from all the rest of *life,* though. You try to see who you'd be separate from that. I look at my friends. They didn't have to open their legs to their father's mouth from age three to twenty-three." This makes people turn away. There is always a nicer way to say it. My friends are going through the same things I am. Divorce, grown children, what to do with themselves now, after living happily ever after. We knew the story up to the point when the prince carried her off. Now we come out the other end and there are no fairy tales to guide us. And they didn't have molestation.

I stay quiet as much as I can, trying to listen to my mouse movements. The yearnings scratching from the inside. And feel the discontent so deep and dull that I voice it aloud, "Nothing is right. Nothing is *ever* right. Nothing has ever felt right." And wonder, Is this what he did to me? Is this the result of being molested. This uneasiness, this unrest. This never being able to feel that things are *right*. Always pushing ahead or drifting behind. Always ill at ease in the present?

But all my friends feel discontent. It's called the human experience, or predicament. You can't be cured of life's ills.

The sex with Flynn, my father, by itself, as a child, was the most intense I ever felt. The physical sensation of it. No man compared to that. It was as if I were an extension of my father and he knew what my body felt. As if my body were his. I was of him. The same flesh. After that, I learned that men were awkward and clumsy. That they groped and didn't know where any nerve endings were, except in the general vicinity of their own. For some reason, Flynn was accurate. Or did molesting make him so. Or was it because I was a child and my body knew nothing else. My mother confessed in her old age that he never made her orgasm.

Alex was the first after Flynn. He made love like a machinist. He got my body to work. He married me and claimed that while we were dating, I was the most passive woman he had ever known. That I lacked a hunger that single women usually had. They usually began unbuttoning him, running their tongues down his throat. While I sat there and let him and was responsive, "to be sure," as he put it. He could tell by the swelling and moisture that I responded and that excited him. That I gave up, gave in, but did not attempt to initiate. That I made him seduce me. That I was seductive. Sensual... We stayed married for twenty years. After the divorce, I went back to school.

Wolfgang, a foreign graduate student, was well-equipped on all levels. A large head full of physics, large wallet from his inheritance, large heart from his genes, and a large manhood. I was a mature woman and knew what I wanted at that time. I began having orgasms from intercourse for the first time.

Five years later, when I fell in love with John, the Philosophy professor, I learned how to kiss at forty-five. Wolfgang was finally too much younger than me and I longed for a peer who came from the same generation, had the same reference points in society and personal history. Wolfgang was surprised my mother was still alive, my greater age came with so many assumptions for him. John was my age. And I fell in love as if for the first time. My lips were eager to touch his skin. I confessed to a friend later, "John never used his lips or fingertips in bed, only at the table. He'd jab in the dark with the thing that felt good to him. He was not a lover. Only a fucker. But he looked so good to me. He wanted the neighbors to hear me scream when I orgasmed. He'd tell me to scream louder. He lived in a trailer court and there was a family of Mexicans next door. His way to have sex was probing on the inside of me, and at a certain point, saying, "Now I have you, now you're mine." And when it was over, rolling away and acting as if I weren't there at all. That lasted another five years.

And now I sit with Sal across from me over decaffeinated coffee. Me, in flat shoes and a baggy sweater. Flat hair. No more excitement over being *me*, the one I always knew. With previous men, I was on my toes, straining to ward off disapproval, having to hold my own, taking verbal blows and maintaining my identity. Building my identity from their attempt to strip me of a part of myself they didn't like, the one who pointed out things they didn't want to hear. Now with every-steady, ever-approving, never-ready Sal, I am neutral. No more flushed face, except for a fleeting heat at the brief glimpse I get sighting John from a distance once in a while.

Was the only passion I ever had saving myself from men, surviving, and now, survived, all the tension is gone? Flynn, Alex, Wolfgang, John, and now no feeling except a kind of peace, with Sal. My wish is his command. And he is a smiling man, a thing a man has never done before. A constant goodwill that baffles me. It punctures me. Leaves me empty. I find nothing in me to respond. I blame lack of money sometimes. And then lack of love. This time of loving. Sal does the loving now. I let him. It feels nice....

§

"What do we want Flynn to do," I ask my sisters. "Come crawling on his belly and ask forgiveness and give everything he has away?" They agree. There is nothing he could do. They wouldn't want to see him in that position. It'd change their role. It would put some responsibility on them. They'd have to respond, interact, search their hearts. Maybe not find anything there but bile. Bother. They'd have to bother with him. And their time is valuable. It's easier hating him quietly, "writing him off," as one sister put it. Her hating was never appeased by living him down. He is still that young father who "stood lurking in the doorway." But I saw Flynn getting smaller and weaker and finally fading away. He is no longer a threat to me, as he remains so with my sisters.

I say, "I'm not sure why I let him stay in my life. I'm finding out, though, and that's important for me. I could easily get rid of him, but I'm curious now, at this point."

"You're a social scientist." One sister sees it that way. "You're doing a study." That strikes a chord. I consider it. It's a hard cold eye she attributes to me. She says, "You always liked to analyze things. I never did. You liked to get the meaning out of things, like sucking marrow from a bone."

I agree that I did like to watch and see what becomes of people. I could be letting Flynn, my father, live out his life with me so I can daily tally my response to him in my strongest years yet. An adult and aging woman, divorced, self-employed, independent financially and emotionally. Everything the personal ads ask for (by men advertising themselves. So who needs a man—if they want a woman independent who won't cost them a thing?) And a strong daughter. No longer a child, and Flynn transformed into a child through old age, smaller than me, and so weak he can't break an ear of corn in half. He at ninety-two pounds and me at a hundred and fifteen. And the hundred and fifteen all muscle as tested in the gym. Only seven percent body fat left after years of running and working out. Am I watching, mesmerized as Flynn was over me, his child once, him shrinking and withering and almost disappearing as a father. Flynn hasn't been a father for a long time in that way. I haven't needed him (or did, but could not confide my troubles to him). Or needed his need of me. As a child I needed him to need me, they tell me now. Flynn watched me grow and blossom in spite of his deeds, and held onto that. I watch him now frail and shrivel, and I draw away, but let him stay. Isn't that the way of parents and their children? The natural process? They bring us into the world and we usher them out. The fathering Flynn did was to become my friend. He made me laugh, although men after that said my laughter was raw, not the refined kind you're taught in the parlor. A real tickle and giggle, not a feigned chuckle.

Losing each man left a dull place in me.

I tell my sisters over the phone, "It's this big house. And he helps. He knows how to fix everything...." It's met with a sigh, as if they are waiting for me to know something they know.

Alex, Next Door

The New Wife

Alex sleeps less than fifteen feet away. I haven't paced it off but he's just on the other side of the fence I put up last year without a gate. I can hear the familiar snort in the morning, and even hear his TV at night when I'm in bed with my TV on. Some mornings I hear a big splash in my backyard, and know it's only Alex taking a "bath." That's the way he wakes up, jumps in the pool. Or if we're on a favor-for-favor-behavior, I'll hear my name, "Mother" called from the deck outside my bedroom door asking if he can come in and take a hot shower. When we were married he used to say that was the greatest invention of civilization: hot running water. He has no bathroom in his camper. At fifty, he finally gets to camp out and be the naughty boy he always wanted to be as a kid. All he had to do was get a brain tumor, have an operation, and all expectations from his proper mother and sisters were dropped. I can hear him whistling away over the fence. Or shouting at his new wife.

His new "wife" is a little alcoholic Irishman, who had nowhere to go, so Alex let him move another camper onto the property and earn his keep by helping him build the house. Similar to what he allowed me to do twenty-six years ago. This little man is a lot like me back then. He's small and obedient, and doesn't have a dream of his own. He's become dependent on Alex and serves as a helpmate. He has attached to Alex's dream and doesn't mind playing second to the eccentric Kraut in Alex. I hear them over the fence now. Alex giving orders, and Jack, the new wife, hopping around to please him, just the way I used to. Jack couldn't make it as a man. Are alcoholics cowards, or extra sensitive, or what? The guy couldn't face holding down a job and supporting a family. His grown son comes down the field to visit him every now and then, and they get into a screaming match. Two little alcoholic

Irishmen. The son trying to get pride back into his father. Jack yelling back that "The man wants it done, and I'll do it." I peeked through the fence once and saw the son's eyes, hurt more than angry. I wanted to go to him and say, "That's okay, Alex is not such a bad husband. He feeds your dad, and cares in his way." Remembering the way it was for me. The dream first, and people next...

I hear Alex trying to get Jack to line up the tarp on the framework. They were almost ready to lay on the plywood when the sky clouded up. Alex has been rained out before. "You're not listening... now pay attention. Pull, pull on it, Jack, over there." The same irritation he used with me for not being an instant extension of his own body. "Pull on it, get the corner there," he hollers almost out of patience. I hear Jack go begging the issue, pleading that he's trying to do it right, same as I used to.

But Alex doesn't lose patience altogether and curse Jack's very existence, all his forefathers that could have bred such a creature, and even the wretched future Jack will have for being so stupid, the way he would with me. And Jack doesn't go away in tears, slamming doors and cursing Alex. The difference is Jack doesn't have to sleep with Alex later, and try to love him. And there's no reason for Alex to insult Jack because he doesn't have to try to make love to him later, in spite of all Jack's inadequacies.

They finish pulling the tarp over the entire superstructure of framework. And then go to separate campers. Turn on separate TVs and do their separate lovings of themselves: Jack souses his brain with booze, Alex turns on the news and souses his brain with the world, and then Channel 10, to souse it with science. Neither one says anything about the other's tastes. And in the morning they're back to building the house: Alex and Jack.

Influences

Each man left his mark on the place. The showerhead went through transition. John used the short low one to ridicule Wolfgang. Wolfgang stood about five eight. John loomed six feet with big bones. His legs like tree trunks, the same size all the way down. If he'd starved to death he'd still look thick with those bones. He should have been a steelworker thug, just like his dad instead of going off to Yale on a merit scholarship and becoming a professor. He prides himself on his 300-pound uncle's threatening the Fuller Brush man with an ice pick. As a professor, he does the same thing to his students—"ice picks" them to intellectual death. Do Ukrainians need big bones for some reason? Do their parents throw them out of the door as babies? He called Wolfgang "The Columbian Banana," and changed the showerhead to a big elaborate one jacked up on a high pipe. When I took a shower, the water would shoot over my head unless I stood at the back of the tub. After breaking up with John, Alex got shower privileges again. For his headaches. Funny now he knew John was out of my life. The way a tomcat knows there are no toms in the neighborhood. Pheromones. Alex never said a thing, but one day I got in the shower and there was a small spray coming from a small nozzle which rotated nicely on a wobbly little head. I asked Alex where that came from, and he announced, "That big nozzle your gentleman friend had was a piece of shit, so I put a water saver on for you, 'Mother.'" He stood five eleven, glancing down at me to see if there was any appreciation on my face. I went in the house with no interest at all.

Flynn takes a tub bath maybe once a week. He says, "Whether I need it or not." It's in the other bathroom on the tenants' side of the house. Flynn goes in there engulfed in steam, windows tightly closed, door sealed shut, mini-blind

25

down, light on, and cigarette smoke emitting from the keyhole. He is still afraid to catch his death. Still from the days people died of getting all wet and sitting in a draft.. and he so skinny. I went out to his "shack" one night to call him in to answer the phone and saw him through the slats of his mini-blind before he could cover himself. No flesh at all. Auschwitz.

When Flynn first came to my house, looking for a place to stay, in the manner of the grasshopper and the ant: even though he worked every day of his life, he never wanted to own a house, chose to rent, turned down three houses offered to him by bosses and girlfriends, didn't want the responsibility; never wanted to plod or be domesticated—I was in disbelief. I knew I wouldn't turn him away. I knew he couldn't go to anyone else's and be accepted. I pretended it was just for awhile. And it was right after Alex beat me up. I knew Alex wouldn't come near the place if he saw my father's car there. This was about six years ago. Wolfgang was still in my life. In fact he was sitting all day on the couch in his bathrobe doing physics calculations. He was out the afternoon Alex "tussled" with me. That was Alex's word. I had hired a mobile locksmith to open the storage Alex rented to hide out one of the biggest assets of the marriage: his workshop, all the tools and machines. About twenty thousand dollars worth. And I needed about twenty thousand dollars to make it come out even so I could have the house and Alex could have everything else, which was a lot more than he wanted to admit. The locksmith came to the storage and, without a question, picked the lock. Then the auctioneer I'd hired did the appraisal. Sure enough, twenty thousand dollars worth of "assets." My lawyer had told me to get the appraisal. Then I went for a run.

I took the back road to get more hills in and that's where Alex came screeching to a halt in his new car and jumped out and grabbed me. He said he was only trying to get me in his car so he could take me to the police and turn me in for breaking and entering. He couldn't get me in the car. A witness later told the police, "I thought the guy was crazy, he kept throwing her at a rock, see that big boulder over there; I was afraid to interfere; I thought he'd kill me." Alex was on the run after that. A warrant out for his arrest. A felony, for attacking with a deadly weapon. But the rock was stationary. I was the object thrown. I remember Wolfgang thought it was just one more shenanigan. He didn't say much, didn't miss a penciled calculation over it, and when I told and retold the story it got funnier and funnier. I had him laughing. He said I should do stand-up comedy. Alex was really a joke back then in his greed. Then Flynn appeared. It took me three years to get over being afraid to run the back road again. I'd run but with no guts. A kind of picked-chicken nakedness, that I was only soft flesh in a carnivorous world. Alex had scared me in a way I'd never been scared before.

Flynn heard all about it. I told him what happened and he said, "I always knew he was capable of that sort of thing." I refused to have my coccyx X-rayed. The ambulance broke down on the way to the hospital. They taped my head down to a stretcher, across the forehead. When they had to change ambulances, they pulled the tape off and I felt they ripped off my eyebrows. At the doctor's office, I had to bend over. A very beautiful young doctor examined my tailbone, and, sure enough, I had a broken coccyx. Alex followed me with a camera after that and took pictures of the running, to prove in court he hadn't hurt me. And I was too strong for my own good and refused to play weak and injured. The only thing I could not do was sit down. The tailbone hurt in that position. The lawyers were having a good time with us. Flynn was helpful. Everything on the place broke and he fixed it; septic system, gas pipes, plumbing, electrical. I avoided him as much as I could, still polite as he'd taught me to be, to his position as father. Then with Alex at my throat, and Flynn underfoot, something came loose in me and I tore into Flynn one afternoon. I ranted and yelled and told him he would have to go for counselling for what he had done to me. That he couldn't just move in and expect to act like nothing had ever happened. That I had to have him understand the molesting. I drove him to his first appointment. He said he was sorry. I said sorry means nothing. It's too easy: twenty years, my whole childhood and you're sorry…? It was a group rather than an individual therapy. He came home each week with more and more vocabulary he'd learned from the other "offenders," "victims," and therapists. He was disgusted with the other men. He said back then, "They tell me that I am 'angry' with women. Now that is the dumbest thing I've ever heard. What does angry mean anyway. What do they mean by that." He said one woman cried the whole session, remembering herself as a child and what her father did. He said, "That's just self-pity. But the therapists were letting her do it…." Through his eyes I learned what he was learning. I was kind of proud of him in a way. He knew I meant for him to find out about himself and stop trying to pretend nothing had ever happened. He went for about a year and then dropped out, saying, "You have to do it alone." He was well liked by everyone. His therapist called me and said he was very honest and intelligent. I think he was the oldest "perpetrator" they'd ever had, at seventy.

I told him he could stay if he'd continue to be the repairman. I added, "To earn your keep," as a joke, and he never let me forget it. Every time he fixed a leaky faucet or a singing toilet or lifted a finger, he'd say, "Well, I'm earning my keep," without a smile. It took him awhile to wash his own dish. That was women's work. And to get his own food. All the cats in the kitchen encouraged him to simply eat out where the counters were sterilized. There was no humor between us. He needed a place to stay, and I had a big house that was falling apart after Alex got through with it, and his twenty thousand dollars worth of tools he justified getting over the years of our frugal marriage, by saying he was saving so much in repair bills. "If you have a repairman come out to the house, they charge you about forty dollars an hour." He never got around to using his tools much after building onto the house. Places are still unfinished. He made lists of repairs to do and then had a brain tumor and didn't have to do any of them.

When I lost in court and the house was ordered sold, I appealed to Alex that it was the *home* and after all the ugliness, the children should at least have a place to call home. It would be financial suicide, that the lawyers just wanted cash so they could take theirs. When he was convinced he'd been out-smarted by his lawyers, he determined to outsmart them and refuse to "liquify" the assets. He let me have it then, in an act of grandiose benevolence. He said, "All I wanted to do is show you that I could win." So I got the house and he got the money and other property. It happened that the property we owned was right next door. He began building his own house, using my electricity.

The giant umbilical cord has been plugged in for six years. Once when I got mad I ran out and jerked it out of the outside outlet. Alex came out of his camper like a troll. I'd made him miss a part of a movie he was watching on TV. He plugged the extension cord back in and I've left it out there, threatening to unplug it if he doesn't keep the pool equipment in order. It is a symbiotic relationship now. He does the pool and I pay his electricity and water. My hose goes over the fence. And once, raking, I saw a cable cord going under the fence. So he tapped into the TV too. I try to ignore it. Flynn has four lawn mowers lined up back by his little room by the pool. He keeps pick-ing up an extra one at a backyard sale just in case one breaks. He'll have parts for a standby. For some reason he has taken to keeping the lawn. He's never mowed a lawn in his life. We never had lawns when I was growing up. Maybe a weed patch for one and crabgrass, but Flynn didn't care about keeping a lawn. Now he has begun to take pride in making my lawns look nice. I'll come home and see them all mowed, and he'll announce it to me proudly if he happens to run into me. I've caught him looking like a real grandfather at these times. A nurturing and caring kind of nice man, and tender, or one who tends.

A friend came out who knew about my past molested by Flynn. She went roaring around ripping out her throat about how he should be hung up by the balls and castrated. I was offended. I tried to explain how the punishment, if that is what everyone was looking for, came. "He spoiled any chance for closeness with him. I have a natural aversion to him. I don't like to be around him. The damage was done when he did what he did. Mother Nature takes care of that. He would like me to come rushing in eager to tell him things, to share my life with him. To throw my arms around him the way you can with your father, but that is what he ruined. I keep my distance. Not because I try to or want to, but because it's been done: the damage. It's as if I was poisoned once and almost died, or suffocated, or strangled, and there's a natural avoidance now. It's that simple."

One woman said she learned about how damaging her incest was in graduate school. I said I learned by my nervous system. No one told me what it'd done—I felt it. Only one person ever understood how I could allow Flynn in my life after what he did, and he was a spiritualist. My women friends only smirk and shake their heads. Their dads are still happily married to their mothers, and they are still their darling daughters. I say, "I would like to be able to be close to my father like you can, but that is the hurt of molestation. Just this, later, the loneliness and estrangement. I don't even sunbathe out by the pool when he's home. I can't stand to bare my body where he can see." Nothing but cow eyes over these explanation to these women who have their daddies who never violated their privacies.

Flynn resisted his role as caretaker here for a long time. Maybe the first three or four years. He'd walk around still expecting the elder respect from one of his children. He'd also try to get attention by having a nice big depression right in the middle of my life. But I ignored the talk of fear of dying, needing to take Valium and assigned him duties to do (I was overworked) until now he assumes his new role with some pride. In a way he has come down on his knees And I'm glad when he protests if I should act too bossy, if I go too far. I'm like Aunt Frances, the family nag. The Aunt Flynn could never tolerate. And now he is in a position to take orders from me. I nagged him once, "You told me you knew how to fix everything and now you can't even fix a leaky faucet; I'll call Alex then." He shouted "Shut up," once when I was 'castrating' him this way, by attacking his intelligence, and skills.

Then he apologized, and said, "I guess I am too stupid to do anything right anymore." I saw his hurt and felt both ashamed and glad. John scolded me, back then, and told me I had no right to treat Flynn like that no matter what he had done.

The Place

We always called it The Place. Whenever we traveled we'd talk about what we'd do to the place when we got back. We'd fix this or that, or build on, or change one thing or another. We were full of the place when we were away from it. We talked for a hundred miles to Los Angeles and a hundred miles back. In Japan we saw little things that Japanese did with architecture. I would picture doing something like that to the place—Paper Partitions. In Mexico we saw things the Mexicans did with the architecture and I would long to have that structure added to the place. A veranda, an outdoor decking, an open air living room. In Hawaii I was sure when I got back I would get everything wicker and bamboo and floral. And then we would return and wake up together in bed. Alex and I for years, would get up and get busy and be overwhelmed by the place. Anywhere we began seemed to defeat us. He got mad about everything. He made lists he couldn't finish in a day, and had other lists waiting for the next day. "Two steps forward, and one step back," was his agonized chant, which I couldn't tolerate without nasty comments on "being so negative." And I kept violating the place by going outside it and making contact with other people who had nothing to do with the place. Adult Ed classes, the schools as a substitute, Unitarian Church lectures, UCSB foreign films.

The place seemed indestructible. It began destroying us. Alex's health broke after fifteen years. His head exploded inside. A pituitary tumor; he was on his way to work when it infarcted. His brain surgeon was a stutterer. Every time he said the word "infarcted" he got held up on the "far," and it hung in the air threatening to sound like fart. His sisters thought I had slept with the doctor to give their dear brother a lobotomy, and that that was what really happened to him. They took me to court. Alex lay in the hospital out of his head and never knew what happened to him. When I told him later, he chose to believe his sisters. Not that he was given a lobotomy, but that I had slept with someone, maybe not the doctor, but one of the sisters' husbands. He couldn't remember me sleeping in the hospital room for a month while he came out of it. Some woman at the hospital whose husband had a head injury had told me then, "They won't remember anything that happened afterward. It's all blotted from their memory." I was in the waiting room, in the beginning, I remember now, and they kept wheeling men by on their backs with sheets over them, and their noses sticking up, going into surgery or coming out of it, and I remember I was waiting for Alex to pass by the door on his back, so I would look up each time, and the women kept saying, "Is that mine or yours?" and then with laughter, "Oh that's someone else's."

It took Alex three years to get mean enough again to give me the nastiest divorce he could muster. I nursed him back to health. I had him running seven miles a day within the first year of recovery. He looked beautiful, blonde high color; but his brain chemistry was out of whack and he'd get a cunning look like an animal and I would fear for my life, and quietly go out the door until it passed. It took Alex seven years before he remembered that he smoked. After the operation he never thought of smoking. It's as if they cut the will out of him. The Alex that went in and the one that came out were two different people. They cut out empathy and compassion too. He came home, selfish and childish, and without that altruism he'd been known for.

I call Alex on the phone and ask him if he wants some wheatberries and shark. He laughs. "What?" He comes over and takes a whiff and declines. "Oh, Honey, I've got food over there." I've seen his stash of food, all canned. He doesn't want to tell me it's disgusting to him, the food I've prepared. He was a hamburger man when we were married. He says now, "I don't trust fish…" And goes back over the fence. I put up a fence without a gate during the divorce. He put up a ladder…. He is building his own *place* now. His headaches are back. He eats canned foods again. The news is on his little TV every night just like it was when he had his big chair in the living room here. The *place* is now my *place*. And I have become Alex. After each man I've found, I become him. Without Alex handling *the place*, I have had to think about all the broken things and how to fix them.

I've gotten nasty, even used some of his lines. And when Wolfgang lived here and was unable to do anything around *the place*, I became the man. I would go to the door to investigate sounds in the night. When it rained I would worry about leaks instead of enjoying the beauty of the sound. When the wind blew, I would toss and turn and find it hard to sleep. Wondering what was being ripped off and thrown across the yard. Wolfgang took my role, like a wife, "Oh, Benny just relax. It's only wind, only rain, it's beautiful." The very words I used to say to Alex. I found myself using Alex's lines, "I'll have to spend the whole day fixing that damn pipe, now...." and cursing. It was the only thing that made me respect Alex again after the divorce. I realized that he was actually *afraid* of all the responsibility of those years. He was caught and hooked into it for life and he couldn't see an end in sight. His life was being used up and his wife was an ungrateful bitch, by his estimation.

Chores

The next thing to go out now that the house was hers, was the gas line. When she overheard Alex and her brother Louis, who had come to her rescue, referring to the gas line to the house as "hers" her heart leapt with fright. Mine: Mine? The house scared her. The place that had been a haven when Alex lived here had become a test of her intelligence. She had learned where her gas main was, and the water meter, and the electrical box. Just in case. She heard the men talking about her in third person within earshot. She began to think of herself in third person. To see herself as this little woman out there. To these men who deferred to her because of the past roles of sister and wife, and now, present tense, because of owner of the property.

She has to get up in the morning and go about the way Alex used to with responsibility. She feeds the little dog. The big dog. The birds. Takes two swipes at the algae behind the calcium build-up in the jacuzzi with the stainless steel brush, peeks into the big workshop to survey the progress with the County plans. "Comply with the County" is a phrase she resisted learning. She takes a quick look at all the pool chaises and visualizes the snap-maker one more time she will get from Sears with her card, and how, with a reinforced eye, she will lace nylon twine through all the holes and shoestring it underneath, and repair all the lounging chairs by the pool with pretty colored canvas. Canvas, which will eventually be soaked with coconut oil suntan lotions by the tenants and family and maybe a friend or two who come over to enjoy the premises. She vacuums around the birdcage. Fries a steak and egg breakfast for her son who visits, to assuage her mother conscience for awhile. Rakes leaves, sweeps leaves. Alex always wanted to cut down the only thing pretty in the yard, the weeping willow tree that is so old and lazy it gets all over everything. The leaves clog the robot's throat in the pool. It is a thousand dollar a gadget she was talked into, to eat algae all day long in a random water-instigated heartbeat. Once a little plastic palate is set in motion it never stops, just flops back and forth with water- suction action like the play between the auricles and ventricles. Nothing more than what keeps her heart going.

When she first put that thing in the pool, she'd see the men standing back there just watching it with boys' eyes. She had written the check. They could marvel without the complicated emotion of responsibility. She'd go out there and say, "Hey, stop staring at my algae-eater. It isn't police," and they'd shuffle and shift a little and smile at her on her exposed aggregate poolside slab, chuckling in an "Oh, there she is" style. "It's just her." A mutual understanding flowing in their veins for a woman they had all had, and still kind of wanted, but didn't know for sure, but who wasn't available anyway, except in this way of letting her smart off and own everything and paying them to work for her. They, each in turn, had supported her. And she had been theirs. First was Flynn, her father, for twenty years, then the next twenty she belonged to Alex. And there they still were. Flynn and Alex. Both white-haired, Flynn with age, and Alex with German genes. Men who once hated each other and fought over her. Each pull-ing on an arm, so to speak, until she became unhinged. Alex finally tore her away from Flynn. And then she tore herself away from Alex. And on and on. It was the typical story of growing up. So that at her age now she is finally just turning twenty-one emotionally and beginning her independence. All her women friends tell the same story. They leave one thing out though. They never slept with their father. But that is the only difference.

She continues to see herself through the men's eyes, in third person, as they put their heads together. She used to hol-ler at Alex. "If you cut that tree down, the yard will be ugly. Don't you know that is the only thing that separates this yard from being a barren field like all the others?" She would ges-ture toward the big old swaying creature. "Do you think it would be a pretty shaded lawn without the tree?" He would curse the leaf fall-out and the caterpillar droppings and the fear of branches cracking off and falling on the house. Curse bumping his head on the lowest branch when he'd go into the shed to get a rake. And the big job of fertilizing it with those spears of nitrate which amused her. They were solidified bull piss, essentially, the ingredients read on the labels.

She liked thinking of how they did that. Remove all the fluid from the urine and collect so much of it it would be a one foot core you could pound into the ground by the great willow root system and it'd bleed out and feed the tree. Nature supplied bulls hanging around bases of trees in real life. But here we were so far removed we had to go out and buy an artificial pissing system, or the tree would pale, eventually grow weak and fall on the house.

Alex had a perfect goose step when she talked like this. As soon as they got divorced, as soon as he got the field next door, as soon as she put up a fence and one tentacle from the— now her—tree ventured toward his property line, he got out his chainsaw. She heard it and came running out of the house back then. It was a sound she hated. And the kind of man who used them. Real adrenalin rushes in killing, mutilating, stacking up in neat rows, a thing that used to play with the air, feel and dance to the atmosphere, do photosynthesis, so that in nature films in slow motion, you could catch the sensual response of a baby branch, a nubile leaf, feeling it's way like any baby, toward light and warmth and growing. Searching. A living creature, knowing. And she shrieked at Alex over on his side of the fence, "Don't cut, my tree." But he, with his rights now, legally seared through the air with such a pitch it pierced her ears. And the languid frightened tree lost one of its largest limbs.

Alex's eyes were triumphant. Like their sons had been when he got his sisters to squeal. Yet, he feigned compassion the way the Nazis did as they simply had to destroy what was destructive. "Oh, Honey, I'm going to put a wall here and build my house, and I won't have termites jumping from this branch to my roof...and your side will grow better now. Look, it's mostly dead wood anyway." She went back into the house.

The only thing Alex liked about that tree was a woodpecker that used to come there when they were first married. They'd be in bed in the morning and hear it riveting away, and Alex's face would be soft with privilege over a woodpecker choosing "my tree" as he called it back then. Never "our tree." That was a concept he learned later in the divorce court.

She loved the woodpecker, too. They would stand behind the window and spot him up there and marvel over the obvious question: How can its brain function if he does that with its head. And they'd laugh. She would climb the tree later and look up close at the holes and wonder about the hidden insects being found and not safe at all and worry a bit over the way that was. Alex called it sentimentality, and smiled back then. They were so young, in their early twenties and had never owned a tree before. They would climb the tree together in the middle of the day when the kids were in school, all through their thirties and make love up there. It would just happen while playing, being hot and adult and married. And there was privacy. They could see the whole neighborhood through the leaves, but no one could see them. She would simply unbutton her pants. Like any primate.

48 Years Ago

Alex and I are standing at The Church of Christ on Chapala before the preacher who looks like Abraham Lincoln. He is saying the vows we repeat to marry. He says he knows our marriage will last. Forty-seven years later, Alex and I are standing over our son's casket in the same church that has now become a mortuary. We are crying. A son was born just nine months after our simple wedding. He was a twin, with a sister who still lives, if you can call that living. The babies were a month early. I got pregnant that first month. Our son had just died of a heart attack. Forty-seven years ago he'd had to be taken out with forceps due to his twin sister kicking him over to the side so she could occupy the whole womb. Forty-seven years later, same thing. The boy and girl were four pounds each back then. He died at six-four and 230 pounds. His sister is well on her way in over 200 pounds of greed. Alex sits over there occupying the whole half acre the son had paid half for, for years. The daughter made sure lawyers overturned the deed, so she could have the whole space for herself once her father died. Just like in the womb!

But, back to 48 years ago, and Alex and I standing in front of the preacher to become man and wife, saying the words the law wants to make it legal and later, if there is property, lawyers come in and see that, in California, it is divided in half. Neither of us had property at the time. I was a new teacher with two months' worth of teacher pay checks saved. That was five hundred a month. I had a thousand dollars. Maybe Alex married me for my money! He had a G.I. Bill that was paying for his college. He drove a bus to make a little extra. He lived in a Silverstream teardrop trailer at High Tone trailer court on Punta Gorda Street. I lived in a studio I rented with my first year of teaching in Orcutt, just a hundred miles up the coast. I gave notice, married Alex and moved into his tiny trailer. That first month, Alex took out a gun and held me down with his first drunk, and made me look into the barrel as he clicked through the cartridge. Still I put the thousand down on the little house we found out by the polo field. It was a half acre with fruit trees. I was tight-throated over the thrill that my baby (didn't know it'd be twins) would grow up "out in nature." Alex worked at a boat company that was making plastic hulls. Plastic was brand new back then. After a couple of years he applied for a job as pilot with three airlines. He got them all and chose United. Our good times began, although, he never apologized for the gun episode. Much later, he tried to shoot our son. He shot our family dog when the twins were toddlers, for knocking over the neighbors' garbage can.

I was a mindless fifties housewife and went on, as if I had good sense, yet knew I couldn't live with a man that had that kind of crazy rage. I was indeed trapped with the twins and now a little girl just twenty-two months later. She also lies in a grave after only 41 years. She'd married a man just like dad. He was her flight instructor. She got her pilot's license. She pushed him to get a job with an airline. He did. The money came in. They were finally worth two million dollars, when she filed for divorce. He was dating flight attendants, getting violent at home, hurting her in front of the kids. Alex and I had hidden his violence from our kids. We had the *don't tell* policy to protect them and pose as the perfect family. Alex's underlying rage drove me out of the house. Our youngest daughter stayed for the sake of her young children. It was a fatal mistake. Forty-eight years ago today Alex and I stood before the preacher and vowed for better or for worse. Better was good. The worse was worse. That rage destroyed his brain.

Layers (Heads)

I thought I wouldn't be here by now. I didn't want to grow old here. I pictured myself never growing old anywhere and never in one spot, but avoiding it by moving around and never letting it get me. Sal comes out and was walking around my bedroom in his pajamas and I went out into the living room to sit in front of the heater and be alone. In the dark I remember myself as a young mother. I was sitting right there on the couch we had at that time, 26 years ago, breast feeding my two little babies. Back then, I remember, I was trying hard to imagine them grown up already and how it would be. I held them at my breast and pictured them six feet tall and walking around, and me, a little old lady by then, grey and short and looking up at them. And now I sit on the floor in front of the same old wall heater, drying my still brown hair, and wanting the impact of the time passed to hit me. But I am so dull. I turn and warm each side, and then stand on one leg and warm my feet. My thighs are hard and thin. And my torso like a strong vine. Sal thinks I have forgotten to grow old. He has marvelled over the fact that I have three grown children. He says he has to keep reminding himself. He says "You are thirteen, going on fourteen, look at you.... All arms and legs. The bedroom an orangutang cage...."

After he leaves I have the place to myself and can sink into my moods. I hear Alex's camper door slam next door over the fence, and Flynn's car grumble out of the driveway. The stillness in the house soothes me. I need to be alone and to try to remember what is going on, where I am and how come I am still here. Early, he was on the pillow beside me. This time a sweet Sicilian from New York City. A gold backing on his front teeth glistened a little as he slept flat on his back. A kind of confusion was there in me over him. What was this man doing in my bed? Where did he fit in to anything in my life? I never had him figured into the whole thing. All those years I'd gazed at Alex as he slept beside me. Yellow chick hair and beak, closed and stoic, an angel-face on the pillow until he flickered those piercing blue eyes as soon as he awoke. Asleep I could admire him, awake I only feared him. His wrath was deep-rooted. But he was my husband— it was the right head then. For fifteen years his head was there. And now he slept alone just twenty feet away within hearing. After Alex, Wolfgang's big furry head appeared on my pillow beside me. A baby with a cherub mouth all puckered and pink, an abundant beard, brown, shiny, tangle of curls. Like the head of John the Baptist, they brought on a platter. The great Jewish nose in the middle of everything. That was four years going on five. Next was the large grey head of the professor. Mama said "This is your mature love." It turned out to be the most fitful and childish of all. At nineteen I was more grown up than when I met John. We were both forty-three, going on sixteen, beyond our responsibilities of wife, husband, mother, father. Our kids were all gone. We had nothing but time. He taught two or three times a week, and had nothing to do but walk around and sit in cafes and feel his testicles pulsating in his 100% cotton campus jeans. And watch the co-eds' breasts bob. He brought out the teenager in me. He was tall and big and thick, a big daddy. The one I'd always wanted. One I could be proud of. I fell in love with the way his clean wrists came out of his ironed cuffs, truly a white collar man. Flynn still strode back and forth in the yard, a blue collar taking the dark stain of his nicotine sweat. Was there really something in me that craved John for what he represented? I did not want to believe that at the time, but I felt then that I had finally found the man I had always wanted. That I had "arrived." His big ruddy profile, twice as big as Flynn's ever was, stuck out like Mt. Rushmore. A superman. I couldn't gaze upon it enough. His young daughter asked once, "Why do you stare at my father so much?" John's head was on the pillow for five, going on six, years. He always looked like stone, chiseled and granite-textured, rugged flesh, exuding some smell that I craved to inhale. I breathed him in, and when we broke up I longed for that odor. I slept with one of the t-shirts he'd left behind. His sweat was in the neck, under the arms. All through it. We had gone for a run. I saved his smell and wore it for months. And then saw him with another woman and threw it in the washing machine. I knew I had to break myself of him. He liked women too much. There was no having him for myself. If Mama was right, it was in a way she didn't mean. I grew up with John. I finally matured. We came out of it together at fifty. Went into it in our early forties and ended it hitting fifty. Went in young and came out old. But more than age I learned that I couldn't have what I wanted for the first time. What Flynn and Alex did to me paled next to what John did. I finally got hurt and knew it this time. Now we both walked down the street with people beside us ten years younger, or more. John's head on my pillow was the head I wanted there. His grey hair, silky curls, not old grey but silver, shiny, sensual. And the bald spot at the back of his head. Sometimes when he slept on his face I couldn't figure out what that was, that bare spot. If I got up and approached the bed from headfirst. He looked like a featureless face. No front or back, just that bare spot and nothing else visible.

Each man has had a big head, except for Alex. Alex's head is small and tight and compact with tight yellow curls. A head you can take up into the sky and twirl around and around and it never gets dizzy. But on the ground it exploded one day. It was a head that needed to dream and when it was grounded, all the daily things that needed to get done, there wasn't enough room inside, for all that energy, and they had to open it up and unjam it. He even talks about his operation like it's a jet engine and he's a mechanic. When I met Alex, his head was full of fantasies of escape. The South Seas, boats sailing away, salvaging "All that metal the military had left behind rusting in the jungles." He married me instead and took on this property. Now his own junk is rusting in the bushes out back. Twenty-seven years of dreams that went awry. The boat long ago chopped up and burned for firewood. And I've let so much bamboo grow around the pool since Alex moved out that it has choked the leachline. That was one of Alex's battles over the years, hacking down the bamboo I had planted from a little sprig I found in the sand jogging on the beach. An impulse on my part, which overtook the whole backyard. Once it got rooted it came out everywhere. Just when he thought he had it dug out and under control, it'd shoot up behind him and take him by surprise. He'd curse it, curse me, curse the whole world. As soon as I put a fence between us, he got out his shears, electric hedge trimmer, ladder and whole storage shed full of implements for reducing foliage down to nothing, even the shredder, and begin to sever every limb and leaf that stuck over the fence into his property. He sawed off the arms of my weeping willow tree that overlapped the two properties. The pittosporum hedge I had planted twenty-six years ago got butchered. Now, divorced, he could ignore my cries of protest and threats, female beggings to "Please leave that plant." The borders were clear, written upon paper, he had a legal right now, to keep my mess away from himself. The small, tight, pilot head of Alex never lost one hair. His head still blonde, kinky, profuse. John used to snicker and say Alex looked like he had a marcel wave. He could always turn something "good" into something "bad." John himself viewed the side and back of his own big head with mirth. His head was so big as a child, they thought he was hydrocephalic. He'd comb his hair straight back from his low hairline (which Alex, the Aryan , called the Mongrel Breed, Ukrainians are lowbrow Slavs), and say, "My head looks flat in the back," and chuckle a bit. I privately thought he looked like his car. He had some souped-up midnight blue thing in the driveway with a big nose and flat back. The car tapered off the back just like the back of John's head.

The only thing small about Wolfgang was the length of his legs. He told everyone that he had polio as a baby, and it was true. He was related to Itzhak Perlman on his father's side. But I wonder if his legs would ever have been long. He had a great big head, big heart which was attached to his big brain, unlike John's whose head was attached to his testicles, and bypassed the heart altogether. Wolfgang had a big wallet and a big manhood. He was born equipped on all levels.

Wolfgang used to remark on the American men's legs. "They are so long." he would say. He came from the country of short people. Men grew maybe five nine. Most were the same size as American women. I used to say, "The legs only get in the way. It's everything else that counts." And that would please him.

I ran into old Larry, the only rich man who wanted to marry me. He wouldn't speak to me. I felt like a fool saying hello and having him look off over my head as if I wasn't there. It had been eight years. He is still mad. I had just met Wolfgang back then going back to school. I didn't want to be with an old man who had already made his million and wanted to settled down and dress and feed some little frantic ex-housewife. I had just gotten free of Alex. I thought I was going to set the world on fire. No man in my way. It was like leaving home for the first time. I was forty. Wolfgang had energy, a future, not a past. Larry had only his past. He seemed dead at the time when he offered me life. As he knew it. French restaurants, fancy wine, Macy's, gold chains. I remember losing or giving away everything he ever gave me, except the psychiatrist. At the end he was furious and wanting to insult me for not falling in love with him. He said to go and get a psychiatrist and he would pay for it, to find out why I was attracted only to "half men." He meant Wolfgang with the "sawed-off legs." Larry rocketed way up into the sky on slightly knock-kneed stems perching his big horse-head six feet four inches above the ground, (both tall men, John and Larry seemed to always bring up size as a point of ridicule when talking about other men). So I went to the psychiatrist and sent Larry the bill. He paid for about two years and then refused to pay anymore. I never did discover why I liked "sawed-off half men." The psychiatrist just laughed. Eight years later, Larry is still seething. The only thing he says to me with his well- placed words, when he lowers himself to look down and acknowledge that I am there, is "I've often wondered how many men you have had since me." And, "I've seen you with another little short guy, and think, 'She still likes those little short half men!' " It always hurt my neck, dating Larry, looking up all the time. I

45

look up now and say, "That is the same guy, Wolfgang. We still see each other." He puts up his hand to block any explanations. I go on. "I've only had two men, Wolfgang and then a professor. Four and four years. I'm not the way you think." By now he is turning his head like blows are hitting his jaw. I feel very small, short stubby, puny. I always felt this way, next to his elongations. I ask, "What is wrong, why are you so angry." He is very English, like Huxley in appearance. A mammoth old bony head with long lines down each cheek, a neck that has loosened, the skin no longer adhered to the pattern of the bone. He only lacks a pince-nez at his high bridge with the hump on it between his eyes. He says, "Why, you broke my heart, you know that." I am silenced. No, I didn't know that. I remember the look in his eye back then. A helpless gaze, probably the kind I turned on John, later which his daughter noticed. Larry looked silly actually I recall. Being in love. I didn't want to believe it. I didn't know what to do with it. He offered me everything: a house, to put my kids through college. But the timing was wrong. And he was too old. I felt dead around his grey hanging flesh. Everything pointed down to the ground, ready for the grave, gravity-tired. A big man with no muscle, and skin too big, staggering around inside it. And all that money. My kids liked Larry. He drove a big white Cadillac with a telephone in it. He called up and made reservations for dinner at quaint little French restaurants or big fancy places where you had you wear a bib to eat lobster. He coached me on needing to learn to waste when I'd ask for a doggy bag, getting glazed-eyed over the rich food. He watched me order foods I'd never eaten before and took in my naivety with fondness, a man who enjoyed his wealth only through a poor waif's experience. I ordered snail and quail in the same evening once and went home and threw up. He had a sales lady dress me at Macy's. I was humiliated. When my daughters saw the clothes they put them on immediately and never gave them back. I was glad. I didn't want them. He wanted me to do my hair. He wanted to make me over. My kids said then, "Marry him, marry him." Dollar signs danced in their eyes. I scolded, "You would sell your mother?" They nodded, back then, at thirteen and fourteen, with their own father home from the hospital and not himself. I tell Larry, "Well, let me tell you that I had my heart broken recently. Maybe that will even things up. And it wasn't some little short guy." Larry didn't seem interested. He ambled off on those long Huxley legs in grey slacks, his wallet not in his back pocket but at his breast over his heart in one of the rich-man pocket-lapelled jackets.

Before the Fence 1

They're drinking over there on Alex's side of the fence. I'm thinking over here on my side. That fence my old father erected to separate me from more ridicule and abuse. Before the fence, Alex would stand over on his side of the property, with his toes on the line he'd had surveyed by the County to make sure none at my plants touched his land, and chide me. I'd be out mowing my yard and he'd point and say I'd missed a piece, that I should get closer to that tree trunk, or something. And when I'd ignore him, he'd laugh at me just the way he laughed at me on campus twenty years before when I ignored his chiding. Or, if I'd respond by telling him to shut up, he'd laugh even louder, gleeful that he'd gotten a reaction out of me. The laugh was, of course, not a laugh, but a feigned laugh to make a buffoon out of another person. His family was good at laughter if it was to make someone feel the fool, to put themselves in a superior position. They laughed, not because something was funny, they saw no humor in life at all, and all its sweet funnies, but like jackasses, to egg someone into awkwardness. Before the fence, Alex lived in the family camper that stunk of butane. He was starting to get his headaches again. I'd go over there and open the tiny windows and air the place out when he wasn't there, or even when he was lying abed, in the overhead space on that foam rubber pad. He couldn't smell anything, he confessed; as a smoker, he'd lost his sense of smell. Even with our estrangement, I had a heart. A weakness to try to help keep him alive and well. Why help my enemy after a nasty divorce where he squandered the college fund I'd put away for the kids while he was recovering from pituitary tumor surgery. Before the surgery, he'd thrown away any extra money in the stock market and never saved a cent. What money he had when household expenses were paid, he'd spend on himself, buying yet one more tool or machine, while I went without any extras for the house. The fights we'd have, if I dared to buy a pretty throw rug, fish tank, new curtains, bedspread. He watched my "extravagant indulgence," as he called it, buying "junk" that'd have to be replaced in time, and ranted how the merchants were laughing their heads off over housewives like me trying to keep up with the latest colors and styles to decorate their homes. I would cry back then, feel ashamed, believe in his words, try to learn; while he justified his purchases because they would last. As soon as we divorced, I bought all the pretty things I'd ever wanted with my own money from rentals and teaching. Before the fence, he kept looking over at my life going on by the pool, in the yard, people visiting, tenants coming and going. He knew all my business. He'd brood, sitting in the second new car he'd bought with the kids' college fund money— which his sister told him to buy to use up any bank account so I wouldn't get the money in divorce court—listening to Bach and Beethoven tapes with the volume turned up so all the neighborhood could hear, sipping vodka and getting drunk on how sweet it is to be past responsibility, have a brain tumor excuse not to have to work, get a guaranteed income— the very thing he hated my sister on welfare for—in the mail every month from UAL, and buy the best car stereo and all the tapes he'd ever wanted of classical music, and marinate in the bitter sweetness of being set free to be. "Free to be" is a quote from his mother. Early in our marriage, she told me she was always prodding (literally) Alex, whom she called Skippy, to get busy and make something of himself. He'd answered one day, as he sat doing nothing under a tree, daydreaming, "Can't I just be?" She didn't learn from that, but never forgot it: this only son, wanting his life to be his own, with no one expecting him to be doing what they wanted done.

Before the Fence 2

Alex was 29 and I 23 when we bought the house with my first teaching checks. The field next door was just a grassy empty lot whose soil sprouted an abundance of wild mustard and turnip. The array of the yellow and purple blossoms those weeds brought forth, filled us with a sense of abundance. The sort, forty years later, even after ten years of boarding our horses there, lies fallow, flattened, cracked in places from dryness. The whole area used to be an Indian encampment, they told us. The easement next to my house was their burial ground of yellow clay used to build adobes. Indeed, we found the granite and sandstone grinding stones with the holes in the middle: the legend being that upon death, the grinding stone was punctured and buried with the user. In the easement, that was once a riverbed, other small artifacts surfaced over the years until one day Alex came riding a bulldozer home and shoved the whole front yard off into the dry riverbed; thus creating a front yard that no longer needed the concrete retaining wall to hold the upper yard from the lower yard where we entered the front door. The one standing weeping elm blew over in the first wind and was cut up for firewood. Old trees, Italian cyprus and that furzy desert tree lined my property, creating a canopy teeming with birds. The half acres hold small houses, built in 1947, standing east-west on the front up by the street, stretch for two blocks without sidewalks or street lights. In County Records, you can see on the map our rectangular half acre plots with a view of the mountains on one side, the ocean on the other and the freeway and railroad in between. There were no fences back then, forty years ago. In just seven years, our girls would get horses and ride up to the top of the ridge, through sage brush, oak trees, lemon and avocado orchards and later cherimoya and grape. Now fences line the roads with *keep out, no trespassing, private property* signs posted. New, much larger houses are being built: higher into the hills and even down in our neighborhood. Still, the length of my redwood and pine fence stands, that Flynn build at 70, dividing my half acre from Alex's; and on good days we trespass; and on bad we slam and lock the gate and feel safe on our side of the fence. Legal rights protect us. We do not dare trespass on days when we feel transgressed against. Tempers flair, old hates ignite, and vows renewed that we will never set foot on the property on the other side of the fence. On my side, I let the bamboo sway in the wind. I have let an elm grow and lift up the pool walkway. Two eucalyptus grew from pods and share air space, swaying with families of yellow nesting birds in season. Morning giory creeps along the gutters of the out buildings, finding ways to hang on and lift up edges of roofing. Bougainvillea, ginger, banana palm, trumpet, nasturtium, rose bushes. and jade, tropical potted plants put in the ground to survive on their own, and potted palms all share my half acre with eight cats, three dogs, and five people. A pool and jacuzzi take up the middle of the half acre where we used to grow a garden. All that weeding now turned to floating in water. The horse stall underwent changes from his shop to my studio. Once full of manure to a concrete floor covered with table saws, drill presses, lathes, to my three computers on desks under the skylights I had installed. This after the divorce. It stands behind and attached to what was once the garage, and now a small studio which is a rental. Once a family home, now partly a commercial venture. On my side of the fence, I wear my fingers and bare feet to the bone, maintaining all the life I've allowed to thrive here. On his side, clay, no trees or pets. Weed and gopher poison. Killing of life over there.

Precision

Flynn is like the cleaning woman who doesn't do windows. He doesn't do borders. I would still have to get out there and pull weeds and grass around all the edges of the sidewalks. I leaned a big broom on the front porch where he sits and smokes, hoping he would get the idea, but he never did. He also doesn't empty ashtrays. Some things are women's work. It is ingrained in him. He disables himself. The way Alex does by not cooking. Alex can't cook. That was what a wife was for, and without a wife he buys packaged foods and heats them in a microwave, or canned foods he opens with an electric can opener.

Alex gave me a weedwhacker for Mother's Day the last year we were married. Paid forty dollars for it to save my hands after fifteen years of pulling weeds. Then during the divorce he stole it back. I never saw it again. Then John gave me an electric weedwhacker for the last Christmas we were together. He saw it on sale for fourteen ninety-five. He gave me a plastic chicken beak to go with it. The beak had a rubber band so I could put it over my nose and walk around and be a fool, which I did because I was in love with him. It was a great joke, this beak and the weedwhacker. Even his kids laughed. But they didn't laugh when he opened my gift of hand-painted jockey shorts with a dead goose painted on the fly.

One morning, Alex woke me up with a lot of noise sounding like a grumbling Italian over the fence. A ynaa, ynaa. Real loud. I thought, "Oh, my weedwhacker." So I climbed over the fence to see it and Alex laughed. "Oh, that cheap thing wasn't any good. This one is a gasoline engine. It's got power. I then remembered the little electric one with its plastic whipping string that would always get short and have to be pulled out. In a kind of demanding voice, I insisted that he let me borrow this new one then. "Why, sure you can, Mother, heh,

heh," he was amused. I accused, "Well, you stole the one you gave me. Look at my hands. I'll get arthritis. He scoffed, "It's your genes. You just have big knuckles. You didn't work that hard." It was the old stuff. I'd worked 15 years as a wife. He never gave me recognition.

He begins to the sound of "You had it pretty good with me...." but I am back over the fence, and vow I will never talk to him again, and *never* ask him for a favor. He always said "You'll never make it without me." And then revised it, when he saw I didn't become a bag lady to "I was the best man you ever had." And then revised that to, "What are you going to do when you're old and ugly. I'd give you about, maybe, hmmmmmm, let's see," and he'd look me over, up and down and fold his arms, a "A good ten more years, give or take some."

I'd raise my voice, "I'd rather be old and ugly and alone, than with some old and ugly man...." And then he'd throw back his chicken yellow head and laugh out loud. A horse laugh. To my stomping off.

I shout now, "Bring the weedwhacker over tomorrow so Flynn can use it." When I get home the next day the yard is bare. No fringe of grass on the borders, no weeds around the trunks of trees and shrubs. In fact, even the good plants are shaved pretty close. That night Flynn is beaming. He's a kid again. He ventures out, without giving himself away, " I think I'll buy one of those gasoline engine weed-whatever-they're-called-whackers" I give him the first praise I've ever given him since he began doing things around the place. I say, "Yes, the yard looks pretty nice. Now I won't have to ruin my knuckles anymore." He beams. I have never wanted to give him nice words, afraid that there will be no end to this need for them. And I'll be like I once was, holding him together with them, even lying and letting him think he's better than he is. But that was all I knew once. Now I try to speak briefly about my borders, and do. "They look nice." I don't say, "Daddy." And I don't praise him. That is too intimate. I keep the formality between us. Ever watchful of his need getting on me. I make him stand alone. He prances around the kitchen floor. The cock of the walk for ever so short a moment. But, I notice after that he can't start the little engine enough with a rope starter and swing it around the yard. Next thing I know he has gone out and bought a weedwhacker of his own from Sears. "It was one some customer returned so I got a forty dollar discount on it." Usually I provided everything, and I was determined to use Alex's weedwhacker to use it up, as a kind of getting something from him.

Over the weeks, Flynn talked about his little gasoline engine weedwhacker. His elbow hurts from starting it, pulling the rope. His flesh-less arms carted it from place to place and I'd hear that whine of power. Once I looked out and saw him clear a whole space of tall unruly grasses standing waist high. They lay on their sides in a split second. Flynn looked triumphant. I told a friend. "They ought to supply all the old age homes with weedwhackers, so much empowerment with so little effort."

Flynn is turning my yard into the Nevada desert. "I'm afraid to tell him to take it easy. It's the first time he's taken the initiative. He comes in at night and has a hearty appetite. I cook a crooked-necked squash and a baked potato and a yam. Anything he can gum down, as a way of thanking him for taking an interest in helping out. When he first moved in he never noticed my predicament, only wanted attention for his depression. I was work worn over the place—all the maintenance. I'd have to look prostrate, as if I really needed help. Then I'd have to ask him. He'd usually give me some reason fixing that thing is impossible. "It'll entail turning off the water for about ten years, or taking off one whole wall to find out what's wrong. Or that corroded pipe won't come off after twenty years now. You'll have to replace the whole thing all the way to China." I'd slam out of the house, cursing under my breath, then I'd go to Alex and get his opinion "Well, Mother, if I were you, I'd replace that whole unit—it'll only cost about two thousand dollars," and "Oh, Mother, wait let me explain…." I'd be shouting by now. "Then why didn't you replace it when you had the house…." Alex always got by, and now his solutions for me are to go "whole hog," as he calls it.

After the lawns are mowed and properly whacked, and the whacker is lined up with the four lawn mowers out by the pool, snug against Flynn's cabana I hear his old car dust-covered deepthroat its way down to Carrow's. He putts away for a cup of coffee. My new roomer Sal says, "Your father is kept going on artificial stimulants of caffeine and nicotine," to my arguments concerning health food. I say, "Isn't my father an example of everything you say not being true? He has not given his body complex carbohydrates, amino acids, fiber, trace mineral and all that other stuff you want me to take." He says, "Caffeine stimulates the brain and gives a false sense of well-being, a nervous energy that can serve his needs temporarily, but the quality of his life is not what it could be if he had taken care of himself." Dropping his r's all the way! In his New York, Long Island dialect. "Like your dad," I say, seeing his dad, at 76, like Flynn, but happily married and appearing healthy, although, he, too, is only a hundred and ten pounds, and a rugged little man who has a nice arrogant strut to him. Both men would be like roosters in a pen, if they got together. Both tough, only went to the ninth grade, supported families for fifty years and grew stark white hair towards the end. Sal lets it go. He will not argue.

After the lawns and after coffee, Flynn takes out his bow and arrow, poises it in the air and lets go. I see a paper cup across the lawn has the arrow through it. Flynn took up archery in his old age. It's not like him. He never shot an arrow all through my childhood. And now he has a quiverful of them. Does he need a kind of precision power or what? He stands in the front yard and shoots a tiny paper cup he has placed along one bank about forty feet away. He never misses. He stands all of his height, shoulders so straight—the osteoporosis theory of my mother's concerning his health falls apart—and fits an arrow into the bow with deft fingers. Fingers I don't like to look at. Fingers I hated as a child. Fingers I try to shame myself out of still reacting to now that I am not only grown up, but grown old. He presses his bow out in front of him just so and I hear the air speak of the arrow's speed and I see the paper cup, and there it is. I ask, "Don't you ever miss?"

and wait for some droll comment, like "Only if one of your tenants comes in through the gate unexpected…like the other day.…" I keep moving, never staying long around Flynn.

I survey my lawns. Nicely groomed but speckled with fiberglass filtertips from Flynn's cigarettes. I've asked him not to smoke in the house, when I put in a new carpet, hurting his dignity. I had to paint the room he'd been in for two years. The spiders were dead, their webs yellow from nicotine, hanging low and heavy. I could imagine Flynn's lungs. I moved Flynn out to the pool room. And now I didn't want to insist he pick up his butts. He throws them in the yard. I put an ashtray on the front porch. Some of the butts ended up where he sits in the old chair and smokes. I live with the butts on my lawn. Most old daughters have to put up with something from their old fathers I believe.

Over the Fence

I haven't heard Alex for three days. He lives over the fence. His camper sits close enough to my bedroom window to hear his familiar snorts, and his door slamming as he comes and goes—that little hard-to-close metal camper door.... I am only aware that I hear him when there is silence for a long time. I begin to wonder now if he is down with another headache. He gets them every three months routinely since his head operation twelve years ago.

One time, not long ago, he ended up in the hospital. Only his mother bothered to wonder why he didn't answer the phone. At 86 she got on a bus and came out with her well-shod foot and stepped ever so carefully down the dirt-clod field to his dilapidated camper and found her son in a coma. He had never gotten that bad off before. The ambulance came and by the time I found him in Emergency, after going to the wrong hospital because no one had a record of his delivery, he was lying out on a table like a great slab of the palest white fish, gown open and a nurse trying to find a vein. There was no blood pressure. He was dehydrated.

I talked into his ear, close up, and kind of scolded him. How could a grown man let himself fall apart like that? But there was tenderness I didn't want to face. We'd been together under the same roof for fifteen years and divorced after twenty. He was family. I said, "Alex, what is going on? Why didn't you let someone know?" He mumbled from deep in his trance, his eyelids fluttering like a blue parakeet, that he just took to bed. The truth was that there was no one to let know. He didn't want to bother his old mother and inconvenience her. His sisters lived across the country. I was his ex-wife and was clearly on my own and had my own life. And his kids were off in school and he didn't want to worry them. He had weathered his headaches out alone before and would continue to.

But this time he was not able to keep his medication down. His medication was what he took from the time of the operation and on. His pituitary had been damaged by a tumor and was not able to produce adrenalin on cue, or testosterone or hydrocortisone. Without these he would peacefully drift off to death. This particular headache was so painful he was nauseated, and was not able to keep his medication or any liquid down. I never would have gone over to check. He also had his own life and was now none of my business anymore.

As I stood by his emergency table side, I studied this man and couldn't let it register. His blond boyish head, eyes so blue that when the slits of them opened there was almost no color at all. Just a glint of light. Sky blue and blond as a new born chick. A short beak. He was still young, a boy following his dream at 56. The camper was nestled next to a big house he was building. From over my fence I could see the structure begin to loom up and tower over my little place and cast a shadow on my patio and pool, giving me a short sunset. At times in the late day, Alex himself cast his shadow over my yard, and on me, making me move from my chair to catch the last rays of sun. He was putting shingles on his roof and silhouetted himself against the sky. An absurd visage for any gathering of people I might have in my yard back there. "That's your ex-husband?" people would say, and laugh, shaking their heads. "How can you stand it?"

"It's the shade that bothers me," I'd joke. And there it'd be, Alex's shadow streaking across the grass, elongated by the setting sun, hitting the old work shop and going up it. By dusk he was as long as the yard.

The last time John was out, just before we broke up, he got in the jacuzzi during the late part of the day, something he had never done before (his behavior changed toward the end). Alex was framing then, and trying to get the plywood laid before the rains.

Later Alex asked, "Who was that fat man swimming in the pool the other day?"

I said, "That wasn't a fat man, that was John."

"Oh, Mother, do you really like all that fat?" he asked,

creasing his eyes down in sympathy. "When you were married to me, I remember you hated fat men." He still calls me Mother. He calls his mother Gertrude.

One morning Sal woke up beside me in the bedroom Alex built onto the house when we were married, where he remembered he wanted to be when he was in Intensive Care after the operation, and where we spent many hours making love and talking and being husband and wife, and Sal said, "Sounds like someone just went in the pool."

I had heard it too. "It's just Alex taking a bath. He jumps in my pool every morning to wake up."

Sal is silent. Later in the day he asks gently. "Does Alex ever just come in the house without asking first?"

I tell him "Not anymore." I used to let him do that, but finally he was invading my privacy. He started saying things I didn't like. I'd be yelling at him again just like when we were married. It occurred to me that I didn't have to let him have access to the house.

He liked hot showers. I felt sorry for him. He said, and kept repeating, that the hot shower was the greatest invention of civilization. They helped his headaches. But then he'd start in on what's broken around the place and how there is no easy way to fix it—I'd have to jack-hammer up the foundation just to change a leaky faucet and I chased him out. He can never come up with a simple solution to anything. I'd always end these speeches with, "The only regret in letting you divorce me is that we can't divorce again."

By then Sal is shushing me, not wanting to know, sorry he asked. He is very decent and still believes in talking nice about people behind their back. I don't know when I lost that trait, or if I ever had it. It seems I tell the next man all about the previous ones in a kind of twisted sense of honesty. They all have listened and felt the previous guy was inferior to them, except for Sal. He says, "You will be saying things like this about me...." (Sal is a drug dealer, it will turn out, and uses my house as a hideout! Keeps a ledger and, like a gigolo, hopes to get my house eleven years later. This I learn parts of later when we break up over his stealing my puppies.)

As I stand beside Alex in Emergency, he begins to stir. The IV is taking effect with one million units of vitamin C. He says, "Hello Mother, thank you for coming." Disbelief is in his eye. Wonder, even suspicion. I don't smile. Keep it at duty level. He has already proposed that we get together again.

I don't want him to mistake concern and maternal love for anything else. I knew that after only a few hours together, we'd begin to clash over all the old stuff. After twenty years we each went back to exactly what we had been doing when we met. Alex lived in a tiny trailer then and ate canned foods.

I was running around bare-footed with my hair askew and keeping a houseful of people and animals. I had a rabbit chewing electric cords and leaving pellets everywhere, and a fish net, a giant turtle shell, and I ate anything on the spur of the moment (before we married).

Being together hadn't made us blend or influenced us in any way to take up the other one's style. That had always been the conflict. A competition. From his Intensive Care bed, fresh out of his brain tumor operation back then, he had said. "Well, I guess you won." And I knew what he meant.

He comes to, now, with a sweet face. The scowl is gone. An angelic question is there, as if he's seen peace up in Heaven. Taken out of his own hands for awhile and with a less exacting task master than himself. He looks at me as if we are together. As if I have come for him. As if someone will look after him now. Inside I vow to make him eat more salads and less doughnuts and wienies. More fruit. Like Flynn, he doesn't equate his real earthy flesh with what he does, how he lives, what he eats, what he breathes.

I began then, at his hospital bed, to try to indoctrinate him—"You need to eat fresh fruit and vegetables...."—and trail off. Like with Flynn, love would be the answer. Someone to love and care for him. But both men worked themselves right out of women with their nasty dispositions.

When I go investigate Alex now, sure enough he's been down with a headache for three days. I see myself in bed with Sal all that time just fifteen feet away on the other side of the fence, being loved up. Some guilt comes. I make a big pot of chicken soup and take it by no moon light. The darkest night of the year feeling my way barefooted down the field to the tiny camper. When I enter, Alex raises up on one elbow, his face contorted with pain.

Old Women

I drive by Alex's field on the way home from the gym and swing in and get out of my car. He's in his half-finished house, blonde hair flattened down on top but billowing disobediently on the sides, Tom Sawyer jeans, and some once-nice dress shirt used for a work shirt. Eyes creased down in the Alex style of "so much to do." The house sits way back on the lot. All the other houses are up front along the street. But Alex has started with the garage/workshop first, which was designed to live in while he is building the big house later. That will be up front. As I approach, barefooted, hot powdery dirt feeling good, sunshine all over the place, I talk loud. No one can hear me. All the neighbors are at work, and the ones home are invisible. No one is ever seen in their yards in this neighborhood. Alex lives in his. Foliage borders these lots out here. I feel strong from the gym and eager to heal the world.

I demand, "Let me see your food." Alex cocks one ear. It's what he always does. The jet engines. He can't hear a certain range of tones. He used to curse my voice when we were married. It was too loud and always on the wrong subject. I used to yell back that he couldn't hear if I talked in a normal tone. And I hated repeating myself. I told people after the divorce, "It was because I had to say everything twice." And he had a way of saying, *pard*on?" emphasizing the *pard*. There was a dog food called Pard, when I first met him. I used to laugh then, at him; but even after I explained what was so funny, he never got the point to think it was funny. Now he tips his ear and I am in my most commanding voice. I've had it with his foolishness. "Let me see your food."

Alex is agreeable. He opens his camper door—the family camper we drove to Baja once and into the Sierras once as a young family. Other wives told of their ex-husbands living in their yards, too, in a camper, after their divorces.

We step way up to get in and he opens a cupboard above the sink. It is a small overhead camper cupboard with a very shallow space. About ten cans are lined up. He says, "This is it." Both proud and hesitant, torn between wanting to get pity and being independent. I see Campbell's soup, tomatoes, green beans, beets, corn. Pretty pictures on the labels.

I feel suddenly sad, but go about the business I've come for. I take a can, turn it toward the light from the open door and say, "Listen to this, here's what you're eating, 280mg. of sodium, 49 of sugar, 1 unit of potassium, and 98 calories." I take another can.... and read the same kind of thing. He reaches in and hands me the beets, hope in his eyes. I read 187mg of sodium, beets (but of course), 85mg of sugar, citric acid, and three or four things I stumble over pronouncing, and 102 calories." His face drops. If he could be ashamed, he would, but he only looks defeated, like a boy who tried to act grown up and failed.

I say " Oh, Alex, you're only eating salt and sugar. They only used the vegetables as a medium for these things to have something to put in the can. They have to call it something, but there's no food value. Only calories. Then you work all day so hard, and your cells are crying out for nutrients, and you bathe them in this saline and sugar solution." He looks both petted and scolded. I try to act authoritative, but it's strictly to do the right thing. I don't want him to start trying to put his arm around me. My voice stays sharp, serious, to the point. I could be a home nurse.

"Do you have any real food in the house?" He thinks, and suddenly turns and says that he thinks he has some potatoes somewhere, but that they have probably gone bad. He roots around under a cupboard where his shaver and ten thousand items are crammed, perched, stacked, and stuffed. Clutter— exactly what he criticized me for when we were married. And he brings out a bag of potatoes. I can smell them. White tendrils are reaching through the holes of the brown plastic bag. I take them, holding them away from my clothes. "Here, let me make you a potato salad." We jump down out of the camperful of thirty years of stuff he'd stuffed into this small space. Not that he's lived here thirty years. But next door in my house, once our house. He's lived in the camper about five; I've lost count. But he took so much stuff from the house during the divorce that he filled up the camper and built a gigantic shed next to it to hold the rest. His thirty years accumulation of tools, machines, stored, along with anything else of value he could find on the premises. I saw him coming out of the front window with a pillow case full of stuff once. My mother still laments the "beautiful copper lid" she gave me that disappeared when Alex did, along with the few pieces of "real silver" in the silverware drawer. She gave me those, too, against my protests, scoffing at stainless steel. And the onyx eggs from Africa his sister gave us, and the little wooden elephants his father had given us. It was just as well. The tenants would have taken anything of value later when I began renting out rooms. If Alex hadn't. I never cared for anything I had to worry about losing. Now Alex has to worry about it. He can't leave his property for fear of thieves. And he was known to have told someone after he retired from the airlines. "I could get on a plane today and never get off, and travel for the rest of my life if I wanted." It was the only thing that bothered me about getting divorced. I lost those free passes.

But Alex stands in his field now and keeps an eye on all the stuff, gets headaches, and builds onto his house. It is a life project, I believe. I don't anticipate him ever finishing it. There are still places in my house he never finished.

My brother came to visit once and said. "Well, Alex is finally out standing in his field." I laughed. Even Alex laughed after he tipped his ear and my brother repeated it, saying "outstanding" as two words.

I take the potatoes home. The bag leaks on my car seat and on my clean pants. I throw it in the sink and find about ten good ones out of the whole bunch. I spend half the afternoon cutting up fresh raw vegetables and finding spices and adding salt-free, egg-free, oil-free mayonnaise and good vinegar that will help with the digestion. His gut has a bloat to it. Too much gluten in the flour he eats.

He needs enzymes. I'll give him enzymes. Apple cider

vinegar with residue in the bottom. That'll clean him out. Then I taste the large heap. Sprinkle some more trace mineral "salts" for flavor. Alex has been heard to say, "Maybe people will opt for living shorter lives if the food just tastes good." I peel chicken breasts from the chicken I cooked the night before for my little seven-pound dog that lives in my bedroom. We are about the same age. She's fourteen in dog years, blind in one eye, almost deaf, and is growing estrogen tumors on her teats (I am too, but I won't know it for ten years). I give Alex her chicken breast, placing it on top of the salad in a big pot, and take the whole thing to the ladder in the backyard leaning against the six foot fence I had Flynn put up without a gate during the divorce. I climb up, call him, and hand it over. He looks like I might be giving him a bomb. He says, with steady eyes levelled on me, "Why thank you Mother," and takes it off the top of the fence where I'm balancing it. It's heavy.

I say "Solid vegetables, no salt, no sugar, no fats, no pre-servatives. Just nutrition. And I want my pot back." And disappear before I can hear his reply. I just want him to stop poisoning himself on canned food. He really needs a wife. I am thinking, "No wonder he got married. " I see myself as one of these little old ladies taking in boarders just to keep their habit of serving someone going. You see them in old age homes sitting and doing nothing and their hands twitching in and out, in and out. And their lips puckering and stretching, puckering and stretching. Will I be one of those one day, I wonder, when there is no one to *do* anything for, or talk to. Hands and mouths, hands and mouths, finally coming to a rest but not able to rest, still going through the motions of a trained server. Do they keep moving even inside the casket? Old women used to serving?

Over the Fence 2

Yesterday: Alex and I working together with the fence between us. It's the way we should have always been. Married with the fence as part of the vows. He hands me his long-handled snippers, and a hand saw he swears by. It's not the kind a child draws grandpa using, but a metal saw shape suddenly big. A circular handle and little razor teeth.

It is right outside my sliding glass door off the kitchen, On the west side of the house. The dark side. No sun gets to it. A rambling rose bush so old it's roots are bonsai thick and gnarled and lifting up the sidewalk, I saw off a limb, looking up, standing underneath, getting sawdust in my eyes. Alex delights in the pruning from his side of the fence, until I say, "Come on, this is what I got divorced over, your trimming everything, killing things. I like foliage."

He coaxes and coaches, standing on some old gas tank on his side of the fence so he can hang over, waist-high and supervise me, because I borrowed his tools. "Oh, Honey, you'll get more growth if you cut it way back. Look at that dead wood on that rose bush. Just take it down to that first knee."

"Knee!" I feign a scoff. How fun it is to make fun of Alex again. To have someone so interested in doing everything just right.

I've been around non-workers for so long. Men lying around all day on the bed scratching their balls for something to do, and using their cock's head as a substitute for thinking. Men who lack ideas or ambition. Men who have already made their money and achieved in their professions and now, semi-retired, have nothing to do.

I use my free-weight gym shoulders and Nautilus hard muscles to reach above my head, and thick limbs come crashing to the ground. The largest arteries of the old bush.

"That's it baby," Alex groans from his side of the fence, the way he used to in bed for fifteen years. "Oh yeah, now you're getting it. Ah, just a little bit lower, yeah, now, right now, right there, no, a little lower, ahhhhh. Yes...."

His delight in trimming everything back, controlling growth always annoyed me. He couldn't stand for a plant to do what it wanted to do. Every time a sprig would shoot up and out and twirl in the air, he'd snap it off. I used to accuse him, "And your sisters are the same way. They all have naturally curly hair and what do they do, go to the butcher and have him shave it off so it fits like a cap. Afraid of letting any hair go in the direction it wants to go in. Alex, himself wets his wild, curly, platinum blond hair down each day, and mashes it against his head. When it defies the comb, he asks me to give him a haircut, and in my kitchen, with a towel around his shoulders, I reluctantly cut off his curls so he looks like a Nazi. He scowls into my little bathroom mirror, satisfied, takes a big sniff and a snort of approval, and stomps out my back deck, climbs the ladder and goes over the fence to his field again. He proudly tells me that he will have concrete poured on most of his half acre lot after the house is built, I can picture that. He'll no doubt spray down the concrete every morning like they do at the dog pound, Alex, the sterile, the expedient. When I asked about plants, he told me he will have some very nice ones in pots.

I hold his long-handled snippers above my head and continue to find tendrils that are choking my electrical wires, In the wind one night I heard these branches scraping against the house. I slept restless to the sound of those groanings, and awoke disturbed. They came to me as urgencies, beggings, cravings, sorrows. As I see light glance off my kitchen window again I begin to agree with Alex and snap away at the jungle of entangled pittosporum, loquat, and rambling rose. While Alex gutturals away with pleasure. He finally hands over a ladder, I am on tiptoe, and jumping up into the air a little like a snapping turtle.

The ladder is a cheap one. This is unlike Alex, He spares no expense for equipment. They must have been giving these away as door prizes at the Price Club. It is a bit wobbly. I brace it on even ground and climb barefooted. He used to make fun of my toes, calling them "salamanders." They hold to the rungs now, and I am sure-footed as a goat on a rock. I say, "This is a spinal injury ladder."

"Heh, heh," from his side of the fence, a good ol' Marty always the dour sour attempt at humor. Heh, heh, heh sound. Then in a serious instructor's voice, "See your electrical wires, Mother? I'd say, you have been very lucky the house hasn't burned down yet. You just can't let plants take over. They're destructive." He urges me to look, pointing with his wide, pale hands that are so strong he can hammer boards into place with them. I look, reluctant, I have told people, "I want to write a book about all the things I never wanted to know about my house." I see the rambling rose has in fact intertwined itself all around the wires, my wires now, and the rubber coating is worn off in places leaning against the shingles. "Bare wires," comes to mind as a phrase I've heard. I am alarmed. As I slept little sparks were, no doubt, emitted all night long like dragging a sulphur match along the friction side of its box.

Alex looks sympathetic, "Oh, Mother," He is sad for me. He can see that I cannot take the responsibility of the house with any grace. "Just do one thing at a time, and you'll be able to manage your place." I can hear the relief in his tone that it is no longer his place. And the edge of vengeance, glad that I am learning my lesson, after watching him try to maintain the place for fifteen years and criticizing his style and frustration, and final brain tumor from stress. It is all mine, now. It used to be an Indian burial ground.

I clip and hand him the end of a long rose vine and he pulls; a thread of thorns and leaves and blossoms ripping and snapping as they find their way through the crisscross of branches to Alex's heap on his side of the fence. His truck awaits, I say, "Wait." And step down from the ladder, avoiding thorns, run into the house, find a scissors, race out, and cut a nice bouquet of pink rambling roses. Alex waits, watches, smiles. I can feel his eyes on me. "Oh, there she is. The woman. Roses, Ah, yes." It is in his patience. Then it is his turn.

He says, "Here, Madam," And I look up and he is bowing deeply with a swoop of his hand, as if it is a cap with a feather in it and he is Errol Flynn. He hands me one long-stemmed branch of rose buds.

"Babies!" I cry in one voice, amazed he saved them, and that I overlooked them in my fear of bare wires, and in another voice, lower and playfully sarcastic, "I didn't think you would ever give me a gift of flowers."

"Anything is possible," he smiles. Lays his eyes on me. The word "fondly" comes to mind. And then Alex pitchforks the trimmings over the fence.

Abilities

When Alex was a little boy, he knew how things worked. He saw things in their parts and pieces. And liked to take them apart and put them back together again. But, alas, like in the fairy tales with their gross symbolism he was born into an upper middle class white-collar family in the days when they let babies cry in their cribs and didn't spare the rod later on.

Over the fence now, Alex's ability, which he took pride in while he grew up, but was not accepted by his family who hired bluecollar laborers to do these manual jobs if something broke around the house, while little Alex watched with fascination, is evident. The whole half acre is cluttered with things in disrepair, ready to be put back together or taken apart, or built from scratch. Is it a proclivity gone awry, or finally in bloom? He says he's happy for the first time.

When he first met Flynn, he a said to me "It's a shame about your father and what he did to you, because I could benefit from his knowledge. He knows a lot about mechanics." Louis, the Marine, my brother said, "Alex should have been an engineer, he's got a native intelligence for it." I had to go to college and get a degree to learn mechanical engineering, and when I talk to him, he knows everything without opening a book."

The three of them stand around in my yard now, heads together over how to earthquake-proof my garage, required by the County. There is a kinship among them. It only took thirty years for the socioeconomic barriers, the personality quirks, and male egos to dissolve, so they could find they were all alike. It took me getting out of the way, so I was not an issue of importance to any of them any more. Ownership of a female did much to alienate them and keep them territorial. And their aging and losing enough so their male egos softened enough to listen to another male.

They will come up with some solution to my problem, that I am paying them to solve. No emotional leanings, just professional skills. Flynn will under-fix, Alex, over-build, and Louis, the big brother, once a Marine, will bring in equipment too big for the job, and over-do.

I will go out there and nip at them with words to keep them as efficient as possible. I just want the job done, no heroic efforts, proof of honor, or recognition of genius. Flynn will want recognition of genius, Alex, heroism, and Louis honor. I get so tired of dealing with males and their needs. As an older female, I just don't want the garage to fall down in an earthquake, as the County makes me comply.

Serena

Alex could never get the hedge to grow out front; and he so
wanted to have it between us and the neighbors. It was one of
those blue poison berry hedges with ivy kind of leaves that the
birds would go after, leaving black splats all over the driveway
when the berries were ripe. A flutter of wings landing on that
flimsy vine with the broad leaves. Alex had lists of things to
do, and make the hedge grow all the way across the front of
our property was only one of them, and not a priority. First, he
bulldozed off the front yard and brought it down even with the
front door, pushing the three-foot high retaining wall of cin-
derblock into the easement along with the dirt. We lived along
a dry riverbed that was known as a Chumash burial ground of
sorts, since we found granite and sandstone grinding stones
with holes broken out in their centers. We'd heard that they
did that when someone died and buried them with their pestle
and bowl. I used the few we found, later, as headstones for
dead pets, as each cat and dog lived out their lives on the property until old age. I think the granite one is under my bedroom
window, sunk low into the soil after so many years. It's been
forty-two, here on Serena. If my twins are forty-one. That's
how I keep track of time, anymore. Otherwise all the years
run together and are one long one where he watched my flesh
metamorphose into wrinkles and spots. When Alex didn't
carry me over the threshhold, because we were above all that
silliness, I was 23, already pregnant with babies that would be
born in eight months, a month early, premature, four pounds
each. At that time, the hedge was a few sprigs sprouting awk-
wardly near the shoulder of the road where our property line
began. A small neighborhood road without sidewalks or street
lights. It appealed to us when we were driving around looking for a house to buy with my first teaching money. I'd saved

two thousand dollars from my first teaching job that winter, graduating in the middle of the year and marrying in July. July 13, a Friday. New teachers made five hundred a month in 1961. I lived frugally and it mounted up. Alex didn't work at all; he was back to school on the G.I. Bill and drove a bus after school for extra cash. He'd been an Air Force cadet for three years, and three years into our marriage he went to work as a pilot for United. Meanwhile he built fiberglas boats for a living while I taught until they made me go home. Teachers couldn't "show" in those days. By December I was showing, at five months. Twins came in April of 1963, soon to be followed less than two years later by a third baby. I wanted one more, but was told by Alex that three was enough. We had our boy and girl and second girl, and that was it. Meanwhile, the hedge was inching its way across the concrete retaining wall above our front lawn near the shoulder at the road. Our neighborhood was on a slope, with a foothill a half mile above us, and the ocean a quarter mile below us across the freeway and railroad track, with a frontage road in between. The retaining walls were everywhere, holding the earth back lest we slip into the blue Pacific. We had earthquake warnings once in awhile. One night, a neighborhood crier knocked on our door and warned us of the earthquake in Japan causing a tsunami, or tidal wave along the California coast. Alex gathered up his new little wife and babies, packed a large jar of peanut butter for food, and headed for the foothill road. It was three AM. I was disappointed when the wave didn't come, hoping for a little excitement, a break in the monotony of daily living. All that happened was boats being knocked around in a high tide in the harbor, and a few of them beached.

Alex was a malcontent who wanted to build a vehicle of escape. In the first years of our marriage, he sat in his big chair, as men had in those days. The head of the household had the big easy chair, the wife a side chair a little smaller and less distinct, and the children, a variety of lesser chairs. That's where The Three Bears got their story. Men, it was believed in those days were bigger than women and children in every sense of the word, in importance, size, intelligence,

73

and responsibility out in the world. They were the ones to go to the door if there was a bump in the night. They were the ones to protect the women and children. After the Feminist movement, a man said, referring to the sinking of the Titanic, "I'd get in the lifeboats first; the women and children could fend for themselves." He meant it. It was the generation right after Alex's. By then, women were opening their own doors, picking up their own tabs, earning their own money, taking birth control, relying on penicillin for sexual transmitted disease. This freedom would go on until AIDS. The only good thing about AIDS is that it made herpes look good! Morality was based on antidotes for behavior. When those ran out, suddenly, the old abstinance returned. Life was good, death was bad; therefore don't do such and such if you could die. It was the *Old Testament* all over again, which I called *The Old Testicle*, written by men, for men. Women were considered lesser creatures back then, not to be listened to. "It is better to live in an attic than to be nagged by a woman," or some such quotation was often recited and chuckled over, to make a point for any wife to stop talking at him so much.

It was the early Sixties and Alex occupied his big easy chair with a drawing board on his lap, an ashtray resting on a chairside table and a pack of cigarets in his shirt pocket. He wore the slacks and cotton dress shirts of his people on the east coast. Levis and t-shirts were California style that never caught on with him. He'd muse into the evening with the news on, sketching on blueprint paper with the little squares. Smoke would fill the livingroom. The kids and I would inhale it while we ate dinner, had baths, dressed for bed and had a goodnight story. In the morning, we'd inhale it over breakfast. Alex was never without a cigarette. He smoked Kents. He coughed in the mornings and cleared his pipes by blowing water over the basin through his nostrils. I used to call him a sperm whale, the way he'd splash the tile and leave it spotted with his morning routine of dousing his nicotine head with cold water to clear it for the days work. Work was going off to the boat company and painting on fiberglas layers over boat molds—until the company folded. Alex contracted mononucleosis and lay abed for weeks. We got by. When he recuperated, he joined the Air Force Reserves and flew over Viet Nam before the war. Later he applied and was offered a job by three airlines. He chose United. We were making money now, which freed Alex up to begin laying out a fiberglas hull for a two-man scuba submarine that would work like a fish bladder, filling with air and water in separate compartments to descend and ascend, speeding faster than any small submarine of its day. He fell asleep with *Mechanical Science* magazine on his chest every night with the lamp on. I'd creep to bed at a late hour after finishing my duties, writing, and exercising in front of the Johnny Carson show.

Alex would look at the vine absently and then consciously shake his head, cursing under his breath in disbelief that it grew low and close to the ground and stopped halfway across the front of the yard. This, on the way to the car, which we parked in front then. The vine that wouldn't grow represented something to Alex that was a constant irritant.

If

If I went back to Alex it'd make everything easier. If Sal wasn't around I'd consider going back to Alex. I feed him heaping plates of food. I buy him bags of supplements and vitamins, I wash his clothes. I do everything I did as his wife except sleep with him. I sleep with Sal. I sleep with Sal only because he's there. I wouldn't sleep with Sal if he would just go away; but he won't go away. I've tried to scare him away and still he won't go. In fact, he holds on tighter; I can't get out of his sight. He's the way I wanted Alex to be when we were married, possessive, jealous, telling me he loved me all the time. But, back then, Alex was arrogant, right out of the Airforce as an officer and thinking I was lucky to have him, even though he was the one who pursued me until I married him. I didn't even like Alex. He convinced me. I was amused by his ardor. And flattered? And already an old maid at twenty-one, in those days. Had just graduated and was teaching school. I remember the biologies—I was simply ready. My body did it. I had no mind. When I finally had a mind, I left him. Or, I made life so miserable for him he chased me away. I never would have left Alex, I've never been able to end anything. Not even letting Flynn hang around. Wolfgang still calls. Kevin would if he hadn't shot himself. When I went for counseling all I heard was, "You hang onto the past." My kids look in the garage and see all their stuff from the time they were born. Their first scribbles, first everything. Boxes and boxes of things going bad. Right up to the present. Now they count on it. They all bring things home and tell me to save it for them. And they tell me to be good to their dad. "Dad's not like you, Mom," they say, "He needs someone to take care of him."

If I went back to Alex would it prove failure? Would he rub my nose in defeat? He always said I couldn't make it without him. He's watched me break up with two men, each five year efforts at a "relationship." I've called him to tell him all the details, and he's sympathized one minute and swelled up with conviction the next, knowing only too well what the real problem was, so that each man got away "before you did them in." But he knew better than to say it.

If I went back to Alex he could worry about the house. He likes to worry about it. He's made that way, with those ears, that nose, those hands, like clubs. I've watched him hammer a nail into a wall without a hammer with those fat fists in a fit of temper. He was made to keep tuned into the needs of a house. It exercises that insane energy and skill he has, a sheer determination to conquer inanimate objects that try to defy him. And make them obey. He used to love it when something broke. It would stimulate that bad little boy he always was, the one his parents tried to beat out of him, the one who would take clocks and radios apart, and steal up into the attic without permission and get into everything and make a mess. The Alex who could prove again that he knew how to fix things, but more: *knew how they worked*, "The mad inventor" someone called him once after seeing some of his solutions to problems around the house. His innovations would make the visiting Flynn, back then, snerf.

If I went back to Alex he'd take this place in his stride. Not like when I got up last week to the sound of the refrigerator making an animal sound. A wail and gnashing of teeth. I went to it in sorrow and empathy to help it. It let out a continuous high-pitched whine and whimper so poignant that I thought of calling the vet. I thought maybe an animal was caught in there, in the motor. I went to it, opened it, looked in, poked at it, touched it all over and could not soothe it. The painful howl and yip got louder. From work I called Alex. All he has to do is step over the six-foot fence without a gate I built during the worst part of the divorce when I stopped speaking to him and hated the sight of him. I used my damsel-in-distress voice (sweet and weak and about to expire from being overwhelmed by reality. A reality that is no big deal to a man like Alex. It even humored him.) It got to his King Arthur place and he rode over on his steed and later told me, "I didn't have to do anything. It just stopped by itself. Probably a slipping fan belt. Sometimes they'll do that." I felt a "My savior," flutter in my breast, but quelled it. I sighed out loud instead. What is a disaster to me is nothing at all to Alex. And it never ceases to impress me.

If I went back to Alex he'd do something about my septic tank, too. It's nothing for him to rent a back hoe and dig up the whole backyard and put in a new system, pump out the seventeen months accumulation of solids since he left, and then come in, wash his hands, and wolf down a pot of spaghetti, sixteen oatmeal cookies, a half gallon of ice milk, and sip B&B all night while sucking down two packs of cigarettes. It would be all in a day's work.

But, alone with this house, I look in the yellow pages for men to come out and solve my problems. They charge hundreds and hundreds of dollars. I lie there at night and stare at the dark calculating what it takes to keep this place going. Each man takes such a toll I begin to wonder if I've done the right thing.

The only problem, if I went back to Alex, would be Alex, himself. Could I stand having him under the same roof again with all of his quirks, the old hissing under his breath, cursing the world all day (or is he over that, by now?) Was that just the younger Alex, before he was broken, when he still believed he had a future to get to. Has he accepted *life* by now. He said, not long ago, that he is happier now than he has ever been. He's got a guaranteed income for life and nothing to do except what he wants (That's what he hated my little sister for —being on "welfare."). That is what he told me he wanted when he first met me. At that time he was just out of the Airforce and back on campus with the G.I. Bill. And driving the city bus. He owned nothing but an old blue Chrysler convertible and a TearDrop trailer. He lived at The Deluxe Trailer court on Punta Gorda Street, which I'd always called Fat Point Street.

If Alex could have seen himself up here now, then, on his half acre, living in a camper, with one of his dreams manifesting itself in the shape of a big house looming up and out and away from him into the air, would he have eased up? Back then it was a Big Boat he dreamed of. He wanted to sail all over the world. Thirty years later he's flown all over the world. In a uniform sitting in a cockpit, and alighted in each country to be taken to a hotel by limo.

It was not his idea of adventure. He wanted to pit himself against the unknown. The unknown turned out to be marriage and all the responsibility, and he cracked under that. Alex was never happy being a pilot for an airline. There was no challenge to it. Once again he and his ingenuity was left out. He was "just a cog in a wheel," he used to say. Now, if he'd been a bush pilot…He used to complain that his future was all tied up, written out, (Like Flynn refusing the free lunches provided for senior citizens, saying he doesn't want to have to be anywhere at any certain time in the day.) Alex used to say that he knew what his life was, could see the whole thing laid out, as long as he worked for a large corporation. That they owned him. So he fixed that. He broke. One day he keeled over in the front seat of his car just as he drove through the gate to work. The guard called the ambulance and Alex was taken to the nearest hospital. Now, twelve years later he is just fine, on an early medical retirement (the guaranteed income he wanted), and nothing to do but what he wants. He and Flynn are always underfoot. And now I'm the one earning the living with all the responsibility. I see that it amuses them, to see me so frazzled. Yet they feign sympathy.

At one point Alex tried to put his arm around me with a patronizing chuckle working in his neck, "Now, Honey, if you'd just relax you'd be able to handle your place just fine. You take it too seriously. It's not going anywhere. There's nothing so bad it can't be fixed. Nothing's going to happen. It'll all work out, just go easy on yourself. You're scared, that's all. I thought you'd mellow out by now, but you've gotten tighter…" I twisted away from his big paw grappling at my shoulder. Did it show that much? I wanted to say how I was not made for all this. That all I wanted to do each day was get up and let things register fresh on my senses, to feel, not know. That it was having to know things that was driving me crazy. That it killed me where I cared most to be alive. I stomped away to Alex's outright laughter. Do I look so funny to him, taking *responsibility*. And after all those years of trying to get away from him to prove that I could handle my own life. I knew he would say, "this is what you women wanted, remember?" if I stayed around.

Alex

Everyone thought Alex would travel when he was medically retired, "An early retirement." Everyone said it at least once, as if he were a lucky man. And I urged him to, not long ago.

I said, "What are you doing stuck in this field, living in a camper, and getting headaches again, when you have all those free passes?"

He said, "Now what would I do travelling. Yes, it would be nice. I'd like to see China and the Eastern European countries, but so I'd go there and see them and then what? Now, if you'd go with me...Then there'd be some reason to do it."

I said, "But, I thought you were a loner. What is this?"

"Travel is something you want to share with someone," he said. I went back into my house and left him in his field. Since when did Alex want to share with anyone? When did he become such a mush? The whole time we were married he dreamed of going off on his own and leaving me behind. That's when he was 35 and I, 28, Now he's 58... That was before his tumor.

I go back over the fence and into his field later on and say, "Besides, I'd want to go to Africa and India. Not all those countries with their history. I want to see countries that people can't tame. Where the land is stronger than they are, while you love any historical site." Alex majored in political science, history, philosophy. He loves cathedrals, ruins, old forts, sunken back into the earth, museums, any remnant of man's fear and aggression. He knows all the names and dates and details of each battle, each effort. I tagged after him all through Europe, all over the islands, poking through history. I hobbled over cobblestones in my clogs, listening to him rant about the glories of these achievements. I carried a camera and took 850 shots of people. Alex took shots of places. I said, "but you can buy those on postcards." I remind him of all this now, our differences, and he just puts an arm around my shoulder and says, "shhhhh. You do go on...."

Flynn is committing suicide, Slowly. He has been for seventy-seven years. It is too pitiful to watch anymore. When he was an able-bodied man, it wasn't so bad. It looked like he was getting away with it. All the cigarettes, coffee, and no decent food. Now he blames his condition on "old age."

Alex 2

A couple of years after the divorce, after Alex and I had calmed down, and could speak again, I had a strong desire to share my few new experiences with him. I'd been taken out on a date to a cello Master class. It opened my eyes, took away many assumptions I had about classical music and classical musicians, and left me in wonder, awe, and respect. Respect for all my former ignorance and how much I had to learn, even at my age. I was thrilled, watching the students play their cellos, and then having the Master come in and correct them right there in front of us, making them play a piece over and over until they got the composer's feelings into it. And I was surprised that even I could tell the difference, and could especially distinguish the Master's cello playing as superior to all of them.

When I drove home I passed by Alex's field and thought, "Oh, poor Alex. He didn't have this revelation. He is still the way he was while I am now a new and better person for it." For what, I wasn't sure, but, I ached in a place that was becoming more and more available to ache in: all that we could have done as a couple together, instead of working and fighting. Why didn't we ever go hear a cello concert together and know this together? I felt I was going on ahead of Alex and leaving him behind in the squalor we had created together. He never left his trailer, except to race to Seven-Eleven to buy a hotdog. I had this pang in my throat of knowing I could never return to that same woman who had battled Alex during the divorce, who lay in bed at night picturing getting even. I could never think those thoughts again after listening to the live cello class. The students faces were still shining in my eyes, as I watched their effort and pursuit of this fine thing called *sound*. And my own efforts of greed and revenge, grovelling to survive made my face grow hot and red.

I called Alex that night. Just over the fence, I could hear his phone ring. I could hear him talking to me out my window while we talked on the phone. I told him all that the cello class meant to me, ending with "I never knew. I thought music was music. But the musician's interpretation…" I trailed off into wordlessness. Alex was silent, listening for more than what I was trying to say. I think he was chewing on something. I could hear his teeth working. He finally said, "That's nice Mother. You're getting out and doing things.…" Like Sal, he missed the point.

Everything stinks. I pay a tank truck to come out and suck up all the solids from under the house. One tenant said, "I think something very large has died under there." I have to leave the room and go laugh out loud in my bedroom, and say to myself, "Yes, an elephant." She doesn't know the septic tank is under there. It is one of the many illegal things Alex did to this place when he lived here. Cut corners. Now, over in his field he is doing everything right. Every time there is a story on the news about poisonous gases leaking up through the ground in a housing tract because it was built over a waste site, I cringe. We are all breathing our own flatulence. A perpetual gaseous cloud encompasses the house. If it had color no one could see us.

I come home after the truck has been here and the smell is still there. I call and the company tells me they have to reschedule because the driver didn't have a flashlight, and that the last time they were out, there was no addition to crawl under to get to the tank, that their map no longer applied, and that they were not equipped to find the lid.

They come out the next day. I come home from work and the smell is still there. Flynn says, "It takes awhile." I say, "Why should it? If the source is removed, how can the smell linger?"

It is one of Flynn's best days since the hospital. He is his old self, meaning strong enough to feel bad again. For awhile he was too weak to carry his head around in his hands and complain. It was all he could do to breathe and stay alive. The smell of my house is the last thing on his mind. I tell him my car stinks. It has a funny smell. Like the septic tank in fact. And there is a new sound now. It sounds like it is breathing, an air inhalation sound.

Flynn doesn't flicker an eyelash. I say, "I left the keys in the ignition. Would you mind driving it when you go down for coffee?" Even though he doesn't drink coffee anymore, because it goes hand in hand with cigarettes, which he has had to give up, he goes to the cafe anyway and has something, sometimes lemon pie.

He agrees to listen to my engine, and later tells me he couldn't hear anything at all. "What about the smell." I ask. He says he couldn't smell anything either.

I say, "Well, at least you didn't say, "there's nothing wrong with your car that a ballpeen hammer couldn't fix." Flynn doesn't let that register. It is his old humor that still resounds in my ears. I have just come from the gym and I smell of sweat. The gym air was thick and alive with smells. The drive home was heavy with sea air and fast food grease. I tell Sal that I long for fresh air. He thinks I am kidding. I tell him I passed a woman who smelled so clean that I turned and stared at her from the back. It was an artificial clean smell. Some perfume.

"The thing that's missing in my life is something that smells pretty." That week he walks me through the rose garden at the Mission. I bend to smell the roses while he watches. And then we leave. The heavy smells of exhaust and the town are there again. My own body smells are there.

I have fallen into one more routine with one more man. I wonder why Sal wastes his time with me. He is seven years younger. At forty-three he needs to be finding someone to have his baby. I considered having Wolfgang's baby at forty three. Now at fifty, I see I was young at forty-three, but the big number scares people away. Yet it hasn't scared Sal away. He says he was scared the first time he entered my property. It was dark. There were no lights on, and I led him through the gates and doors into the inner rooms.

We had been kissing in his car. He'd been celibate for five years. He was nervous coming home with me. I didn't want to bring him home. He didn't want to come. But we had been dating for a couple of months and I was curious about him. Why was he taking me out and never showing any interest in touching me. Why was I letting him take up my time when he wasn't that interesting. The talk was guarded and polite. He didn't understand my foreign films and I didn't understand his vegetarian restaurants. Pizza-without-cheese kind of evenings. He was too soft-spoken and so well-mannered. I was reminded of the Fifties when the high school boys came to the door.

It was this consideration and propriety that made me keep saying yes to his invitations. He showed up in clean ironed shirts, impeccably groomed. He held the door for me, asked me what I wanted, tried to please me. I discovered with him that I couldn't be pleased. After losing John I refused to be pleased. John, who didn't want me, who made me beg for his affection, and contort myself to get his attention. Even so, I had fallen into a routine with him that lasted five years.

Each man lasts about five years. After the divorce it has turned out that way. I wondered if that was a natural cycle for a primate in the wild, and only a goose mates for life. Alex and I spent twenty years having offspring together. I wondered if that was the natural cycle for that kind of nesting. It took them twenty years to leave. Chronologically the figures add up. From twenty years old to forty with Alex. Then from forty to forty-five with Wolfgang. Forty-five to fifty with John. And now beginning with Sal. It's been one year. But this time I don't want to be with anyone. I want to be alone.

Friends say, "You have always defined yourself through a man." They've read all the books. I am offended. I say, "I've always been alone."

"When?" they ask.

"With the man," I say. "I always felt alone."

They say, "You don't know who you are without a man. You have no self."

I say, "I have a whole self that has nothing to do with a man…. But it's true," I agree, "The self that has developed around a man is a well-developed self. I know how to push all his buttons and watch him go off." Laughter on both sides of the line. I add, "It's fun, it's hard to resist, a lot of power in it, but it's taken up too much of my time. I've got to get busy doing other things. There's a lot of things I want to do and men are in my way now.

They ask, "What do you want to do?'

"Go teach in England, Africa, India, Join the Peace Corps, Vista. You know, go see the world," I say.

"But you've already seen the world. You travelled with Alex."

"Don't remind me," I joke, "This time I need to go as myself, not as a wife."

When Sal hears me talking this way to my women friends he gets sullen. And then he begins with his, "You can be any-where in your mind" business of the yogi.

I argue, "I don't want to transcend everyday life. I feed on everyday life. I'll get cancer in my denial organs if I do. I want actuality, not to live in my avoidances."

I have fallen into a pattern once again on Serena Avenue. Once again there is a man in my bed. Sometimes half awake, I forget which one it is and have to use logic, do arithmetic in the wee hours. Oh, yes, this is Sal. I'm up here now away from Alex, Wolfgang, John. This is the new one. I remember the old ladies my mother took care of after her divorce. They couldn't remember who was who and began calling their hus-bands by their brothers' names, and sons by their grandsons and great-grandsons. All their men became one man. They were all alike enough to have no identity after awhile, when the mind dulls and begins to cross-associate. I sometimes call Sal Wolfgang. They are alike. And Alex, John. Those two were alike.

One friend said, "You always choose short dark men, "who are kind of quiet and let you do all the bossing."

I had to remind her that was not true, I said, "Only two were that way. The other two were the opposite. Remember?" She had met Alex and John in turn, And Wolfgang and now Sal. I said, "It's every other time. A dominant one and then a passive one, and then dominant and then passive." She laughed and we shook our heads. She was with one exactly like her husband had been. I wanted to say that at least I hadn't done that until the second one.

Sal was afraid of the that first night. Later I knew it was of my body. He didn't know if he would be able to get it to work. He was afraid of the job ahead of contending with all my parts. When he tells me he was afraid of the premises, how dark it was feeling our way through the gates and doorways, of his hesitation because he didn't know me that well, I know now he was afraid of not being able to please me. He never admitted until later that he was afraid of me, the woman. But I discovered it that night. The way he felt his way along under the comforter, sensing and unsure. He wasn't like the other men, mounting right off, after doing their routine preliminaries. A bit of exploration and they suddenly know their way around. Just another female body. Old hands at it, literally.

Sal had few women. Some perfunctory sex in Viet Nam, never knowing if the women took pleasure. Just released himself in a matter of minutes and then parted, sadly. Sex, being a necessary evil to him when the pressure builds up.

Then he married at thirty-five a twenty-two-year-old waitress in another town, who was never without a cigarette and cup of coffee, who had such mood swings and crying jags, he retreated into himself. As a meditator, this wasn't hard to do. He rarely made love to her.

He never knew if she had an orgasm when he did. I said, "No wonder she was a wreck. You can't let a woman go that long. And at twenty-two she didn't even know what was wrong. A woman needs to be taken down by her male. Each day, at least, mounted and made to know that she's his, that he wants her."

Sal listened. He never knew this. I said, "A woman gets meaner and meaner the longer a man, under the same roof, doesn't overpower her and take her." I don't tell him until later how John took me morning, noon, and night. For five years. How my women friends finally said, "That's a sick relationship. That's all you ever do," And later, when Sal put in his opinion, he said that it sounded like I was just a sex slave.

"Just," I laughed.

Sal was light-weight, lithe, white-fleshed, smooth as a young woman, in his flesh that night. A body never soused with alcohol or nicotine or animal fat. His muscles were hard and solid. I said, "How long have you worked out?" "Nevah." He told me brown rice has nucleic acid that tones the muscles. He had been eating brown rice for twenty years.

That night he did his best and when I gave in and let go, the release scared him. He lay very still, not knowing what to do or what it meant. I asked him, "Haven't you ever felt a woman have an orgasm before?" (Sal's penis was so small I told people later, he was his mother's daughter—after we broke up and he stole my puppies.)

"Nev ah." he admitted in his Long Island dialect.

"I scared you." He was silent, I knew he was curious. But he doesn't ask direct questions.

After that he was single-minded in pursuing that moment of climax in me. He was a cunning animal, knowing just where it lay hiding. He became skilled in finding it. I enjoyed his enthusiasm. He became a man. And I had fallen into yet another routine with yet another man.

I think of John teaching co-ed after co-ed how to find their orgasms at the University for twenty years. How that is probably the only thing he has ever taught. G-spots?

Poo or No Poo

Alex comes over to meet to meet the Rooter-Rooter man and
direct him through the leachline, if he ever shows up. We drink
horsetail tea from some bush, leaves I buy from the Bee Man,
and wait. Alex muses in his once-kitchen with me at the stove.
I, with a sober face. Dour-mooded, all business, even somber.
Actually morose, or melancholy. Or, just not feeling exuber-
ant or very happy at all. I cut up the makings for a vegetable
stew. I clean out the refrigerator bin and get rid of all the old
carrots, broccoli, and leeks. It all goes into the pot while Alex
perches on a stool and says, "This tea isn't bad."

I see poo on the newly mopped kitchen floor. Shoe prints
of it. I say, "I think you stepped in something." He turns his
sole up and sure enough. Great eruptions of curses from Alex,
even though it's my floor and it's nothing to him. He is still his
mother's son and hates to be the one dumb enough to step in
it and track it around without knowing it.

Still I'm dull, quiet, and it doesn't matter. It's all just business. This isn't the life I want anyway. Poo doesn't matter, Poo
or no poo, It's all the same, just business and duty. Where is
the love?

About ten years ago, I chose love over money, and now have
neither. Alex still snorts. I remember now. A familiar sound suddenly up close, right in my ear, right in my kitchen. I've only
heard it from over the fence, faintly, in the past ten years.

The Rooter man never comes. I announce to Alex that I
must run in to TG&Y and get two sink tubs to catch the water
in the clogged sink. Again I am surprised by my lack of caring. There is no passion stirring in my blood. Where did all
my excitement over *life* go? What used to get me all worked up
so that I poured out words in such profusion, so that Alex was
tantalized listening to me, is gone. What used me up? Even
Alex looks twice to see that I have changed. Usually a clogged

sink would be a pivotal point for all else to hang on. He used to say, "You can get more out of things than anyone I've ever seen, Mother.... It's great. You seem to manufacture meaning from the slightest thing. That most of us miss."

On the way out, I tissue up the poo spots with Alex's sole imprinted in them, and Alex poses in the doorway on his way back to his field, and turns to look at me. Before his words are out, I can hear his editing, haltering, and final courage, "Why don't I go with you?"

"Okay," I say, saddened by the no enthusiasm on my part and his fear of asking. His vulnerability that I might turn him down.

This lackluster bloodstream of mine, full of vegetable matter, no stimulants, no animal fat, no dairy. No chicken coop eggs. Nothing a monkey in a tree wouldn't eat. Alex gets in my little car and the only *feeling* I've had all day that I can *feel* (a concept Sal doesn't understand) flutters itself. It is irritation over big Alex in my small car. He reaches for the levers and his seat shoots back to make room for those long German legs. Legs covered all over with white fur. He curses the smallness of my car ever so quietly under his breath. I drive in silence. A built-in curse in general for everything.

Together we make out dual checks to rescue one grown child from in between jobs. Alex makes an ear-deadening proclamation like a knight with a sword, minus bowing, "I am going to cut these kids off when they turn thirty. I tell you. They can sink or swim. They are draining me. Every time I get a little money ahead to work on the house, it's gone. They're blood-suckers, I tell you. I'm not going to give them a penny after they turn thirty. I'm cutting them loose." (He means one daughter in particular. He is still supporting her when she turns 50, and that year when he dies at 80, she takes all his property and the 50 years accumulations of the tools he cherished.)

Again it doesn't register in me as anything at all. Just some male animal blowing out some sound. A bull in a field maybe. Am I really immune to Alex now, except for his size inside my belongings?

In TG&Y, I go kind of blank. I have trouble remembering what I've come for. Alex stands in my way, following me around. Every time I look at a shelf full of stuff to remind me by association, his long blue hulk blocks my view. I go down a different aisle, and here he comes. Like a little boy with his mom. When did all the men in my life become decapitated so that they need me to lead them around? Where are their big ideas about everything that they used to force on me? Where is their leadership? As soon as I don't belong to them they don't know anything.

It comes to me when I go down the plastic wares. Oh, yes, the tubs. The clogged sink. To catch the water, and even when the sink is fixed, to catch the water and throw it out the door on the plants. To conserve water. There's a drought. It all comes back. I've had a bucket in the sink for months, and the tenants don't like it. It's awkward. With the tubs that fit the sink, they will have no choice but to empty the dishwater on the two margarite bushes that wait. It is all taking up space inside my head. These thoughts. And Alex takes up space in the aisle. I separate two shiny black square plastic tubs and think out loud, "Black won't show the slop in the water."

It's Alex's cue, "But, they'll look too dark, Mother. That kitchen is already dark. Your tenants will go in there and get depressed with all that black. Honey, you want to uplift people. I'd get the blue."

"Not with that green tile. I'll get the light, green, then." I tug at the tubs and finally thrust them at Alex to pull them apart. Like morons we finally separate the two I want, and I watch Alex carefully stack the others back in place. Again, that haze, as if I'm not really here. That it isn't Alex and me thirty years later. At the check stand Alex stands gazing at the earring rack. As if he's from Mars. He asks me what they are. He doesn't recognize merchandise now. Tiny dots with prongs on very small cards.

A Walk with Alex
on the Three Mile Foothill Road

"I've always loved you."

"I know, that's what you say anyway. You like to think of yourself as that kind of man, a one woman man. "It's true, I'm surprised myself, but I still love you. I am a one-woman man." "So everyone else is promiscuous, right?" "Well, I am amazed at how many men you've gone through since our divorce.... And I know you don't like to hear it, but during the marriage. That's what ended the marriage."

"You ass. That's a general statement so you don't have to admit that anything was wrong with you." "Well, what do you mean Honey. Nothing *was* wrong with me."

"You had the brain tumor, you Jerk. I didn't, That's nothing?"

"Yes, I did, didn't I? It was all your affairs you know. It was hard to take, I think I held up pretty good, considering your carrying on."

"You are blind, you know. Name *all* those men. All those affairs. There were only a few. There was Kevin, Yes, I'll admit that. I loved him though; it wasn't a one-night stand like your women, I mean, we match one for one on quantity; the only difference is that I fell in love and you just screwed. Love is decent, anyway. I didn't just have hot pants as you need to believe, I needed love, and you couldn't love me. In fact you hated everything I was according to your prissy background. I represented all the slop your mother made you hate about the farm, and you were never on a farm and neither was I. It was your mother you hated. And then me,"

"I loved you. My heart ached for you."

"Yeah, I believe that; but as soon as we were married you turned into a husband and father and couldn't love. You just copied your own father, You lorded it over me. Got to be a power-monger. And finally your head exploded. What do you mean love? You had temper tantrums, You were so afraid of all the responsibility...I mean, don't you remember? I was miserable, everything was always my fault. Kevin loved me. Made me feel I was a good person. You made me feel I was never good enough for you. I worked myself ragged trying to win your approval. That's love? Service?"

"Yes, you were a good worker and a good mother, If you just hadn't had so many men...."

"So many, you ass. Count them, The same as your women."

"Let's see, there was that boy, what was his name, who came to pick up his sister... Oh, Mother I don't want to go on...."

"Of course you don't because that was it. You just want to believe I had a lot, and that it was that, and not your frenzy that ruined the marriage. You were always so negative, and work, work, work. No fun, no laughter. A maniac making lists, wishing you could get a slave for Christmas. Wishing you could sleep while you worked and work while you slept. Wishing you had an old man chained in the basement to beat the hell out of, the way your father beat you. But, of course, my few men wrecked the marriage, and you are a one-woman man,"

"Oh, Honey, let's not go on like this. I did love you. I always loved you, and I still do,"

"Oh, yeah, Okay, Great."

Mansur

A Minimal Man

I said, "A minimal man"...It's funny. I don't know why I need a man in a small package. To be the least a man can be...But that's what I am getting out of these small men. Mansur had only one testicle. He was so thin, his arms smaller than mine. Six feet, no, five-eleven and only 135 pounds. Incredible. Small bones. Small, elongated bones, except for that one (ha ha) ...He had such a small penis the rubber hung sadly on it. He didn't fill it up. It was like a flat-chested or small-breasted girl trying on a big lady's bra. I felt sorry for him. And after he came I held the rubber up to the lamp light and there was hardly any semen in it. I pressed it with my fingers to see and it was almost empty. From one testicle, there's not much fluid; I don't know. But the whole thing pleased me. I enjoyed how little he was, how little fluid he had, how singular his testicle was..... The only full and ample thing about him is his mouth. He has a nice thick sensual bottom lip, and a big tongue. When I feel his tongue I think of Lebanon and giant lizards running on hard dry ground, rasping with their toenails. His tongue has ridges along the sides. Like a lizard. I figured it's the way Arab tongues are. I also thought of a disease, but quickly chose to believe it was the way men's tongues must be in his country. Big and strong. They're so vocal over there, and political, at least on the "News." Always yelling and throwing rocks.

There's something about all this smallness of his, and also, I forgot, he ejaculates almost as soon as he puts it in, and sometimes before... that's another element of his meagerness. I hardly get a chance to feel the little that he has. And I am glad. Isn't that strange. I've always had powerful men before, with so much to press at me, insist I take, have, be.... You know? Big wallets, big ideas, big dicks, big cars, houses, big pressures on me to receive all their bigness. And now thin

Mansur slips silently into my empty studio with nothing to offer me (even though he doesn't know this), I quite enjoy the absence of everything. The beauty for me is in all the things that don't matter. That are harmless. That can't make demands. He's covered with hair. Black, curly fur, It disguises his thin elongations.

Hair can't hurt me. I can lean against it and it's pliable. It gives way. It's everywhere. All over his head, chest, belly, completely concealing his private place. Yet, he confessed he was afraid he might go bald. Luxuriant, is the word they use in pornography books about women's hair. Well, his is so extravagant. Such thickness, and the smell of cleanness. I wonder what nature was thinking to produce such a man.... I look for the meaning of him, you know? The way what any animal means by the ways it's made. How it's supposed to be in the world. So, here's Mansur, the Arab, from Lebanon with a very small penis, a very large rough tongue. An aggressive tongue, and shy penis. The tongue can go on for hours, keeping its moisture, holding its heat. He loves to kiss. A wet and hungry passionate mouth and a penis that quickly gets the orgasm over with and then lies quiet and shrivelled and safe, watching the erect tongue taste all the pleasures. It's funny. And then the thinness. And the abundance of hair. And the most delicate hands I've ever seen on a man. Tiny white narrow fingernails, long thin fingers. He is a man who turns the pages of a book. He reads a lot. He has enormous eyes. That's another thing. I guess he was created as a head kind of creature. All the organs of his head and face are opulent. Like jewels. A very large razor-edged nose, which starts at the top of his forehead and curves all the way down his face.

At first he reminded me of a camel. Up close, kissing him, he would considerately place his nose to one side of mine. He did this carefully, the way one handles good equipment. He would bat his long eyelashes, and his eyes would go half-mast, round, blue eyes, and I had to try not to think "He's a desert camel," so I wouldn't ruin the moment. If I let myself think that, I would have started laughing, and he'd wonder what was so funny....And what could I say....I'd have to make up something else, and he'd think I was silly, just a giggling woman. So....

Nature made him a long, lean, hairy, big-headed, big-featured male with a big deep voice, and very delicate hands and privates. To me that means he's a seer, a hearer, a breather and smeller, a kisser and taster, and big talker, And it's true. He's getting a Ph.D. in politics, and heads the organization for Arabs on the West Coast. I asked him, "Aren't there such things as Arabs majoring in art?" He gave me such a camel look, I thought he might spit at me. He oozed out, in his Arab accent, it being a "lugsuray," a thing not to study but to do, art is." His voice is the most sensual thing about him. So heavy and thick and smooth and creamy, like almond butter. It's what made me turn to look at him in the first place.

I was sitting and having coffee at the Student Union and ignoring everyone when I heard this voice behind me at another table. It massaged my ears, petted the back of my head and neck and shoulders. God. It was so beautiful, like a deep brook, heavy waters over solid rocks...working around every piece of space, filling it up, rolling, continuous. He was talking politics in his language. I couldn't understand a word he said, but I turned around just to see what that sound was coming from, and there he was. I thought, "Oh, how disgusting. An Arab. And a weird one at that. Not even dark and masculine, but scrawny and pale and blue-eyed, with such a nose...I didn't see the camel in him yet. I sat there finishing my coffee and listening to his voice. I liked not knowing what he was saying. I have heard too many words from men already. Now I just want their sound. I will put my own meaning into it. His friend would intercede with high rapid-fire like a machine gun. Kind of a midget's voice. A comical sound. It was a serious discussion because a war had just broken out somewhere over in their countries. I listened to the music they made together. High and low notes, different tempos. It made me like the deep voice even more, hearing the high one with it. I sat there becoming aware of male voices, and developing a discerning ear, and coming to certain conclusions. I grew very opinionated and discriminating. I suddenly knew exactly what I liked and didn't like about the male voice. I liked the deep one I heard. Exactly that one. When there was a lull in the conversation, I turned around and said, "That sounds very interesting." He focused those enlarged eyes on me and said, "What do you mean?" I said, "Everything you're saying." He said, "What are we saying? Do you agree or disagree?" I said, "I don't know or care one way or another. It's just interesting to listen to you." He half smiled to be polite and looked at me then at the table, and then at the cigarette he was smoking. I had interrupted their train of thought. His friend stared at the ash tray, avoiding me, waiting for Mansur to handle the situation.

I said, "So, what are you going to do with all your ideas, go back to your country or stay here and use them." He said, "I don't know yet..." He was irritated. He wasn't sure if I was being smart or serious. I wasn't sure either. Partly I was curious and partly wanting to annoy him. It would be good to hear him try to say something angry to me with that beautiful voice, I was so safe, as myself. What could he say or do to hurt me. It was fun. To interfere and confuse him. The coffee shop closed and we all had to leave. I walked out with them, but they went up a flight of stairs and I went the wrong way. I discovered alleyways I never knew were there. I dreamed about his voice. It stayed with me. For some reason. I wonder why? What is it I was needing to be so taken by that deep beautiful sound. The way it resonated in his neck and chest, promising what kind of treasures? His calm, steady tone. An authoritative yet benevolent, reasonableness. He understood, waited his turn, offered his words, always with sureness....Was it his confidence. His knowing for sure. His manliness. Such maleness? Or my interpretation of a language I couldn't understand. Did I give him more credit than was there. The surprise later, to find he had nothing to back it up with. That was a curiosity to me. Such a delight. For a man with such a voice to be so ineffectual in bed with a woman. I guess it was my private, special discovery. A kind of triumph over him. He sat like a little king among his men...everyone looking to him, coming to him at his table, deferring to him...and even I being intrigued by the command of the sounds he made…and then nothing. He was nothing… It's what I needed to find out. I needed to know that. Among men he is equipped to deal. With women he has nothing to offer, not even very much of his time.…He is so stingy with his time. The best thing he gave me, the only riches, and that was only because I encouraged him, were his childhood stories. Each one like a gem. He told me how his parents sent him to boarding school when he was five, and he didn't see them again until he was fourteen; and the only warmth was when his grandmother would come get him, and his brothers, and take them to her house in Tyre, on the sea. The school was in Lebanon, and his parents lived in Nigeria.

Money was to be made in Africa then. His grandmother would cook anything he wanted to eat on those holidays; and at night she would prepare his bed by going outside and picking the white blossoms off some exotic bush, did he say Frangipani? And tossing them on the blankets. The whole room had the beautiful scent of these blossoms. It was the only time he smiled. His voice rose high, as if he were still that child in wonder. I leaned my chin on his forest of hair, detecting his heartbeat beneath, a rapt audience to his memories, I saw no posturing of the deep-throated male he had become as he talked about these things. I felt sorry for his poor frail body. It hadn't grown properly. There was no mother to care if it was nurtured or not. No response for the effort the flesh made back then in his boyhood. The flesh must have someone tending it personally. Only these rare times with his grandmother. When I touched him after these stories, I thought of this. And touched him in a way to help make up for all the touching he never got when trying to grow. Trying to be in the physical world. No wonder his head grew so large. He lived up there. The nicest thing he said to me was, "That is the best touching I've ever had." And then, "Where did you learn to do that?" I said, "I never learned. I just did it right now." A slight scowl of suspicion crossed his face. Did he think I was a professional? Was I? Am I?

This long-distance call to my sister, to tell her this, cost me nine dollars.

Before I Met Sal, and After Mansur

I went out to dinner with an old man. Even at seventy, he hadn't given up on love, but specialized in love-with-an-unattainable-young-woman. I was that to him, he told me later, and he threw himself at me. I ate the French food and made it clear to him that was all I would do. He gave me a poem, a short story, his bleeding heart writings. I pretended I didn't notice his "love." And said he should send these writings out. He finally went away. I have always wanted to give his dinner back to him.

He was a retired geologist, had gone to an Ivy League college on the East coast, had a grand career, and was still dabbling in a gold mine in Mexico. He was weathered and clean from outdoor exposure, instead of crusty and damp from sitting behind closed doors, so I went out. And he was French. He ordered from the menu in French. He ordered a nice bottle of wine. His eyes were young. I saw him as the man he used to be, as he talked and listened to his words, and it was pleasant. Why did I fear his age? I knew, of course, because it meant I was old too, and he saw that and that is why he had asked me out. And because, he told me later, I had retained "a certain vitality, a good set of legs, a trim body, strong arms, and a still lively face with eyes that missed nothing, and spoke in words that struck their target." He said he liked my "direct ways," too high shoes, mood swings, excitement of any kind, and real passion for anything. Later Sal says, "These are all evidence of poor eating habits and lack of proper brain chemistry."

I think of that night with Pierre, and the French food. I asked Pierre to order for me. We drank deep red wine and I wallowed in the company of a generation ahead of me that I had known so well. Those older men, before they retired and got too old. They had all the same reference points I had.

Knew the same actors, songs, Presidents and more. We shared the same understandings.

With Sal there is always a tug-of-war, as he comes along with no real experiences in taming anything. Pierre gave me leeway. He wasn't threatened by me, but, instead, amused, and stimulated. Sal is always on the verge of panic, lest any of my "irrational" tendencies get out of hand.

John

When I Was with John

I looked at myself and saw this worried little woman. And I wondered what I am so worried about. I take inventory but without interest because it's what people tell you to do to reassure yourself that everything is alright.

My kids are fine, the birds are fine, except for the one that got eaten by the stray cat my daughter brought home from her trip across the United States. She found a starving kitten in Mississippi. An orange coon cat I think they're called. It's now a long, lean, rangy hunter with eyes the color of its coat. Before she left, she talked me into buying a whole cagefull of parakeets. So I did. The house sounded like a morgue. Now it's full of chirps and squawks.

When I got the news that her cat had eaten one of these parakeets, I felt sickened beyond reason. It was only a bird. But I couldn't shake the feeling of doom. Everything I attempted now seemed to end up a mess. Every day I'd go to the cage and count the birds. It was a bad habit, and I wondered why I'd do that. I even wrote it down, that I went to the cage and counted the birds each day and when they were all there, I felt better. Then I called home and heard one had been found, or the remains of it, out on the rug, a feather still caught in the cat's foot. When I got home, I went to the cage and counted the birds, and sure enough, one was missing. I felt beyond sad. That doomed feeling.

My daughter told me I was taking it hard. She said, "You sound depressed." She could pass it off. She still had her whole future to recover. Lovers to have, babies to bear. Cages full of birds. All the cats she wanted. She didn't understand that this cage full of birds was an extravagance I couldn't even afford anymore, financially or emotionally, and when it was destroyed I would not be able to replace it. Or so it felt to me. But I didn't explain that to her, because she would have scoffed, and shook her head and been disgusted. She wants a mother who's happy. Who can continue to fill up birdcages and not blink an eye. And I'd like to be that way.

Besides the birds, the only other evidence of life are the dogs and cats. I see that they are all still here every day. The big dog in the yard that I don't want, who cases the place. The tiny dog that lives in my room, blind in one eye and, of course, can't see out of the other. She's going deaf. When I whistle she always turns in the opposite direction and looks confused, so I can't bear to look at her struggling to find me. I have to go up and touch her. Each day I go off to work I think she will be hit by a car by the time I get home. She always gets out and sleeps on the hot paved street. And there is no one at home to watch her. I remember all the cats each day anew. Over twenty-six years we've had many cats. Great clans of them. Now this is the last of all the family pets. There's old Babe. If I don't see her I forget she exists. I think she was one that died awhile back. Then she shows up, sad-eyed, because she is no longer the family pet because the family is gone, and I remember, "Oh, yes I'm still at this phase of my life, with that cat in it."

These animals. If they were all gone, I'd be fine. It's keeping them alive that bothers me. I am afraid of coming home and seeing the end of one of their lives. It doesn't stop—death, even when I am doing everything I can to keep them alive, even when I am tired of it myself. Tired of everything passing in spite of my efforts to hold it still and have it.

The way I was clinging to John. No wonder he shook me loose. Those comic books with the dead coming out of the ground clutching onto the living with their bony fingers. Sometimes when I was loving John, I'd see my hand like that. When we'd fall asleep, he'd say that I slept so close and held him so tight it's as if I wanted to be him. "If you could get inside me, I think you would," he said just before telling me to get out of this life and leave him alone. And left me wondering why he wouldn't let me *have him,* that way. I wanted him to make me safe? He was big and thick and always warm, even in cold weather. He took care of himself. There was nothing threadbare about him. I did like to lean against all that substantial flesh. Why wouldn't he tell me that everything was always going to be alright and let me feel safe. He'd get nasty. He said, on the trip back from Mt. Whitney, where I out-hiked him to the 14,500 ft. peak, that he was not going to reassure some middle-aged woman that she was still Daddy's little girl. I wanted to slap him. I was driving down the mountain road going fast around the horseshoe curves and he was afraid. He finally shouted at me to slow down. I was surprised. I wasn't driving recklessly. He was just knowing he deserved to be hurt, too. I looked over and said, "You're afraid of me, aren't you?" He didn't answer. I knew he knew I should be mad as hell at him and take joy in killing him. He knew why.

When we reached the bottom of the mountain and eased into that small town, he breathed easy again and even suggested we stop for coffee. I watched him eat. We'd been on trail mix for three days. He wolfed down a hamburger and fries and gulped and guzzled coffee. He was no John Muir. I was, though. I abstained. I was leaned-down with the trail and trail mix. I felt pure. I didn't want to ruin it yet. I wanted to cry. There was John, the man I loved, getting rid of me, and here I was sitting across the table from him watching him make himself more *here* than I ever would be, and he not wanting to let me be part of the way he knew how to do that. I saw my small self without him and a lump formed in my throat.

He dropped me off at my house with the threadbare birds, cats, dogs and strange lonely tenants. It was good riddance. I saw him later at a sidewalk cafe in a new down mountain jacket eating yet another half chicken special at Gustav's. I said aloud, "He's got the Down Syndrome." A big hunk huddled over his plate. So solid a form. I drove by in my skimpy car with nothing in my stomach and no desire to eat until he cared if I did. When he sees me again, I will be almost not here at all. And when he asks how I am, I will tell him that my bird was eaten by my cat. He'll have that told-you-so look. The well-read professor who knows where to place people in terms of emotional contexts. All that literature he's read over the years. He's already lectured me on my animals and what they mean and why I keep them, and why I don't get rid of them. I have already cried over that "accusation." My motives are never good in his estimation. All based on fear and dread and then the opposites, greed and the need to slash out and hurt when I don't get what I want. Always the symbolic meaning.

I go to the cage and count the birds. They're all still there except for that one, of course. And the cats are perched on the porch looking at the cage. And the dogs staring in the doors for food. I take lettuce to the birds, refill their water, curse the time because I'm late and don't have time to take care of the birds. I throw ham fat out of the door to the big dog, and chew up little bits of it for the tiny dog in my bed. I think of John all the time. He's right. I do want to be him. And I get a lump in my throat. Why can't he let me?

A Temporary Permanence

All the things he tried to do for a kind of permanence toward the end. He bought an economy pack of razors and placed them on my shelf, saying firmly, "There, now I'll have something to shave with when I stay over." I was petted. He'd never said that before. It'd been over four years. He'd stay reluctantly at my place, complaining about everything. I'd hear how low my shower head was for a big man like him. Implying there's always been shorter men in my life. And the razors. He'd say, "Which ones are the new ones. Why don't you throw out the old ones." Ridicule in his tone. I was always nervous having him as a house guest if I can call it that. He'd usually not plan to stay, come for one thing or another, maybe to borrow a tool, left over from my ex. End up eating dinner (I'd rush around trying to make something extra nice to please him) and he'd snicker at my red face and quick manner. Telling me I looked "jerky" doing things so fast. I'd hide the hurt for a while and then say, "You look sluggish, moving so slow." He'd blanch, and my silence that followed these quips would settle in him. Wonder on his face. Did she really mean that. I'd clarify it. "There are so many more words to use for someone who is quick, you know." He'd smile ever so slightly. "You're the Philosophy professor. You know what words do."

I can't say we ever got along. Toward the end, though, he said maybe if we could be more tolerant. That was his idea of trying to make it work. I scoffed, "I've been tolerant for too long, what do you mean." And the argument would be off. He'd cite cases of my intolerance. And I'd try not to point out all the times I was still there after he'd been with some other woman. That was the unmentionable. If I said it aloud, he'd always slam the door, justified to have prowled because, of course, see how you are.

Part of the effort to hold things together when he

sensed the end in sight, was to go on and on about computers, until I felt I was part of the dark ages, still chiselling my words in stone, clacking away on an old manual with the touch button set at *heavy*. I'd always pounded away. And the computer keyboard required a light touch, which I didn't think I could develop. Also the cursor, pulsating on the luminous screen, waiting like all the dogs on the porches all my life, needing, wanting something from me. My dumb, mute typewriter was loyal. And didn't require indirect action. What I did came out. The computer wouldn't do anything unless you did something other than typing. But John hammered away on all these "romantic notions about yourself," as he called them until I spent over a thousand dollars for one that sat on my desk purring and humming and occasionally sounded like a slaughter in a hen house. The printer. My room vibrated with the life of this machine. And my simple words were nothing compared to its importance. So I rarely went near it. Introducing me to the computer gave John the opportunity to talk for weeks, uninterrupted, about all the features, and possible features of the future, in those "ports" with all the programs available. I couldn't argue. As my friends said, "It's the first time he knows something and can be important to you without you saying he's wrong." I wondered when I had ever made him feel that way. I kept my ignorance about the computer to myself, to escape his ridicule. He was a cruel teacher. Once I said, "I'm afraid to let you know how much I assumed a computer could do, and show the amount of magic I believed in about it." He looked up from the monitor (I later told him I thought a computer did everything without anything having to be put into it. When I learned that it did nothing without a program on a disk, I felt cheated.) I'd attributed robot intelligence to it.

John's neck is arthritic, and he can't turn it half way to give me a sidelong glance to see if I'm serious. I'd be smiling. Playing the fool. He'd say, "Was that an attempt at humor?"

He'd say we'd marry if I was pregnant. He'd never said that before. We never used anything. He had a low sperm count and could hardly cause two pregnancies twenty years ago. I knew I had been fertile and got pregnant the first time I made love. My babies were born eight months after I was married. They were a month early. But now, who knew? I'd wanted to see if Mother Nature would do it. I'd respect it, if it happened. I said, "It'll probably be born grey-haired with glasses with your old sperm and my old ovum." We were running our five miles that night. He said, "Sperm never gets old." But of course. I ran behind him and watched his 50-year-old Ukrainian broad hips and fat waist above his hips. I loved this fat man. He thought that to be a man you have to keep your ego big, by minimizing everyone else. That's how he did it. And if I wanted him to make love to me tonight, I'd have to hold my tongue. Let him believe anything he needs to believe. It got tiresome.

So toward the end, he bought a new shower head and a piece of goosenecked pipe and put the shower way up high. So no one would forget he was a *big tall man*. I said, "What's the next man do, get a ladder?"

Over the four years he bought several flashlights, a set of knives, always complaining the lighting was poor in my house and yard and that he couldn't cut anything. He gave me a corkscrew for the car glove compartment. And several clocks which my grown children took with them when they moved out. He gave me a large red clock for the kitchen and then stood looking at it, saying how pretty it was. I'd point out, "You don't say 'pretty' except what you've given me." He gave me a little stick-on clock for my car. "So you won't be late," he said.

And radios. He supplied me with music wherever I went, buying a stereo system for my room and installing one in my car. It was always knives, flashlights, clocks and radios. And once a shower head. I gave him a big Chinese comforter, pillows, a huge skillet, an industrial vacuum and lots of sweaters, flowers and pretty bowls and kitchen things.

Now he's gone. There's an empty spot on my desk where

his printer used to be. The razors are still here. And the shower head was changed by Alex to a water-saver. "Who put this one on, it's a piece of shit!" Alex said. My children took all the lights and clocks and radios. as they were needed. I'm back on the typewriter. I never took to the computer...

I Remember the Last Supper
with John

He had already started eating. I rounded the corner in my high heels and spotted him where he said he would be. He was hunched over his half-chicken special, well into the barbecue sauce. And he didn't look up. I locked my eyes on him. Seeing him was always physical; a physical pang. And I couldn't not look. I towered above his table and said, "You've started." He mumbled with his mouth full that he was hungry. I wanted to turn around and walk away, but sat down.

I felt cool and long and lean and beautiful, deserving of love even at my age. I tried to join him. I sat at the table. I was there. He just kept eating. Looked up with a brief glance and talked at me into his plate. "Are you hungry, go get something."

I said, "No, not if you are already eating without me. I don't want to eat." He threw down the bone he was gnawing on and pursed his lips, then turned and eyed me with hard eyes. "Are you going to get something to eat or not?" I brushed it aside. "No."

He froze, immobile, and then thrust his hands back into his plate and went after his chicken again. I got up, ordered a fresh-squeezed orange juice, waited in line and peered out the paned window at him, as he kept chewing away, eating here at his sidewalk cafe.

He did not look up once to see where I had gone or what I was doing. When I returned with the juice, he was in the same posture doing the same thing. I had watched him chew his way through four and a half years. Chomping down food as if he were starving, then complain about his weight. He came from Ukrainian people who could weight 280 in old age. They were all from Ohio; so he took little pills to curb his appetite, be California trim. I sat and sipped and swallowed

115

the juice in a few gulps. The tartness stung me just so and felt healthy. I sat in silence, glad that he was eating grease, that his father had died early of a heart attack, and that if he did I could finally be at peace again.

He had called and invited me to have dinner. He said, "I called to invite you to dinner." I knew what he meant. He hadn't called for half a week after insulting me. He hadn't wanted to call. The insult had been about my volunteer work. "You're regressing," he had said. "I thought you had given all that up."

I'd tried to explain that I didn't know why, but that I still wanted to work with abused children. "The whole thing is embarrassing to me, just embarrassing to hear about all this," he said. "Embarrassing?" I was appalled. We parted angry. When he called, I just had swallowed a lettuce sandwich, and was not expecting to hear from him again. Four and a half years was a long time to be not getting along. We seemed to have stayed together just to argue, as if he had it in for women like me, and I had to finish up business with a man like him. We agreed on nothing. And finally I hated the way he ate with both hands as if the food would disappear if he didn't eat it all immediately. He hated the way I wouldn't eat most of the time until I was so hungry I'd be irritable. He also hated my shoes, the way I walked, talked, and I think, loved him. Or so it seemed. And I hated the way he hated. He loved to hate things about people. We had fallen into a nice "adversary" friendship he called it. People who knew us said we picked at each other and it was unpleasant to be around us for fear a fight would break out.

I had been monologuing all week about saying, "Fuck off, asshole," if he should call; but when I heard his voice I said, "Where?"

"What did you want—a red carpet?" he sneered.

I didn't know how to tell him I just wanted some show of his being glad to see me. Instead of hunching over his plate and eating. I doubted my rights to make this demand. When he was through eating, he farted, burped, and picked up the paper and began to read, as if I wasn't there at all. I looked at the back of his gray balding head and wanted to stomp out. But if I did, he wouldn't care. So I sat there wishing I could make him care enough so if I left, it would bother him. Even kill him. More burps, more farts, which I fanned away with his unused napkin. He licked his fingers clean and turned the paper so the last of the evening light would hit it at this sidewalk cafe. We weren't even married. I could have accepted it if we had been married. Only a husband's behavior. But I tormented myself with visions of all the women he would be treating better than this. I knew he would not ignore a woman on a first date, or that prissy woman he worked with, or the "cheap slut" as he called her that he lusted after, or anyone else, an old friend from out of town. Me, though and he turns his back after eating audibly. After ordering dinner before I arrived. Ordering it just for himself. But we had been through these things before. Once it was at a movie theater. I waited and waited out front for him to show up, missing the first part of the movie, to discover after the movie was over, that he had gotten there first, bought his ticket, and sat down, thinking I'd find him in the dark, after buying my own ticket. I'd screamed obscenities at him then, and he'd happily stomped away and didn't call for a week. When he finally called, I was grateful. I'd decided that I had a problem with my temper. I was confused. Was it unreasonable to expect him to wait for me so we could go in together? My friends shook their heads. There were no rules, just courtesies. Again I had plagued my brain with all the other women he would have waited for and escorted in, and even bought their ticket.

The Last Year

In my last year with John, he became increasingly narcissistic. He bought more mirrors and had some old photos of himself when he was young, enlarged. He hung them on the wall. And he bought new lamps and wall lighting. Indirect and direct kinds of lighting. There was one large new mirror hanging above the couch where most people hang framed pictures. And several door mirrors in his bedroom, bathroom, and along his closets. All those new mirrors and lights and the large photos, and his constant saying he was old and fat and ugly, so I would be compelled to disagree, with him. Once I did not disagree, and he waited and I stayed silent. He turned, and looked directly at me, which was a rare occurrence, and said, "So you agree, don't you?" I was hurt and angry enough that day to say, "Yes." Now he waits, too, I imagine, for me to run myself to death and look very bad.

Over Him

I had a nice description of John worked out in my head about the way it would be to see him again: Cowpie. He'd be all settled into his flesh, grey and sinking, I'd be encompassed in Sal's "love." Instead, adrenalin goes right to my knees. My eyes have made contact with him as he goes up the street. I keep my eyes steady and become motionless. A deer spotting a coyote. The optic nerve goes off in my brain. *It's him, it's him.* And bathes those cells, that had been so deprived so suddenly I am stunned. The alcohol I sip lodges in my joints. I sit there ticking with energy. He is too familiar. Like looking at myself. This man hiking up the street, red-faced and shiny with oil. Where is the cowpie....? And then he is gone. I get up to take a piss. In the bathroom mirror I see a smirk on my face. It was the way he stared at Sal. That *he* wanted to see, too. I didn't expect that of him. I try to know what it means. When I return, I ask Sal, "Did you feel like someone was drilling a hole in you just now?" He doesn't look up from the paper, but inhales, so I know he is responding to the question. Without missing a word of print under his nose, he mumbles, "Uhhmm."

"Well, John just went by and couldn't take his eyes off you."

"Come on," he says. "Don't go on about it."

"What if your ex-wife went by? Wouldn't that mean anything to you?

"Not anymore," he says. "It's been seven years. I guess I would look at her."

"Out of curiosity, you mean? To see if she was a wreck or not?"

"No, I don't look for that sort of thing. I don't know. I guess everybody would look at someone they had a life with once. But I don't want to start talking about John."

I shut up, but the sighting plays on my emotions for the rest of the day. I tell everyone over the phone. First my daughter, then the other daughter, then my son, then my mother, then my sister, and then locally I call two women friends. My phone bill is always a hundred dollars a month. Each recipient of this information, told as if I went whale watching and *saw one*, is silent, at first, then reluctant to share my stimulation.

Mama laughs. Any kind of passion amuses her. It gives her a tickle that I am still reacting to him after two years of not seeing him. She asks about Sal. I simply say he's nice to me, but.... "I know" she says. She always understands. And then tells me about some other woman being lovesick over some guy that she did all kinds of crazy things.

No one had patience with me. I could hear, in their silences that they thought I had deceived them somehow. That I was still in love with him when I claimed I was *over him*. I hung up disappointed, thinking that I have not honored my love for John. Instead I violated it with Sal.

That night I turn my back on Sal and try to stay private. An annoyance runs through my body. I don't want to touch anyone.

For two years I talked myself out of John. Convinced myself he was an ass. Dwelled on the "abuses." Then there is his face going up the street, glistening with heat, pink, striking me, making my blood race.....

Tea. Sal got me off coffee and on tea. He got me off red meat and on fish. He got me off dairy and on sesame seeds for seasoning. He watered me down to no sensation at all. Spring water not juice. Just going through the days so calm I wondered where I was. What became of that wild woman John used to torment? The one with the violent jealousies and fits of rage over his affairs? The one who poured weed poisoning on the potted flowers his other woman gave him? The one who tried to ram his trailer with her car when she found out one more time about one more woman? The one who stood outside his window at night and screamed obscenities at him until he opened the door and pulled her inside?

What killed Flynn was closing off his heart so he couldn't be hurt. Not that he's dead on the outside yet. But, when he gave up on love and stayed safe, he died. He got mean. He went sour. He lived only to protect himself after that. He tried to live the lie, to pretend he didn't care about women anymore. He stopped giving. He dried up....

I was giving love with John and not getting it back. Now it's the other way around. I can see Sal is blossoming, loving me. And I go around with a sour face, letting him. Even Sal's mother remarked on how handsome he looked lately, and how much weight he had lost. She chuckled. Love, always a joke. In photos his smile is dazzling now.

He never cracked an open smile in any photograph before. Just a curve to the lips. But now, in photos. with his arms around me, both rows of teeth are visible, and a gleam beams from the eyes. Like the pictures I have of the with John. Mama points, when I visit and look through her albums, "Look, you were so happy then."

"I was a fool, is all," I say, remembering.

When John's face went by, it's as if my eyes had been on a private search, separate from me, and they locked ahold of him and hung on. Giving a message to my knees to go. Go get him. Or was it to run from him. But I sat with grasshopper legs and went a little numb, controlling it. A fleeting gratitude trickled in. It made me form the words, "Thank God there's still someone in the world who can make me feel like that. Who can make me *feel*. And he still in the world.

I wonder: Am I going to be one of those old teachers who come back to the school after they retire, and beg to read to kids, and tell them stories, and listen to them talk? Like those parakeets that finally get loose and fly around lost and alight on a cage with a bird in it down the street and want in, recognizing the feeder and the water tube, and not understanding anything outside on a bush?

I suddenly become a crouching grinner. Sal has been watching my face as I think this. He says, "The wheels are turning a mile a minute." He wants to know what is going on inside my head. Sal, who spends money on me. And treats me so nice I feel guilty and get mad at him for no reason he can see.

Look how the calcium supplements settle in my nails, in bunches, seeping irregularly, filling in where it's been depleted. And look at this one hair on my arm. It's three times as long as all the rest. Is this what I need? Mottled fingernails and one long arm hair?"

He gives an instant Sal smile. My eye glances beyond his head. He turns and looks to see what I am seeing. Nothing. But my eye keeps a look out for John.

One Night

Men leave me alone the older I get. I can go places without being bothered. I can sit at a cafe and the whole population of men under forty will usually glance a bit, and then lose interest. It gives me a privacy I never knew I missed until now. And a safety. I don't excite the senses enough anymore to be killed by men. In a few more years I'll be invisible. My forearms have gone bad. Men look away.

One night, I tied my hair back, took off my high heels and followed John down the street without him knowing it. It was right after we broke up. No one noticed me without my hair and shoes as signals. I became just someone taking up space on the sidewalk.

I stayed a half a block behind. John is near-sighted, even with his glasses, so I knew he couldn't detect it was me, although, whenever he turned, as he did, to talk to the girl he was walking with, I'd stop behind a palm tree or phone booth. I didn't take my eyes off him. I watched the way he flailed his arms and worked his jaw in her direction. I'd never seen him with another woman. I could see he worked at it.

With me he had been poker-faced and limp-armed. And silent. I called him Mt. Rushmore. I followed him three blocks before I realized they were strolling to the Ready Teller. They disappeared around the granite facing of the bank and I waited.

John and the girl appeared again on the opposite side of the street. I could see them face on. She was tall and beautiful in a poor student way. A waif, taking his Philosophy course, no doubt. She was run down in the heels; wore a shabby dress. There was no fun in her clothes and I could tell that she cared nothing for John, who was still knocking himself out to win her over. She would not look his way so that he had to bend in front of her face to talk. I wondered what he could be talking about with such animation. They made their way back up the street and entered a sidewalk cafe where a tableful of young men and women were seated. I peered from behind a palm as John stood, politely and pulled the chair out for the girl, dipped his head and asked her what she wanted, a bit hard of hearing, took out real money and laid it on the table. Then he excused himself and headed for the rest room. I entered the cafe and through the shadows made my way toward the rest-room and waited. In a short while John emerged, eyes on his own prowess, lips rehearsing lines. He had a little smile as he muttered. When he saw me he jolted. I said, "Your daughter would be very proud to see that her father can date someone her age." He threw his head forward like a horse with blinders, and I heard his scowl, as he plowed ahead, "Go away. Just go away."

I went outside the cafe and across the street where I could see the tableful of students and John on the patio. They were not California types, but a group of kids with pimples and parts down their heads, and their parents' idea of how to dress. I watched, feeling the night around me. Hot from the sleuthing, red-faced from the confrontation. I could hear my own heartbeat and breathing. Whipped and entertained in one. Broken and made whole in one. Hot-faced and icicle-fingered. Satisfied and ripped apart. Now I Knew. This wasn't the woman I had known about. It was still another one. This one. The one he told me about was my age. This one was young. Just a girl. I wondered how many more I never knew about. I would go out of town at times. And he'd never be home when I called.

John did a strange thing. He got up, excused himself, and made his way down the steps of the cafe. He was heading for his car in the parking lot. I ran across the street and entered the cafe. I thought, he left because he's afraid I might make a scene.

I took a table next to the students. I listened in. One of the boys asked, "Who was the old guy?" The girls giggled. One of them said, "He's our professor."

She was clearly proud of her conquest. The pretty girl told

the boys, "He buys our drinks, what the hell. And it's good for an A in the course." The silence made the other girl go on, "Well he deserves it. He's the proverbial lecherous professor. I mean he came onto me in his office. I may as well say it. He wanted me to masturbate for him. Can you believe that."

Somebody laughed, "Did you?" Everyone laughed. The first one laughed loudest. I thought I recognized her laugh. I'd been a teacher for years. It was Eleanor. She's outgrown her acne and combed her hair over one side of her face, so it acted like a veil. But there were her teeth and nose. She never had a date in high school. The mention of her name would make the boys make throw-up sounds back then. Now she had linked herself to this tall pretty co-ed and had John chasing them on campus.

Both girls got up and headed for the bathroom. I got up and followed them. Once inside the tight space, the light revealed me to Eleanor, "Oh Mrs. Lansdowne, How are you?" The tall pretty one stood and stared. She was a bit empty-eyed, afraid of her own beauty it seemed and hid behind it. I said, "You're with the Professor—John?"

She gushed, "Oh, he won't leave us alone. I figured after I saw you with him, remember that afternoon? I thought he couldn't be all that bad." Then she stopped and introduced me fondly to the blinking beauty, as her former track coach. She said, "John and I have been running all year together." I am stabbed. He never told me that. I remember his silence when we ran into Eleanor that day at a cafe. She says now, "I thought it was shitty that he didn't act like he even recognized me then. I was insulted."

I'd come into the relationship with John, trusting, after twenty years with Alex. Alex had taught me that all men don't betray you. After being raised by Flynn I thought all men were cheaters. That was part of the trouble between Alex and me. I was on edge, waiting for him to prove he was like Flynn. But Alex's mind was on his inventions, building things, working with his hands. Once he had a wife, he never looked at another woman. There were circumstances, but he never would have been unfaithful. I think I pushed him to live out my expectations.

The ugly girl looks triumphant. She has proved to her beautiful friend that she means nothing at all to the professor. She wants to go on talking, "See, what did I tell you. He had you convinced you were special. You're so naive: I knew it. I'm so glad we ran into you Mrs. L." They interrupted each other going on and on telling me how they played a game with John. "He takes us to Happy Hour every night, right after school, after we make him hunt us down. And after we're seated we time him. It usually takes him about forty seconds before he starts talking about sex." The pretty one says, "Once it was only twenty seconds: that's the record." The ugly one says, "The one who wins the bet gets to sit by the window on the ride home. He has a kind of smell, very unpleasant, we always laugh and he asks, 'What're you laughing at?' We have an agreement that she'll never leave me alone with him, but one time he insisted on giving me a ride home. He was so upfront about sex, kept grabbing at me and touching me and wanting to kiss me. How old is he anyway?"

John used to say, "Vanity: everyone celebrates their own mediocrity."

Sal

Everyone

Everyone in the world must know when I'm having sex: my tenants, the men I've known, my grown children, the neighbors. Sal comes calling with his overnight bag. He brings his pajamas. He likes a lot of clothing to take off. That's all part of it. Then he likes me to walk him out to his car the next morning when he leaves. He always reaches over, kisses me goodbye. Mrs. Jones is always at her window. Last year it was John. He was six feet tall and a hundred and ninety-nine pounds, grey and balding. Sal is five-five, a hundred and thirty with thick black hair and much younger. John never carried an overnight bag with his pajamas. He would come carrying his professor bag full of books and papers to grade. And if there was any kissing in the street where the neighbors could see, it was me, reaching for him after he was in his car and ready to back out. Sal parks on the street. He thinks that is discreet.

In the house, Sal likes to sit at the table to eat. I haven't sat at the table to eat since the divorce ten years ago. So there we sit with our plates full of macrobiotic foodstuffs: beans, rice, vegetables, and in walks Mike, the electrician who lives here. He's fat, shy, and now embarrassed to come upon his landlady in the middle of a "romantic" dinner. He has never seen me eat. I always take my food to my room and lie on the bed, eating with the plate on my stomach ("like a sea otter," I tell Sal), the TV on. But Sal likes to sit up. He prides himself in liking me for more than sex. He wants to sit face to face and eat and talk; I prefer side by side. He says he's a man with old-fashioned blue collar traditional morals. And he is Catholic. John was an atheist and proud of it. But he always said it like a big crybaby. Some giant toddler who knew there was no Santa Claus and was going to show everyone how he could take it just fine.

Sal has introduced me to organic foods and cosmetics. I've spent a fortune. He has taught me to eat no animal fats in any form and cause no animal suffering (even to Scraggles...). He brings non-alcoholic champagne and roses as a gift.

John brought wine and french bread and together we ate more animal flesh than I'd ever eaten in my life. One night he tore a baked duck in half long ways with his bare paws and we sat on the couch wolfing it down stark naked. John had no respect for anything.

Sal reveres everything. He is so kind to his dogs it is almost cruel. We went over there yesterday where he keeps his dogs. He rents a woman's yard and garage and employs her to feed them raw meat and vegetables and apples! In the agreement, which he pays her for, they get to come into her house at night and have the run of the living room. The first date we had was to go to see his dogs. I went just because I couldn't believe this was true. A man loving his dogs so much that he wants to take me to see them.

Sure enough, in some woman's backyard there are two dogs waiting as Sal and I enter. A mother and son it turns out. Both medium-sized shepherds of mixed colors. Well-brushed, thick-coated and deferring to Sal, their master. I conceal a smirk. It's a comical situation to me for some reason. The mother dog is jealous of me right off. She smells another female around her male, Sal. The male dog slobbers all over me. Sal is oblivious to any of this response to me of his dogs and goes about picking up their poops. He has a contraption made for the job, and is very efficient at it. I watch the way he walks, the way he holds his shoulders. He's very straight. Has male proportions the way males are supposed to be. John was big. But his hips were as wide as his shoulders, and he was growing a hump on the back of his shoulders behind his neck like some male hoofed beast. Sal now strides easily around this rented yard doing his chosen duty. John refused to own a pet. Said it would tie him down. He never went anywhere anyway. But he kept thinking he would someday.

Sal gives his dogs vitamin pills. The mother spits them out with guilty eyes. She keeps her head low and her eyes up and hopes he won't notice. I take her side and tell him she doesn't want it and he should respect that. He gently shames her into swallowing it and then pats her for being good. "She's not good, she's just pleasing you against her will," I protest. He takes my comments with silence. "You're killing her with kindness," I say. A slow smile stays on Sal's face.

Sal is a combination of Perry Como and Mussolini. He's pure Italian. John was pure Ukrainian. In a report I helped my son with in world ranking of health, Ukrainians have the highest incidence of suicide in the world and they rank highest in heart attacks. Italians died of cirrhosis of the liver the most. Sal simply said, "The red wine," when I told him that. He is a nutrition specialist. A consultant. A biochemist. He knows what happens in the body when it takes in nutrients. He told me many stories already. I listen and go sliding down the esophagus with a piece of starch as he talks. He is a good storyteller of facts. I see little cells assimilating complex carbohydrates, and the husks of brown rice, scritchy-scratching the lining of the lower intestine ushering waste products out. John talked about Philosophy and how sexual energy was always at the root of each philosopher's dilemmas, as the driving force and the destructive force. Both subjects turn out to be the same thing as these men talk. John talks of the heart. Sal, the nucleus of the cell. (Wolfgang of the origins of the universe, and Alex focused on entropy and almost self-destructed on it. And Flynn of love, and hates women for not loving him.)

One daughter calls and asks, "Are you in love?" I say, "No, in like."

The other daughter calls and asks, "How are you doing with Sal?" I say, "Fine."

My son says, "If you ever go back to John, I'll never respect you." I am silent.

When Sal looks at me, I'm so self-conscious I can feel my face cringe. How long can I go on laying down layers of living. With each man, I thought it was *the* man, and that it would last forever. I pictured us old together. Little by little, Sal learns of the other men. And they learn of him. Alex comes in to measure my bathroom pipes. He is building a house next door and is about to place hs plumbing in just so, and needs to know how far away from the wall certain junctures need to be for county inspection. He knocks on my bedroom door slyly. He knows Sal is with me. He knows Sal's car. He asks permission through the door to do the measuring. And I give it. While Sal sits straight up in shock. "Is that your ex-husband?" he said, disbelief on his face. Still the gentle voice. We lie down again, and after awhile the slow methodical footsteps of Flynn are upon the deck outside my bedroom door. Then the sound of the sliding glass door. "Just my father," I say.

Sal has met my father already. It was the first time I invited Sal home. He sat in the front half of the front room and acted like company. I said, "No one ever sits on that couch. This is kind of a no room space. Come over here." And we went into the back half of the front-room. The skylights brightened things up and he could see into the backyard where my lawn was depleted of nutrients. A very sparse lawn just holding on. He had just met me and with his professional eye told me what to do about dry skin, brown spots and every other flaw he tactlessly saw and spoke about. Yet, he kept telling me I was beautiful. He stood on the deck now and saw my dry lawn. Then my little dog came stiff-legging it out of my room where she lives on my bed, and rolled over on her back to scratch her dry spots. Two large tumors were displayed on her underside —the only things doing well in the whole house. I simply said, "She's too old to operate on." I could see his frustration. A man whose profession it is to cure ailments with emollients and he sees one depletion after another.

Then Flynn comes in the front door, ever so slowly. At 76 he is down to 99 pounds. Sal looks up with those Perry Como twinkly eyes and never erases the quiet smile on his face. I introduce one more case of depletion to him. They shake hands. They spend half the afternoon talking about Flynn's psoriasis and how many pints of predigested vitamin C he can take to get rid of it. I say "Who digested it first?" Sal is quick, he says "chemicals." Flynn hangs onto his condition as if Sal just might take it away from him with cures. Then what would he have? I ignore them as they talk and then I take Sal away. He has survived seeing my face, my dog, my dad, my yard and still wants to see me again.

The first time John came out, was as a tenant. He took one look at me and rented the place out back. That's what he told me later. He wanted to get to know me. He eventually thought everything was stupid in my life, my dog, my dad, my yard, my ex-husband next door, and even my face. He finally moved out.

Sal says never to say "Sal said…" He says that makes me sound stupid. But I tell everyone. "Sal says brown rice is the answer to everything." My women friends laugh. "Is he any good?" they ask. This time I don't think in terms of living happily ever after. Everyone can see I will do this over and over.

Food

Flynn sits feeding on a TV dinner like a sick grey buzzard on the down side of a hill at the zoo. He perches on a stool and forks in $1.50 worth of dead matter (even though I have a pot of steamed rice on the stove.) His false teeth snap up the pre-fab franks and beans like a desert tortoise. He is surviving, just staying alive. His meager intake irritates me. I fed him with all of me at one time. And flee now to my room from his need to be fed. An upright ancient infant. He's never learned to feed himself. He would rather starve to death and fall on the kitchen floor within reach of a pot of whole grained rice, and let it be my fault. Everyday he goes to the store and selects one TV dinner from the frozen food dept., comes in the front door about five o'clock with it, and puts on his glasses, and with a lot of racket taking off the plastic bag from around the little package, reads the instructions. I try to avoid the kitchen at this time, but was caught in there briefly. He leaned into the print on the package and said, " Poke holes in the apples."

I said, "Poke holes in the apples? What apples?" And glanced over and saw some discolored applesauce in one section of the tray. He squinted his eyes to take a closer look and then shuffled across the kitchen floor and pulled open the silverware drawer, ever so careful. His every movement is pre-planned. Getting from one point to the next, and finding implements is an act of thinking for him. Methodically he selects a fork, strides back across the kitchen floor like he's doing the one-step, and I leave the kitchen before I hear the holes being punched in the cellophane that covers his once-a-day meal he must puncture before it goes into the microwave that kill the oils that float free as radicals in the body. I go to my room and spoon in *life*, I eat brown rice with amino acid soy sauce, low sodium sea salt. I get away from Flynn's sounds of hunger, his feeble attempt to live.

Flynn also hates the sounds I make. He is repelled by the way I hunch over the steaming pot of rice and slurp audibly, as I'm stuffing in sustenance. Usually, I am too impatient to put food on a plate. When I was under Flynn's roof I was never allowed to eat out of a serving dish or cooking pan. Now in my house I eat the way I want. Flynn looks at his hands or straight ahead as if I am not doing what I'm doing.

Sal comes for a nice little salmon steak dinner one night. Flynn has already done his TV dinner routine and gone out the back door to his cabana by the pool. It is a room I had added for my son and sits there forty feet from the house. When my son left home, Flynn moved in. He calls it "the shack." "I guess I'll go out to my shack now," he announces to no one at all each night, and out he goes, sliding the sliding glass doors ever so deliberately so the sound is the maximum length of time. When he is gone, I scurry around and try to make a simple little vegetarian dinner for Sal. It is the first time I cook for him and he says he will eat salmon. He has instructed what to buy and how to cook it. I asked him. For twenty years I did family cooking of the regular American diet: meat, salad and potatoes. I was heavy-handed and high-flamed. I would beat, bludgeon and attack the meat. Alex used to complain about how fast I could cook, and always making too much food. I cooked in vats. Now Sal says to simply steam the vegetables and broil the fish a few minutes on each side; the leaves and roots and fish are delicate. He will arrive in a little while, I decide to go ahead and do it all myself and not act nervous or like I don't know what I'm doing, even though I get fluttery as if it is the first meal I ever cooked. I run the sink with water and begin rinsing all the bok choy, chard, mustard and collard. Then I pull out the broiler and see the damage the tenants left. I have to scrub that. I grow more nervous, hoping not to look frazzled by the time he steps in the door with his Perry Como smile and Mussolini need for controlling things.

And I have bought a bottle of wine, even though we don't drink. I find all the different kinds of lettuce I bought and begin tearing them up. Sal said to get oil. I painstakingly read labels and came up with olive oil. When Sal finally gets here, he shakes his head, "You want the extra virgin olive oil," he instructs and explains the first press kindly in his Long Island, no "r," dialect. His smile stays. His words do not smile. He smells the fish. I pull out the broiler pan and he sees two fine fat salmon steaks and a great slab of filet of salmon. He says, "Mmmmmmmmm," with Mafia intonation. He lifts a lid and sees the vegetables steaming. He sees all the lettuce in a bowl. I bring out the wine. He stills me, holds me in the middle of my kitchen where Alex used to make love to me on the sinkboard, and where Wolfgang used to follow his nose and stand and heap his plate, and then John stood smirking and supervising my efforts, with his literary-critic fault-finding, always what's *wrong* eyes, and Sal wraps his Italian arms around me and looks right at me and says, "Hello." I'm stilled. I can't remember what to do. He asks when I put the fish in and when I tell him he rushes to the pot holder and quickly slides the broiler out and pokes it with a fork. I hear low notes of disapproval. I quickly turn the flame off under the vegetables. He begins to make lemon and olive oil dressing and asks where the salad is. I had put it in the freezer to chill. I pull it out and it is frozen. The delicate sprouts are stiff. He grumbles beneath audibility, but I see his face. He puts the bowl in the oven. I begin to laugh. He just smiles, not looking at me. Eyes like a yogi with light flickering from them: brown at night in this light-bulb yellow, light and pale in the day light. And when everything is set out, the sound of the sliding glass door begins, ever so slowly and Flynn appears from out of the dark living room into our yellow bright kitchenful of smells and goodwill and sexuality going on. He steers himself up to the counter and takes a big inhale and says, "That sure smells good, what is it." Sal is all hospitality. Soon Flynn is part of the nice little romantic dinner, saying "It sure gets lonely out there."

Flynn is full of stories no one wants to hear. His whole life's experiences are there inside his head and no one is asking to know what he did, how his life went.

But tonight I am trapped and Sal is polite. Flynn says, "When I was about seventeen, me and Jess went for a ride in his car and the steering wheel came off in his hands and we were going around a curve in the mountains, and we run right up on a hill and come to a stop and both got out without a scratch."

He goes on, his false teeth giving him such a bad time that he takes them out and puts them in his pocket. "Another time I was way up on Mt. Baldy and lightning began to strike. I was with my sister and boy was I afraid. I used to be so scared of lightning. Pearl said 'If you're afraid of lightning it'll strike you,' and I was never afraid of lightning after that."

That night Sal holds me again in that eye-to-eye contact, so I will not forget who I am with, that it is him and not any of the others. He sugars me up and turns me into a silly woman. A kind of sweet person after all.

And the phone rings. It is Wolfgang. I let the machine get it. Suddenly there is the big molasses voice. Spanish accent, honey-dripping words. The familiarity, the pet name he calls me. "Benny"—from Benny-Hill predicaments I get into! Sal simply walks into the other room to give me privacy. I pick it up and talk for a half an hour.

Later, Sal gives a little speech, "When someone is trying to bond with someone and there is this kind of experience, someone you have bonded with in the past and are still bonded to, it is very difficult." I can see he is hurt, and the only language he knows is that of the nutritionist. It is the structure of the biochemist. This equals that. Equations: this goes in and that is the result, and therefore this is the solution. He suggests very politely that he will leave every time the phone rings. "I want you to have your privacy, Dollface," he says, in his Mafia Long Island dialect.

Flesh

Sal is taking his father to the doctor. It is called "preventative medicine." I protest. "If I took my father to the doctor they'd find everything wrong with him. But as it is, he walks around just fine every day." Sal has a way of not responding to pig-headedness. He simply explains that his father goes for regular check-ups and they are going to do a routine procedure to check for anything wrong. The next day they have the 76-year- old man on a fast so they can do a dye enema. I say "See, if you go in they always find something wrong. A lump in the bank and they find a lump in your breast. Your poor dad. You've probably opened a can of worms."

The ignoring gestures of looking off at something else, but I can see his ears twitch. He is getting ready to give a speech about the value of catching something in time. I say, "My father probably has every disease known to man, but because he doesn't know it, they don't show up; if I took him in and they told him his lungs were full of cancer, he'd probably die tomorrow." Sal tells me his father had to give up his one glass of wine in the evening. I ask, "Now what will he do to be naughty?" He's faithful to your mother, what? fifty years now? The only willful act he had was that glass of wine at night to make an *I statement* with." Sal looks straight ahead, as if I am not really talking. But he is silent, so I go on. "My father was told to quit smoking for years now and every doctor who told him that dropped dead within a year.... I mean, my father smokes because he wants to beat the system. If he gave it up, he'd be cowering, fearful. There's something to be said for men like that who try to outsmart..."

And before I can finish, Sal says, "God," and laughs out loud. He finally looks directly at me with his brown Italian irises rimmed in blue, and sees that I am on a soap box. I go on, "You are expecting your father to be like you and respect something greater than himself, but our fathers are each 76 and from that generation of little gods. They bow to nothing. That is what keeps them alive, not health, not food, not good living, just their idea that nothing is going to push them around...."

Sal took his mother in to the doctor and they discovered a prolapsed uterus when she turned seventy, and they took it out. He took his dog in for a hip x-ray, and the vet discovered a dislocated joint. He himself went to get an AIDS test after he began seeing me. He asked me to go. I said I didn't want to know. He was silently furious. He consoled himself by finding it was negative and brought it out to show me out of "respect," he said. He now wants me to have a mammogram. I am afraid to tell him I haven't been to a doctor in ten years. That I am afraid of doctors.

Sal tells me, "You are cardiovascular, have you really run for thirty years?" I say "thirty-one." I have never been described as cardiovascular before. I picture myself as a few ganglia attached to bellows and hoses. I've lost fifteen pounds in the last six months. It was over John. My heart was broken. Then Sal came along and said I was the perfect candidate for the perfect health with that kind of oxygen intake for so long if I would make sure I got "essential oils and complex carbohydrates." I say I have been eating lots of protein all my life. That I love protein in the form of big juicy sandwiches. He shakes his head. Animal fats in any form are bad for me. The answer is in grains. So I went from feline with John to bovine with Sal. I have never grazed so much on leaves, grains and sprouts. I tell him, "I used to think it was cheating to take care of yourself. I'm like my father that way, I guess." He sees how long he can get by on nothing." Later....

Sal says, "Honey, Sweetcakes, why don't you run every other (*oth ah*, with the Long Island *r*) day. You don't need to burn yourself out." I am confused, thinking he admired my running. I say "Yes, I do. I need to strain. I need to push against it. I need the circulation. The flush. The rush, the pain. I need to come back from that...or I get mean. I can't just stay the same temperature all day. I need to change. To be all wet with sweat and then get all dry. To be hot, to get cold.

"You are a furnace," he says looking away, as if he has more to say, but will not deal with my reasons now. He thinks I have reabsorbed my muscle mass leaving no fat, I turn muscle into energy so my skin is getting too big for me. Patience is his style. In time, he believes, he will gently wrestle my beliefs away from me. I am suddenly sorry I have insisted on my way. I soften it, "Maybe I am too much like my father. I have learned to run on empty and make my body do what I want it to do. I treat my car and dog in the same way. I've never liked pampering myself. I will reward this animal body only after it serves me. After I abuse and punish it into submission. And it's always done what I've made it do. There'd be no end to pampering it if I ever started, but there is an end to the abuse. I know the limits. It's automatic. I simply can't go on any more. Exhaustion comes. And I finally have to give in." Sal looks apologetic. Bloodhound-browed for a moment. Something has crossed his mind. Sympathy? He has lived in moderation. He sits there brand new at forty-three. I could run circles around him. It turns out I'm older than he thought. The first time he saw my face…his face fell open in surprise. He had been following me. He says, "There is the law of accumulative effect."

He tells me he talked to a woman who teaches Power Walking who wears padded socks. I hee-haw him out of the room. When he comes back in, he waits for more ridicule. I say, "Why don't you just get into a desensitizing chamber where you can't feel anything at all. You know, they've done experiments." He is quick: "Or just run barefoot on the pavement and hammer your cartilage into the bone."

I am pleased. He fights back. I say, "There is a middle ground." He says "But not for you there isn't, oh Sheena of the jungle." And has the last laugh.

So I try not to think about it. I say "It's just hard for me to back down. I was running 10 miles a day at my peak (at 40) and coaching tack and working out. I never wanted to let up, but my fingernails were turning up. I figured I was depleting my body of something, so let up. Now I only do 3 to 5 a day.

I have to see that I am on the other side of my peak. I don't like that. And then menopause. Now Mother Nature is going to dry me out, wring me dry. I hate that. I like being bloody, juicy, alive. What if I began to worry about myself and buy padded socks, and have a mammogram? I'd probably get crippled and tumored. I say, "Everything begins with trust. You say you trust some larger thing, but you go around with a full tank of gas, a cupboard full of food, and run to the doctors to tell you everything about yourself. I thought you admired the "birds of the field," and…whatever you quoted that time in the rain about animals being taken care of.

The next day at the store I see a sign for "boneless rump" on sale. I have burned up my rump. I have no ass at all, and now agreed to give up meat. Sal has plenty of meat on his body. All hard and white and untouched by being alive for forty years. I say, "Where does your living show? Even Viet Nam? You haven't began to tap into your baby fat yet.…" He isn't sure if I mean it is good or bad. At fifty I have honed myself down to the bone. Flynn, the one I look like, is a walking skeleton.

Sal's House

Sal wants to show me where he lives. He likes to come out and pick me up. He says he has never had a woman meeting him anywhere. He tells me that I am a "California" woman. "On the East Coast a man comes to the door." I tell him no man has ever picked me up. I have always met them. They don't come to my door. That I have never dated in that way. That I like to drive my own car. That I don't like being a passenger.

Sal picks me up at exactly two o'clock. He comes to the door and actually knocks and waits for me to open it. I feel giddy. It makes me nervous, this formality. I open the door and laugh out loud over the absurdity of it. This house, full of tenants and Flynn, and sometimes Alex traipsing through with a towel over his shoulder on the way to or from a shower.

Sal instructs, "When you open the door I would like you to do like this," and he demonstrates an eye-to-eye greeting with a little kiss. I grow silly and giggle like a girl. And protest.

"No I can't do that. It isn't what I do. In fact, what do I do?" He demonstrates by going through the motions of opening the door and stepping aside to let him enter so I am side by side with some distance between us. I kneel over laughing, seeing how he sees me. I never knew I did that. As I approach the front door after his knock, I always spy him outside the window waiting there and my throat tightens, and I see how dapper and dark and quiet he waits, his eyes flickering with a yogi kind of light, and he tries not to look in the window (John always peeked in like Peeping Tom, not knowing I could see him.). Protocol utmost in Sal's demeanor. I try to learn about myself from Sal. I tell him that he might make me into a lady yet. The daughter my mother wanted. One who wears pretty dresses and has good manners.

He opens the car door for me. I try to take the handle and

get in by myself wondering why he is over here on my side of the car in my way. No man has opened a door for me yet. Not that I would have minded. John used to go first and let the doors slam in my face. Now Sal and I vie for the same door handle and again I laugh like a silly woman. He renders me physically weaker in these small acts.

Once at a restaurant I left the table to go to the rest room and when I approached the table again he got up, walked around to my side and stood by my chair. I then went to his side of the table and sat down in his chair. He was appalled. He said, "I am holding your chair, what are you doing?" I was truly surprised. I told him I thought he had changed his mind and wanted to sit on that side after all. He didn't smile. He thought I was joking. I began to laugh again. That nervous laugh. It was the first time a man ever held a chair for me. He could not believe it. I was in the habit of accommodating the man. John always took the best view. Alex sat at the side that gave him the most room to stretch out. And Wolfgang liked to have the best lighting so he could do calculations at the tables. I always sat wherever they didn't.

Sal drives his vintage Dodge so slow that I grow sleepy. The wide leather seat is warm and his heater makes the front seat too cozy. I prop my legs up on the dashboard and close my eyes, he sits very straight behind the wheel in his ironed shirt buttoned all the way up to his adam's apple, his hair combed back like a black city cap, and his fine baby skin well-doused with emollients, and glances at my bare feet on his dashboard. "You are a California woman," he says with his Mafia voice.

We cruise to a stop in the very clean garage affair in the front of his parents' condominium. He explains that they have lived here eight years and he has moved in with them to care for them since last summer. He tells me about the little place he had in Venice before that. I can't picture him in Venice, California. He says he never went to any of the clubs there. I can believe that.

We go up the well-swept steps and enter through what seems an impersonal door. Just any door, not a home kind of door. Once inside I am struck by the stillness. His parents have gone to yet one more Italian wedding. It is a big family of relatives with the younger generation getting married early and going right into adulthood, unlike my own California kids who are still adolescent in their middle twenties. Still in school, still haven't worked a day in their lives.

I am embarrassed in Sal's house. I am afraid of my own judgments. Afraid that I will see how stupidly he lives. Or see how much I fail by comparison. See evidence of something that will make me not like him. Or not like myself. He has told me how important it is that I see where he lives, how he lives. I stand there now in the middle of his living room and blank out a little. I suddenly am overcome with sleepiness. He wants me to go through his files and see how much information he has accumulated on nutrition. He places the cardboard files on the dining room table which has a central location. The condominium is small. Everything can be viewed from where I am standing. I go to the table and look at the files but do not touch them. He opens the refrigerator, which is the largest item in the house, and suddenly there is an illuminated array of very clean, shiny, containers with every kind of vegetarian delight. He lifts one from the shelf and opens the lid, and sticks his finger into some goo and puts it in his mouth, closing his eyes and saying, "ummmmmmmmmm, nectar." He holds the container there for me to do the same. I stick my finger in and take a big scoop and taste it and go back for another scoop. It is yellow and thick and tastes of garlic: He closes the lid and puts it back and takes another container out and we do the same thing. This time a green mixture with curd texture. I begin that laugh again and ask what his mother would think if she saw me sticking my fingers in all her properly prepared and stored foodstuffs. He doesn't answer. He closes the "fridge" and we turn, like a dance, and he throws open the cupboard behind us again. I am struck with such neatness and organization that I grow sleepy. I do not want to see this. I knew his house would look like this. By the comments he made about my place, the suggestions he made of throwing out everything I own and beginning all over again with the right products, that his house would contain all this. Nothing extraneous. No excesses. Everything making sense and used. Everything in its place. I begin to protest.

"I can't live this way. I have to have a backlog of stuff. I'm used to it. It makes me feel secure. You live right on the surface. I have to sink down into layers of living, heaps of clothes that I'll never wear, cupboards of food I'll never eat." (Sal opened one of my cupboards and a moth flew out. It was an old bag of brown flour that was hatching weevils. I remember he broke out in a sweat. I said, "I don't want to kill them, wait," as I grabbed the bag of flour and raced out the door with it, threw it over the fence into Alex's yard. The weevils could eat all they wanted, and then fly away, or do whatever they do. Alex's yard was so ample it could absorb anything I didn't want. Rotten oranges, rotten potatoes. Mildewed rice. ("For the ants," I told Alex, once when he caught me.)

Sal says now, "We are not in competition, I am not accusing you. Don't go on the defensive." Sal takes me to his room. There are double beds, neat as a pin. So neat, my toes grow cramps, thinking of getting into one and not being able to pull out the sheets, and have to sleep in toe-dance position all night with that military tightness.

I sit on one bed. He carefully slides open his closet door. Inside there is a row of ironed, cotton, clean, long-sleeved dress shirts. I recognize all of them. He has worn one each time he came out to the house, and no matter what time of the day it is, even at night, it was as clean and ironed and polished as if he just put it on. He never works into a sweat in the course of a day. My closet at home is full of "skins," t-shirts and sweaters I can pull on. He asked once, "Do you have a wardrobe?"

"That's it, I said, pointing to the stacks of t-shirts and jeans. Sweaters and tights.

On the shelf above a row of shirts, and also the row of pants that he wears, all ironed jeans, are several boxes, stacked just so. The lightness, the space between these boxes, the way they are not crammed together, or stuffed, but simply sitting there with ease and no effort, nothing bulging, again fills me with a wave of sleepiness. I yawn, and then yawn again. He removes one of these small tidy boxes and with the same gentle movement the boxes themselves seem to have sitting there, he takes a stack of photographs and invites me to sit on his bed. The other bed is his father's. I have already heard that they no longer sleep together, his mother and father at 73 and 76. I have already made comments about why they have their ailments then. No sex life? Two Italians? I thought they were passionate people? He has already poopooed my notions.

Sal begins shuffling one photo after another under my nose and I see him in Viet Nam with a military haircut and immaculate uniform. In picture after picture he could be interchangeable. The same serious smile, the same angle of the head. The good guy. The nice guy. The clean guy. The Italian guy from Long Island. Even his sergeant liked him. A black guy from the South who let him get away with impersonating his dialect. Then there is Sal on a horse. Same turn of the head, same expression of goodwill on his face, same readiness to have his picture taken. I laugh again and ask, "Don't you never get caught off guard. Aren't there any candid snapshots of you?" He lets it pass. We do not speak the same language. He lets most of my comments pass.

Once I asked him if his mother was going to be worried when he didn't come home at night. My little dog was snoring by my side of the bed. He said he would let her snoring be his answer to that kind of question. He quietly puts the box back and takes down another, and as I yawn again, he lifts the lid so carefully and gently, that I almost fall backward in a deep sleep. His deliberate hand movements are like a massage. Inside the box are safely stored his "hippy" years. My eyes pop out. There is a very sexy man with so much long curly hair he could represent the whole Sixties movement. "That's one thing hippies could do alright," I say, "grow hair." Then I ask, "Who's that?" He notices that I wake up. He's pleased. I can feel his smile. "Is that you?" I snatch the photos and go through them studying his bare chest. Tan, jeans, hipbones, sensual face, a beard so thick his Sicilian eyes jump out.... He could make Charlie Manson look bald.

After Sal puts this box of photos away, I go around to all the walls and peer in closely to all the framed and enlarged photos. It is certainly an Italian family. Everyone is Italian. It's like that black woman I went home with once. All the photos she showed me of herself were black. For some reason I thought there'd be a let-up on it sometime and she'd be white in some of the photos. But, there she was in her ballet dress at five, black. And at her piano at seven, still black. And her albums were full of black people. She pointed out her brothers. They all looked alike to me, but were different sizes and had the same names, Razmus, Tashia, Aquita and Haza that kind of sound. Now the same with Sal. There is his Sicilian grandfather, a very big head, short body, and a mighty, and proud, look on his face. Truly a male. An Italian woman beside him, very serious. Some assumption inside me popped. I thought Italians were full of joy and music and singing and dancing. I see this family very pokerfaced and sober, looking into the camera as if it is a momentous event. No smiles, no clowning.

All my photos at home, bags and boxes, chestfuls of them. I snapped everyone all the time in any position. Laying them out in a row, it would make a moving picture. And everyone smiling from ear to ear in bright beach clothes, Hawaiian prints, fruit colors and making a two-fingered ear behind everyone else's head. Big grins, silly poses, and some impatient "hurry up" expressions. A party every five minutes.

Sal's Napoli grandfather on the mother's side also looks out at me as I peek in close to a very formal brown and white photograph. A studio sitting. Again, the big head and small body and a very straight, dignified pose. Life: a very serious matter. And his wife beside him, proper, no nonsense. Presented as non-sexual. Only a face above miles of cloth. A male-dominated family. In my photos all the adult males are missing. Only women running things. And there is Sal's father on a horse in jodhpurs. Same face as his Sicilian father. big head, very sober, but a bit of humor around the eyes and mouth; carefully guarded. Even the horse looks Italian with a very serious expression, looking at the camera, too, as if this photo is important to him. The horse also has a big head and a small body. I conceal any mirth, and swallow my comments. I have already shown Sal some of my photographs and he has already marvelled over the intimidation he felt looking at them and knowing that in Long Island, this California blond family, looking like this—"The affluence was so far from anything he knew, and had only heard about, that it overwhelmed him. That he was here now, with the woman who had lived in the middle of it all, and created a whole world of her own out of it. We have already talked about our different beaches. I have already said that East Coast people don't know how to go to the beach right. They wear three-piece, button-down bathing suits, and their tans fade as fast as their seasonal grasses.

"Our lawns and wild grasses are here to stay. But with the first cold wind your grasses and tans die. So frail." Always a disgruntled look, like he could come back with something that would hurt me, but he holds his tongue for now. My skin displays the damage of tans. A confusion of pigmentation, all freckled and spotted.

I fall into a deep sleep on my face on Sal's bed. We had planned to make love in his bed, but he does not disturb me. He passes time. So quiet, I wonder how he can live like that. No stirring, no movement. He breathes short and shallow. I've never seen him heave in the air except the time he told me to look at one of the breathing exercises he learned in yoga. Suddenly he was bent over, a hissing exhaling and then inhaling sounded and when he straightened up his rib cage was standing out like an Ethiopian refugee and his stomach was a deep cave. A hairy fur-lined cave. Otherwise he doesn't make a ripple on a day, simply moves through it with that big head and straight proud body, and his belt up around his waist, wearing ironed jeans and cotton dress shirts buttoned to the neck.

I sleep and lose myself. I forget where I am and wake up to his silent house with the pattern of his bedspread on my face. He is simply in a chair, waiting, looking at me. It is as if I am in a hospital and he has come to see my recovery. He says,

"Hello Sweetiepie." I can't help but smile. His voice is sooth-
ing, and his calm is an emollient to my nerves. He has a look
on his face like, "Oh, honey, it's too bad what's happened to
you. What did they do to you?" Does he see what my life
has done to me? What I could have been? What injuries have
been inflicted on me out in California? And me not knowing
better and so willing. He has spoken often of cures. He tries
to teach me another way to be. The way blue collar Italians
treat their women— with respect. He has told me if I'd grown
up in the ethnic regions of Long Island I'd be twenty pounds
heavier and know my place, what to say, do, think. "I would
have cherished a woman like you." He has been alarmed by
the stories of what the other men have done. He shook his
head slowly back and forth in disbelief. He has offered to take
my hand and lead me to another kind of life, where all the
cupboards are organized, the angry words have stopped, and
tranquility reins and men love their women. We began with
my giving up coffee, "which shatters the nervous system,"
and animal fats, "that run rampant in the body and cannot be
digested, so lodge and turn rancid in older women and show
in the tissue of the face and body." His voice has always been
soft: I've listened as if it's a kind of fairy tale. A voice far away
calling me to come back from a kind of insanity I got caught
in. He speaks to some part of me that wants to hear what
he has to say, that wants to take his hand and be shown the
way. Even dragged, kicking. Only in bed does he take me with
less than gentleness. Less than persuasion. Only then does his
Sicilian take over and leave all the stuff he learned to say and
do in the '60s behind. Only then does he lose himself and live
the way I live out of bed.

We return to the California home I have created all
around me. A life style. John said he never heard that expression until he came to California. People had a life in Ohio,
but not a "life style." It was never used. A colloquialism on
the West Coast... I am relieved to get out of Sal's parents'
environment. I say, "Your mother sacrificed her life for your
father. She even irons the dish rags, you told me." "He wants
her to do that. He knows if she is doing that, she is not getting

into trouble." And I let that hang between us in the air of his warm front seat. In the silence, I believe Sal is also wanting me to teach him another way, too.

As we enter my house the sounds of parakeets scolding each other fills our ears, and Alex's saw searing the air next door vibrates our bodies. The cats race in ahead of us. A tenant is flushing one toilet. Sal reaches down and picks a bit of something off the floor. Flynn has been tracking in pittosporum seeds. A sticky pod he doesn't seem to notice on his plastic sole. I decide we will make a fire in the fireplace tonight. There is a chill in the air. I do have a home. It can be comfortable if I go to the effort. I ask Sal to follow me out to the dead space behind the pool to the wood pile. He is surprised by the big grassy area hidden by the fence. And the two sheds...full of my *past*.

Mind Centers

Sal questions my motives in taking the potato salad to Alex. He is out of town and calls me from San Francisco. He tells me what he did and I go on about what I did, and I tell him about the potato salad.

Sal is researching brain clinics. They are called Mind Centers. The brochures advertise them as "keeping more than the body in shape." They offer a life balance course. There is a feedback graph for mind fitness. It is a new wave in stress-reducing programs for businessmen. I make the mistake of joking about the old program, which was to call up a girl and have sex in the office during lunch hour. "That was great for the nerves." Sal was not humored. I felt vulgar. I argued, "You're too moral. Like a boyscout. But your morality is all in your head. In logic. Real morality has to come from the heart. You can tell when you are violating yourself that way." I hear his silence on the other end. Finally he says I give him so much at once that it would take him hours to form a rebuttal.

I scoff. "Just say it. Forget about how to say it." But Sal is very orderly in his language and in his person. His shirts are ironed, and his pants never show a smudge or crease or missing button. When I first saw him, I thought he looked like those men who drive a bread truck. There are hundreds of tidy men, staying close to their activities, not getting too far away from exactly what they know. But as I got to know Sal, I discovered he knew all kinds of things that weren't tidy, but handled them in a tidy way. It held my attention. His pre-planned speeches seemed to flow out of a history of real thinking and study. After the hippie movement swept the country, it left a bunch of men who didn't know anything for sure and questioned everything so much that I stopped "believing" in men. Sal tries to be spontaneous now, for my sake.

151

In the beginning I asked him to tell me about his life. He began. I remember we were in his car, in the frontseat with the heater on, about December. And I couldn't hang onto anything he said. His words didn't stick in my head. He went on and on, stating the exact year and month, and sometimes even the time of day something happened. Dates, places, times came from his mouth and I got them all mixed up. When I responded and got a fact wrong, like was he married first and then went to Viet Nam, or did he wander across the United States barefooted and then go to school, or what, he got so frustrated, I laughed at him. But he blamed me. He accused, "You're a college graduate with a Master's degree nonetheless. An educated woman who's a writer and a therapist, but sometimes, I mean, I wonder…"

I feel my face change color. I have spent all my life with men who think there is something wrong with the woman if they are unsuccessful with her. And now here is yet one more man doing that. I say, "Your words are without any graphic detail. I don't get any picture of you in school, hitchhiking, running from bombs, or standing at the altar with a twenty-two year old bride. I need to *see* your life. All you've done so far is listed the activity and chronology. Where's the entertainment," I am raising my voice by now, and like Alex used to, squeezing out the last ounce of air on my defense.

Sal sits on his side of the seat behind the wheel and looks ahead. He is pale with black hair and eyes that take the light during the day, and now at dusk have taken the dark. He looks very Italian. In fact, I knew he was Italian when I first heard him talk, because he wasn't sarcastic. At first I thought he might be Jewish with that coloring, but his words were too kind, not cutting enough. I feel stronger than Sal, and see that he can't understand my need for visual language. I calm down and say "If you think I'm retarded, then I think you are dull and dry and factual. A travel guide. I would retain every word of what happened if I knew what you were thinking and feeling through each event, if I could see the faces and reasons and motives behind the names and dates."

He shouts now. I am startled. "I don't know why things

happened the way they happened. I could spend ten years sur-
mising about why I did something, or what was behind my
wife's behavior, but I still wouldn't know, no one can know
these things. Things just happen. It's only guess work to try
to delve into what someone was thinking or feeling. And how
can I tell you how they looked? It would take all night."

I smile. I didn't know he could shout. I am glad for him. I
continue to push. I say, "I mean why'd you show up suddenly
at Northridge and begin studying biochemistry? What was
going on inside you? People don't just show up at a school
and start studying something out of the blue. What turn of
events? Causes?" He pouts, or is it just that he has a pouting
lip that looks sensual most of the time and now juts out like
a pout.

In a very controlled voice he says, "I don't know what you
mean. I never thought about what I did. I never felt anything.
I just did it." I pull down the sun blind and study my face in
the mirror attached to the back of it. I cringe. It makes me
want to be nice to him, I'm getting too old and ugly to still be
giving a man a bad time. And he is younger, sweeter, kinder
than others. I iron out the creases at the sides of my eyes. I"ll
never have money for a face lift. I'll really have to just crinkle
up and do nothing about it. Will a man ever help me again?
I know that they won't. Either I won't let him, or he won't
offer anymore. I look at my upper lip. How many lines can
an upper lip get in it anyway. I have been watching mine for
some years now. It started in such a subtle way. A tiny crack
that disappeared when I smiled. Now I have to stretch my
lips across my face to smooth them out. I turn the blind up
again. I'm humbled. In a nice voice, soft, a little helpless and
high, the kind that men have responded to in the past, a sweet,
hinting at pleasing voice, I go on, "Never?" This time it isn't
with ridicule, challenge or on the defensive. A real concern.
Some sympathy. But not too weak. A man doesn't like a weak
woman, just one that doesn't always challenge. "Provoke" is
the word Sal used. He said, "You are a provocateur," once. I
have scared myself. I am ready to listen.

He softens. He explains as a kind of apology, "My father

(fath ah, the Long Island no r) was a yell ah (yeller). He was a yell-aholic. He'd come home from work and yell and humiliate all of us, my mother and my brother and me. Insult us all through dinn ah, and we'd go up to bed silent and sullen. The next day he'd hug and kiss us and go off to work. He'd nev ah even remember what he did. He nev ah apologized. He never even knew what he was doing. His father's father was an illiterate peasant. A blue coll ah worker. He poured ta ah to fix the streets for forty years. He yelled at my fath ah when he was growing up. He had to sign his name with an X."

He continues because he can see I am all ears. "My moth ah was a quiet woman. She came from a household that had music and literature and conversation. But in those days a woman knew her place. She never spoke up to my fath ah. She would come upstairs later and give us a cookie and kiss us goodnight. We knew she was sorry he was that way, but she never spoke against him.

I picture his mother going up the stairs; the house dominated by the out of control hard-working Italian father, who was never unfaithful to his wife and worked forty years as an electrician. I've already asked, "You mean your father didn't make goo goo eyes at some housewife all those years when he was fixing her thermostat?" Again he was poker-faced.

I ask him, "What did your mother talk to you about when you were growing up?" He says, "Oh, the usual things. Time for school. Eat your dinn ah. Things like that."

I control my sniggering, the cutting edge. I pull down the mirror again. I sigh. Will I really have to be nice to men from now on. I turn to Sal and ask, with respect, "You mean she never pointed out who did what to whom and why? She never painted vivid pictures of this old prune and that sour pickle and some other face like a bulldog?"

"Nev ah."

I picture my own mother frothing all through my childhood with juicy tales and full-bodied reasons behind every action and the whole human condition. She bubbled over with so many words I couldn't wait to get to school where the teacher never talked, except to say "turn to page twenty-

154

seven and do the questions at the end of the chapter." Mama made me see the world and its inhabitants in all their greed, lies, deceits, betrayals, and anything else that was right under our noses.

I fall silent. But that was when I was getting to know him. Over the phone he asks, "What do you think your real motive was in taking Alex that potato salad?"

Party

Flynn turns seventy-seven, I buy him a new blanket, pillow, pair of Levis, and two Hawaiian shirts, two chocolate cakes, and insist that Louis give him a juicer. Louis comes for the party; Sal is there, too. Everything like this always happens around my kitchen counter, that borders the livingroom. Louis cooks sukiyaki. I take Flynn down to the beach in his new Levis and Hawaiian shirt. The blue one first. And photograph him by the mile-long row of palm trees. He has always painted beaches. I have given him a canvas to paint a picture of palm trees for me. The canvas has sat there untouched for over a year. This photo will leave no question as to what kind of palm trees I want in my picture.

When we get back, Louis has the sukiyaki ready. Flynn eats a bowl. We each slurp it up, and are ready for the party. I can't find the candles. We use one of Flynn's cigarettes in the middle of the cake as a candle. Our voices blend in song. Flynn smiles, snatches his cigarette from the cake and licks off the chocolate from the filtertip (He never smoked filtertips until he got old). We all laugh. He takes the small cleaver and cuts the cake. No one eats cake but Flynn. Louis goes outside to sit on the porch in the setting sun. Sal retires to the base-ball game on television. I stand in the kitchen with Flynn and watch him eat first one slice of cake from the layered cake, and then another from the torte. Flynn loves cake. I serve ice cream and champagne. Louis comes back in and demonstrates his juicer. I have bought a bag of carrots and celery. Sal comes back in and watches. The juicer is noisy. One carrot after another and it sounds like a tractor going through the kitchen. Finally there is one quart of bright orange foaming juice. We pour Flynn a small glass. He sips it and then drinks it down.

Louis, Sal, and I all breathe easy. He likes it, Like the ad on TV. Now Flynn will be healthy. I go to bed. Louis goes home, and Sal says, "I am really surprised your father liked that carrot juice. People not used to eating healthy food, they usually can't stand the taste of carrot juice." I say, "Flynn likes anything sweet," and that's a quote from Mama.

The next day, Flynn comes home scared. He says, "I almost fainted at Sears. I went out to pay my insurance and I was walking back to my car when all of a sudden everything started to spin. I thought I was going to fall down. I leaned against a car, and kept leaning against cars until I was back to my car, and got in and sat down until I got my balance."

"What do you think it was?" I ask. "I think it was that carrot juice. I was alright until I started trying to do something healthy. I think health food can kill you...."

Later on, when Sal arrives, I tell him this story. He agrees with Flynn. He says that Flynn's intestines are probably so ruined, that the juice began to clean them off, and he got a full dose of the sugar in carrot juice, and it made him reel. I laugh. His body is a cunning little animal. It's spent seventy-seven years doing without and balancing itself. I will probably end up killing him by feeding him right.

§

Sal has a fluttering in his ear. "Like a hummingbird wing," he says. Flynn takes an interest. He likes to talk symptoms. Had all of them, with his nervous system. But was never sick a day in his life.

Sal says he's never had anything like this before, in his quiet voice, not liking to talk about ailments. "Energy follows thought is his saying." I say he has never had me talking in his ear for eight months before. He comes from a silent family. His father now old and no longer raging. A smile stretches across his face and stays, Perry Como style.

Flynn pursues the subject, glad to be a resource to Sal. It's a role reversal, Sal is usually telling Flynn, "A man of your age and genetic heritage and present condition (meaning a "wreck") would benefit from..." Now Flynn feels triumphant. Sal the nutritionist, the biochemist, the vegetarian has a "ringing" in his ear. Flynn says, "Tinnitus."

"No," Sal says, "not a ringing. This is a whirring every once in awhile." He speaks of it in awe, baffled. (Later he discovers it's the hot mustard!)

Flynn recalls all the times he's had sounds in his ears saying, looking directly at Sal, "When I've taken vitamins. The doctor says it's too much niacin." He remembers the only time it sounded like crumpling cellophane. "A crackling noise. It never went away. A sound like that can drive a guy crazy if it goes on too long." He pauses, looking back into history. "I was working for Dick Cabeek at the time, right after all you kids grew up and left home, about when Irwin got killed." Silence, remembering Irwin, "And I was on my creeper under a car, some big bucket of bolts, pile of junk Cadillac some idiot tried to take across the desert about a hundred miles an hour with no oil or water. They should'a stayed home. Some people got no sense. So I was trying to turn a bolt in 120° in the shade, and all of a sudden this crackling sound starts up. It was so real I thought my boss was opening a parts package or something. And I look around to see the cellophane wrapper drop on the floor, but he was nowhere around. I kept listening, and it was in my own ear. I just lay there listening to it. And it never stopped for about two years. Then it just went away. 'Bout the time I moved up to Springville and lived on Louis's place."

Sal has waited patiently and when Flynn finishes talking, he says, "This is like a hummingbird's wing, right here..." And he gestures toward one ear. Flynn looks at Sal like he's the gooniest guy he ever saw. Some geek who doesn't get the point and never will (the point being that Flynn is special, has a special condition, and any story coming from him isn't about health at all, but about him, like coming from a guru. As if Sal doesn't know who he's talking to: that Flynn is Flynn, and people who know him, know that about him, that he isn't just an ordinary person.

Flynn doesn't know Sal has read all the Eastern religions and carries a booklet of sayings to live by in his car, tucked up in the sun visor, and by my bedside, which he reads every morning while I still sleep. If he knew Sal had any leanings toward gurus, he'd say, "Ah, those guys don't know nothing. Over there in India with the bottom of their feet turned up in their laps. What do they know about Life unless they live it. The greatest teacher in the world is hard work. Ain't none of those rag heads did a day's work. You can tell by looking at them. They never use their hands except to eat rice and turn a page in a book. Now you get up at six every morning and put your tools away at six every night, and do this for fifty years. Then you know what Life is all about."

Sal's milk-white hands are doling out the brown rice and green salad I've prepared while Flynn talked. Sal goes softly into the livingroom where the TV's on the baseball station with the sound turned down. Flynn sits at the counter, perched on a stool, some kind of authority on something anyway, as I disappear into my room and solitude. He is left alone in mid oration, the look of "the younger generation…they don't know nothing" smirk on his face. Perplexed that he has lost his audience. The setting sunlight, golden, slanting in through the blinds above the sink hits his ruddy complexion. The sliding glass screen door is open with the summer air coming in. A kind of disbelief is in his eyes. He's so full of his life's experiences with Japs, Communists, Roosevelt, one of the first Social Security cards ever issued in his flat wallet, white supremacy, a good day's work, no queers, no welfare, and eat anything you want, "It ain't gonna hurt you. Your own mind. Now *that's* the only thing that can destroy you."

He goes stepping through the livingroom on his way out to his room by the pool, knowing without looking, that the baseball game is on for Sal. He says, "I never could get interested in chasing some ball around…the silliest thing in the world." His antlers itching to engage in battle and show who's still the mightiest. Sal smiles. Doesn't speak. In his yoga way he gives "the old man respect. He doesn't honor him with a good argument. I come out of the bedroom, thinking Flynn is gone, he moves so silently and speaks so softly. I see his small straight back in blue shirt, Levis flat and showing no human inside.

Humiliation in his bearing, but pride. He's got his god, too.

Sal has been known to say, "When someone says something hateful, silence will let it resound in their own ears and they can hear themselves and feel ashamed." And I've said in response, "Did you read that or come up with it yourself?" to which he was silent.

Flynn stops just before going out the door, sensing me behind him. He says, "I'm the only one at Carrow's that can walk in under my own power and sit down and get up without help. Most of the old people can't get up if they sit down, and can't sit down if they get up.... and they all tell me to stop smoking.... " He lights up, and goes on out the door, inhaling deeply.

I look at my old father standing on my deck smoking, defiant wondering where all his importance went. No one thinks anything he knows is of any value, "unless their cars break," in Flynn's words. And I wonder if what he did, the molesting, is still ever-present in everybody's mind. Can he ever live it down. Will anyone ever forgive him. Is that why we all still turn away?

Sal

I ask Sal, "After five years of celibacy, how do you feel having a regular sex life now with a woman?"

He says, "It's like I never stopped. I don't remember my celibacy. This seems natural." Offended that he left me out. Didn't get the meaning of my question. Wanted to hear how he likes sex with me.

I am silent. Then I say, "When Alex first married me, right out of the 50's when women weren't "giving sex," he was so happy to have this woman, me, anytime he wanted me that he came home all hours of the day for it. All the young husbands said that at that time too, in the early 60's, exclaimed over the access to sex after being single. It was a delight to them. I was that to Alex."

Sal takes a few moments, I can hear his brain grinding on my words. He finally says, "You can really weave a trap. You are a master at twisting the meaning of the words I say and catching me so what I just said sounds like something else, your interpretation is setting me up to castrate me."

I ignore him. We are in bed, about to fall asleep. It is late, and he climbs in beside me as if we are married, lies back and assumes that we are just fine. That we will fall asleep and be all settled in for the winter like fogies. When I do not respond to his response, he reaches over to pull me around to face him, and finds that I won't budge. My shoulder is concrete, legs ballast, and torso steel. He cannot make me face him. In a rush of wind as the covers lift, he throws himself back, flat on his back and shouts to the ceiling, "Come on. You manufactured this whole thing. Now kiss me goodnight. I don't want to go to bed this way."

"We are already in bed," I say in a deadpan voice, pinching off a smile, "Go to sleep, I mean." I ignore him, scowling over on my side of the bed. He lifts himself up on top of my corpse-stiff form, naked to naked, and I turn my face away. He blocks it with one Italian flip of his Mafia hand. I feign anger. He never knows when I am testing. And I never know when I have stopped teasing and mean it. In disbelief, that the evening has been ruined and we will not chortle eachother to sleep, he leans over to see if I really mean it. If I am really offended by his response to my question. When he catches sight of my face, feigning anger even harder, he increases his physical effort to overpower me and bring my face around.

The more I resist him, the harder he fights to win me back and prove his love. He says, right in my face, so that I can taste his breath, "Don't I show you how much I care about you. How I love to make love to you."

I scowl, "You just said it's old stuff, just ordinary, as if it's always been in your life. No big thing."

His shout startles my startle reflex and I jump in shock. "I did not, I might have said it was *natural*, but I didn't say it was not important to me."

To tone down his intensity so my tenants won't hear, I use my deadpan voice, "Yes you did. Now get off and let me sleep. I just want to sleep.... forget it.... it doesn't matter anyway.... it's okay that I'm not a big experience to you.... that you can take me in stride.... that even though you went without it for five years and are now in my bed every night, you aren't thrilled or grateful, or think it is special in any way...."

His voice pierces my ears again, and I am startled so that a fright leaps through my chest and warms my belly. "That is not what I said," in his Long Island-shrill-enough-to-wake-the-dead, tone. And then after he has uttered some gutturals of protest beneath language, choking up in disbelief, he finally adds, "You are very skilled at using words to paint a negative concept, when that was not intended." He sighs and flops down.

I say, "Don't be clinical. Just say, 'I don't like what you just said!'" This causes him to laugh. It is always a surprise to him that you don't have to be tactful in California, that you can just get to the point and say it straight. I pretend awhile longer to play hard to get and wounded, until he has covered me with kisses and filled me with I-love-yous. Like a rider who gets control of his horse and brings it back on the trail, he rests, assured, and we fall asleep, heads together and arms intertwined. In spite of myself there is a smirk on my lips.

I sigh. John called this kind of behavior, "chasing you through the bushes," and would never cooperate. He would not be manipulated. And Alex would just get mad after getting frustrated, and go read a motor manual. Wolfgang would know I was only kidding, and say a few consoling words about my needing him to be demonstrative. But, Sal, he believes it until I almost believe it, too.

Storybook

The bleeding came late and Sal took hope. I laughed. "I'd have it just to see what Mother Nature could come up with," Sal looks hurt. I say, "I'd like to be in the *Guiness Book of Records* as the oldest woman in the world to have a baby." It appeals to me to be on the cover of one of those supermarket magazines.

But the blood finally came and Sal was both disappointed and relieved. His parents, at 75, with a daughter-in-law at 51, having a baby. It even embarrassed me to contemplate it. I tell Sal, "Come on, I can see it in your parents' eyes. You introduce me as your girlfriend; and they somehow still expect you at forty-something to bring home some sweet young thing. I don't like scaring parents. Go find yourself someone in her thirties. Or your own age. There are hundreds of women who put careers first back in the Sixties, and now coming up on their forties, are desperate to have babies. It's on every channel on television. Their briefcases full of paper work and heads full of facts in the business world can't take the place of that organic little critter they long for.... I've already had mine." He stops me at this point and goes through his amazement routine. He sits and gazes at me and shakes his head slowly, and kind of whistles, and rolls his eyes up, saying he forgets that I have those three great big, full-grown human beings as my babies grown up, and that I did all that. He tries to imagine me back then up to elbows in diapers, and young and like a little girl myself, playing house. He's seen photos. He wishes he had known me then. The same thing Wolfgang said. And Wolfgang snatched a picture of me from one of those albums to carry in his wallet. I saw it the last time I visited him, and exclaimed in surprise, to his embarrassment. He said, "Well, you were so beautiful..." And I feigned hurt. "Were." Then I asked him why he didn't carry a present day photo, to which he was silent, saying finally, "Well, you still are.... "

Sal pouts without showing it, his head slightly lowered, eyes raised and focused on the ball game with the sound turned off. He remains silent so I go on. I believe he is learning from me. I cannot resist: "The timing's off. You need one of those women like yourself, who hasn't marked herself by stages and ownerships, babies and duties. Even if we were the same age, I'd still be older than you because I went through all the steps I thought I was suppose to go through. That marks me like rings on a tree. You haven't done any of that. You aren't marked by time. Nothing shows on you because you haven't felt all those feelings you feel when you do all those things. You're still an adolescent in a way. You haven't had kids grow up taller than you to make you shorter and older. You haven't paid off a mortgage for thirty years~month after month, and come out on the other side of that. This house, those kids. I've had a life. You haven't. I feel that all the time I am with you, your inexperience in emotions even at forty-three, have it all ahead of you." He shuts me up with a kiss, jumping up from the couch and closing off my mouth with his so I can't go on.

I squirm away, raising my voice, now that it has become a game, "And all your Italian relatives being so nice at those get-togethers, but behind their eyes they are slightly curious and amused and horrified.... There's even a sitcom on TV now where the mother says out of the side of her mouth to someone when her son introduces her to his new older woman girlfriend, "I hope this is her mother." I am backing into the bedroom by this time and trying to slam the door as Sal dives for my mouth again, to shut it this time with his hand. I fall on the bed and begin kicking in sharp slices so he cannot get near me. He begins to laugh. I give up, and he flops down. We roll around awhile, and he finally throws his hands above his head and sighs. I leap up, race to the door and usher out the rest of my words, "And all your cousins. They went to school with my kids. I don't want this to be the unspoken understanding in your family... that your first wife was too young, and now this woman is too old."

I think this will provoke him to chase me, but he just languishes. We've been through this before. He has already told me, "I don't think of you as older. You're about thirteen." Those were Alex's very words years ago, except he added, "brat." Alex used to say I was arrested emotionally at age thirteen. He would chase me around the room but not in fun, to close my mouth back then.

At those big family parties Sal took me to, there were couples my age (a lot of 50-year-olds). They'd all been married thirty years. I sat with Sal, being, their age, but with him, this younger cousin of theirs. All his cousin's children were there, my children's ages. They all knew me as my children's mother, Mrs, So and So, and asked about my children in the course of the party. They all wore black MTV stretchy dresses—the girls, while their mothers wore the loose mature dresses of mature women. I wore a stretchy dress. I went to the bathroom and looked in the mirror after a glass of wine, and shook my head. I had to laugh at myself. In between everything now. Not fitting in anywhere anymore. But did not regret that I had left Alex and was now moving around the room with Sal to parties like this. I detected in the wives a certain comfortableness that I was glad I had lost. I remembered it well as Alex's wife. I felt safe then. Now, I peer at this creature in Sal's relative's bathroom mirror and hardly recognize myself. I am thinner than ever; even gaunt at certain angles. And the bones do something to my eyes. I look a bit tormented. Maybe nuts, in a certain light. But I knew I would not trade places with any of these women here laughing beside their big, bald, bellied, and domesticated husbands.

I go back out and slink through the crowds of festive people and find Sal, who sits erect-backed waiting for me like a dog waits for its master. Nose to the air a little, to detect my whereabouts. I join him on the couch and say, "I wouldn't be a married woman again. Look at this. Everyone's just pretending, you know. That uncle of yours, or is it a cousin, just made a sexual innuendo to me. And there's his wife dancing with that musician." Sal smiles. Always Perry Como. And I know it is front. He hushes this kind of comment. These are his people. He tells me it is innocent flirting, that no one means anything by it. That they are all happily married and have been faithful to each other throughout their marriages. I ask him how he knows this. He says that in a family like this, word would get around, and the men would put pressure on the unfaithful man. That they are all hard-working family types who love their wives. I watch Sal's face as he tells me this. He believes what he is saying. I tell him I have never known a man who was faithful to his wife.

I change the subject. I say, "I hate it when a man thinks he can trade his bad side for mine. I haven't come this far and made this much effort to put up with some man who has lost his teeth from sheer neglect, grown a gut from sheer gluttony, and is simply lecherous because he is too lazy to develop a personal morality." Sal turns and looks into my eyes to see where I am looking. He follows my gaze to one more of his uncles or cousins, in the throes of living it up right before us with a very young girl. Maybe it's his own daughter.

"You are a severe task master. That's his niece." Sal sits as stoic as a sentinel. I am shamed by my need to make these comments. I go back to the bathroom again after the second glass of wine, and see that my rouge hangs in my cheeks, every pore not bearing up under the weight of gravity anymore. "Never again will I walk into a room and have people ask, "Who's that?" As I make my way through the room again a reddish freckled woman bumps into me and makes a big fuss over having spilled her drink down the front of my dress. She wears a repetition of all her freckles in a copper bracelet of little dangles that look like extensions of liver spots, and a watch band with a series of red sections inlaid around it. I am blinded by the blight of pigment she is and wears. As Sal suddenly appears at my side with a towel. With his warm hand under my bare elbow, he takes me off to a porch, where there is only a patch of sky to view. He watches me to see what I will say now. I just sigh. He looks around like a coyote, over one shoulder and then the other, and then wraps his arms around me to give me a big hug and kiss. I turn my cheek and nudge him away. Is he afraid someone will see? I say, "Your body language confirms all I say."

On the way home from the party we are silent, finally I say, "I don't have a life. I have not created one yet. I am still doing what other people want me to do, so that they can be a part of it. I need to arrange things my way, so that I look forward to waking up in the morning."

"I have nothing to say to anyone any more." Sal says. "I don't know what you mean."

Short Cuts

Sal and I couldn't be more polite around each other. I try to violate that, the smiles, like whistling in the dark, sweeter than sweet holding hands and pecks on the cheek: I never wanted a brotherly love with a man. Am I only used to brutes? Sal turns me into an invalid with his kindness, as if I'm delicate. There is a lie in that kind of unnecessary politeness. I want an opponent. Mama says I "learned to fight Daddy."

When I met Sal I was afraid to show him my life. Afraid to let him see who I was. Afraid to show him where I lived, what I drove, and what I ate, and how I ate, and what I wore and how I got dressed. I was afraid to show him how I acted, and afraid to show him my skin, my closet, my shoes, my hands, my breasts. I was afraid to show him how long I wore a pair of shoes (until they were worn out). I was afraid to show him my father. And the fillings in my teeth.

A therapist would have said, (if I wanted to pay forty dollars hour on the sliding fee scale) "Why, you're ashamed of yourself and your life," separating them. I would half agree. I had been a therapist for seven years. I knew the words. I would say "It isn't shame so much, as the way I cut corners. I don't dawdle. I live quick and without ceremony. I am immediate, direct, expedient. I leave room for company or for a lover, I have no in-between life in bathrobes, chairs. At tables. I eat on the run, never sit down, and take off my clothes and go to bed at the last minute."

The therapist's eyes would reveal argument, but he wouldn't interrupt me. I would go on, "That was the main quarrel in my marriage. Alex was taught to make a production out of everything. Dinner was to be just so. Going to bed was a ritual of hanging the clothes over a chair, draping things around the room and on the bedposts. As soon as we divorced, I gave the bed away and got a futon, folded down the

169

table and put a fruit bowl in the middle of it, never to be used for dinners. Gave the bathrobes to Drug Rehab Thrift Store. I'm always in a hurry." The therapist would ask, "Where are you going?"

But I let Sal come home with me. He didn't seem important. One more set of eyes witnessing my existence and how I did it. I finally didn't care, or tried not to. I would scare him away and that would be good. I could see in his eyes that he believed all kinds of things about me based on appearance that weren't true. He looked up to me for one, as if I were somebody. I pretended for awhile to be more than I was, and have more than I did, and know more than I did. I didn't want to see the belief go out of his eyes, even though it made me nervous. I knew he would discover how make-shift my life was. How I was just getting by. He eventually learned that I didn't have a wardrobe, just a stack of t-shirts and jeans in the closet. And a bunch of tights. And one pair of shoes. Not like my women friends. When they bring a man home, he is impressed: satin bedspread, matching furniture, newly uphol-stered. Nighties, Undies, Lace Bras, Teddies. And all those pretty things I don't know about filling their bureau draw-ers. Beautiful dresser tops. Perfume. Fancy bottles on glass tops. And ceramics. Little female things decorating the walls. That makes the man get an erection just entering the room. Men have told me that my room looks like a storage place for everything I can't put anywhere else. I remember the bedroom Alex and I kept. It was masculine. A big brown desk covered with his electronic devices for adding up money, and storing papers. Two big overstuffed chairs for sitting before going to bed. The bed equipped with an electric blanket. Lamps for reading, once in bed. And the TV hung up by the ceiling so you wouldn't strain your neck, the way they hang them in hotels. And drapes with all the rods and ropes and paraphernalia that come with them. Very serious. A room that was Alex's. When he left, he took the taller-than-man wardrobe with him. A sturdy, dark, formidable piece of furniture his mother had given us. Everything was up high in that room. As if Alex was still a little boy dealing with adult furnishings.

Marty

Pitbull

I keep forgetting that everything has been ruined. I well up with good will and see Alex and me, or Flynn and me, having a nice get-together. I know Flynn is around today. I heard his old car throat into the driveway. (All his cars have had this same sound). I busy around the house and because all the windows and doors are open and the sunshine and warm air and cats are coming in and out, I am filled with well-being. That everything is all right.

I get an impulse to join Flynn on one of his coffee breaks. I'll walk out the front door and step in beside him in the drive-way and say, "I'll go, too. I need a break." And we'll sit on stools at the counter and lean on our elbows and sip and chat and laugh. He is still very funny. I still laugh in spite of it all, over his droll comments about people or a play on words. And just peering out of the same eye, together. He was my father all those years, and I learned to see what he saw. We used to laugh a lot. When I've told people about that in the past, they are silent. I can hear the cranking and ticking of their brains as they see the molestation. And my laughing my head off. A half-wit. With all that was going on in the dark all those years, it was supposed to take away from any enjoyment of Flynn in the broad daylight. I wonder myself. Perhaps they're right. These people who fall silent whenever I say anything good about my father. The silence of holding the tongue to allow for a poor creature, its pathetic nature. Letting it pass.

But, even so. I conceive of being with Flynn in this way, on this sunny day, at a cafe. Sipping good coffee, even though I've given up coffee. Having a real moment of living always has a coffee smell to it. And my time has become so janito-rial. I get through a day. Day after day. The same movements, thoughts, behavior, road signs, names on everything, faces. Sounds.

I maintain because not to maintain is to simply stop. And how could I do that. My musculature wants out of bed, wants to take to the roadside in a run, wants the resistance of weights at the gym, wants to wrap around Sal, or someone, at night. And my nervous system goes on poking around and investigating things, touching untouched places, rooting around. But *I* don't get out of bed in the morning. My body does. Something has gone out of me. I don't see progress. Is this the age one feels that way, after so many years of doing things. What do they call it? A plateau.

So I think maybe I can have a moment again of pure feeling like I'm living. One of those moments I used to have where everything is exactly right: the air, the person I'm with, the feel of being safe. I haven't felt safe since I stopped obeying men.

I think today I could recapture a moment like that. And with my own father. He stalks the place. I can hear him. All he lacks is dragging chains from the crypt, or the bandages trailing and unravelling of a mummy. He's been preserved already in flannel plaid and levi denim and pickled in caffeine and nicotine. And disgrace. He can never live it down. And he keeps on living.

I am the woman, the daughter, the "happy one," the one with a future as he sees it. It's my job to go to him. In my own house. He doesn't dare come to me. That was forbidden when he moved in. Going on seven years now. He was not to disturb me. I was to have my privacy. He was to keep his mouth shut. If he disapproved of anything, he was to keep it to himself. And he was to make himself useful. That was the rule when I lived under his roof in my childhood. And now, even though it was unspoken, it was understood it had to be that way for him under my roof.

Today, I let up a little. I forget that things were ruined a long time ago and no matter how much I try to deny it, I cannot like Flynn.

Now, out of sight, I picture Flynn the way he always was, and I picture us being able to go have coffee. So when I heard his footsteps, as he passes up the walkway toward his car, I go out the front gate and try to stride up beside him, but I get one look at his face, and change my mind. I always forget that he is that old. His near skeleton-thin face blinking and twitching a bit, and his old legs trudging in his shoes like they're boots three feet deep in snow. I see his face and my heart falls.

Where is my father. Where is Flynn? The Flynn of the daytime? The one I liked?

He looks surprised to see me. He says, "Do you want me to gather up all the hoses and put them under lock and key. Your tenants keeping washing their cars when you're gone."

I stand there, and kind of scold out, as if that is what I came out for, "Yes, that will be good. I can't believe they'd do that in this water shortage. We'll be fined."

He goes on toward his car and I go back through the front gate. I hear his old car grumble. If this was still his father's time, he'd been getting old Jenny or Molly, and riding her down to the country store. But it's Flynn, here and now, in my day, in a car I gave him, a car named after a horse that waits faithfully for him, and then goes sputtering off down the road exactly like Flynn moves. How does he get his car to creep along and lean around corners, and head forward with such a bleak look on its desolate old hood. Headlights corroded over with dust and bugs. But I can't say that about Flynn's eyes. Flynn's eyes are still getting attention. People always ask me if he wears blue contact lenses. His eyes are still bright as a child's and blue as a color crayon.

Flynn is still a child, sullen and hurt. No one likes him. No one. And I am still his adult. I let him go off for coffee alone. That face, that voice. Both grey and dense with his pain. His age ever present, even though he goes around saying, "You never know how long someone will live. I might have another five years. Or someone younger could die before I do." And I've said that could be me, in jest. Now I wonder. When you finally bury your parents you're so old yourself you hardly care anymore. It's a kind of relief.

After Flynn's gone, I imagine dashing to town and running into him and swinging up on the stool at Esau's or Foster Freeze, and joining him after all. I am stubborn today. I want things the way they were supposed to be. I want a father I can love and feel good with. But I remember his face. Too grim, too impacted. Completely absorbed in himself. An ascetic who's denied the flesh in every way but sexuality. No food. Only poison. And private angers.

§

Sal is new to the situation. I take a certain pleasure in watching someone who doesn't know Flynn try to treat him like everyone else. Or just anyone. And see how Flynn will wrestle them around until he gets them in exactly the position he requires them to be in around him. Not unlike the owners of pitbulls. To someone who thinks all dogs are poochies. I am.

Sal is watching the ball game on my little color TV in the living room when Flynn comes home. And Sal is a friendly fella. "Fella" suits him and I've never used that word in my life. When he hears the front door open and sees it is Flynn, he speaks right up, "Hello, Mr Lansdowne. How are you today?" I can hear some bass rumble like a hi-fi set tuned wrong. It's Flynn lowtoning it. Then silence. Sal stays chipper.

"Mr. Lansdowne, did you ever follow sports when you were young….. like the ball games, baseball, all that?" Silence. Even from the kitchen I know Flynn is waiting like a pitbull for Sal to get too close. "Did you ever watch Babe Ruth?"

No one ever talks to Flynn, and if they do, he turns their words into them like a knife. He says, "The only interest I have in baseball is taking a baseball bat and swinging it around and knocking about four smart-alec kids in the head with it."

Silence. I come out just to see Sal's face and smile at him. I see Sal's jovial smile fade around the edges, because he sees Flynn means it. Then Flynn says, "I was going into Thrifty and these boys were standing around, and they say, 'Hey Mister, will you buy us some beer?' And I tell them, 'You want me to go to jail? I can't do that.' And then I walk away, and I hear them yell, 'You old fart.' So I turn around, and they're running away. I just keep walking toward them, and get up close and say, 'Which one of you said that?' They're

176

hiding behind a car and pointing at each other; I see they're scared, and they finally apologize, but, I mean, a fella can't even go to the drugstore without having some kids call him names. The kids today don't respect nothing."

Later Sal will diagnose Flynn's anger and bitterness as, "A quality of life induced by the deterioration of the lining of his stomach walls and intestines from the intake of caffeine and nicotine."

"Your father lives on the stimulation of these drugs. It gives him a false sense of energy."

Rats

I'm getting grouchy in my dotage. Sal slips an article about menopausal symptoms on my bedside table under the reading lamp. I don't read it. I was never this way with John or with Wolfgang, I was in love, both times, then. I want to believe I am grouchy now because I'm not in love, and only live practically with Sal. And that John hurt me so bad with his betrayal. That it's not menopause coming on; I don't want to dry up. To be infertile.

Last winter, Sal dragged me to a series of lectures on losing estrogen. All about older women. A sea of white heads filled the auditorium. Like Flynn I didn't want to be around my own kind, it was a grim bunch of talks about all the things that will inevitably go wrong, shut down, give up, let go, drop, and wilt and die before the woman, herself does. All the grey heads bobbed. They understood some of these occurrences already. I wanted to walk out. Sal steadied me. Made me listen. Like a nice boyscout ushering an old lady across the street. I jerked my hand away. I didn't want to be helped into old age.

The only talk I liked was the one half the audience stomped out on. A bright-eyed young Berkeley professor had done research on animals and showed us slides. One experiment was on rats and under eating, He put rats on a near-starvation diet, and found these rats lived one-third longer than the normal control group. He built a theory around breaking the genetic longevity mechanism. Once the rat forgot how long it was supposed to live by trying its hardest to survive, it got beyond the body countdown. The little clock that ticks away gets pushed aside, its meter snapped and hanging limp, and the rat can go on until its flesh wears out. It has no limit. I thought of Flynn.

These rats looked broken down and rangy, undersized,

scraggly, with threadbare coats, but they went on living way beyond their "healthy" normally fed rats. A slight rumble of humor went through the remaining audience, as we saw pictures of these sorry creatures: battle-worn, and noses straight ahead, surviving. But out-smarting the system. They looked a lot like Flynn.

Hamstrung

Finally I sleep. With my sprung hamstring all night. Laying it this way and that, to be comfortable. While my little dog sounds like a cat that sounds like a frog beside me, sleeping, too. She sleeps near my ear on my pillow. Her estrogen tumor so swollen and smelly that the stink enters my dreams. I dream of John coming into my room where I am trying to stuff all the red meat he left behind, into a refrigerator. There is a vivid memory of folding the ribs, a great row of them, in white butcher paper, and surprising myself that it all fitted away so I could close the door. He never spoke. He turned and went away.

In the morning I take my hamstring for coffee. It can move sideways but not backward and forward. On the way, I take a niacin, and get a pin-prickling rush of blood to all my cells so I'm on fire. I think it will ruin coffee time, but I sit in a glow, instead, warm from the inside, under an awning, having swallowed one of Alex's pastries. They were still fresh and in my front-seat, I begin to wonder what they put in them so the flaky crust never gets hard. And now that ingredient is inside me.

I remember a sixth grade the day before, that came at me all day, the students like jackals after a wildebeest. In my little high-heeled hooves, they tried to get me down, nipping and going for my ankles until I did finally trip over one of their Reeboks stuck out in the aisle. After school I went on my run, doing the foothills for extra release, and the Bodosy dogs came at me. It seemed an endless screaming and flailing session where time stood still. I finally, unable to scoop up a rock, because they were at me so close, gave a kick and heard and felt my hamstring rip and pop. I hobbled home. A man in a truck stopped to help. I felt foolish. He was half-handsome and my age. He said "You were really in a bind." I agreed. He drove off.

On the way home I began to laugh and tell it. Do dogs really notice when you limp and the instinct is to pick you off? I've run that hill for years. But I never limped before. And the kids in the classroom. I've taught for years and never did I have a class circle my vulnerability like that before. I laughed too hard. Back in the street I got my walk under control. All those neighbors waiting for me to come crawling home, old age catching up with me. People would ask, "Whatever became of that woman who ran all the time." And the answer would be, "Oh, she was killed by dogs after she threw all her bones out of joint." And they would be glad that they never were foolish enough to take up running. That they stayed in their houses where they were "supposed" to be.

Even Alex waits for me to go crippled, get osteoporosis and curve forward, as a result of my running. And Flynn. Everyone waits for the bad effects. I take to the roadside while they drive by and wave, with a smirk for a smile. I am their private joke, but they won't say so, But I see: *sooner or later* in their eyes.

The Neighborhood

I am walking the last block so as not to be running up to the front door. I pass by Brown's place and see the grown and growing older daughter in the yard with a young man up on the roof. She turns and says hello. It's been years since I've seen her. We moved in thirty years ago when she was just a teenager. I see grey in her hair. I ask how her father is. She says he died. I ask when, and exclaim that no one knows anything about anyone else in this neighborhood. As soon as I say that I regret it.

I know there are rumors about me. I haven't spoken to my neighbors for ten years, maybe more. Since the commotion over the marriage ending, Alex's brain tumor, my boyfriends, the eyes were averted, greetings withheld, and we began to unknow one another. I welcomed the distance. And now Brown, the daughter, has moved into her father's house. I ask about her father and her mother. Her mother died a few years ago. Again I never heard. And the man next door? He died, too? I tell her a story about that old man. I was running through the neighborhood a few years ago and he was out in the street with his three poodles bouncing around his ankles, and he called out to me in a gravel-throated greeting. He asked how my mother was and I told her she had a hip replacement. He shook a bony finger and told me that he *knew* that if my mother had kept running the way she did that he knew something like that would happen. That she was a fanatic. Then he asked me how I was and told me he remembered when I broke all the track records for my school in girls track, that I looked great and that I should not overdo it like my mother. I decided not to confuse the old man by telling him that I was my mother and he had me mixed up with my daughter, and that I was still running, and he had just complimented me.

Brown laughed a bit, but not much. She liked the old man, and I could see that she took a dim view of my running herself. We parted. I walked home, a few doors down, and felt her eyes boring into the back of my body. I didn't turn around.

Later, I tell Sal that story. He just looks at me. Finally he says, "You love this kind of thing. You just love it, to be mistaken for your daughter." Later, too, I call my daughter and tell her. She waits for it to sink in and then laughs ever so slightly. I realize she is seeing only herself, not me, through their eyes.

I ask Sal, "What if Hitler's aging daughter sweetly said, "Daddy can't chew so I stew his meat... would everyone think, so what, the bastard should be dead anyway. Can a daughter of a *bad man* ever say any mundane daily thing about her dad, or must it always be seen in the larger view?"

A fellow teacher said, "Why is he at your house? Why do you allow it? He shouldn't be there. Why don't you just throw him out?"

I say "He has nowhere to go."

"So what." She searches my face for evidence of dementia. Is this woman retarded, completely warped, good-hearted, insane, or what? Is she missing something, or has an addition of something? Is something very, very wrong with her, or very right? It's all there in her eyes.

A not knowing me, after all, enters her vision. She averts her eyes, as if I'm an impostor. We've worked together for five years, and she has just learned about my father. She was one of the full-time teachers who had been drawn to me in the teachers lounge, over the years. She has sought me out, laughed at my "guts" as she called it. Guts, to her, were simply comments I'd make in general, and my clothes, hair, shoes.... a kind of style. Now, she draws back, hesitant. All these same peculiarities suddenly are attributed to my secret, which she never knew until now. The way she swallows makes me think she feels betrayed. My whole bearing is now translated through this new bit of information. My facial expression, hair, clothes, shoes. She interprets it all under the dark cloak of molestation. The unspoken words are *Oh, now I see why she is that way.... why she's different.... now I understand.* I've been tricked. With some guilt as we part, I think, *Should I wear a t-shirt with I Was A Molestation Victim, or more positive: I am a molestation survivor on my chest, so people won't think I've deceived them. Do I owe that to my friends, to tell them in the beginning what happened to me?* Later this teacher will call to me over the heads of children, "My mother was a sadist, my therapist says."

It had come out as simple chit chat. But it was like dropping a stink bomb in the middle of the space between us. We were just talking. Her boyfriend had committed suicide and she had been in intensive therapy resolving it. I told her, in jest, that Sal was too nice, that I missed the abuse of John. She asked if I'd had an abusive childhood.

It took me off guard. I'd answered honestly, "Yes, molestation."

Flynn

Cheshire Cat

Flynn is a hero. He saves my little dog from drowning. I come home to my room, as usual. But he seeks me out. He dares to go near my door. To invade my privacy. I have left the door open a crack to listen to the house. He is careful not to look until his voice precedes him. He asks, "How's Scraggles?"

I prick up my ears. "Why?" I'm hostile. He never asks about her. She is sleeping on the pillow by my bed, as usual. At fifteen, the tail-end of the household pets, blind in one eye, and deaf in one ear, she sleeps her life away, except to wake up when I come home. Then, like a tiny puppy, she hops around in the kitchen urging me to feed her. Today she sleeps.

Flynn's story begins. Flynn is a spinner of yarns when he can find an ear to listen. "Well, I was painting in my little shack, working on that landscape, trying to get the shadows just right and having a hard time at it. And I keep hearing this sound." Flynn swallows, blue eyes looking right at me, gestures of a cigarette smoker, not allowed to smoke in the house anymore. His knuckles and tendons and cardiovascular system clearly visible through his seventy-seven year old skin in his hands. Flat nails poised in the air, chest high, his voice so soft I get irritated trying to hear it. His presentation commands attention. His voice placing each word with accuracy, precision, and equal space. The pace is too slow for me. I urge him on with uh, huh's.

"Kind of a..." And he makes the sound, "and I think it's something over in Alex's field. A turkey maybe. But I think, what would a turkey be doing over there, so I try to put it out of my mind, but I keep hearing it. And I can't identify it. It's a sound I've never heard before. But I keep painting and I keep hearing it, and it begins to bother me. I can't place it as any sound I know. So I goes about my business a while longer, and then decide to go have a look around. Maybe Alex has a turkey over there or something. He pauses for a laugh. We still keep an unspoken joke on Alex. The joke is that Flynn is skilled and smooth and able to handle things, while everything seems to defeat Alex. Alex's style is a joke. It would be like him to have a turkey over there. I give Flynn the expected snerf. Is it the last remnant of our once intense loyalty to eachother. A token on my part?

"And I pass by the pool, and there's Scraggles just hanging on by her toenails. The most pitiful little sight I ever saw. She'd fallen in the jacuzzi, and been hanging there for I don't know how long, so I pull her out, and the poor thing's just shakin' all over. I felt so sorry for her. Scared to death."

I say, "And Sal made me trim her nails the other day. She probably could have gotten out if she still had her long claws." This is a new joke between us: Sal. Flynn gets a chuckle, even though very quietly, over this new man in my life, and I am more than willing to paint a funny picture for him.

"Oh, no," Flynn insists. "She was just about to go under. She couldn't have hung on for another minute. I come along just in time."

I say, "Thank god you were here." And Flynn goes out the door grinning like a cheshire cat, but hiding his pride ever so carefully.

To his back I say, "Alex can't hear high sounds, you know. The jet engine's high whine ruined his ears."

Flynn low tones, "This wasn't a high sound. A kind of a low moan." Out on the deck, Flynn lights up a cigarette, and goes off toward his shack by the pool.

I've been thinking lately, who will watch the place when Flynn dies and Alex moves away.

Right in Her Oriental Sideburn is a Big Mole

I don't run or work out. Life ebbs from my body like life from my little dog who finally died. My energy, so feeble, I feel my limbs at night in bed too weak to lift and turn them. Only a day and I am drained. So that I see now, all my effort at the gym and the side of the road, is to keep pumping energy into me (not out of me, as Sal believes). I blow myself full, like a moth's wing, so I can take the blows from students, my own kids, everyone, it seems who come at me, as an object in their way, to be removed. And to stand my ground. I work the weights into my body, so I become as dense as I can get. And now I lay limp and light and empty. And my little dog is dead. Sal praises my complexion in this state. He says I don't look so dark-skinned when I don't exercise. He says my face hardens with circulation, and darkens when I overdo the exercises. His voice holds some disgust. I lie under my comforter looking at his pallor.

I need to catch the young male cat to have him neutered, because he tore my tenant's cat open. Sal says he will do it for me, since I don't seem to want to get out of bed, "Where you are playing with the idea of weakness." I don't believe Sal can catch that cat. The cat is like me. It wants to do what it wants to do without restriction. Sal is not sly. He is logical. He is out in the open with his observations. He isn't always darting his eyes around in case a door snaps shut. And sure enough he does what I expect. He catches the cat, puts it in the big dog house, and places a board in front of the open doorways. He leans it gently and leaves a crack or two for air. In the morning the cat is gone. I have gotten up, and survey his handiwork. I try not to scold him as if he's a little boy. I try to be adult to adult. But I have become my own Aunt Frances, a female voice always chastising, admonishing, scolding, scoffing at, disdaining. Sal says, "breaking my balls"; Louis says, "Castrating men with the sharp edge of your tongue."

Aunt Frances was on Flynn's side of the family. When I arrived in the family, she was already jelled in her role of "hag, nag, and bag." I never knew her any other way. The hierarchy was set, and she was always there as one of the prime and primal matrons.

Flynn's side of the family was patriarchal. Ruled by and for men. The women were silent, obedient, god and man-fearing, and hard-working. Except for Frances. She didn't have a man. He had died of orange orchard spray poisoning early. Frances was the only daughter of a family of seven sons. She ruled from birth, until her brothers went out and got wives. And she couldn't be appeased. Her need for power and dominance permeated everything.

I slash Sal now, and wonder where this need to control comes from. When did I stop being passive? A female who could be manipulated by Flynn first, and then Alex. John called me a "tyrannical bitch" and bought me a pair of steel-tipped high-heels as a joke. And then laughed when I put them on. Wolfgang never challenged this part of me. He went silent or went away. He simply said once, "You are very emotional sometimes." He called me a mare!

I tell my friend, Suzi over the phone, "I've become a bitch, everyone is saying so….Well, it's a luxury to be a soft-spoken, innocent woman who doesn't know where to unplug her washing machine when it's running over….I know more than I've ever wanted to know about this house and the limitations of men after all. It has cluttered my mind, this information. I haven't been able to think about what I want to think about since I've taken on this responsibility. I've lost the smile in my voice, and even feminists keep this. And discovered that men didn't know how to fix anything….they all have added to the breakage in fact. Flynn has wrecked my life but fixed my car. Alex has ruined my nerves, but can fix a faucet. At least Wolfgang never led me to believe that he was handy with his hands. And now Sal can't keep my cat trapped overnight."

Suzi says, "Sell that place. Just sell it and live off the

interest of your investments." She tells me how she did it. She sold the Big House after her divorce, invested the money, and now draws a monthly check in the tiny little house she can handle just fine. I listen and remember her big house, full of all our kids, all the noise, all the abundance. But she stayed in that house only a few years, and then moved to another big house. She did not get attached to her house the way I did.

I say, "But, thirty years. This is more than a house. My kids were born here. It's like a homestead. How can I just sell it?"

Coma

The funeral gives Flynn something to do. At first there's the phone call. Dotty is in a coma. It's her kidneys. "Septicemia." Louis, the Marine has read a lot and calls everything by its name.

"You mean poisoning by her own piss," so tired of my brother's brain. We're all in our fifties now. And he's still proving up like a student. Flynn says, "It's the kind of coma you never wake up from." Intrigue in his voice. Something is finally happening to break his monotony.

I snap, "Well, then, she's dead," And add "Essentially" to soften it. We are all in the kitchen and I feel we will cook up a lot of juicy tidbits over my cousin's death. Flynn has been known to get a laugh out of such grim subjects. Louis, the Marine, who spent his time thirty years ago in Okinawa, is cooking up sukiyaki. He makes it every night, while Flynn watches and finally is doled out a portion, and will show Flynn the grocery receipt and have Flynn pay for his bowlful. I am steaming brown rice and tofu. Sal sits in the far livingroom with the baseball channel on, reading. I fight hard to hold my tongue around Flynn and Louis anymore. Or any family subject. Dotty never took care of herself; I don't want to be sacrilegious though. Sal has poopooed my "ruthless and vulgar" comments on life's most precious and tender" goings on. He has tried to shame me out of accusing people of everything that happens to them, as their own fault. He wonders how I ever got so angry with everyone. Where's my sympathy?

"Instant Karma" being ever-present on his lips but he says it another way. "You have a beautiful house, beautiful children, both parents still alive, all your brothers and sisters are intelligent, industrious and healthy. Things aren't bad for you. They're very good, in fact, most women would envy you. Why are you always talking bad, saying how bad things are, grumbling?"

(Sal always talked about my house and turned out to be a small time gigolo at the end, waving a ledger in the air of every cent he ever spent on me to claim "commuity property.")

In the kitchen now, with Flynn and Louis, I try to stay neutral. Flynn's whole demeanor has changed with the news of his niece's pending death. He brings forth statements he, otherwise, never would have uttered.

"She was the sweetest person. Always did for others. Never thought of herself." But his real fascination is the coma. "They say you can tell everything that's going on when you're in a coma, you just can't do anything about it."

As the evening goes on, Flynn gives more focus to the subject of Dotty's coma. His mind is kicking into gear and building a thesis (not unlike the ones on campus John talked about as an Philosophy professor, "you build on an idea, gather data, get a bibliography...") Now Flynn comes up with reasons.

"After her cancer surgery, I guess, that left the kidneys in bad shape." Conclusions are flying around in his head, he wants to understand this. I sense, underlying his concern, is triumph. Once again he lives. And out-lives. With each death, especially, of someone younger, he is validated. His ways. Everyone has always told him that he is killing himself smoking and drinking coffee all day long. Now, at seventy-seven, Flynn is still strong and alive. And as surprised as any of us.

Little Flynn

There he is, entering Dr. Finklemetz's office in his new red Pendleton shirt I got him for Christmas, so he looks like a rich country boy instead of a poor one in flannel. There's an old rich skinny Englishman in Montecito who looks just like Flynn and smokes away over coffee. Finklemetz comes over with the poorly coordinated contraption of a body some Jews get as their birthright: sprattled pelvis, like an old woman, and he is only a forty-year-old man. A humpback from bad posture, wide gut riding along his trouser tops, the flesh folding in on itself (Sal says Americans carry forty pounds of waste matter in their intestines). He's an example of what could have been prevented. I've stopped believing that doctors are intelligent. His long narrow skull is emphasized by a vertical long narrow beard and moustache and head of hair slipped back from his forehead, all blending, leaving no neck. The beaked face holding thick lenses with eyes magnified backward to pin points is the only personal presentation he offers his patients. He and Flynn stand together ever so briefly to check some paperwork at the front desk, and I see how young Flynn's body is next to this already old young body. At seventy-seven, Flynn's frame is straight as a kid's and as flesh free. No curvatures, caverns, cave-ins, distortions, bulging, saggings. All bone and true to his English-Irish heritage. His people, mountain men, were all five-eight and stood tall. For little men their pride ruled and dictated to their spines and shoulders. The straight back Mama fell in love with Flynn for. It was their innards that were ruined by their habits, mainly smoking. None of them could hold liquor. None of them tried. It was the Bull Durham sack that finally did them in, but not until they'd lived out their lives anyway. Now here's Flynn shoulder to shoulder with his antithesis. Flynn's doctors are always Jewish and Flynn, a bigot. But I witness how Flynn reveres this man. And I turn away. Since he's been in his care, Flynn has never felt worse. Flynn's usual joke about doctors is, "A doctor treated a patient for yellow jaundice until he realized he was a Chinaman."

They disappear down the short hallway and into a doorway and I can hear Flynn monologing and monotoning. I have never accompanied Flynn to his doctor before, but am here to challenge the medication Flynn takes. I can see Flynn's reputation: the nurses laugh at his words, the comical cynic, and the doctor cajoles, as if Flynn is truly frail and not a bull dog. The thinness gets them every time. He's gotten by on being near-to-death in appearance all his life. "Worn-Out is how you're supposed to look if you've been raised in the hills by California homesteaders. The mopping of the brow, the prostrate grimace, as if you've done a days work and that's your row to hoe and there's no other way. And if you've retired, like Flynn, and don't work anymore, you're supposed to eke out and work the day anyway, milking and squeezing remorse and consternation, and angst, and what's-a-guy-to-do, and somebody's-done-somebody-wrong, and all the woe you can muster. Just work it and wring it dry. He won't let me talk to his doctor.

Flynn sits on the couch all day, but not in a relaxed sit. He leans forward, resting his elbows on his knees, and puts his face in his hands (the bony gnarled, many-crisscrossed mechanics hands with the wide flat nails) and rakes his fingers through his hair. I've never once looked at Flynn, as I pass through and seen him in a pleasant posture. He all but wails and gnashes his teeth. His jaw works, sawing and gnawing like a rat in a wire cage. While his bright blue eyes, flat with the anguish I know so well and turn away from, stare and then blink, as if with wonder, a mere child, still in awe over his life. No one can rescue Flynn, but he doesn't know that. He still thinks if he ordered the world he'd be happy (even though he's been heard to say there is no such thing as happiness, it is only a byproduct of accomplishment). He'd be like Pinocchio on the Island of Jackasses; all women would have eyes only for him. They'd all be virgins and he'd never have to worry about being betrayed or deceived. His children would be happily married to one oaf or another, the daughters faithful, and the sons getting something on the side (although it turns out the opposite). His parents would be dead, that's okay. His brothers and one sister would dote on his every quirk, calling regularly and kissing his ass. The waitresses would rejoice with big smiles and compliments and applause as he entered, and beg him not to go so soon when he was through. They would press on him an extra piece of pie with extra whipped cream, free of charge, and refill his cup before it was empty, never letting him see the bottom. They'd never let him run out of sugar and cream, and they'd understand that this is *Flynn*: this man *is* his coffee…. like a cowpoke can't be separated from his levi's, horse, tobacco pouch, and other doodads he puts on the bedside table at night. This recognition being of utmost importance (memorabilia they call it after he dies).

Therapists would say I'm mad at Flynn for getting old and feeble. That I blame him for the inevitable. That I envision some other way Flynn could have aged and still retained his composure, shown courage, and pride and kept his looks and physical strength. Kept his youth as well as die of old age. And what do I do with this anger? I take it out on Sal, they would say. Or they would ask, "Why are you so angry?" And they'd lead me around to describing Flynn lying and dying at Christmastime right in the middle of my livingroom. In the middle of my middle age, in the middle of my *life*. My grown children and their guests trying not to notice out of politeness and a desire to have a "normal" Christmas, as one daughter put it, so afraid her friend would witness some family scene (as only Alex and I could create from her experience in the past, beginning with Alex's brain tumor and the eventful separation and the stages of divorce, ending with the finale of Alex next door like the homeless in a camper and me in a houseful of tenants.)

Flynn's collapse on the eve before Christmas eve was a minor scene compared to her worst fears. It was only her grandfather stepping in through the doorway in his dark fleece-lined jacket and swaying forward suddenly, so that everybody reached out to catch him before he hit the floor. Sal rushed in to find me in my room, wrapping packages. I sighed, and went out thinking, "this is where it is going to happen then. Flynn will die right now, when everyone is gathered around the hearth, the tree ablaze with lights, scissors and tape and string askew, and the hubbub of cautious merry-making in the air.

I rushed to my father where they had placed him on the edge of the big couch like a little sick kid. He was shaking. I thought of Mama's word "palsy." While everyone watched to see what I would do, I stood over Flynn and demanded, "What's wrong? What are you feeling? Tell me."

He mumbled," I'm cold. I can't seem to get warm. I don't know why I'm so cold and can't get warm." I thought of Socrates dying, feeling cold at first. But he had taken poison.

I said, "Come over by the heater."

Flynn tried to rise but couldn't. I wrapped my suddenly big hand around his arm, and through the fleece-lined jacket, felt all bone.

I could lift Flynn and carry him, but I wouldn't yet, not if he could walk. I helped him to his feet, feeling large and strong, while Sal hovered on the edges in the shadows, a scowl of concern on his face. And the grown children glanced at my responsibility. "It's her dad," was in their manner. I pulled out the desk chair and placed it by the wall heater with one hand while I held onto Flynn, who stepped all over his own shoes in an effort to be guided physically, while he was confused about what was happening. I could see he was out of his mind like a stray cat almost frozen to death in the creek bed. I sat Flynn down, flipped the thermostat up to high, came back and helped him out of his jacket, flung it onto the desk and felt his arms and chest. "A living skeleton, like ice." I could hear Mama's words. I commanded again, "What did you eat today?" Flynn moved his lips, but like a child afraid to answer, said nothing. He mumbled, I couldn't hear him for the blast- ing of air from the heater. It didn't matter. I knew what he ate. Nothing of value (It was a bone of contention between us). I said, again in a loud voice, as if Flynn were somewhere deep inside this human predicament, "What fuel do you have inside you to warm you?" The blower came on and the heat poured out and I moved back. Broke out in a sweat, and took off my sweater, standing there in a t- shirt, just looking down at my little father. He began to tell it in his Flynn way, "I don't know what happened. I just didn't know where I was or who I was."

I said, "It's that damned medication. The doctors are killing you."

Flynn said, "That's kind of hot now" and attempted to move his chair, but careened off. I grabbed his shoulder. Sal moved in to help me position the chair. I announced, "I'm getting you some chowder…it's nice and hot, and I want you to drink it." I go off toward the kitchen thinking: We were all making clam chowder, the fireplace crackling, rosy-cheeked, and high-peaked, while Flynn was freezing and starving. A disgrace, that I wouldn't notice, and that he would let himself get this way. The next day I discovered he had parked with two tires on the curb. He was disorientated. It was 22 degrees outside. He had a few crusts of McDonald's chicken wings inside him.

Flynn slept for three days on the couch, through everything, waking in the morning to pick the paper napkin off his false teeth, on which he lay them, trudge off to the bathroom, and then back to the couch with his heating blanket wrapped around him, heater on, logs in the fireplace aflame, and still he felt cold. We opened presents all around him, ate Christmas dinner, calling him to join us, and he lay like a corpse, in a daze, an Ethiopian refugee in the land of plenty unable to partake, gone too long toward death to backtrack. I brought him juice and eggs and protein powder, vitamin C powder, Green Magma concentrate, and carrot cake. I made him eat, "For fuel," I bullied. "So your body can create heat," "I'm so cold he kept saying. "I don't know why I can't get warm. There are icicles along my spine. It feels like chills. "I don't understand."

Only once, late one night, he got up and without a jacket, in his long-handled underwear, he headed for the sliding glass door that led to his little shack out in the back. Sal came again, to tell me. I came out of my room, and sure enough, there was Flynn, the no weight of his body, and his unsteadiness on his feet, making his movements robotic. I said, "Where are you going?"

His words floated out as if from the crypt, "What about my things?"

He balanced, swaying, thin and white. Sal shook his head and again scowled with more than concern. Disapproval. Later he would say, "Did you see how skinny your father is?" As if I didn't know. Hadn't known all my life. Skinny is what Flynn did.

"You are *not* going out, You will freeze to death. You haven't eaten enough to keep a bird alive," in Mama's words. "And what things? No one's going to touch your things. They're out in your place. What do you need." He stepped toward the door; I held him by the arm. He leaned toward his shack like a turtle toward the sea. There was a tugging in his body toward his stuff. An old male and his territory. An instinct. And I believed Flynn was dying. The urge to travel. To go. Without his coat, with bones exposed, heading out the door, a last migration to crawl off and die. I restrained him. I felt the tugging ease up a little. I lay him back on the couch. I knew he would have gone out in the cold, that his time had come and he was answering its call. I'd seen it in the dogs and cats that lived out their lives on this piece of property. At the end they all got that look in their eyes and headed out. The wandering instinct, their frailness. No common sense anymore.

That night I gathered Flynn up like a baby in a blanket and took him to Emergency. He wasn't getting warm. He was getting colder and weaker. I coaxed him. "You might need antibiotics, you might have an infection. That ache in your back." Sal stayed out of sight, but coached me from the sidelines, and kept a watchful eye, knowing Flynn would hate him being a part of anything to do with this weakness.

In the hospital they discovered pneumonia. We almost smiled. Is that all? Flynn and I: our self reliance and belief in the myth, in Flynn's infamous life-long condition, and my insistence on health. A belief system that the two of us could somehow solve the problem of his coldness. We had done our act together, one more time, father and daughter, while one more family watched. I'd tried to keep Flynn alive, as I had done all my life, in my own way, not believing anyone else could. And suddenly in the hospital, they cut through all the sentimentality, myths, the romanticizing temperaments and find the simple reason, a germ in his lung. The right lung almost full of infection, the left one okay. And the doctor does not console me with agreeing that it was because Flynn is so skinny and it was so cold, and that Flynn doesn't eat, and used to smoke two packs a day. He can smell family foolishness and isn't sympathetic. He simply says it's communicable and that Flynn exposed himself to the germ. He brushes my need to explain aside, "It's going around," is his final say. And then he turns away to go to the next patient. Flynn will live. They hook him up to an Electrolyte I.V., take blood tests, and go about their business. Antibiotics trickle into his veins and he sleeps, warm and peaceful without a blanket while they examine his heart beat and blood pressure. He opens his eyes once and smiles, with an angelic smile. Later he will say a Chinaman turned and coughed in his face at the Carrow's coffee counter, and call it the Asian Flu.

Skin and Bone

Finally a doctor that looks like a doctor. White hair, glasses, a preoccupied stride. He goes off down the hall. For five days there have been troops of interns coming and going with their instructional masters, looking at Flynn, their specimen. They call themselves "teams," And they examine the organ they specialize in. Flynn, the thin; skin and bone, in his hospital gown. Flynn so weak he looses himself in the confusion of keeping his balance, and exposes his privates to anybody. He doesn't know who or where he is. At first I try not to look. But I've never been successful in not looking, unlike Sal who actually puts his hand over his eyes and turns away and walks out of the room, respecting another man's dignity. But I see, in Flynn's dilemma, what I saw so much of as a child, something that was once so familiar, and now a complete surprise. It is full and large, I thought it would be as withered as the rest of his body.

Sal says, "It's not an it." I exhale audibly. That night I can't make love, I'm numb. Sal goes through the motions and I feel only his efforts on top of my skin, and down underneath there is nothing. In the morning I say, "It must be the aversion, being around the hospital, so fleshy. The impressions. They were there. There must be some memory, I've forgotten, still at work. I couldn't get the images of Flynn exposed, naked, hurt, scared, frail, out of my mind. His body. His mouth. His hands. All the things that almost suffocated me as a child. Stunted my growth. Took away the world. Was always on me, having me. I guess it's all still there somewhere in me. That avoidance of him now. And there he was having to deal with his real body, all of it, his mouth gaping like a fish out of water trying to breathe. His hands, squared-off finger nails, so primate. So ape-like. So animal against the sheets. Dark as soil and marked by what he's done, what he's touched. His feet. His legs. The psoriasis. And all the doctors coming in using him as an example to teach their students about what becomes of you if you've smoked for sixty years. Going beyond, past Flynn to his particular parts.

And each new doctor being annoyed by the inconvenience of having to consult Flynn in order to get to the organ he's there for. Even disgusted that it is inside this little human being covered all over with scales, blackened nails, false-toothed. And Flynn being a storyteller, a monologuer of what's happened to him in the slowest and quietest of voices.

The heart doctor is the most heartless, telling Flynn to be quiet so he can listen, putting the stethoscope all over Flynn's chest in little stainless steel moves; and the big wide young blond intern putting it all over Flynn's back, and learning to tell her patients to shut up in the same cold manner, when Flynn composes himself enough to make a wisecrack, "Don't you have a backscratcher attached to one of those stethoscopes." No one laughing.

All week one team after another come and learn from Flynn's real flesh. Interns too young to be calling themselves "doctor," but learning to. The word so new that they lay them carefully out in the air and see if anyone laughs and when they don't, believing it themselves a little more each time. Their student status already learning arrogance and bedside manner outside of the class room.

The kidney team comes and does a "sonic boom" and finds one kidney "significantly smaller" and both functioning fifty percent capacity. The heart team does a sound test, too, to find the same thing. The infectious disease doctor comes, trailed by a short weasel-faced intern and a tall, skinny freckled one with merry berry eyes right in the middle of her face. Each seem to radiate their mother's pride and joy, until Flynn begins to talk. The weasel gets smaller and smaller as Flynn drones on about wanting a cigarette, valium, Enderol, his caffeine, enough sugar and salt, complaining that they've taken all the pleasure and pastimes from him and left him with "nothing to lean on." The weasel attempts to console. Flynn asks, "What do you have without cigarettes?" He means it.

The weasel shrinks into himself with a kind of horror, while his voice stays smooth and trained, denying Flynn these addictions.

The master doctor, a Walt Disney cartoon of a bigbellied, rolypoly, nice guy with bucked teeth, rolls with the punches. His kind eyes show no horror, only some humor. He seems to have nothing but time and patience for Flynn's dirge-tinged tales about how he was born nervous and has been a depressive all his life and self medicates with a very small amount of Valium, and has for twenty years now. The freckled intern, with an Irish name tagged to her crisp pocket, gawks and keeps an open-faced smile of endearment. Later she will tell me, "he's so cute."

Each woman says the same thing at one time or another, "Oh, your dad's so cute," They all call him "Honey." They bathe him. They wash his real skin. Skin I haven't touched since I haven't had to, they salve down the "crusty" disease that covers him from head to toe. And when they're through, I come in, and he's asleep in a twitchy position, as if muttering to himself, like a wounded animal turned inward, too far gone to lick his wounds. And I don't want to look.

But I look. I am so tired of seeing Flynn's condition. I don't want to know it anymore. The truth of Flynn. A man who's reduced himself down to a sick miserable little ruined bunch of frayed nerve endings. Like a fox with his nose under his own tail, Flynn is consumed by ailments he has created by determined ignorance . And now justifies and defends, even in the face of dying. He loves every bacteria, the fluid filling his lungs, the enlarged heart, the one kidney left. Any amount of breakdown of his health tells him again and again how special he is. How delicate, how intelligent. How important he is, How deserving of attention he is. His swollen feet scared him a little, though. But he has passed it off as "Just one of those things."

I look at Flynn asleep, like the infant he was seventy-seven years ago. It's true, the family history. He was born sickly. And he is still that sickly infant. A hundred and three pounds. Seven pounds of fluid made him weigh in at a hundred and ten. He took hope until they told him about the fluid. Flynn is still the bad baby that controlled his world, his parents, his brothers and sister, and later his wife and kids, and me with his condition. He was taught to feel sorry for himself. He got his way by evoking pity. Now he's caught in his trap. If he gets well, the attention will stop. He is still that child who was catered to and given in to by his well-meaning but ignorant mother, who favored her sickly baby.

Flynn sleeps on his side, fetus position (but, of course), oxygen hose under his nose, I.V. of body fluids in his arm. Sustenance. Still kept alive, but this time by a very expensive mother's tit, medical style. And I am still here calling him "Daddy." I was his tit for the first twenty years of my life. He sucked me dry. And I feel the pull again. just entering the room, seeing his small form, and pathetic nurturing he gave himself on his own, the near starvation condition he let himself get in when there was plenty of food around, the tugging to fill his needs is still there. I feel such anger over it. I question it. I want to leave. I'm so tired of knowing Flynn.

Raw

Flynn is rendered raw. Stripped of his habits, made to stay in his hospital room, and denied any of his usual drugs, he turns red and quivering. A premature infant in an incubator. I come in on the fifth day, and what I've asked the doctors about has begun to occur. Withdrawals, Flynn's famous *nerves* are on their own with no help from Valium, nicotine, caffeine, salt, sugar, or Enderol. He's running under his own chemistry. And he's scared. His hands shake. His thick white hair stands out from a frightful sleep where he awoke to see that his night-mares were true. There is no escape for him.

Is this the bare infant he was seventy-seven years ago that his mother tried to comfort. Was he born raw, no cushioning between himself and some invisible torture no one else can see. One granddaughter researched the disease after Flynn died, and educated us all. It was real and caused all his life-long symptoms.

I see why he's an addict. The fear in his eyes, shaky hands, jutting jaw, as if he has a grinding, slow motion Parkinson's. The no reserve of his body. As if he's skinned and salted. I round the corner and as soon as I enter his room and spot him in the middle of all the hospital equipment in his cotton print gown, I feel the tension. The family term was "high strung." An old-fashioned concept we used to tag certain people with for lack of knowing what else to say. I am not prepared. He's like a beetle in the bush on a summer day, radiating a silent vibration that fills his room. A staccato in the air. Intense, beyond hearing.

For five days I almost enjoyed my father. He was finally clean. No black under his nails. No black in the creases of his hands—even white. He had become white-skinned in this white hospital, adapting to the habitat like any animal to camouflage itself. My eye had trouble spotting him until

205

he moved. He was becoming the father I'd always wanted, submissive, asking rather than telling, listening to everyone instead of talking about himself. Obeying orders, observing with fresh eyes, his mind finally not made up. He seemed intelligent, curious, not only a collection of prejudices.

The old hot-shot defiance of "nobody's going to tell me what to do" was gone. Gone was the cloud of smoke around his head that I'd had to breathe all my life if I had to be in his company. A serenity prevailed. He had surrendered to his broken health and given in to the hospital staff. I had even ventured a goodnight kiss on his brow and learned that his skin was soft and even sweet. Gone was the cigarette smell, the male smell. A grandfather's innocent forehead. When had Flynn become a soft, kind, old man and not the predator I remembered.

It surprised both of us, my sudden gesture of attempted affection, an awkward bending forward of just any daughter kissing just any father goodnight. Then I fled, embarrassed and confused down the hall, wondering how I could have kissed my enemy so. I rushed to my car in some wonder and disgust. Am I such a weakling of a female as to reach out and try to tend the male who violated me all those years. I could hear chastisement from my friends, everyone I knew.

"Oh, how could you do that, he doesn't deserve it. He should be hung by the balls and castrated," And they'd continue, "It's the same thing, his old pity, making you, once again, touch him."

I thought, in some instinctive place, that Flynn really was this nonsexual little man the nurses adored now, and the doctors kind of admired in his heroic fight for life, defying their tests, and taking credit alone for surviving. Not antibiotics, but will. And everyone chuckled, professionally. Flynn, who had lost his will and looked to others for answers, then, gently refusing their solutions.

On the fifth day, though, Flynn is back. It is the Flynn I know. The one who doesn't fit in the world, can't blend. And can't isolate. And can't get comfortable in his own skin. I stand there, an audience to it again, and protest rises in my blood. I feel it fill my face. The words come as accusation. "You're having withdrawals."

Like Dracula getting the beam of light, Flynn writhes and winces before my eyes in his bedside chair, "Don't say that. It makes it worse, I'm trying not to think about it. I'm trying to put it out of my mind," My mother tells me later on the phone, she used to ask him when they were first married if he wanted love or pity. That he was always telling her not to say anything that might make him *worse*.

Rage fills my chest. It's hot shooting out to my fingers and toes, I have the urge to kill this stupid little man still taking his illness personally, as if he can think it away. I say, "It's not a thought. It's organic. You need your body chemistry balanced, that is all. I'll tell the doctor. I'll call the psychiatrist assigned to you. Everyone has been waiting for this. They know what to do."

He visibly lurches and jerks in restless helplessness, and raises his otherwise mellow voice. It is an effort to keep things his way. His nerves are so familiar to him he's afraid to have them soused in anything but Valium. He shouts, his pre-throat cancer neck working, "No, don't do that. There's nothing anyone can do, I've always been like this. All my life," Does he think I haven't noticed? He finishes, "No one who hasn't felt this knows what it's like. There is nothing anyone can do. No one understands." His teeth fall down, the uppers cutting off his words.

I say, "Depression and anxiety *can* be treated!" Flynn stiffens. He has always been afraid someone might be able to take his *condition* away from him, and then who would he be. It has been his calling card, Flynn's expression for other people's idiosyncracies. His identity. Here I am, nervous, temperamental, sensitive, artistic, genius Flynn. Like no one else in the room. I knew the myth so well.

I say, "There has been a lot of research. You aren't unique. It's not because of what you think that scares you. You think these scary thoughts because of your depression." His prominent collar bone begins to stand out even more. The empty pockets, where flesh should be, growing darker and deeper.

The ego of his illness is gathering forces. I let my words fill his ears, lay against his eardrums, ride up the famous nerves, enter his brain. Stick. He tries to throw them off. This concept that he is not *special*. That there are hundreds of depressives out there. I say, "It doesn't mean anything about you. You are not your depression." I had talked to his psychiatrist years ago, telling him that Flynn had gotten his intelligence mixed up with his sickness and could never separate them. To take away his anxiety was to say he was not that brilliant, sensitive person he was known for at one time. A time before I knew him.

It is a tug-of-war, I hold my ground. He holds his. The only thing I can do is what I have always done with Flynn, hold out. It is my only leverage. He needs me, now, as before, in his weakened hospital state. He called it "dependent." He said he had never been dependent on anybody before. Mama scoffed over the phone when I told her that.

Flynn cannot get up and walk out with his pride at this point. He is too weak and he's hooked up to the I.V. and oxygen machines. Later, my brother will say I kicked him when he was down. And I will say that is all mans' stuff. That I'm not a man and I don't follow their rules of combat~ That I have to use what I can to win.

Win? That word stands out and my brother reminds me we are doing what we can for Flynn's good, not to win.

I stand there and hold out. It is my old fear. Flynn could get me again. I could begin pitying him again. I hold out now, not because I care if Flynn is depressed or not, but to protect myself. I always thought I could be free of Flynn and go my way.

Keeping Flynn Alive

Flynn is starving to death in the Land of Plenty because of freedom of speech and all the other Civil Rights. He is allowed his ignorance, and the merchants are allowed to sell dead food. He came in, before ending up in the hospital, with one more McDonald's burger or a corn dog and malt under his loose belt. His shoulder bones look like shoulder pads that got bunched up in the wash so big and bony and bare of flesh they are. And he's scared. His white hair, newly butchered around the neck and ears by some cheap barber on the Mexican side of town, stands up like a Mohawk, as he leans against the counter and eyes the "salad" supplements (or in his case, substitutes) I show him.

"These will give you your greens, since you can't chew real lettuce," I say. He squints, without his glasses, at the labels, Spirulina and Wheat Grass, "one is from the sea, the other from the fields...Like a cow, munching," I add. His teeth drop down as he begins to make a comment. I want to say, "Why don't you use glue?" Instead, I say, "And this one is brain food," I tap the big can of amino acid powder. "It's pre-digested, so it is very easy on your body." This time he nods, open mouthed, in desperate trust, *finally*. Flynn is trying to learn.... what is good for him.

I say, "It ought to be illegal, a health hazard to let you, in your condition, be able to buy food that's full of nitrates, sugars, salt, and white flour," A gnat buzzes around my mouth when I talk. It is a gnat that has been with me all day. If I didn't blink, it'd walk on my eyeballs and enter my nose holes, lay eggs, suck blood, and nest in my mouth. I bat at it, and Flynn looks up to see what's going on.

There is a kind of contest between Flynn and me. We have never said anything about it, but I sense that he is biding time until my ways, all this "health stuff" doesn't work and

I fall flat on my face. In the hospital, to console himself, he said, all of a sudden. "You never know. I might out-live you." Alex said the same thing once, from his hospital bed. He had said, "Well, you win now, but I might just get well and outlive you, you know."

Flynn

Every morning since the hospitalization, Flynn wakes up a different person. Another wash of body chemistry taking him over. He says he doesn't know himself. He was prescribed four medications. One for the heart, one for the kidneys, and one for fluid, and one for bowels. And, of course, Valium. He has given up coffee and cigarettes. He drinks two glasses of orange juice instead.

Flynn asks Sal to listen to his pulse. It's racing. Flynn leans back on the couch, flushed, closes his eyes. Shakes his head. He says, his voice grave, "I'm gonna die....I'm not gonna come outta this."

I say, "It's the doctors, not you. If I took one of your pills. I'd spin out too. Anybody would. You were fine before all this medication. They're killing you." And then I begin like Aunt Frances, in that hawk voice, "Have you taken your protein powder?" He shakes his shaggy head, slowly back and forth resting against the couch, and tells me in his slow, metered voice that he doesn't want any of that stuff. That it doesn't taste good. I turn on my heel and go into my room and make him a vitamin C tonic, bringing it out in a little glass of bubbling water and I tell him to let it clear and then drink it. In the tone everyone, including I, hate, I tell him that it has a thousand units of vitamin C. I preach, "It'll lift you up."

"What's it for?" he asks, innocent as a child in a high chair, and as suspicious and stubborn. It's this willfulness that enrages me about Flynn. He will clamp his mouth shut and no one has the right to open it and pour in something that's good for him because he is an adult and needs to give his consent. The desire to overpower him and force the vitamin C down passes. I stay composed.

I say, "Vitamin C...Your body can't function without it. It will help all the processes: circulation, exchange of nutrients

211

into the cells, oxidation." He sips at it before it stops bubbling. He probably is reminded of Alka-Seltzer.

"Not yet," I warn. "Wait a minute." I stand above him, looking down at his small body on the couch, holding the glass, expectant. He wants to live. I let him believe that vitamin C will do it: save his life. I almost believe it myself. Then I say what Mama used to say to Flynn when I was a girl at home. "Give me that shirt. I'm doing a dark load. And those Levis, and that t-shirt."

He says, "It's too much trouble, too much an effort, right now." I say, "Come on, they're dirty. Look at that stain." He looks. Have I shamed him. Made him feel like an old man who doesn't know he spilled soup down his shirt? He begins to amble one hand toward the buttons on his blue plaid shirt. A left-handed gesture without looking, fumbles, and I end up helping him. There is no strength in his movements. I hurry, half annoyed, undressing Flynn, trying to be simply expedient; but feeling uneasy. To treat Flynn like just a father and to try to be just a daughter is a lie; it is built into me. Yet I do, anyway, just as Louis, my big brother, walks in. I quickly withdraw my hand and let Flynn undo his own shirt. I do not want Louis to see me touch Flynn. No one in the family has ever seen me touch Flynn, or Flynn touch me. No hugs at departure or arrival, no handshakes or claps on the shoulders in greeting. No contact at all. Contact with Flynn was only sexual, and in private. And kept in secrecy. Even as a child, there was no smoothing of my hair with his big father hand, no pats of approval. Only searching for my sexual places in the dark. When we walked together we never held hands like some fathers and daughters did. And I envied that kind of affection at one time. Now, the thought of any consoling touching irritates me. When my own children leaned against me, I would move away. They told me this later. I hadn't noticed that I did that. I loved them very much and felt tender, but touching was only for sex, I had learned early. So that now, at fifty, thirty years after the last incident of molestation, I am shamed to be caught trying to "nurse" my ailing father. And Louis is trained. He looks askance, as if he never saw anything.

I face my brother as he comes striding toward me to see what he wants, stepping away from my father, protecting us both from knowing that I was anywhere near him, while he is undressing. I protected Louis all through my childhood. He was always red-faced, and gulping his Adam's apple over anything to do with "girls."

Even now, as adults, we have never talked about sex, except in the context of health that Vitamin E and K are good for the prostate. Louis has come in for a measuring tape. I open a drawer and hand him a ruler. Alex took everything he ever bought from a hardware store, and I never bothered to replace it. Louis is fixing a hinge on my garage door that the last strong wind ripped off. Sal is out there, too, helping Louis. I've just been video taping their bare backs, as they work together in the hot afternoon sun. Now I stand near the utility room door and say in a loud, impersonal voice, "Let me have your shirt, hurry, the washer is starting the cycle." Louis goes back out, and I see the naked backs glistening in the heat beyond the glass doors, out by the pool. I am awkward in this large cover-up movement, to hide from my brother the fact that I came too close to Flynn's body, as if there could possibly be some devious motive on my part.

I throw Flynn a clean shirt and pair of pants, and grab my video camera and head out toward the men, to record the fixing of my hinge, and their friendship in working together. And for what other reason? To prove to Louis that I am not with Flynn?

Pending

When you're going to do something as important as die, someone should be making something of it. But Flynn, a living corpse, strides through our days and no one shows any sign of knowing. My tenants are more worried than I am. They come to me and ask if Flynn is alright. "He looked better yesterday."

Flynn lies flat on his back on the stiff-seated couch, folds his hands over his chest, nose straight up, coffin postured, and takes a nap to the sounds of my making dinner in the kitchen. "The sounds of a woman in the kitchen," is what Flynn missed most when he divorced Mama, he said.

When Flynn was first divorced, he dated a little. A fellow mechanic, old grey-haired Hank, was a new widower and wanted to double date. He fixed Flynn up with "an old lady." She laughed at his tie and said, "Don't you know big fat ties are no longer in style. Little thin ties are." And later in the evening she hit him on the arm and teased, "Why are you so skinny? Why don't you eat" He never went out with "an old bag" again. His tie was too fat and he was too thin. And Flynn's once-confident ego was too frail to laugh off the criticism. He still remembers it today. I have been asking why he didn't remarry so he'd have someone to take care of him in his old age now. I already knew why. But I wanted him to say it and know it aloud. He remembers dating a girl with a baby after the old woman. The young one was some wild, divorced 21-year-old who got him to try smoking pot, and thought he was a cute and funny old man; he made her laugh. He said she wanted to marry him. I ask now, "Why didn't you marry her?" knowing the answer, too. He said she would have hurt him eventually. The old ones he didn't want and the young ones he wanted too much to take a risk with. So Flynn sits alone in my house preparing, in his way, to die. He says, "You always want to be with a woman you can walk away from… Who can't hurt you."

Flynn's baby brother, Bobby, only 72, five years Flynn's junior, just got married. His wife of forty years died less than a year ago. Flynn has passed judgment on his brother's folly. The woman is as old as he and has seven good-for-nothing kids, all grown and out of work. His brother has a little money in the bank. He has never had children of his own. Flynn says, "She only married him for his money,"

I say, "Oh, no, Bobby is lovable. I went to visit and I could see how she felt about his bright blue eyes, and tousled head of hair. They seemed very happy together." Flynn will have none of this. He holds that Bobby is afraid to be alone, and married "that squaw" just to keep him company and cook and clean. And that no one can take the place of his first wife.

I agree with him. Pearl, his first wife, was a gem. We'd laugh over that. She never lost her looks, and babied Bobby for all those years. He was naive. I tell Flynn that Bobby thought all women would be like Pearl. He was like an adolescent at 72. He had no experience whatsoever. And now, he is eager to find out what sex is like with another woman. Flynn falls silent. We have never talked about sex. I never mention the word around Flynn. But I am tired of pretending that it doesn't exist, and that I can't let Flynn know that I know about it and think about it and like it and can easily talk about it. Flynn's ears prick up when I hint that Bobby has confided in me about his sex life with his new wife. The whole kitchen stills like a morgue. Flynn has been near death, and I decide to give him something else to think about.

I say, "Bobby told me that when Pearl had her mastectomy, she got frigid. And then he went impotent. It was upsetting to both of them. Then she died, and he thought a new woman would bring his sexuality back." Flynn is all ears. He got a new short hair cut, and his ears are as prominent as a fox's. I go on. "So he got a prosthesis, you know, an insert, put in." Flynn's back has been turned to me, to keep distance as I talk, and he pretends to pick at something on the table. Now he turns to look at me. His stiff old neck cranks around in disbelief. It is the first time he has shown interest in something beside himself since his bout of walking pneumonia. I say, "It turns out that it was more painful than they told him it would be, and continues to be painful. And the worst part is that his wife, Olive, has a prolapsed bladder and uterus which she will not have operated on, so that if he tries to have sex, it is painful to her, so, in fact, they have no sex life." Flynn is facing me by now, and staring into space, picturing this whole business. It is something his brother would never tell him. It must be understood with those brothers that everything is just fine in the bedroom. Flynn's face is as full of wonder as a child's in the classroom, watching a dead frog's leg jump when the nerve is touched with a needle.

He begins to shake his head back and forth, and slowly forms some words, "They are worse off than I thought they were." It is all he can say. I tell him that I told Bobby it was probably Olive, herself. She is one of the most unattractive women I have ever seen. I tell Flynn that if he had chosen just any old ugly woman he couldn't have picked one like Olive. That she had an addition of ugliness, not only an absence of beauty, Flynn agrees. We were in awe over his brother's wife from the beginning. Was he blind, or too lonely, or what? It wasn't like a Lansdowne man to choose a woman for simply character.

Since Flynn is now an astute student, I cannot let him drift back into his morose mood over his pending death. I say, "Bobby told me that Olive is mean and cruel, too. That she is not only beastly, but unpleasant to deal with."

Flynn rises to a bit of humor. He says the expected, "If I was that bad looking I'd be mean, too." I laugh.

That's exactly what I told Bobby. That she probably feels so bad about herself that she covers it up with an attitude that beats him to saying anything about it. Flynn gets up, goes to the sink and rinses out his cup, and takes a sip of water. His manner is buoyant, and voice light. He says, "Well, I guess I'll go out to my little shack. I feel a lot better now." He hesitates, and adds, "Now that I know people have worse problems than I do."

216

Die

What am I supposed to do, come home and find Flynn dead? Is that how it happens? He'll be out in his little shack dead in his sleep, teeth in his throat and eyes open. Or sprawled on the kitchen floor with the wrapper of a microwave dinner half off. Or will it happen out in the driveway on his way to his car, or in his car, going down to get a coffee substitute. Or at a coffee shop, toppled over at the counter, his white hair askew. Is that the way it's done. And what am I supposed to do? Will I have that helpless feeling I had when my little dog of fifteen years died in my car on a trip, when she began to pant hard, and I pulled off the freeway, and watched her have convulsions, and then her eyes went flat, no light coming out, debris collecting immediately on them. And her whole body so still, my eyes thought I saw her move. Will I be afraid of Flynn dead.

Sal poopoos this kind of supposition. I say, "I will call Louis. He will know what to do. He will handle it all. I don't know what to do. Who do you tell when someone dies? And what happens. Does the body belong to the law? Can they take it away from you?.... I am not going to have a lot of people take over and go through all the expensive formalities."

I get annoyed at that point "No one will even come to Flynn's funeral." That's the worst part. Maybe some waitresses who will come up to me and tell me how sweet my father was, how he never got like other old men, his mind was always sharp, and he had a sense of humor and made them laugh. My sisters won't drive all that way just to see Flynn dead. They don't like him much. Maybe both brothers. And my mother can't, although she wishes him well over the phone and talks to him each time she calls. She always says she remembers the good times up in the mountains when he was young and handsome, before anything happened. She recalled his beautiful back recently, telling how she was riding the school bus and looked out of the window and there was this beautiful back of a handsome young man. Golden tan, beautiful strong shoulders, tapering waist. And black hair with blue eyes. The face, when he turned to talk to his friend. She remembers falling in love at that moment. Her eyes sought him out after that. But she is crippled now, rides a wheelchair, cannot leave her stroke-weak husband.

When the Time Comes

So many times I wished Flynn were dead. As a teenager mostly. Never as a little girl. I was too afraid not to have a father then. But after puberty I wished him out of my life. I hated his demands. And restrictions. I learned to curse him under my breath. I hated his smell of nicotine. Now, he comes in, telling a story of clawing at the air in town after having a fish sandwich at McDonald's, and going into Radio Shack to buy yet one more transistor radio just because "some little kid might want one for Christmas," As he made his way out, he lost his balance, felt dizzy, and reached out to steady himself, but there was nothing to hang onto. He has us all at attention over his plight, as he takes his time to draw a breath, and measure each word, knowing we are waiting to hear what happened, even though we can see he's here and made it alright. He goes on to say that the Radio Shack man came running out, asked if he could help, and steadied him to a bench where he rested and recovered, but not before two policemen came over and asked if they could call the paramedics. We laugh on cue, as Flynn commands our audience with his standard line about being in this shape in the first place because of the paramedics taking him off to the hospital a month ago for having an irregular heartbeat, and the new doctors putting him on another new medication. "I never felt dizzy before I started taking that new pill. I don't even remember what they said it was for."

When the time comes, and wherever it happens, my mother will send a card. She has a whole bunch of sympathy cards. She buys them in bulk. At seventy-five everyone you know is dying or sick or having an operation. I found all those cards while cleaning her house last summer. It made me stop and draw back my lips in a grimace. As if someone had smacked me. I took them to her and held them out and told her how grim it was to keep them around. She just looked surprised, smiled over my response, and learned from me. She had forgotten what it was like to be young enough not to have to send sympathy cards all the time. At least she didn't say what Flynn says when the age difference is blatantly pointed out at times, "Just wait. Someday you'll be in my position, old and sick and dying. It'll happen to you, too." He just can't stand not to be young. It irks him to death that it's his turn to be old, and a living joke.

The Aged

Flynn always had a cruel eye for the aged. Especially for old women. Now Flynn knows he fits the description of one of the names he himself, has called old men: "geezer, codger, lecher, old fool," He suffers in the amount of criticism he carried all his life. And now protects himself with, "just you wait…" Like casting an evil spell over all the young.

That night there was a program on mountain sheep. Like on a snow white mountain, Flynn perched on the edge of the couch, too small for the large couch, so he was dwarfed to child-size. He watched the young males challenging the old leader. Each male in turn locked horns, banged skulls, snorted, frothed, panted, and finally one beat the old male. The camera followed the old male as he took off to stand alone, looking down in a kind of confused stupor, as the cows went mindlessly off with their new leader. Flynn got up and left before the program was over.

Later I ask Sal, "What about your father? He's not bitter and angry and sour. He doesn't hate old women. Why do you think he is so at peace and content?" Sal is silent, thinking about it. Before he met me and all the men I talk about, he never thought much about people at all. He never questioned, compared, examined, analyzed, or cared about the happiness or unhappiness level of any human being. He mostly thought things were the way they were because they were just that way, and there was no reason for it. Like the mountains and the stars, by some law of nature, but nothing to think about for any length of time. I finally answer for him, "Your father doesn't feel betrayed by women; he hasn't felt their fickleness. He never put himself out there. But my father used to strut his stuff. Be the "cock of the walk." Your father stayed with your mother all these years. Was never unfaithful. He "did right by" your mother. So he enjoys her,

221

even as they grow old." Sal looks a bit stiff-lipped, as if I might be criticizing his parents. I add, "I think they compromised a lot to stay together and never ventured out and found out anything that wasn't approved by the other. But that's what they knew. Flynn wanted more. And my mother, you know, is difficult in her way. She was not content to just let Flynn lead."

I ask Sal, "What do you think my father is? A geezer? A codger? or a lecher?" Sal exhales in the tedium of having to answer at all. So I answer. "A geezer maybe. His jaw is that sharp, especially when he takes out his teeth.... He definitely is not a codger. Codgers are old fuddy-duddies. Flynn's too alert for that. What about a lecher?" I wait. Sal sits with his eyes glancing at the ball game on their TV screen, annoyed but trying not to reveal it. And if I should ask, he will deny it. I answer for him. "A lecher lusts after anything female. Flynn is too bitter with all females for rejecting him in his old age to give them the attention required to be a lecher. *Any more.* Maybe he never was a lecher. Lechers are hungry. Flynn always got what he wanted, so he didn't go around leering like looking in the bakery shop window." Sal looks at me to see if I am through. His soft Italian eyes show sorrow. He has lectured me on making fun of people. He reveres his father. I go on, "A geezer is only a physical predicament. Not a mental one. I'd say he's a geezer."

Like shouting way inside a tunnel to Flynn's agedness (so the past can hear it). I raise my voice when talking to Flynn. I can see that Flynn has lost hope, confidence, self-esteem. As I do with school children, I take him around and introduce him to the world. It is a brand new world. The one he knew has disappeared. He has never been 77 before. I take him along the boulevard on Sunday to show him what's going on in the arts with the local artists. "See, everything is Santa Fe now, coyotes howling at the moon, barrel cactus (he corrects with "soriel cactus"), and adobe haciendas.... Just what you always painted." I want him to see that, as an artist, he is still in style, not out-dated or dated. There is an urgency in my throat to do so.

He asks, "I wonder why Santa Fe is so popular?" There is an innocence to his voice. Truly curious.

Outback

Flynn with a new respect for life. The great Whatever is reigning and reining him in, slowing him down, and beginning to close his eyes. He fights to stay awake during the day. He will have a benevolent death. Flynn holds onto the dead shrub as he tries to step down the concrete steps that lead to his place outback. It may as well be the Outback in Australia for the time it takes him now. A great expanse of space where before he never gave it a thought. Now he concentrates on each step, staying steady so not to fall, and looks ahead as if his shack is far, far away. The effort takes all his energy. I tell him to hold onto me. He gently clasps my arm, and we go off into the night toward his bed. At the steps, though, he insists on taking hold of the dead shrub, the shrub that died in the drought and freeze. The freeze that took Flynn's lungs, that killed him in October (but he never fell over…one of Flynn's old jokes…all his old jokes being on him now.). He says the shrub is reliable. He is sure of it. I say, "What about me." He doesn't answer. His breathing is shallow, and we stop every couple of feet. When he catches his breath he tells me he always thought that he'd die of a heart attack, or something sudden, not like this, slowly, barely able to walk or breathe. He laughs a little at himself walking like an old, old man.

It was the pink dress and jacket that made me frail and questioning like one of those old English ladies. As soon as I got home and put on the tights and t-shirt, I became capable and wide-awake. I felt my body take muscle and blood come surging back. Superman rips off his business clothes and there's the muscle. I had sat with my knees together all morning in that dress, Suzi's dress. And watched my hands sticking out from the sleeves. Folded in my lap. The raw flesh, very much like buzzard heads. I studied the blue and greenish veins, network of crinkles and cracks and lines. The enlarged knuckles. So much going on there in my lap. Garish and pulpy. Spotted as a frog's back. Diamondback rattle snake heads. And on me. Of me. My hands showed everything. I had stopped trying to hide them. A pink dress at Suzi's son's wedding....

I am taking it personally, Flynn's pending death, as if I have failed him and it is my fault. And Mama's leg. That too, as if somehow I could have helped her more and it wouldn't have happened. I am believing deep down that they don't *have* to die, that it could be prevented, "Oh, Gawd, oh, Gawd.... "the words form in my head.... I can't ask for everything to stay alive, so I have to ask for the courage to take it when it passes.... Where are all the new babies, puppies and kittens, ducklings and chicks. And colts. Just Flynn dying, and no new life to take its place. Like the yard. Only dead grass and then it stays that way.

I remember how reluctant I was to learn Sal's phone number. I didn't want to go on without John. "You want to hold onto the past," they keep saying. Finally I tell them it's the present I want to have. And then I have one good dream. Of strength. My little dog, the one that died in the summer, is running beside me. We are on a ship, running as fast as we can. She is on her hind legs, ears blowing back in the wind. I look over at her and it's as if she's happy to be so strong and keeping up with me.... There is more, all about food and hunger...but that is not the strong part of the dream. I am never able to choose the food, while everyone else takes portions and goes to the table to eat. I want too much, and everything. I end up taking a serving dish by mistake, and have to put my plate down. I am making my way to the table with a big pile of slop in a half watermelon shell when I wake up. I swallow and my mouth is full of saliva; I am starving....

Mama writes, "Build yourself up, Honey." I tell her I went off all the charts at the gym. That they did a fitness test on me. My supervisor laughed as she recorded all the scores in the margin. She says they don't have a chart for me yet. That these are old charts before women were working out. That I would have to use an athlete's chart for my scores.

Mama sighs, "Leave all that for the younger women. Just sit and relax."

Sometimes I think of John. Belonging to that world of trained thinkers. Splitting hairs over a word and it's context. Taking literature apart the way interns dissect cadavers, and everyone arguing in a very specialized language about what stories mean. He slept with a literary critic: They talked all day in the campus coffee shop and fucked all night. Two trained brains. The training to analyze words in their heads side by side on the pillow. She read his articles and fell in love. He read hers and praised her. They talked about me once and what I meant to him. I came out looking pretty bad. He told me once he was sorry he discussed me with her. She became a woman and said some nasty thing. I think he expected her to be a literary critic all the time.

I call roll at a rich school. All the names are like anatomy: colon, anus, appendix. Or Jewish names: Sam, Joshua, Adam...I am so used to the Hispanics that my own people sound odd to me now. I used to have trouble with the Spanish roll call. The students would laugh. It was full of Jesus and Maria, and, Xochi and Alejandro and Alejandra.... The Alternative School roll with all the ex-hippies' children was the hardest to pronounce. They had names from Africa, India, and ones they made up or re-spelled. And the parents would stay and watch to make sure you weren't indoctrinating their child with any idea they didn't agree with. At the rich school I give a lesson on the space shuttle: pulling against gravity falling toward the earth, the pull, the attraction, magnetism... until it's outside the atmosphere...then—no pull, it goes into orbit. I begin to think about John. All the time the pull. I couldn't stay away from him. I begin to miss him just talking about gravity... And thinking that's the way it *should* be. That it is wrong being with Sal. The kids bring me back to earth. "It's time, It's time.... to go to recess." I go out, thinking, "Of course there's a cake pan in this fat teacher's room."

"You left your dishes, grease floating on top of the cold dishwater, a mess.... I try to sleep and keep thinking of the sloppy tenant leaving her dishes and her boyfriend behind...

The words float in my head. I try to think other words, but I'm already practicing my lines to tell her to clean up after herself. Words I will never use…. I will let it pass, I will clean it up. Someday. One day…I will speak up. Sal says to be glad I have a house. (*Later, I will learn that he wanted my house.*)

I blot out the tenant by remembering the faces of the children in the classroom. I like watching their faces as they learn. There was a student teacher, so I had the luxury to sit back and watch. Each child taking in the information according to the temperament. The shy one peering out, careful, a fearful one holding back, looking for danger, a bold one already challenging the facts, the little student teacher fresh out of methods courses…. Some faces are still open, closed already. And all with glistening eyes, baby cheeks, and tiny pink mouths and innocent noses. Trust, suspicion, inadequacy, and sometimes pure joy and eagerness. One boy who has never been to school, from Mexico, radiant, with the miracle of education. As if he's in Disneyland.

Flynn's face appears in the doorway. Beyond agony and anger now. A soberness I never thought he would be capable of. Life is very serious toward the end, now that he can see it coming. Like climbing Mt. Summit. The "suffering" he did all his life over death was an abstraction. A man playing with the idea of the inevitable. As long as it kept its distance. Now it is upon him and there is no rhetoric. No pastime contemplation. He didn't know it would have ahold of his body, pulling him down so that to stay up took all his effort. Not knowing was always one of Flynn's angers. He did not like to not know what was ahead. Now that he knows, there is a kind of peace. And a sadness he won't express. I ask him how he feels about his condition. It is a stupid question. "Something from that therapy stuff." He doesn't honor it with an answer.

A tenant drops a plate. I think, "Good, that's one less thing to worry about." A man comes to the house carrying a white paper sack and an aluminum tray. Each has #31 written on it. It is Flynn's low-sodium, doctor-prescribed lunch. Another man brings oxygen. The silver and blue tank sits on the porch glistening in the sun. Flynn cannot be found. He is off in his car. People are beginning to ask, "Does he still drive?" I learn from them. Flynn, the feeble, now. But I am not going to be the one to separate him from his car. As long as he can get a license.... I remember they would have let Alex drive home from his brain tumor operation. No one bothered to see how he was getting home. I just happened to be there, or he would have taken the wheel.

Flynn leans on things now. He's always leaned emotionally, and now he leans physically. There's a chair by the front door he grabs ahold of as he enters, stops and rests, leaning his weightless body against it. He's ninety pounds and still can hardly pick up his feet. I suddenly remember I have a cane. It's been leaning against the wall by the big bird cage so long I stopped noticing it. I say, in an impulse, "Here, use this." He takes it with a grim face, trying for some humor. His hand feels like parchment as I hold it so he can get ahold of the cane. Flynn takes a step for the novelty of it. He looks good with a cane. A gentleman. Wearing his gabardine slacks and the lightweight plaid flannel shirt. He leans across the living room on the cane and then quietly places it against the wall, and goes on out to his little shack. The fun over. Later I ask him why he doesn't use the cane. He tells me he will if he ever has any walking to do.

I plan ahead a little. Just fleeting thoughts which I try to put away before they go too far. I will play Flynn's tapes.... He recorded "On the Wings of a Snow White Dove" when he and Ernie played in that band. And the big black preacher can say a few words about Flynn finally being at peace, a tormented soul, sick toward the end. He doesn't have to know anymore about Flynn than that. I could tell when I met Flynn after church that the preacher just thought Flynn was a nice old white man. He can talk about being released from physical bondage. And everyone can have their own thoughts and memories. His sister, who "didn't want to make two trips." She'll be there. Everyone likes a funeral. All they have to do is sit there and be entertained by the preacher and then go over to somebody's house and eat all the casseroles up. She didn't want to come see Flynn alive and then just come back again for the funeral. She said over the phone that it would be too hard on her so she would just make "the one trip." If she came when he was alive she would have had to do something, take him out to dinner, talk, listen to him, maybe help him make his bed, help him walk. It would have been work, so she'd wait. She had her own heart to think about. Flynn's big sister at eighty: a cross between Benny Hill and Margaret Thatcher, in looks and droll sense of humor and well-placed wit, not willing to see her brother alive when it could get messy, but chose to wait until he is neatly put away in a box, all dressed and still with his needs ended, hands folded, eyes and mouth sealed. Nothing to do but look. She could handle that. Her brother packaged and preserved.

Flynn's eyes show some sparkle now that he has everybody mad at everybody, trying to keep him alive. The family divides down the middle into the health-nuts to the doctor-lovers. We bark at each other over the phone and begin feuds we will go to the grave with. I determine never to forgive Flynn's brother, my nicest uncle, for preaching to me about giving Flynn ice cream, white bread, salt, anything he will eat, "He's starving to death, And vitamins won't do him a damn bit of good." It was a personal attack on my beliefs.

That night I offer Flynn wienies, ice cream, white buns, and all the chocolate Valentine cake he can eat. He finally declines towards the end of the dinner, saying he's had too much of "That stuff." I press him, asking, "What stuff?" Playing dumb. To see if he'll call it what it is. He looks to see if I mean it.

Flynn Again

Flynn just smiles sweetly when you come upon him unexpectedly, as if he's been found and rescued, a domesticated animal in the wild. I go out to his little place now and then to see if he is still alive. But I don't tell him that. I ask, "Did you eat?" or I tell him about my day, which is something I have rarely done. It was too intimate to "share" life with him in that way. As I stand in the sliding-glass doorway, I see that he has both electric heaters on now, the expensive one and the cheap one to run. I have consulted the electric company. They say no electric heater is "cost effective." It is evil to think in terms of expense when it is your own father. It made me think back. Flynn paid utilities all our lives, growing up, and I never heard him mention it once. I picture him taking out the dollar bills and handing them over to someone. He never had a bank account. The money earned was to be spent each week. Friday was payday. I never knew anything about Flynn's finances. He never talked about it. He sits now, flanked by my two heaters, squatting on his short-legged stool, on which he has placed a folded towel for cushioning. He is in his long-handled underwear, listening to the news on one of his many brand new portable stereo recorders. Every month or so he will come home with another "good deal." The radios are still in their boxes stacked up on top of everything, all sizes. It's as if Flynn never had any money to spend and now he does. I never remember Flynn shopping or buying anything but gas and cigarettes and a cup of coffee. He was never a spender until now. And now only for this particular item. Sometimes I'll come back to check on him and he'll have China on one of his more expensive sets. He'll be grinning and turning the knob, and feeling grand, saying how many countries he can pick up on this one. Or he'll be playing tapes. Old songs from the fifties. He'll be listening with a musician's ear, leaning in to hear the lyrics and the guitarist, really admiring the skill, and "the way they used to play...."

"There's no mail," Flynn says as if it's important. I only get utility bills, and he never gets anything. But at his age even the paper delivered is something happening. One tenant gets the *L.A. Times*. It gives Flynn something to run over in the morning as he backs out of the driveway. I say that we are a family that is ashamed to tell any bad news, and no good news has happened so no one writes. In truth, my sisters tell me that they will not write to Flynn again until he answers "my last letter." He never writes, they complain.

One night I want to cut Flynn to the quick. He is hacking away and saying, "I've got something that is going around." I am still waiting for him to admit that he smoked sixty years and is sorry because he is now in this condition. I want him to acknowledge that, at least. So I take out my video camera and tell Flynn I want to have a session: I am taping Flynn, interviewing him like a journalist would. As if he is somebody. It is mostly so he can hear himself, see himself, reflect on the actual. Although I picture myself watching it after he's dead.

We sit on the two couches, the camera perched on my shoulder and Flynn across the way ready to respond to my probings. It is in these shootings that I have heard him say things I would never have heard otherwise: bitterness over certain parts of the past, mostly to do with women betraying him. Tonight I ask him about his condition. He is near death, and still we make an exercise out of it. He is more than willing. His oxygen tank stands by. He inhales with effort to prepare his talk. Flynn says, "I wish I could draw a breath." I say, "Take out your pencil."

His voice is slow and deep, but this medium takes his words into another realm, where it is no longer talking, but recording. He seems to see himself through someone's eyes in the future, and wants to have his say, be understood: I let him tell about the difficulty in drawing a breath, the weakness he never expected to happen to him, the fear of it all, hardly able to walk or breathe. I then ask what he thinks caused him to get this way. He sucks in as much air as he can and, with a whimsical look of sorrowful musing says that you can't smoke all your life and not expect to have some kind of problem.

I take my eye out of the lens and look with both eyes at Flynn. I don't want to miss this. I bring him in close so his mouth is framed in this shot on video as he goes on. "Well, sure, nobody can expect to smoke that long and not have something go wrong eventually...I'm no exception." I push telephoto and push Flynn away to full-face and ask him if he would smoke again if he had it to do over again. He hesitates, not to gather his thoughts but to gather air into his lungs. With dignity, looking down, taking his time to place each word just so—he says he would smoke again.

"Why?" I ask.

With his eyes still downcast, meditative and alert around the razor-sharp jaw, his wide, once sensual mouth jerks and twitches a little to express exactly what it was about cigarettes, "That was the only time I really felt like I was living." I know what he means but I ask him what he means, "Well, you stand there and reach into your pocket...I still do that, I keep forgetting I don't carry cigarettes anymore. I still reach for them.... " He looks up at the camera and laughs a little, self-conscious. He goes on, "You light up, you have a cup of coffee right there, you sit back..." I can see the nostalgia. His chin is high and he sees himself at a cafe or standing in the shop all those years, inhaling deep, sipping hot, sweet and creamy coffee. It makes me want to do it. I know that moment, too, but with different drugs. John was that to me. That moment of pure being or whatever it is. Of *being there*. Flynn is as awkward as I am in accuracy of word. Or maybe it can't be said. Biochemists would call it one thing, psychologists another. Philosophers still something else and social workers something, too. And preachers another. I always saw it in Flynn as defiance, having a say over his own death. Alex smoked, as a rebellious act again his Quaker father. I never took to smoking. But I agree down deep with Flynn. Of course he would do it again or he wouldn't be Flynn. I don't want a sorry father. Sorry to have "lived."

When one eye is weeping from holding it shut so the

other one can peer through the lens, and Flynn is wheezing for air, we stop, "To be continued," I say. And wonder if he will live that long.

Last year Mama called me and said she had her first orgasm with a man, "He reached for me.... uh.... in his sleep.... and touched me, tender...and he was...uh, you know...It's the Dopamine..."

I say, "Oh, Mama. He was asleep? And on Dopamine, And you are interpreting that as really caring at last, as he's at the end of his life?"

"No, he loves me, I could tell. He was so tender, And..." Mama never could talk about sex. But she was no prude. I try to wake her up about her husband's affection and rob her of her fantasy.

"It was a moron's hard-on," I say: babies, baboons, and invalids get them. Morning erections don't count. They only mean pressure on the bladder, not love.

"Oh, shhhhh. Don't say that,"

"Well, he doesn't know what he's doing if he's asleep. And with his stroke, even when he's awake. And if you turned back the clock he'd still be the way he was with you.

"Oh, you shouldn't say that..."

"Well, if you want to believe he really cares, now that he's dependent..."

Mama admitted to me when I asked, just recently, that Flynn never made her have an orgasm. I was astonished. I thought about it a lot. That's all he did with me. I couldn't believe he didn't "make love" to Mama the same way with the same result.... I remember her saying, "All he ever wanted to do was use his mouth, that's not romantic...."

Marty

From Mrs. Jones's Window

Mrs. Jones lives across the street and her kitchen window faces my house, Mrs. Jones sees me go out to greet a car. A dog owner and a dog get out, and my dog comes out, and both dogs sniff each other's assholes, balls and begin pissing everywhere, and following each other around, sniffing each other's piss. She sees me laughing and talking, taking the dog owner into the house, come out later, laughing and talking some more, and then the dog owner gets back into the car with the dog and drives away.

I don't know what it looks like to Mrs. Jones. I'm renting out a room, and have put "allow pets" in the ad. Everyone coming out has a big dog. My dog is not really my dog. It is a big dog that was left by the last tenant two years ago. I don't want her, but cannot take her to the pound or find anyone else who wants her, so she cautiously tries to belong to me, sniffing visitors, putting her wet nose in my clean hand while I'm too busy talking to notice, and too many people around to push her away.

Mrs. Jones's head is always in her kitchen window. I laugh over the phone to a friend. "She probably thinks I'm being sexual somehow, all that sniffing and laughing and talking and disappearing."

"You should move," is all my friend has to say.

She couldn't have that many dishes. She lives with her old husband. Both of them retired now. She married into the Jones family fifty years ago. Back then Jones owned all the land as far as the eye could see.

But each heir sold off a piece until the piece across the street from me is the last wedge left. Old Mr. Jones, though, carries the family legacy inside his head. And walks around jovial, fat, drunk, and flirtatious. A wheeler-dealer still. While Mrs. Jones, a retired school teacher, plays Grandma. She was just going back to teaching when I came home to have my babies. She took my place at the schools. Then I went back to teaching ten years later, and she came home to retire. Now little toddlers run around on her nice new lawn. Mr. Jones has built her a new house. Is it his last offering to the pure and devoted Mrs. Jones? She is one of those tidy, pale, never mussed, quiet women who finally don't know because it's not nice to even think so. So for the twenty-six years I've been across the street from her (first she was in that little house, then the one in the cul de sac a little bigger, and now this great big one), she'd never said anything about anything, except when she could say something nice. While I've been across the street saying everything about everything, not because I wanted to but because I had to or I would have been destroyed. How did Mrs. Jones get away with such nice manners. Why wasn't she ever pushed to vulgarity?

We've watched each other grow old over the years. Although once she thought I was my daughter and inquired about "Your mother."

I said, "I am my mother." I was in the jogging shorts and in that neighborhood a senior can be mistaken for a child if she wears cotton, and no polyester over blouses. Mrs. Jones herself has faded, erased by time. Her pantsuits are the same shade of pastel as her hair. Pigment being vulgar in old age. Anyone retaining color or form regarded as sexual in this neighborhood where the farmer's daughters married the lemon picker's sons, just a hundred miles from Hollywood.

Canned Grapes and Asparagus Tips

Sometimes I think of turning myself over to a clinic. A staff that knows what to look for in hands and feet, arms and legs, necks and backs. Like butchers to a chicken farm. And I picture them, these nice people who care and are paid to care, taking my "poor little body" and massaging and oiling and tending it, the way they did Jesus's feet when he came off the desert, all asweat, baked and cracked around the heels and toes. And I hear Mama's voice, "…all your hard work…."

But because Mama's fat, I'm thin. And because she's crippled, I run more and more the older I get. And because she never learned to drive, I take off in my car as soon as something doesn't please me. Men have shouted at me as I slammed out the door away from them. Mama couldn't walk and she couldn't drive. She was always trapped in one place where she accumulated flesh and became a large, hot mass. Because of her, I fast all day and keep moving. I never sit down until night, and then I don't sit, I lie down and sleep hard until the next day when the thinness and the mobility begin all over again. The only man who matched me was the one I married, Alex. But he raced through the days with the American Dream coursing through his bloodstream; and still does. The men after him were sitters. Each, in turn, sat and read while I dashed around taking care of all the practical matters.

One night I tried to intercept myself, to fry a steak, take a long, hot bath, and lounge about. I didn't run, or go to the gym, or jump back into my car to race out into the night to see a film. I stilled myself at the stove and it was the first time the kitchen smelled like a kitchen was supposed to smell since I stopped eating animal fats. The kitchen Flynn knows: bacon and eggs frying in the skillet in the morning, meat and potatoes frying in a pan at night. "When people were normal and ate bologna on Webber's Bread," as Flynn said.

Flynn is opening the smallest can of anything I have ever seen. I lean in and read the label. Canned Grapes. He then opens a taller can with a picture of asparagus on the label. I say, "It's too bad you can't chew this or you could have some of it." He edges closer, and like a whooping crane, knee-deep in swamp water, perches his head as if he's about to spear a fish, his long nose at the same angle to compensate for the distortion of water magnification. I warn, suddenly greedy to have all the red meat for myself. I have eaten fish for a year. My teeth tickle for the texture of muscle, and tongue drools for blood, I say, "Oh, wait...don't try it unless you can chew it." He withdraws himself. Goes back to his cans. He has heard my selfishness. That I don't want to share. It is unlike me. He averts his eyes to allow me my greed in privacy. As if I'm in a cave guarding some fresh kill and intend to fight for it. My hunger surprises me. I am always hungry, but not like this, I have never not pushed my food toward someone else if they wanted it.

After the divorce, I remember not wanting to share a whole pizza with my own children. I tucked it away in the refrigerator and hoped they wouldn't find it, and baked it when they weren't home, and when one came in and saw me eating, I hoarded it, and reluctantly gave pieces away. I was filled with guilt and shame then, and they looked at me funny.

Now Flynn knows that I would eat the last morsel and let him starve to death if it came down to it. I begin to cut off pieces of the steak and fork them into my mouth before they are done, I sop up the blood in the pan with each chunk and poke a few holes in the meat with my teeth, and gulp it down like a dog, as if I have four stomachs. Again Mama's voice is there, "You've been running and working out too much just look, you're down to the weight you were in Junior High School. You need to build yourself up. You always had a tremendous appetite, because you go, go, go."

Then Sal's admonishment when he first met me, "You've cannibalized your own muscle mass for years by over-exercising and under-eating. You need more protein."

Mama accused Sal last summer, "You're starving her to

death. Look at her. She used to be voluptuous. She needs iron, liver, butter, almonds, raisins. Not just brown rice. She's used to protein. What's wrong with cheese. She uses up a lot of energy, but not you, you never move, just sit all day and read, you can be a vegetarian. But she needs to *eat meat*.."

All this is with me as I slice off each piece of still raw steak, that is softer in the mouth than anything I've had all year, and gives under the teeth and soothes the tongue like nothing else. *I need this, I earned this, I deserve this.* Have the TV ads for women influenced me? Flynn goes slowly out of the room, to give me the privacy in my orgy over this piece of red meat I can't wait to be done. I am glad. Out of the corner of my eye I could see the way his hands and mouth moved, first pulling back the lids, making way for his fork, the sounds of his taking sustenance were still the same jerky, needy movements he used on me when I was a child, separating my clothing from my flesh, inching in between places on my body. Even though I have tried to not notice gestures of Flynn's, my eyes never miss one. His fingers, his mouth. Like a rabbit instinctively aware of a fox? And to show appetite with Flynn in the same room. I usually won't. But tonight I am ravenous. I try to interpret Flynn's mannerisms as a simple feeding of himself, but after he leaves, there is a relief. I felt naked. And he saw that I wanted to have without modesty or moderation.

After Flynn is gone, I finish up the meat, and with some disgust, wash the pan and try to relax. In my room the irritation over Flynn's movements stay. I feel vulnerable suddenly. He saw me naked again, I am thinking. It is the same thing. Both of us in the kitchen. He, exactly the way he used to be when he used to touch me. The same slurping and smacking and slopping sounds, while he took in faulty sustenance. The only difference, is that I usually take my food into my room and eat in private. Even Flynn seemed embarrassed, and walked away... Some anger flairs up and I feel my fingers and toes take the adrenalin, Flynn is still in my life. It comes to me again, as if it is a brand new concept.... I can never get used to it, yet it is the most familiar thing. A disbelief...This is *not my life*.... ?

From Flynn's Point of View

I look at Flynn and feel what he is thinking. He thinks: "Oh, she's home. There she is at the stove, cooking liver for her cats. She'll ask me if I want some, and if I say I can't chew it, makes some slight about my eating habits. About getting glue for my teeth. Try to push vitamins on me, or offer to fix something else, but I'll refuse because her cooking doesn't have any flavor since she's been listening to that Wop. Leave the salt out. My only choice, though, is just to be tactful, keep my mouth shut. Someday she'll be in my position. Her kids are selfish. They'll treat her like this when she's in my position. She doesn't know it yet, but it'll all come to pass. Oh, she's in her tights. Must have been out running or at the gym. She thinks she's getting somewhere keeping herself like that. And running around showing her legs and crotch, and letting her hair go like that. When she was growing up I kept her like a lady. Smooth hair, modest dress; now men look at her and think she's cheap, but she has a heart of gold. They put the two together and try to take advantage of her. But no one would listen to me, I couldn't tell her anything. Kids won't listen to you after they grow up, think they know it all. I'll just bide my time and they'll all find out on their own what it's like to be in my position. I've done some things I'm ashamed of, but everybody does...."

From Alex's Point of View

I gave Marty the house. She didn't deserve it, but I did it for the kids. She never liked the home, however. She was always running away, out chasing some man. I know she doesn't like to hear it, and doesn't like to think of herself that way, but it's in her blood. She goes from man to man. I wouldn't have believed it myself, but I see it's true. Since the divorce, she's had three boyfriends now, I don't know why she doesn't want to hang on to any of them. There was only one that was any good, that was Wolfgang. But she did to him what she did to me, started seeing another man, this professor guy. What's his name. He was just a big toad. I never could see what she saw in him except for the prestige of his job. She always wanted an intellectual, I guess. But he turned out to be just like her, seeing women on the side. I felt sorry for her. She couldn't seem to break away from him, I didn't understand what was holding her.

Everyone could see that he was stuck on himself, and just a fat and old, sluggish bald-headed toad, *a toad.* It took her a long time to get rid of him. And now she's with this new guy, what's his name? He seems too nice for her. But he'll get smart sooner or later, He'll learn. He won't take it after awhile. And that house. She's never found a man who could help her with that house. She always goes for these types that don't know how to do anything. They just want to get her in bed. And when something breaks, she calls me. I'm the best man she's ever had. She'll never be able to replace me. I'd take her back if she'd just keep her mouth shut. Or get a tracheotomy. She's kept herself in good shape. I'm really surprised. She's kept her looks. In fact, I'd say, she's better looking now, as an older woman, than she ever was. She's slimmed down, I'll tell you. I have to admire that. When most women are going to pot, she seems to be just waking up. I don't know.

I mean I'm really amazed at her. She looks good. That's the kind of woman I'll marry again: someone who's taken care of her body and has an interesting mind, just like Marty.

Fried Chicken-Chips and Donuts

I teach sketching. First use your pencils. Then the crayons. First the lines, Then the colors. They follow directions; So do I. I joke with the kids, saying, "I can see better with my eyes painted on. I can talk now with my mouth drawn on…" They smile, laugh, look serious to see if I mean it. They see that I do. They wonder about it, ask to see my toenails. School children: they want to touch you, their teacher, feel your texture, pet your hair, lean against you and look at your skin; my skin compared to their mothers' is all the colors of the rainbow.

"Which color now!" I slip out of one shoe and show them. Again the innocent quizzical faces, beautiful childrens' eyes, soft cheeks, full mouths, silken hair, curious about this teacher who paints her toenails all different colors. Why does she do this? They want to learn how to be and how not to be. Every morning I paint my face flesh-color and rose and red on the mouth and black around the eyes. All day long I look to see if I still have a face. If the eyes and lips are outlined, and colored in. Like a child's drawing. I do it shamelessly in front of the school children.

These schools and all those teachers all the time. Their silk shirts, pleated pant legs, cuffs, collars, long coats of denim, belts, chains, buttons, ribbons, scarves, bracelets, earrings, and closed-toed shoes with flat heels. No one on heels except the short dark ethnic men teachers. Sneakers and socks, and jeans and those awful blouses. And soda pop. The big machine standing there taking their quarters all day long. That big vice principal, a mean-looking woman, going right up to it all day and putting in her coins, pushing a button after deciding which one, the slot opening and her can of pop hitting the stainless steel pan with a final stop. Then she's pushing the pop top in and sipping, walking back to her office, smiling and saying, "Is this only Wednesday," to no one at all, not to me especially, since I am not staff and we have no rapport. She calls me a "guest teacher" to the students, "Aren't we fortunate...."

I watch her go by on her breaks, in her long skirts and blouses, sealed calves in nylon, shod feet, a little wobbly on the polished floor, pock-marks on her cheeks. And her taste for fizzle water. I can see her having a stiff one at night when she gets home, in a shot glass, and fading out pretending it's Friday every night, leaning back, feet propped up, that coifed hair on the arm of some stiff couch. A cauliflower man, like an old boxer, scrubbed down, dried off and dressed up in the room somewhere with his highball and highballs resting in his gabardine pantlegs. Mumps. Mama used to say for men who had mumps as a kid; their balls don't drop the way they're supposed to when they grow up.

He'd be in the kitchen door way, the telltale broken capillaries that match hers at the sides of the nose and on the surface of the cheeks turning from magenta to purple. He would have his eye on the microwave, waiting to bring their dinners into the living room.

She told one teacher she had a three-year-old. I can't picture this. There is nothing that tells on her about a three-year-old. No allowances in her movements, facial expressions. If it is three, this child in her life, I imagine it a very old three. With glasses, a back brace, posturepedic bed set, little serious brown shoes with laces and a hat and an overcoat. And grey hair. I feel it could never be young, born out of her.

The teacher who told me this, surprises me. She says, "You are spaced out. What are you thinking about!" I tell her about the three-year-old. She says she knows what I mean, and hurries off to class. I am left wondering why it matters to me at all, this vice-principal's life and the possibility of a three-year-old.

That night I throw the clock. The hands fly off and the face cover cracks in two. There are other little bits of beige plastic pieces on the carpet. The battery is off by itself, as if sulking. Sal watches me have the fit. It was over the way he took his supplements, but I don't tell him this. An instant anger over a pampered man, pampering himself even more. As if he needs to replace anything. He hasn't even *used* anything up in his body. I want to ridicule him, "You do *nothing* all day long. Why do you need to protect yourself. You disgust me, The way you swallow disgusts me. Look at you. An over-kept body: afraid to show wear and tear...." I send him home that night saying I need to be alone. He goes, slamming my door so the tenants hear. I am thinking, how I could not let him touch me under the covers, naked. My body stiffens just thinking about it. A man like that, so afraid to show signs of any living. I hug my breasts. A tear runs down my cheek. I curl up alone. The vice-principal is still there.

The most attention students pay me all week is when I draw a snake on the board and talk about its venom. I tell them if it bites you, you have seven minutes to live. The room is silent. No discipline problems for seven minutes, then all the hands go up asking what do you do in the seven minutes you have left. I demonstrate the venom going from the bite to the brain via the heart. Thirty faces, their ears and eyes glued to me. "A guest teacher, you are so fortunate.... now, how do you treat a guest...."

The cafeteria begins to exude its smells early in the morning. You take roll and make out the lunch count. I have never, in twenty years, eaten a cafeteria lunch. I don't eat at school at all. I refuse to participate in that way with the faculty. Or dress for the job. At noon the soda pop machine begins to send down the cans. I get out my book and sit on the arrangement of couches away from the table in a spot of sun. The room is so cold my lipstick is like ice.

Some days I want what the teachers get: fried chicken, chips, doughnuts, all covered with grease, sugar and salt. It looks so pretty and smells so good. Sometimes I reach out and grab some of the teachers' food and tuck it into my cheek before I can stop myself. I swallow it down and have it like a nice wad of what *everybody* else gets. Privation sits deep in me. And *never getting*. And never having what I want, even when I don't want it. Or knowing what it is.

It was the lamp that I wanted to throw. Something big: all

that ceramic base to break. I wanted the sound of the crash. The clock simply thumped against the wall. All night I regretted it. Killing an innocent thing. And then I had to call time. It was a number I never forgot. It would be time to get up and go back to the schools, time to go for my run, time to go to the gym, time to chop up something Flynn could chew and cook it, and prepare something for Sal, time to go to bed, time to make love. I'd have to spend five dollars to replace the clock. Time to buy another clock. Time to pay for my rebellion. It was the clock John gave me. I never wanted to go past John and come out the other side without him. But here I was. What I tried to resist for five years happened. I didn't get what I wanted. I had been afraid, this time, of not getting what I wanted. Before we broke up I feared losing John. If I didn't get to have him I was sure I would change into someone I didn't want to be. I learned that he destroyed any evidence that I was ever in his life. He threw out photos and gifts, books, sweaters, "any reminders," as he called them. I had never done that, I had boxes under the bed full of stuff from being with him. And the clock that sat staring at me on the bedside table.

Sal said he would buy a new clock. He hasn't yet. I call the time, or guess at it. After fifty years I know what time it is all the time. And what I feared would happen, happened. I am that person I didn't want to be without John. I pace myself all day, no one thing meaning more than another, since none of it's what I wanted anyway.

Every morning I paint my face and go out to sketch and tell stories to kids. I don't believe certain things work in the school system. I'm confused over all the things a child must learn and where to start, so I begin with stories. They listen and always get the meanings, and they learn to sketch people and animals, houses, and cars, and everything in their lives. There is always their resistance at first: they fear that they can't do it, and then they discover they can. They take their stories and pictures home. The assignment for homework is always, "go tell this to your parents and see if they understand it."

One teacher called to me across the parking lot one morning, "I envy you. You never carry bagsful of materials." My students keep drawing and teaching the other kids.

The colorless part of the day comes. I see it out my bedroom window. The weeping willow turns grey. The six o'clock sky pales and takes its time staying bleak. The yard is cold. I almost want to bring it in and warm it up. But it must stay there and take the winter, over and over again, each year, without a let up.

The news comes on. Sal uses the remote. Flynn comes in saying, "Kill him. They ought to just go in and kill him," about Saddam Hussein. I begin cutting the vegetables. The vice-principal must have her feet up by now, and that ex-boxer and three-year-old eyeing the microwave.

I Could Outrun Myself

All the fussing in the evening around here. Cutting onions, getting out the big iron skillet, bending down so my knees pop to find things in the vegetable bin at the bottom of the fridge. Sal on the periphery with his rules on how a woman should serve a man food to honor him. His father believing the same thing twenty miles away. If Sal wasn't kind and generous in other ways, I would refuse to serve him food. But here I am, family grown and gone, husband and ex out of the way, a father who chooses to eat out as often as possible or cook his own little microwave tray full of food cadavers. I wonder over my willingness. What would I do in its place? Is that why I fill up the evenings scrounging up a dinner, to avoid figuring out what to do with the time I'd have on my hands?

Right after John was out of my life, the evenings scared me. I'd come home, it was before Sal, and the time alone, after my job, gym, run, turned into a ringing in my ears, and an emptiness I'd never felt before; I'd get on the phone to fill up the silence. It was the silence, and being with myself that I was frightened of, for the first time in my life. After all the counseling I had done for clients who had broken up and felt this loneliness, I, now, was afraid of feeling it. I didn't want to be in my room. The tenants were over on their side of the house; Flynn out in the back. It was a houseful of lonely people. None of us wanting to talk to anyone else, keeping our distance because we were so close. Fighting for privacy. Even in the kitchen, sharing the stove, at night, we'd say as few words as possible. No one had anything to say that would help. No one meant anything to anyone. We were all strangers by choice and intended to keep it that way. Each would hide in our respective room and try to avoid one another. Flynn would come drooping in the door, itching to run into any of us so he could start a fight. Or, at least, provoke. He especially liked to ride the animal rights advocate activist who lived in the middle bedroom, "What would you do if a child and a dog were in the street and you had to make the choice to run over one?" That man stopped talking to us altogether. And that was fine with me. I had chosen him for his silence.

My room is on one side of the house, the tenants on the other. It's a big room with big windows that overlook the backyard. The tenants have smaller windows that face the side yard, where their big dogs sleep in dirt holes they dig anew weekly. I never have to see a soul walking about. I never had my pain interrupted by the presence of anyone living on the premises. And there was nothing but pain over losing John and not wanting to know it and having to keep knowing it. This knowing it was so continual that I could not escape, even in sleep. The dreams would chase me through the night and sometimes wake me up. Or I would wake up in the morning exhausted, not wanting to wake up. Not knowing which was worse, being awake and knowing it or being asleep and having it come in its own twists and distortions.

Then Sal came along. He entered my room, my bed, used up my time. Sat waiting for food. Talked his talk. Did what he did. Brushed his teeth, put on his pajamas. I'd never known a man who wore pajamas and never wanted to. It was simply a distraction, like a monkey in a cage watching some visitor at the zoo. My eyes followed him around to learn what he would do next. My ears adjusted to his voice: reluctantly. They still craved the sound of John's. And my nose. It was the sense of smell that tormented me more than the other senses. My olfactory lobes had imprinted on John's pheromones. Sal was sending the wrong ones my way. But I inhaled less directly around him. I didn't breathe him in the way I had breathed in John. I had withdrawals of the sense organs. They did not get what they wanted. They got Sal instead of John. It was all an irritation to me that I let happen because it gave me real tangible things to be angry over, annoyed by. It changed my pain to wrath, and my fears from ghosts to reality. I tried to tell Sal that this is what he meant to me. He would say he understood, his serious face pouting the way it does with yogi concentration and transcendence from animal man to a higher being. But, at unexpected times he'd get mad that I wasn't attentive, more considerate, in love.... with him. I would be in disbelief. "But I'm getting over John with you," I'd say. "You know that." He accused me of bluntness. "You just let people have it." He'd raise his voice. The Sicilian would come out. The yogi was nowhere evident. He sounded like I had with John. I became John. I would simply turn my back. I told Sal he was a combination of Perry Como and Mussolini. He ignored me.

I recalled John simply turning away from me. It didn't matter to him. And now it didn't matter to me that Sal was mad. He could take it or leave it. He was no one to me. It's what John used to say to me. "Then go away if you don't like it." I would say that to Sal. And he would go silent in fear. I remember that fear when John gave me the choice to accept him the way he was or leave. I went silent the way Sal does, and then began to cower like the lowest dog in a pack. I'd lick and grin, pretend I didn't mean it. Grovel on my belly, roll over and bare my neck. Sal did that with me. And I would say what John said to me, "Get some self-respect. Go away with pride. Just go away." Without knowing I was using John's lines until after I'd used them. There was no pleasure in the role reversal, as they would call it in counseling. Just curiosity. Perhaps John wasn't such a beast after all; perhaps he was just getting over the last woman by filling in with me. I understood his absence of joy in being with me, the way I had no real joy in being with Sal. The no participation in anything we did together. He was simply going along so he wouldn't be alone? And the same kind of giving in to sex as an emollient to the wounds. I felt used by John. Sal shrieks now and then, "Don't use me."

Recently I asked Sal, "Are you trying to do what I tried to do with John? Hang in there as long as possible, until I get so used to you that I begin to need you, and then you'll withdraw just so you can watch my pain." He said no.

I remember it was a plan that began to destroy my feelings for John. I pretended finally to only love him, hiding the hate and resentment. He began to take to me after a couple of years. He admitted it took him about three years to fall in love. Yet, he was lovesick over every new co-ed in his classes that would recognize the head of cock as he pressed it against his thin cotton fly at the podium in front of his class. He would come to me in the evenings, farting and burping, which was his natural state, as an over-eater and under-interested in anything but pornography on video tape. He bought an elaborate system for copying these tapes, slowing them down, and pausing them at critical moments. The little co-eds never knew. They only saw the Philosophy professor in front of his class spouting Sartre and, what's his name... Wittgenstein. Sometimes he'd have them read a short story about a whore who begged to be fucked to death, and still some coeds didn't get it.

Being Flynn's daughter, I was used to a man in private exposing all his perversions. It bonded (a counseling concept) me to him. At the end, he told me he liked me because he could be himself around me. That I knew his bad side. And that I was still there. And then I betrayed him. It was over one of his many women: I called her one night and told her that she was one of many. She was an academic type and listened like a sorority sister, drooling. I learned that night that women are not loyal to women. She called him as soon as I hung up. He never saw me after that. He sent me a note saying how ashamed he was to know someone as low as I was. When he passes me on the street now he turns the other way. My women friends say, "You really got to him somehow."

So, I bend a knee in my kitchen each night. I get down and pay homage to the vegetable bin, while Sal watches the news the way Alex used to, the way Wolfgang used to, the way John used to. And I prepare food to honor them as the male, each in turn. Using up my evenings, not discovering what else I would do instead.

I'm starting to like Sal, I recognize John in it. It's been fifteen months. We have repeated so many days of the same thing now. A kind of melding that scares me. I could probably connect with anyone, anything. A baboon. You get a rapport going. You feed an animal. It responds. You do it again. It responds again; pretty soon you have a "relationship" you look forward to because it fills up your time. Makes you feel useful. Gives you a certain amount of power, and there's pleasure in that. You don't feed the person. He reacts. You delight that he misses the feeding. Makes a ruckus over it. Shakes the bars of the cage. That fills you up with more importance. You get full of yourself. You mean something to this creature. You get in deeper.

I can make Sal go nuts now, the way John could make me go nuts. All I have to do is talk of breaking up. I talk about a future without him and he sulks. John used to do that to me. He'd say, "I think in the spring I'll go up into the Sierras. I miss the mountains," I'd say, "Why don't you ever talk about *us* going up into the mountains." He'd look over like he didn't understand. But he knew exactly what he was doing. He liked hurting me. I know that now, because I do that to Sal. He sets himself up for it. Anyone who wants you that much. You can't resist. John couldn't. I find I can't. I've learned that about myself. Before Sal, I never had a man who let me hurt him. He'd hurt me first.

Starched and Ironed

A starched and ironed lady in a starched and ironed car backed into my already battered and tattered bumper, leaving a big long black scratch, peeling off the silver paint, revealing the undercoating. She jumped out, or rather, carefully turned and placed her well-shod feet on the ground and lifted herself up and tried for anger, "Where in the world did you come from? why, I looked and nobody was there." I stood looking like a million dollars, all wrinkled and green. My bare feet in thongs were still stained from mowing the grass that morning. She kept the irate voice and permanent crease deepening between her brow. "You weren't there when I looked. What did you do, skiddle in there behind me. I didn't see anyone behind me, and let me tell you something, I checked my rear view mirror before backing out."

I matched her cranky tone, telling her her vices, "You have tinted windows and you're wearing dark glasses and my car is silver. You car sits up high, mine down low."

This took her a minute. She was one of those elderly wealthy ladies whose formal dress ages her even more. Someone able to afford that big gas hog of a Buick Le Sabre in off-white, or is it cream? Cream exterior, cream interior. She wore a cream scarf, if I recall, in some splash configuration making the fashion statement that she did not have to worry about getting dirty. Or, was it stark black and white. It seems to come back to me as polka dots, or an ilet fabric that costs a fortune. Her aura was all starched and ironed, the kind of garments you take to the cleaners. Her jewelry was the kind you change to fit each outfit. I'd been wearing the same pukka shells around my neck for two years, ever since I bought them for a dollar off a kid in Mexico.

Instead of being intimidated anymore by this kind of social status, instead of unreasonable respect, I told her that

I'd been there all along and kept honking, getting her to back down off her huffiness. That worked. Instead of maintaining her lofty place above things like this, she came back down to earth and began a tactic to keep it out of the hands of the insurance companies, telling me too much. "Once, when this happened, I reported it to my insurance company, and even though the damage was only six hundred dollars, my insurance went up six hundred dollars."

I jumped at that, "So, this has happened before."

Caught, she wiggled loose and dismissed it as so long ago she could hardly recall.

Addendum

Sometimes I tell my story in the classroom like a fable, and ask the little children questions: Why does this lady find someone to cook for every night? Why was the lady afraid of herself all alone in her bedroom at night after that man told her he didn't want her anymore and to go away? Why did the lady let the new man stay with her? How does that help her forget the other man? The little children understand more than any adults I've ever told. They have watched the big people in their lives and understand emotion. They had answers; "Because when someone tells you to go away, it makes you very very sad, and when you are very very sad, you get scared. And, "Because when you have to go away because someone tells you to, it's like they say they don't like you and never want to see you again, then you think something is wrong with you, and if everyone in the whole world told you that, you would get very very scared, and maybe try to get another friend real fast so you could forget about what the first person said," And, "She likes to cook for people because it reminds her of when she had a family and that's when she felt good, when you have no one to cook for and you are used to cooking for people, then you don't know what to do when you can't cook." And, "She could think of something else to do instead of cooking, but maybe she likes to cook."

My adult friends say, "You should not try to forget John by letting Sal take his place. You need to go out and do things, learn new things, be active." And professional counselors would say, "Do you have an exercise program daily? Exercise can get your mind off things, give you a fresh view. And write. Keep a daily log. Jot down your thoughts, and pretty soon you will see a pattern in your behavior. That's when you can make changes. First you have to recognize what you're doing wrong. And don't stay in your room, Attend lectures, films, plays, take a cooking class, dance, anything. Just stay active."

I tell my few women friends, "What do you do when you already run, write, and go out into the night to everything the community offers as a diversion from sitting in your room?"

They say, "Yeah, I know what you mean."

I say "I can outrun myself now. At fifty I could beat myself at thirty. I'm used to discomfort."

Coming Out the Other Side

I run one of my old runs. I tell Sal to drive up ahead and stop and wait for me to catch up and then drive ahead again, a mile or so at a time. We make it all the way home that way. I lean against his old wine-colored hoodlum car, a long, slinky thing, and pant, "I wonder why I used to think that was such a long run. It's not long at all. At 50 I could race myself at thirty and forty. I used to believe I was really running. It feels like nothing today."

Sal sits with the car radio on the sport station, white shirt like a choir boy, black slacks. I tell him he looks ethnic. I ask him if he saw that police car, "The cop asked if you were bothering me. He probably thought you were a rapist. You look dark in this car. Very suspicious." He barely hears me for the radio. He's used to my teasing. But I am concerned over why the old runs feel so short now. And he's the health researcher. I insist, "Why was this run so easy. I remember the pain, or the discomfort I used to feel at certain points, the inclines, the certain bends in the road that wouldn't stop. I'd hope for it to go down, and when I rounded the corner I'd see it still went up. Today, I didn't feel any of those things, no hopes or anticipations. Maybe I'm just used to the strain, the no comfort. I used to look for a let up on it before.... I remember that. It was always a test with myself. Now I just run. What do you think?"

Sal says "I don't know."

"But you have to know," I say. "Am I stronger at fifty than I was at twenty, thirty, and forty? Does that happen? And why?"

He says, "Do you feel stronger? There are a number of reasons, from metabolic factors to hormonal."

I say, "I think it's attitude. I'm used to being miserable. When I was younger I sought comfort. Now I don't. I think that's it. I wasn't expecting a release of tension. Any relief at all."

Flynn at Home

Bones

Flynn falls and breaks a leg. It's not long after he said he was better off than Mama, his last words, "At least I can walk." It was the cement ramp Alex poured twenty years ago connecting the driveway with the walkway. An architect friend visited and said the ramp was too steep, that the County would never pass it. And he laughed. It was Alex's way, to do things like that. Flynn forgot to step up and went over, hit the side of the driveway with his femur and couldn't get up. It was eight in the morning. No one was home but one tenant who heard his call for help. She called the paramedics. When I came back I got the news and went out to see him being wheeled into surgery. I held his hand, pressed back his snow white hair, thinking he would not come out alive. The surgeon was a jock, young strong, muscular. Later, Sal, who knows all the doctors in town by business association, said he was an athletic doctor. "If you're an athlete..." We had a few words before he disappeared with Flynn. He kept looking down at my tights. I had come straight from the gym.

The invisible predator had Flynn by the leg now. I'd watched it eating away at him since fall, and in six months time Flynn was running out of strength. Until he falters, fails, and falls. Eight years he had walked that ramp, adjusted to the slant, made it to his car and drove off for his cafe time. On the way down, before he hit the ground, his life passed before his eyes, time stood still, fear prevailed. "I didn't know if I'd ever get up. If I'd be killed or not."

Flynn comes out of surgery just fine. "Tough old bird," goes through the family. Even mama chuckles. Flynn, once again, much stronger than we all thought. Than he led us to believe. We all stand around feeling a bit foolish for the drama of our worry and the romantic pictures we held of his weak and feeble heart....

In the hospital room I have some impatience. I ask, "How can you be so afraid to fall? I fall on my runs once in awhile, step in a hole or something, skin my knees on the pavement, get gravel in my palm. It's no big deal. I just get up and keep running."

Contempt in his rooster-cocked head. His eye speck, looking to peck. "When you get old you can't take a fall," he eases out the words so it's the opposite of sassing back and snapping off my head, which is what he feels like doing. My flippancy settles on his face as pure resentment. Over here on the other side of old age, I chirp. I know it's short-lived, but I still have a little bit of life left even though Flynn doesn't. I can tell he hates me for it.

"I used to like to fall ice skating and roller skating. You just roll and slide across the floor and laugh." I flaunt my "youth." *I deserve to live even though he may be dying.* I have the same mean streak Flynn had, as long as he was fine. He had no sympathy for anyone else.

He says of his mother now, "I'd never been old. I didn't know what she was going through. No one would take her so she had to go to a rest home."

"Why didn't you take her?" I ask.

"I didn't want to put myself out." He blinks, like Montgomery Clift, as if he is just waking up. I wonder at my need to egg him on, to make him fighting mad. To challenge him. To rub his face in his old age. No one else in the family does it. They all coo and cater or stay away altogether. The sharp talk is what our family does. We never learned to comfort in formal phrases. We tease, ridicule, use sarcasm, heckle and peck each other in line. The barbed comment was taught to us to get someone back on their feet. Flynn was one of the teachers. Mama the other.

And now does Flynn really think I'll enter his hospital room with sweet words and reassurances and daughterly concerns. I survived. So can he. I remember the Ishi tribe. That book about the tribe that laughs when their old people fall down to die. I didn't understand it at the time.

I tell my sister over the phone. "I feel like walking into

his room with a mirror and holding it up so he can have the perfect person to understand him. He keeps complaining that no one can know how he's feeling because none of us have experienced what he is experiencing."

"Maybe you should," she says in her quiet way, always reserved. "That's how they rehabilitate criminals." Then she asks, "Are you going to be okay...if he...uh, dies?"

I use logic. I say, "Yes, he's had all of his life and half of mine. That's enough for anybody. A life and a half? She listens for hysteria, the telephone line is still. She waits for me to go on. I sound too hard. She lets me be. I know what she believes. That Flynn has been my burden to bear and the whole family is grateful that I assume the job so they don't have to. And they wouldn't anyway. He would be off dying somewhere and we would be that kind of a family, letting him. I alone am willing to do the job. I will let him die at my house, in my life. The way I let him live all over the top of me. She is gentle in her listening to me bewail my lot. It's what she is able to give—*understanding*. The same thing Flynn wants. In another mood, when I haven't run too far or worked out too hard or taught too long, I enter Flynn's room with some humanity. I want to take him a pack of cigarettes and a cup of coffee, a white bread lunchmeat sandwich, and let him be the jaunty man he was just last fall. It's no good to see even your enemies stripped down to a hospital gown, oxygen tube under the nose, looking twitchy about staying alive, what—another few months? Maybe a year? Flynn has already done the damage that has shortened his life to only seventy-eight. Longevity runs through those English veins. The women in that lineage live to a hundred with their men not far behind, unless they smoked. Their lungs are weak. And Flynn and his father and his father before him were smokers. It was the coming of age. The male rite into manhood. You weren't a man unless you had a bag of Bull Durham hanging out of your chest pocket and a pinched, flat cigarette stuck to your bottom lip, and your eye in a permanent smoke-avoiding squint.

Flynn in hospital garb is how all the men in his family ended up. Louis says, "Ignorance." Sounding like Mama's people. Louis is an alcoholic since being a Marine.

I say, "Custom" How could Flynn be another way. His identity was tied up in all that smoking, coffee, and meat. He'd have been castrated giving it up. None of the men ever drank booze. They were church people. God-obedient. And God never mentioned coffee and cigarettes, except in Revelations. Flynn pointed out early to me, the place where it said there would be smoke pouring from the mouths of people in the last days of sin just before the second coming of Christ. Flynn marvelled over the prophet who got a reading on that in the future.

I tell Mama over the phone, "Sal's parents offered to visit Flynn in the hospital.... .and he said he couldn't have a lot of people 'pouring in on' him.... Said it wasn't like you and your friends who make a social thing out of visiting each other, sending cards and flowers. He just wants out. Can't take his mind off himself for a second. Milks and works and ekes out every ounce of meaning about his broken leg and going down hill and pending death...Why can't he ever just relax and sit back and not try to *survive* all the time?"

Tools

Before Flynn came to the nursing home to convalesce, he said he would be happy to stay on I.V.s and take pills and never to have to eat again. That his teeth hurt and "It's too much trouble when you have no appetite." Then they took him off the I.V. and sent him to the nursing home. I followed the big lift truck all the way over from the hospital. There was Flynn, in hospital gown, perched in his wheel chair way up high inside the truck, and the truck with a window in the back so he could look out. He'd turn and smile back at me and I had to laugh. He did look funny, little Flynn being transported from the hospital to the nursing home in this great big lift with a nice good old driver who knew just how to push levers and buttons and raise and lower Flynn in the wheelchair. In fact he was so good at it that I lost Flynn at the entrance to the home. By the time I parked my car Flynn had disappeared down the corridor and I ran into the driver who was coming out, I said, "Where'd he go?" The driver pointed down the hallway, but not before responding to my reaction to the number of debilitated elderly in the hallway. I made a face of grimness. He laughed. He had made deliveries like this for years. It was nothing to him. My face reminded him of his professionalism. He waved goodbye.

Flynn had been checked in and assigned a bed and was *in* bed by the time I found him…And already complaining about the aides who were ignoring him because, he said, "They can't understand a word I'm saying. They don't speak English. A guy could die in here and they wouldn't care. They walk right out when you try to communicate with them. All I wanted was my urinal over here where I could reach it and she just walked away. I had to ring the nurse…."

Before his days in the nursing home are over Flynn, will have recovered enough to be "starving to death in here," and

267

knowing it this time. When his health broke, he starved willingly. Now, I visit and listen to him complaining that he can't get enough to eat. I look at his tray. Pudding, cake, pasta, canned carrots, etc. He says, "A guy can't eat that slop. It has no taste. No salt. And I can't chew it anyway." I assure him I will go to the head nurse and the nutritionist and find out what is going on.

"They have you on a vegetarian diet," I tell him.

"Vegetarian?" He lets it sink in. "What in the world would they do that for," He sits thin as a stick under his smooth hospital blanket.

I explain that because he is taking protein supplements that Louis and I ordered, the doctor took him off meat so he wouldn't burn out his kidneys. When Flynn throws a mild fit I agree with him. The absurdity of that. The protein supplement is not enough for a starving man, and Flynn's intake of meat would be so small, with those painful false teeth, that to put him on a diet of any kind is a serious oversight by our new organic doctor, with a name like "Crack Pot" or "Quack." I go on to tell him that the nutritionist is upset, too. She has told me that my father is a high risk patient, weighing only 92 pounds. That he could die at that weight trying to live only on vegetables that he won't even eat. She herself would let him "graze." Let him eat *anything* he wanted just to put on weight. But that her hands are tied. She cannot override a doctor's orders.

Flynn takes this tale with wide-eyed alarm. It is the epitome of what has gotten him attention from birth: feeding. Will he eat or won't he. Will he starve to death or won't he. Now a nursing home staff is all awhir about it. His all-time lowest-weight ever is the buzz of the nurses' station. The row of old people perk up with the news that Flynn is down to 90 pounds and might die. I tell Flynn I will go get him something to eat. He has told everyone he is *starving to death*." And this time he is not crying wolf. He is.

A nice young nurse stops me at the nursing station and tells me that she will bring Flynn anything he wants. She says she feels so sorry for him. I say, "Anything hot and juicy and seasoned." We can smell the tray coming as she nears the room. *Potatoes and gravy.*

Flynn almost sighs in satisfaction, and slurps it up with his impeccable table manners. One succulent bite at a time, taking out his teeth and laying them aside; I try not to look.

The next time that I come to visit Flynn there is a dance troop of little girls. Flynn has been wheeled over to the game room. I find him among a sea of grey and white and blue heads. He is the only one whose spine hasn't curved over yet; still the straight back Mama married! And who still retains a mobile face that changes expressions to show feelings. And the only one whose eyes are as round and open as sunflowers in summer. All the other old people are curled forward, eyes closing, mouths drooping, hearing aids plugged in and expressions set in one emotion they have settled on permanently, their faces locked in varying versions of the mask of tragedy. They seem already dead, just not buried.

Flynn sees me come in and smiles then turns back and cranes his neck from the back row to see the little lithe bodies in leotards jump and twirl, leap and cavort. I look at the old faces to see how they register this moving group of youth and see nothing but those solid scowls. Only Flynn lights up, alert and ready to turn to me and laugh if they show clumsiness or awkwardness. Mama was a ballet dancer when he met her at 16. She did all this, backbends, the splits, stag leaps. I can see Flynn's knowledge play on his face.

The little girls' eyes avoid the audience of aged faces, except for one fat girl who must already identify with being trapped in her flesh. I can imagine the girls will be the way I was after that first visit to this world of the elderly, talking among themselves about the audience's absence of response to their dancing. The old people just sitting there. They will no doubt try to mimic the faces, turning down their mouths and haunting their eyes, trying to look vacant and dull. The prettiest girl was the most distant. A smugness and severe judgment oozed from every pore. She was glad not to be old and never planned to be. Sure of it. She reminded me of some part of myself, believing somehow, *I'll be old but not this way.*

After the performance the attendants come in to get their patients. I take ahold of Flynn's wheelchair asking, "Do you want to or do you want me to, wheel you." He gives me permission. And as we go out he gestures toward the old bobbing white head in front of him and says, "She looks like Aunt Osie...she had white hair like that." One old man grabs ahold of an old lady's chair and she turns around and lashes out at him with a growl. Like naughty kids the old people leave, daring anyone to bump into them. One woman begins her permanent social response to the crowd, "Go to hell, go to hell." Another begins hollering for help, like a peacock. "Heeellllppp." I ask her if I can help. She goes quiet and then groans, "There's nothing you can do," and goes back to hollering for help. A passing nurse smiles at me. Flynn laughs. He tells me they are all nuts. That he can't wait to get out of here.

Flynn marvels, "Tools to put on my shoes and socks." He shakes his head. "I can't reach down anymore so they give you this special tool so you can learn to pull up your socks and put on your shoes." Flynn is once again lined up with all the other old people watching the nurses. The heartbeat of the Home. People with jobs, still performing for society. Not yet sluffed off like dead cells...

I say, "Let's go out on the patio. The air in here smells bad. Like urine and pea soup." He has wheeled himself into the hallway to get away from the loud groans of his new ninety-two year old roommate. He says the old man just lies there and you can hear him all over the Home. I ask what happened to cause so much pain and Flynn tells me he broke his leg. "Same as I, but he got infection in his, they think. They're going to take him back to the hospital." Flynn, by contrast, begins to take hope again. He says, "I should have made a motorized chair before I broke my leg, just in case. He contemplates the possibility of being able to walk again. His mind races around devising ways to innovate what used to be ordinary actions. "I'll just get a string for my socks. To pull them up. That's what they use here, like suspenders.

Flynn's broken leg is the first *real* thing that has ever been wrong with him, *something he could put his finger on*. He is now so taken up with the phenomenon of having a real foe instead of his psychological ghosts, his psychosomatic symptoms, that he thrives. He has real sutures he can *see*. An actual place where his hurt is coming from. And it is the first time the family can respect him and give some concern. We can all sympathize with a broken leg. We could never sympathize with his personal bogeymen who could only be assuaged by our doing something for him about them that we didn't want to do and that didn't help anyway. Now he needs only assistance getting from his wheelchair to his bed. Before he needed assistance in not being scared of his own head. And we didn't like lying to him to make his fears go away....

Remembering the chill they called walking pneumonia when his car broke down, when he was in the hospital the last time.

Soon enough the nursing home wants Flynn *out*. Six weeks is all he qualified for, by the insurance. The head nurse says he is ready to go home. He has told them that I took him to Bob's Big Boy on his trial run and how he walked in by himself with his walker. I grow embarrassed trying to keep him in. He can't walk alone yet. I see myself trying to do things for him I don't have time to do. The nurse assures me that he will get "home care."

Flynn tells me that he wants to get in his car and drive into town as soon as he gets home. I tell Sal this and Sal tells me to tell his doctor, and to have him restricted. I simply tell Flynn he can't walk, is weak, shouldn't drive. As soon as I bring him home, he makes his way, like a turtle, pushing his walker ahead of him and gets in his car and goes putt, putt, putting down the street. I look at Sal; I feel some real pride for Flynn's spunk. In less than a month he will be on one crutch and soon after that back on both feet. Everyone will be surprised at his recovery...

Naked Chest

The old Persian tomcat dies in my room. Like Flynn, he comes to me at the end, holes up on my bed, in my room. For two weeks he talks to me to tend him. He knows it's the end before I do. As with Flynn, I do everything I know to prevent his death. I spend a hundred dollars on tests and cures. The old tom lies around waiting. First behind the big TV, next, in my closet. Finally on the floor by my bed. Sometimes on top of me while I sleep, I call my daughter. It's her cat. The last of the family pets, "He's only twelve, that's not old." She begs me to do anything. "An I.V." I draw the line, trying to keep perspective. It's only a cat. I forget who's human and who's not. I take the same urgent energy I have generated for Flynn, and distribute it to the cat. But in vain. In spite of all the sweet talk, brushing and vitamins and supplements, iron and liver, tuna and salmon and fresh fish heads, the cat gets a faraway look in his eye one night. He doesn't respond to petting. Won't eat. Looks distracted and irritated. I feel bones under his thick coat. Ribs that are tiny. And tiny pelvic bones. I try to sleep, but the restless cat wakes me. I take the once big tomcat to bed and hold him under the comforter to quiet and warm him. His bones are cold. Only his ears radiate heat, Is it fever?

The cat lies still against my naked chest. I've held a lot of sick or lost animals there, in belief that the sound of my heartbeat will comfort them. Hairless gophers dug up by a backhoe, baby rabbits from the nursery school, stray cold kittens tossed in the creek by some other mother, and always baby sparrows, featherless, fallen from their nests. I was the one all the neighborhood kids brought their findings to. "The temperature's right," I used to tell them when the animal would disappear into my shirt.

The tomcat sleeps, then wakens. Like Flynn, he's vigilant.

Doesn't want to miss the signals. Wants to stay ready…to let life out. I doze and wake, hold the cat and try to calm him, and finally let him pull away. He cries out and crawls out onto the bedside table and knocks over the phone, driven by instinct, mouth pulled back, baring his teeth, breath shallow. The world has fallen away as he listens to the call from the other side. He slides to the floor with a haunting look I never thought a cat could have, and stumbles toward the TV table. This is where he will do it. He knows. There is something in the angle of his head. As if he is following instructions. I sit up in bed and watch. Sal covers his face with a pillow. He curses. He won't accept it, that the vet didn't save the cat. That he, himself didn't do more to save the cat. That the death of the cat cannot be stopped. I shout at him. *"This is… life… death is… grow up… I thought you were a yogi."*

He hides in disbelief under the feather pillow I bought for him, a year ago saying then, "And what about the poor goose?" So against kapok and polyurethane he was.

The cat weaves, making a thin line of a form, and attempts to leap onto the TV table. He falls back, gets up, steadies himself and with all his will, leaps up on the table, finds the long slim place behind the TV that fits his body. I go to him, put my hand on him. His shallow loins heave. He turns toward me to do something. To help him. A yowl comes out. And then a growl. I see that it is hard work, to give up, give in; but he must. It is written somewhere inside him. He pants, cries out. And then he lies his head down and a deep sound crawls out. Yellow urine makes a pool on the white table. There is no heartbeat under my hand. The eyes go blank and the mouth stays in its fanged gape. I say, "He's gone. Dead." Sal rears up and curses. He doesn't get up and look. I feel like a midwife. I call my daughter. It is three A.M. I leave the cat there and try to sleep. I will bury him tomorrow. I sleep fitful, wondering if this is a preparation for Flynn's death. I think of Flynn at the nursing home, skin and bone. The nutritionist said he was at risk. She had never seen a patient that skinny.

I tell Flynn about the cat the next day. He listens like a farm boy. A cat means nothing to him really. He used to have to drown bagsful of kittens.... But the subject is death. I tell him after a point you go kind of blank and just watch, that you feel dull...

Flynn tells me he was there at his father's bedside when his father died. "He reached up and took ahold of my hand and squeezed it real hard, and then turned his head to the side and was gone. Just like that. A sound came out. I waved the doctor away. He wanted to come in and keep him alive...but he was in so much pain, Dad was. He had cancer you know. The lungs. Before that I didn't think fathers could die."

When I leave the nursing home, I weave down the corridor between dozens of old people in wheelchairs, caved-in people, grey people. People with no movement to their faces, only the eyes following me. I wonder if Flynn will ever get out of there. Will Flynn reach up and hold my hand with his thin paw that now looks huge on the end of his stick arm, when it is his turn? Will he squeeze real hard and then turn his head to the side and die, half-embarrassed, like his quiet, reserved, dignified dad did. The Englishman still stiff-lipped to the end. And will I wave the doctor away?

Later

No, Flynn doesn't want any visitors. Sal's parents ask. "I can't have people pouring in here." Flynn's not like Mama. Mama's social life includes hospital visits now. Cards and flowers.

But Flynn is fighting for his life and the nursing home is a place to curse while you're there. A place to get out of, not relax in and take visitors. The live flowers I took Flynn the first time he was in the hospital, died. He let them. I came back the next day and the pot was dry and the flowers fallen over. He never notices the needs of other things. And the few cards that came, he told me to take them away. I can't have a lot of stuff around the room."

His mother lived in a rest home for ten years before she died at 96. She kept pictures of her children and grandchildren and greatgrandchildren on her bedside table. All of us there in her room and none of us willing to take her to our homes. I tell Flynn, "I'll bring you home right now if you want. You don't have to stay here, you know." He chooses to stay until he learns to walk again.

"A beautiful woman comes in and tells me she will bring some paints and wants me to paint her a picture." He lights up a little. Yes, I saw her. Not beautiful, but young with a big smile and a way of holding and touching the old people and finding out what their hobbies are. Flynn sits as erect as a woodpecker with hair like a shock of feathers, sharp-beaked and alert, as if he's spied an insect when he tells me this.

That night I lie over on my side in fetus position and try to sleep, but remember the termites drilling holes in my beams, eating my wood and in closer, inside my mouth, one tooth, microorganisms, they're eating it away, too, no matter how hard my efforts at renewal there's this constant destruction. Always the chewing, chewing, chewing away at me and my house. And now my cat, buried, is being chewed up by mouths underground, just under my bedroom window.

Like Flynn did once, I still believe, "Fathers can't die."

Hard

Flynn has his toenails trimmed: Not an easy job. One requiring heavy duty clippers. Hard to imagine Flynn and all these other old people in this convalescent home with a substance so hard it needs pruning sheers and a specialist to use them and the State of California and even the Federal Government to pay for it. Their old claws curling under and around like the wayward horns of mountain goats and big horned sheep. Attacking them like mutinous pirates. Everything turning on them at the end. These weapons growing back into their toes, as meek and confused as their brains have gotten. Delicate little caved-in ladies in feather-light dusters and baby-crib booties of flannel in which hard-as-nails toenails live, growing, growing, growing. Pushing out keratin, unruly grey-green material pouring from each old gnarled toe, still making its presence as a defense implement.

In the small, self-contained world of the nursing home, Flynn can shine. He is one of the twelve per cent that is still conscious, articulate, wide awake, and "three steps ahead of us," one nurse said. And added, "Even though he can't walk."

Louis and I take some pride in Flynn, our father, among all the old people. But we still criticize him relentlessly behind his back about his ignorance over nutrition and his belief in doctors. We get almost giddy over the possibility of his health improving when we hire an organic doctor who treats Flynn with supplements. Flynn takes these vitamin and mineral supplements like medication. The nurse comes down the hallway and administers them in the same little cuplets she uses for the traditional medication. Flynn drinks them down without resistance. We have told him he has a new doctor. Breaking his leg has broken his spirit just enough to get him to try any cure. And to attempt to trust us. As he begins to thrive and heal and begins to walk again with the help of his physical therapist, he takes credit for it. He says, "A guy can't just sit and deteriorate. I'd have gotten better anyway." He doesn't know the extent of supplements we've ordered. He knows them by, "The big blue pill," or the "Little bitty pink one, or "That great big one, I'll choke on that." So the nurse crushes it up with the back of a spoon and mixes it with applesauce. Louis and I watch in surprise. She's on our side. We beam. At home that night, Sal praises us for the health we bring to Flynn, whether he knows it or not. I say, "*But I don't even want to keep him alive.*" I say it because everyone who has heard about Flynn' s broken leg has hinted to me that there is finally an end in sight and I will soon be free of a father who has been too much and too long in my life. I have let them influence me, doubting that perhaps something is *wrong* with me for taking Flynn in and trying to *save him* through one trial after another. "An old pattern?" they ask. And I all but say, "Am I supposed to let him die and smile watching?"

Therapy is full of this kind of justice for child molesters. Nothing short of a horrible painful death. "Throw him out," they said. "Who cares what happens to him. He doesn't deserves anything...." No one has said, "Even though he molested you he is still your father and a human being, and it is okay to be nice to him. That's all over now and there is really no joy in revenge. And it is certainly not healing to kill your enemies..." They have all cried for blood...

Sal shushes me now. "Don't..." He can't go on. He knows I don't mean it. My actions prove differently. He understands that I am "under a lot of pressure." That Flynn is not a nice old man who is easy to handle.

I say, "What if he lives another twenty years. I see the supplements have already given him a vitality he didn't have before. They have wakened up a system that was thriving on drugs for over fifty years. And now he has a "ravenous" appetite. His word. His head has cleared and his thinking is too sharp. He is like a lurking moray eel in his room.

Tundra

If this were the tundra and Flynn a caribou, his broken leg would have caused him to be eaten by wolves. But it's my life he's broken his leg in, and the Oakview Nursing Home, which he calls Oakie View, he's convalescing in. So he is protected and more, nursed back to walking, being a once again upright man. I drive out after work to see Flynn. In fact I see him more than when he was at home. He would be out feeding himself at some counter, or I'd come home and go right to my room. We'd go a week at a time not seeing eachother. Now I enter his room after making my way through all the old people lined up at the nurses station and find Flynn's room empty. I go back up the hallway, and I hear a voice from the line of old people in their wheelchairs who sit all day watching the only life in the place, the working nurses at their station, answering the phone, meeting visitors. It's where everything is happening that is current and worldly, otherwise they have their four walls and other patients, and the nothingness of waiting for the end. I look and see Flynn. He is lined up along with all the others. And I didn't recognize him. Just another old white-haired, skinny-necked elderly in a wheelchair. I laugh. "What are *you* doing out here?" I want to add, "I thought you'd have too much pride to join these people."

He says, "It gets awful lonely in my room. And I want to keep an eye on these nurses. I came up here because they wanted to take my wheelchair away from me and make me walk up here. Now a guy who's just broken his leg can't be expected to walk all day long. It was that nurse right there. The one with the red hair. She thinks if she takes my chair I'll exercise more. And she didn't get permission from the head nurse. I just checked with her on that.... "

I want to say, "But when we first came here we were horrified at this row of old people lined up with nothing to do but watch the nurses station all day. And now you have willingly become one of them. Where is your perspective. How can you not see that you are now like them?"—wanting Flynn to retain his Self to the end.

So to Speak...by Some Definitions

Flynn's listening all the time for any hint that we might slip and say the word "dying." I say, "Wear those clothes I bought for you while you're...."

He finishes, ".... still alive?"

I lie, "No, I meant while you're around here. Don't save them for.... *what*? What are you saving them for?"

"They're my good clothes...in case I go somewhere."

"Where? Where will you go? You're here. Wear them here. They're your clothes for everyday wear," I can feel a tension in my voice of desperation. Wanting to scream, "*Wear them before you die.*" But I go on in a teacher's voice, giving an example, instead, of Rose, his mother-in-law whom he doesn't want to be like. My mother's mother who was known as an eccentric. How she went around in near-rags all the time, just some "bodice" as she called a blouse, and an old pair of pants. Except for her breasts like a pillow under her shirt, she could have been mistaken for a man. I tell Flynn to remember how Rose saved all her nice dresses for a time when she would have to dress up. How she used to say, "in case I go somewhere," And I finish with, "She died and never *wore* them. She never went anywhere."

Flynn flinches. I breeze past the forbidden word. I say, "It's as though she put her real life on hold, getting by, saving all those clothes for a life she thought would begin, but never did." Flynn does not respond. He sits, despondent, on the stool across the counter where he has positioned himself for my company. I never get used to this expectation from Flynn, that I will be his connection to the world, and he will warm himself against my tales of being out there in it. When I come home, I never intend to tell Flynn anything. And if I do, my words turn to anger or criticism. Today I watch him sidle up to the counter with the sole purpose of listening to me fill him up with *news*, and I comment on the old shirt he has worn for three solid weeks. I go over the history of all the clothes I've bought for him. "The ones when I took you to Hawaii, remember? And the ones for your birthday last summer. Remember. All those pretty shirts. Where are they?" I know he hoards them.

§

When he was in the hospital I went through his room and cleaned. I was curious to find all the nice clothes neatly folded and stashed in a half dozen suitcases stacked along one wall. And socks. All those white tube socks. Brand new. And shorts and t-shirts. I thought of all the old men who don't like to bother to change their clothes. Or take a bath. Does maintaining and grooming lose its meaning when men get beyond jobs and women? And they begin to turn the color of their habitat. I see them sitting against storefronts watching the movement of the mainstream, even feeling the breeze of it as we whiz by, not even looking at us anymore. I remember the gold miners in Nevada when Flynn took me through Searchlight and Scullbone, and all the other oddly named ghost towns as a child. They never changed their clothes. Those old men. And now right under my nose, Flynn has become one of them.

Sal calms me down. He says it is perfectly natural for people to have clothes set aside for dress up. It's what people do. That he isn't not wearing them to make me angry. "He's normal, just calm down."

I buy Flynn a wicker rocking chair, I set it out in the sun on the front patio, I say, "Here, try this," Flynn steps right up and sits down. He leans back and rocks, I laugh. He smiles, as if it's a joke. I go about my business and when I look again. Flynn is asleep, nodding off like any old man. The sun beats down. A spring sunshine.

The old tom has come to sleep in the shade of the rocker right beside Flynn. Together the old males, both about the same age, nap all afternoon. When Flynn wakes up and comes in the house he is worried. He says he fell asleep in the middle of the day. He goes on about being afraid he'll start sleeping all the time, and one day never wake up. I say, "What are you going to do? Stay awake for the rest of your life?"

Again Sal calms me down. "The rocker causes the liver to sway back and forth, and in so doing, it releases poisons and as they leave the blood stream and collect in the lower colon ready to be expelled, a relaxation takes over the body..." or some such explanation (an Italian nutritionist's baloney).

That night I dream about wicker. That rocking in a wicker chair causes cancer for women. Their uteruses swing back and forth and there's something in the woven reeds, treated and painted that is picked up by the body. Flynn comes through the living room saying, "I wonder how they make a wicker chair. Look at this, and he rubs his hand over the intricate interlocking structure of the surface of the rocking chair, marvelling, before going out the door.

As the day takes brightness and gathers heat, Flynn comes back in the house looking for someone to tell. In the light of a spring day he tells of toils and turmoil in the dark of night. "I fell over last night and cut my finger."

I am giving the parakeets a scoop of seed and opening the blinds so they can watch the wild birds come and go from a feeder outside the window. Without looking at Flynn, I say, "Was is fun?"

"Oh, a barrel of laughs." I turn to show concern. I look. Sure enough there is a bandage on one of his fingers. I look at Flynn now and listen. "I got up, and it's the strangest feeling to be off balance, and there's nothing you can do about it. I just kept leaning like this, like something was pulling on me, and I fell. And cut my finger."

I say, "I've done that, almost. Got up in the middle of the night half asleep, leaning and veering off and crashing into the door or catching myself against the wall. Especially if I've gone for an extra long run the day before. My body pitches around in the dark. It's *normal*." I can hear Flynn exhale as if he is impatient to be understood. *As if I still don't understand what he is trying to say.*

In this family we never say, "Daddy is getting old" or "Mama is crippled." We still hold out that it's a temporary thing, a condition that will pass and we'll remain the family we always were. Admitting things is hard to do in this family. Denial always got us somewhere. We ignored the facts, and in that way, "overcame" them, so to speak, by some definitions. It didn't decapitate us. John called it willful ignorance.

I pretended Flynn wasn't doing what he was doing. All those years. Mama walked on her deteriorating hip joint all those years, pretending she wasn't crippled. I recall her slight groans of pain all through my childhood. While nothing physical was ever wrong with Flynn, yet he complained all the time of one ailment or another, Mama just twisted and lurched in silence until she hit it wrong, and then the almost imperceptible groan and sigh. Later, in my training as a therapist, I learned that martyrs are not heroines—they get a "payoff."

If Flynn had withered on the bone all at once before my eyes I'd run screaming and tearing out my hair. Instead, it happened gradually, so that I tend him as if he's still Flynn and not this nightmare of himself.

As I watch Flynn grow old and die, am I learning how to do it? His example is all I've got. When I squint my eyes I picture his face doing that. When I make light of it, his pending death, they are his words, the humor he has taught me. When I catch a glimpse of his face from the kitchen I think Flynn is watching television.

He is only watching the drama in his own head in the middle of the living room in the middle of the day. I turn away and busy myself. His look was intense. A concentration. Sal calms me, "Be glad for what you've gotten out of your life." He speaks with consternation, which is a look of constipated concentration on him.

We all laughed at Mama in her little battery-operated cart called Amigo. No one ever said, "It means she can no longer walk." Neither Flynn nor Mama can project themselves very far anymore. They can't walk and Flynn can't yell. His voice is as mellow as his own father's was. The words to the song, "My Mother can't dance and my father can't rock and roll," come to me. I go around singing it.

§

Flynn looks like he wants to bawl like a baby. But he's a man and won't. He quotes Robert Service about when life gets tough and you can keep your dignity.... you're a man, or some such pre-emotional era talk, for men. How can life do this, first your strength, then your only means of movement and power...too cruel. Flynn's alternator goes out. He breaks down a block from the house and comes in soaked from the rain, and stricken-eyed.

It's a life and death struggle now, to the end. A broken generator or alternator or transmission, was nothing to him a few years ago. Just a year ago, in fact, he put in a new carburetor and adjusted his points and changed his spark plugs, cleaned the cable to the battery, and thought nothing of it, except to curse in jest because he was a mechanic for fifty years and lets it be known he hates working on cars.

He staggers in through the front door desperate around the hairline, like an old cowboy whose horse broke his leg and he just had to shoot him. I look up from my place at the stove at that hour of the day and say, "What happened to you? You look awful."

He has a way of shifting his shoulders to get ready to lay it all out in words, but he pants now, and has to lean against a chair to catch his breath. I go to him and pull out the chair by the wall heater. He doesn't sit down. He winds up all his strength and tells in disbelief about his car quitting on him. He could be a savage who just tangled with a tiger and escaped death. His chest heaves with exhaustion. I say, "Well, Alex can help you fix it."

He rears his head up and with all the vehemence he can muster in his weakened state saying he wouldn't let Alex work on his car if he had to walk for the rest of his life, "He's no good at fixing cars."

"Well, then Louis can come over and fix it."

"Oh, he doesn't know anything. I wouldn't let him touch it." Flynn's flair of anger is deep-seated. These two younger men are capable of putting in a new alternator. Too capable. And they are young enough to have learned the metric system so they can work on the new cars. Flynn was outdated, finally, as a mechanic. He's from the old school. He has a special contempt for all the new little mechanics with their computers and whistle-clean shops, as if they are afraid to get a little grease on their hands, and listen to an engine with their naked ear and tell what's wrong by the sound of it.

I remember all the new little feminist professors replacing the old style professors when I was with John. John was from the old school, too. An old male teaching in the old way. You read a piece of literature and talk the old jargon. The new professors were teaching a new jargon, a new way of seeing literature. More technical, less left up to some old male's interpretation. John used to come home with a scowl on his face, spewing nasty words, having to do with women and their brains. On a hiring panel, he kept as many women out as possible.

I feel lonely for that kind of man I used to know. It comes upon me later, after Flynn has calmed down and settled on his strategy. He says he will go analyze the problem tomorrow and put in a new alternator. That he has no choice.

Lonely and a little sad. What became of that man I used to know who knew things and was strong enough for me to lean on. Flynn is just a wisp of his former self. Erased by time, and until he moves, you don't notice that he's there. He's small and his clothes are the color of the walls and furnishings. And Alex. I used to lean on Alex, He knew everything I didn't know—politics, history, philosophy, mechanics, anything that was complicated. He could talk for hours on subjects. And both men are still here. But they are not the men I used to know. Every once in awhile some fear would creep in over that. I want to go find the Flynn I knew, and the Alex. And talk and laugh and be the way we used to be. As each in turn faded, I had to fill in and be them. *I became my own man.* And the trade-off filled me so that I am no longer receptive to them.

I have to hide the disgust I feel when I deal with them now. Is it their fault? I see some disgust in some young men's eyes over me. As if I've grown old on purpose just to repel them. As if I wanted these wrinkles as a lesson in non-sexuality. As if I'm saying "See, you can't make love to me." As if I'm living evidence of the female letting them down. I make them nervous. They have no use for me, they in their prime and driven by mating instincts. Flynn and Alex leave me with the same detachment. A permanent estrangement. They don't apply anymore to my life. I am only their caretaker.

Once a month I remember John with every cell. Just before I bleed. His parts flash on the way coffee did when I gave it up. I'd picture the cup, the steam, the aroma, as they call it. The smell. I could taste it. It was all I could do not go to a cafe and have it. The withdrawals from John came on in the same way. His parts came floating through my vision. His smell. I could feel my lips swell just remembering, the blood there, my face warm with it. But I would cover it with anger. I quelled the sensations with talk of how bad he was (the way coffee is bad as a stimulant, too). But my body still remembers and craves him beyond logic. My *animal* still knows who's master. Sex still has John's face. And I wonder how John looks in my bloodstream now, after two years without him. On a microscopic level. As chemistry. Real molecular messages to my brain. His abrupt exit left something in me still looking for him.

I wonder if John will become one of these men to me when I see him again. That I will discover my passion for him is gone and he is simply there as so much biology before me, just a hunk of flesh time-worn, tired, and useless. If that happens I will be scared. I count on him to be the one left who can quicken my heart so that I can be a woman and not only a female feeding him, someone at the stove. Will I ever feel taken care of again.

Mama says, "Oh, that…after awhile other things are more important. I imagine other things being more important. What can be more important than being in love with a man and feeling all *that*? Mama laughs out loud.

Mama

Eggs

I let the phone ring awhile. It takes Mama time to get to the phone. I can see her in her little blue flowered house dress with the buttons down the front, the belt loops empty, the belt hanging over her front bedroom doorknob. She'll be shuffling fast, kind of hunching along so not to miss the call. She does a heavy kind of skip when she hurries. The X-rays showed her hip bone had broken loose and was rattling around in there, threatening to sever a blood vessel if she stepped the wrong way. It would be her second hip replacement if she went through with it. The 85% success rate chilled her blood. She mainly feared a blood clot going to her brain. The first doctor got defensive when I went to him last summer and asked him why his replacement broke loose. He referred her to the new doctor. The new doctor had a new prosthesis made, computer-exact this time, and dog tested, and scheduled her operation in the spring. It is almost spring I call each week to see how she is doing with the plans to go ahead. She has played brave one week and backed out another. I sometimes lose patience. I have ended up yelling at her about the fact she is younger now than she will ever be again. That eighty-five-year-olds have it all the time and she is only seventy-five. That she is healthy, and if she doesn't have it, she will surely be in a wheelchair all the rest of her life. To this she usually has said, "So what, I've worked hard enough. I wouldn't mind sitting down from now on," I usually end by saying it is her decision. Remembering that her mother died of a blood clot to the brain after a simple knee operation. But she was a cantankerous woman who fought the doctors.

Mama has already gone through six hours of anesthesia with the first operation. I remember her moon face coming out of it. As soon as her eyes glistened as slits in those waking few seconds, she smiled at us, her waiting grown daughters, gazing down. She had never been in the receiving position, and looked sleepy and guilty. (Like that dog that was hit by a car and wagged its tail just before it died because we all rushed over to pay attention to it.)

"Hello?" A lilt to her still operatic voice, "Oh, is it you." She sometimes thinks I'm my sisters. Our voices all sound alike. Even I can't detect who is who on a tape recording. She says, "What's wrong?" I tell her nothing is wrong. I snap. And then tell her: it is coming up on my period, is all. That I feel a little cranky.... She says, "Oh, do you still have that?" I tell her, of course I do. She says, "I just read that a woman is born with only so many eggs and when they are all gone she stops her periods. Again I snap, "But of course." "Do you still have eggs?" And she laughs like tinkling bells. It is the first time Mama has alluded to my age, and has hinted that even she now thinks I am getting *old*. I tighten my voice.

"I'm not out of eggs yet...."

She can detect the irritation. "Oh, you must be," she insists. I wonder over her insistence.

"Well how old were you when you went through menopause?"

"After I met Jolsen.... Or a little before.... I could have had his baby.... I wish I would have. But I thought I was old then. He'd be thirty by now. A beautiful son. We should have had one together. He never knew his son by his other wife."

I mumble, "I can just see him. His life all messed up...." Then I interrupt myself to her. She can tell stories for an hour or more. Little asides I will cherish later, but have no tolerance for now. I say, "Mama, just listen now, I called to tell you something. I called your doctor and the nurse said you have not decided about the operation. You need to decide one way or another. What are you planning to do, wait until the last minute?"

"I'm fine now, I lay out in the sun all afternoon, My leg feels good. I hung out the laundry in the fresh air, It was beautiful.... I don't need the operation. What if I die, or have a stroke? And I don't mind being in a wheelchair for the rest of my life. It'll give me time to do the things I've put off doing, tending to everyone."

"Oh Mama." I sigh. Then I tell her. "Daddy asked when you were coming down."

"Oh, how silly. Tell him I can't come down. What does he mean. I can't even walk. And I can't leave Jolsen. And Jolsen can't travel. This is my home. What a question. What does he mean by that?"

"I just wanted to tell you that he asked. It was spontaneous. Not logical. That he would like to see you again...." I whisper, "before he dies, I think."

Mama is silent, letting it sink in. She says in a soft tone, "Tell him I remember all the good times up in the mountains when we were young. Tell him I am writing poetry about that. I'll send him some poems. I only have beautiful memories. He was happy and handsome in those days. How is he doing?" She is truly concerned. She has sent canned chowder in the mail for him, "He always loved chowder.... he doesn't need teeth to eat that.... it'll help put some flesh on his body...and calcium in his bones.." (The cat's got all the little half-chewed-up pieces of clams that Flynn couldn't chew, left on the side of his plate under the bowl.)

I tell her that he has weak days and strong days. That it's good he's a sly-eyed and sharp-tongued old man so no one has to feel sorry for him.

She laughs. "Well, give him my love. And tell him I'm sorry he feels so bad."

When Flynn comes in that evening I relay the message. He sits in front of the big wall heater, blasting himself with heat and says, "What does she mean, sorry. I'm better off than she is. She can't even walk."

I go away. Before I say something. Everyone can talk freer to Mama. We have to measure our words to Flynn. And make allowances. He needs most things un-said. His ego is frail, where Mama's is robust.

Sal watches me like television, reads me like his newspaper.... He doesn't miss a cue. A year and a half into our friendship he has attached nicknames to me for each observation of my behavior. "The Great Orator's Daughter," he says now, as I get off the phone. "You and your mother trying to say goodbye is a joke." I give him the message and storm to my room. "Ms. Dash," is the name he calls me as I dash around, always in a hurry and getting things done.

"Dollface, Glamorpuss, Beautiful Angel," at other times, and "Mrs. Thatcher," when I snap at him. "Don't be short with me," he warns. Wolfgang called me Benny Hill and Eleanor Roosevelt in turn depending on whether I was in a good mood or doing business.

I can't remember if John ever called me anything, except other girlfriend's names by accident. I dial John's number. It's been almost two years. I still miss something that I can't recall. I am only irritated by Sal's nicknames, Flynn's determined upperhandedness, and Mama's unwavering perking right along even in the face of pending disaster.

I have to look up the number. It rings twice. And there he is. His voice. The resonance around the Adam's apple.... He asks, "Hello? Hello?.... Anybody there?...." waits a bit and then hangs up. A gentle hanging up. And some mirth in his tone. A voice that leaves me out. That makes me know he never thinks about me. That he has forgotten me. That he is in his own life again, while I have not found a new life, just staying alive from day to day and trying to keep my parents alive. How is it that I am always *surviving*. I can tell that John is *living* again. That the period of "breaking up," the turmoil, the dynamic of all that emotion is finished, and he is comfortable and *back* to himself.

I hang up. Stunned and staring at the air. What did I expect to hear? I lean back and remember how John's daughter was in love with me. With the idea of me, back then, when I was seeing her father. She used to smile, more of a grin, and tell her father to look, just look, isn't Marty just perfect for you. John would maybe grunt a little and walk away, or switch channels on television and ignore her. But in private he would tell me that it mattered to him that his daughter liked me. He used to say we were alike, she and I. That our minds worked in the same way. And he liked that. I dream a little about *those days* of being in love with him, and then it is time to make arrangements for Flynn's oxygen tanks to be delivered. And to call Mama's doctor. And to respond to Sal's teasing...

Mama

Mama got easy with money in her old age. She kept saying life was too short to hoard it away. "I'd rather spend it now while I'm alive and everyone needs it." I would tell her that was the problem, nobody needed it, they just knew she had it and until she ran out would ask her for it instead of earning it themselves. "Oh, you're just like Daddy," she scolded.

"You mean I can detect a con artist when I see one?... You used to be able to tell when someone was manipulating you. Now you can't smell a rat when it's right under your nose."

When Mama got "old," in her sixties, she started hugging us. She was never a hugger when we were growing up. But, by sixty, had twelve grandchildren and that placed her in time and made her feel her greater age. As a mother, she had believed in our strength. Now, she believed in her grandchildren's weakness. Because she was growing frail and a little helpless, she saw the small children and younger generation as that. As a robust mother, she made us get busy and earn our own way. She could tell laziness when she saw it. Back then.

As the grandchildren grew up and grew older, she seemed not to notice. They were still the little children, and she doled out money and her sentimental hugs, creating a gang of over-fed, over-aged, and under-worked adolescents. All in their twenties, they were still acting as if they were still fourteen. They were still calling her and asking for money. Not asking, but giving a hard-luck story and saying that it was okay, they would be okay freezing to death, or dying of some dreaded disease, or starving, until she insisted on helping and telling them where, when, and how much money she would send by Western Union. Then she would call me. I had been sending her gifts of money for years until I caught on. She was simply passing it on.

I'd find myself raising my voice over the phone, saying,

"So? Let them stand in a phone booth in the middle of nowhere at three AM with tonsillitis. I don't care.... When I was twenty-eight..."

Or, Mama would say that one of her beautiful grand daughters "Can't do dishes because it will ruin her hands.... ...She models, you know."

"Oh, *Gawd*, Mama, Look at my hands. You didn't worry about my hands. I modelled, too. Everyone models when they're young. I still had to do dishes.... .You mean you just let them sit there and look pretty after you cooked them dinner, while you staggered around on your broken hip and cleaned up after them?"

"Well, they're not used to doing for others. They're spoiled."

"That's no excuse, I learned to be useful early, remember?"

Sadness in her voice now. "I know, Honey. And I'm sorry. You worked so hard. I wish you hadn't now. I wish I could have pampered you."

"Oh, come on. It was good for me. I learned how to be *responsible*." Silence on the other end. "Besides, it wasn't you, the whole world worked back then. We grew up and became adults. We didn't prolong childhood."

"Oh, Honey, you were so good. You were only seven years old when you took care of everything. Right after Vicky was born. You were a sweet little girl. You'd help me all the time. I don't know what I'd have done without you. You were a natural born mother and schoolteacher.... but these girls today are different."

"Because *you* are different, older. You can't imagine the amount of energy those kids have."

"They do eat, I spent over a hundred dollars on groceries last week and there's nothing left."

I say, "You know what finally happened to the woman who wrote *Born Free*?" A little hesitant voice on the other end, as if she wonders why I ask. I can hear her listening. "They killed her."

Silence. "Who?"

"The lions grew up and killed her."

She is speechless. I explain. "She raised those cubs in

captivity, throwing meat to them. They never had to learn how to go out and hunt. But they played little hunting *games* in the yard like kittens, running and tussling and surprising each other. Then when they got hungry they ran to her and she threw them the meat. One day she didn't throw them any and they got mad and attacked her."

"Oh."

"They were spoiled rotten. There are studies on that subject. If you keep people dependent on you, keep them helpless, they finally hate you. They fear nothing because they have never had to. But they really fear everything because they sense their own underdevelopedness."

Mama laughs. She says, "What about your kids? You're as bad as I am."

I agree with her but wince. She always turns on me. I remember Flynn all through my childhood. I was dependent on him, I couldn't break away.

There was a little boy in kindergarten saying, "Never say fuck and shit, never say fuck and shit," over and over, all day long. I had to meet with his mother. She was in tears.... I hang up the phone and say, "Never say fuck 'n shit, never say fuck 'n shit."

She makes me so frustrated. She has given away twenty thousand dollars in five years. I have alienated myself from my nieces and nephews calling them and talking to them about it. I have asked, "What would you have done if there was no grandma." They have thought about it for a split second and then quietly surmised, "I guess I would have had to do without."

"Exactly," I say. And go on to tell them that their grandmother has never owned an expensive pair of shoes, a good purse, and has never really had anything." *But she's just an old lady; it doesn't matter* is in them.

Fruit

Rendered, because of age and isolation, in a state of awe (ah), Flynn is like a yogi, in wonder over the simplest things, as if seeing them for the first time. He does not recognize some of the things he has seen all his life because of his new reverence for life and his acceptance of the media dating him. None of the names, products or symbols fit his memory. He blinks at the TV channel on television. As if he can't believe he is seeing what he is seeing, or understanding what is behind it. Where did it come from. Who watches all this near-pornographic dancing and listens to this music. It leaves him out. An indestructible mailbox baffles him as he watches a bulldozer run over it and only scratch it. He says, "Up in the mountains mailboxes stood for years. No one ever wanted to destroy them."

A bloated apple, rotten, in my fruit bowl makes Flynn turn it with the greatest curiosity, like a child. "What is this?" he asks, his tone innocent. He scratches the surface with a thumbnail, testing

I say. "It's a rotten apple," leaning over the counter, looking closely to be sure. He sets it down, slightly embarrassed.

It is a fruit bowl filled with fruit I glean on my runs along the foothills. It is a big bowl with pomegranates, avocados, lemons, oranges, cherimoyas, loquats, that had dropped off the trees and rolled right out into the street. Flynn never knows what to expect. It could be *anything* anymore in this daughter's house. I can see "she comes up with the strangest things…" in his eyes. "What's that white stuff?" he asks, as I brown it in sauce in the pan. He lifts his nose to catch a whiff and can't detect what it is. "Tofu," I say. "What in the world is tofu?" he asks. "Like a bean curd," I say. "A bean curd?" he repeats. Again like a child learning a language. I stand there peeling a grapefruit, ready to eat it like an orange. I see the unspoken words in Flynn's expression. "You're supposed to cut a grapefruit in half, sit at a table and eat it on a plate with a pointed spoon. She's got her mother's ways. And picking up fruit from the road…"

Treatment, Liver and Onions

Sal's kind treatment strikes my senses each time as a surprise. Like a kicked dog, I marvel over not being kicked. I'd grown so used to it with Alex and later with John. All the bawling out, disapproval, criticizing my behavior, talk, looks, dress. And they made me pay my own way. John never picked up the tab. And, once divorced from Alex, and not earning my keep under his roof, he disengaged all finances. Now I step out the door with Sal to dinner and a movie. Something that simple. And he adores me all along the way with a sweet smile, hugs and kisses. Later the flannel sheets are too rough for Sal, so I get up and put on smoother ones. Mama calls and tells Sal to feed me liver and almonds. "Build her up. She exercises too much.... " He smiles. We laugh. He tells me he has never met anyone like me or my mother before in his life. I tell him I thought Italians were like that, full of words, exuberance, energy. He shakes his head.

John hated Mama. He called her a meddler and a busy-body and a nuisance. I was appalled. Mama who had broken down her body serving people, while he himself never did anything for anyone. He said she was a controller and lived in determined ignorance.... That she forced her ideas on people and most of the time she didn't know what she was talking about. He meant she didn't have a Ph.D. Alex came around to admiring my mother again after the marriage ended. He says now, "If anything ever happens to me, take me to your mother. The way she is keeping her husband alive. I know she'd do everything she could to help me." Sal and Mama locked horns over nutrition, but instead of ridiculing her he put his arm around her and told her she liked to stick to her guns.

The Men

Lonely

Lonely: for the men I used to know. Someone to ask things to. Now they lean on me. They're gone. Those men...

Or: Lonely and a bit scared. Where are all the men, the way they used to be? Alex never came back from the operation thirteen years ago. Flynn is a shadow, taken over by time, no longer the father I had. And even Larry, the rich man who wanted to marry me, who gave me a psychiatrist when I said no, shuffles down the street now, dragging his feet, ashen as a dead firepit. And Wolfgang. No longer the sweet boy with the promise of a brilliant career as a physicist. Over the phone his voice is sad. A 22-year-old broke his heart. At 36 he is turning bitter over "women." I don't count as one anymore. When I was forty and he twenty-five, it was a different matter. He's had too much recreational sex on campus since then. Even I, meeting him again, wouldn't fall in love the way I did. And John? Will he be that man I was in love with, or will he be gone, too? And leave me empty?

Or: Will there ever be that man again? Who knows answers and is *there*. And I can feel little and lean on. Or will I always have to be the one to figure everything out?

"You've gotten lipstick on everything," Sal says. "The coffee cups, water glasses, water bottles, toothpaste tube."

I say, "I don't like to waste time, water, or ingredients, putting things in containers." I go out the door. Instead of an illicit affair, it's an illicit cup of coffee now. And a muffin. Something I'm not supposed to have, according to Sal.

There's a storm. The wind blows and the rain comes down so hard it turns me into Alex. I rush home all a-worry instead of enjoying it. Wondering what destruction is occurring that will cost, cost and cost.

I still miss Alex, the one who was wheeled away to the operating room. He understood me. He had compassion. The one they wheeled out again was selfish and childish. He even vied with his grown children for the breast of the chicken. Someone said, "Well, what do you expect, when you come that close to death, you're bound to want to get things after that."

The refrigerator is making a bird sound again. As if one of the parakeets is in there. Flynn sits and watches the news. I never remember his doing that before. Being interested in the world. I look at him as I pass by on my way to call Alex. I see Flynn is simply glad to still be alive and that he doesn't expect anything any more. The evenings are just more time, not a time for excitement the way they used to be for him. He has given in. Been tamed. Broken.

Alex comes over with a tool kit and my promise of a piece of lemon meringue pie and all the ice cream he can eat if he fixes the refrigerator. He opens the freezer where the sound is coming from the loudest and scoffs. "If you'll clean all this stuff out, I'll see what's wrong." It's not the freezer he kept with neatly stacked chicken pot pies and frozen dinners, frozen vegetables, and bargain wienies. He sees my frozen chickens, a whole salmon, left-over beans, bagels, last Thanksgiving's tupperware of turkey. I quickly remove the contents and he goes down on his knees, his belt tight around an unnecessary bay window. I say, "That's not a belt your wearing. That's the Equator."

He groans, "Come on baby," ignoring my effort at humor (at his expense), talking to the panel that he begins to unscrew at the back of the freezer. His screwdriver slips a little on the ice. I go back and forth fussing at the kitchen chores, glancing from time to time as he works at my feet. Flynn comes in to glower at Alex's efforts as a repairman. Humor in his eye. Alex's style has always made Flynn smirk. Even though, without words, Flynn has trained me not to ask him to fix anything anymore. He'll try but his feeble attempts anger me. Flynn simply can't do it. Five years ago he put up a whole fence. But now it is apparent that he is too *old*. Something I refused to believe for a long time. And many fights with him over getting something done, mainly changing the washers in the leaky faucets. Any job would become a major undertaking. First finding his tools in his storage, long walks back to his shack, then the long trips to the hardware store, then the effort at bending and leaning and twisting. The wrenches slipping and the pipes always too corroded and Flynn too weak to turn them. His talk of the pipes breaking because they are too old and haven't been turned for thirty years. That I will have to replace the whole faucet. My temper. When I was a child, Flynn could do anything. I don't remember his ever changing a faucet. But he could build boats, little cars, paint pictures, sing songs, and tell stories. I just assumed he could do *everything*. I wanted to believe it.

"Come on you cocksucker..." Something in the freezer is resisting Alex. He turns red, holding his breath, and squeezing his shoulders up in a hunch so he can direct all his strength into the twist of his wrist and fingers. It's a sound I am afraid of, this frustration in Alex over inanimate objects. Watching a full grown man have a fit when he can't turn a screw. It's the only time Alex ever swears. To me it is not "manly." He was a kid who had temper tantrums. He'd fall on the ground and turn red, holding out on the unreasonable adults towering over him. After getting to know his parents, I didn't blame him, but I still did not like seeing it in him "as a man." Too often, in the marriage, it would go from the appliance to me. He'd be cursing me for breaking the appliance, which was then using up his life fixing it, while I stood around as a helpless female and then go flitting off to an Adult Ed class and never give it another thought. Alex, the inventor, turning repairman for 20 years in this house, was what caused his head to explode, finally, his family believed. They were glad when he divorced me, got rid of the responsibility of "that damned house and that damned woman." And got his own place with no one but himself to think about. They were horrified when he moved next door to save money and still came when I called.

"Ahhhh." The panel is off and I look. Alex expels sounds of approval. I see his brow is pinched. It is the look of fatigue. I ask him if he has taken his medication. The operation took his pituitary gland, so he takes daily doses of supplements to replace the chemical messages he would be getting if he had a pituitary. Adrenalin is one of those supplements. His body will not supply it on cue. If there is a need for it, such as repairing my freezer and being under pressure to get it done now and fast, his body will not have the resource by itself. "Yessss," he exhales with a dog-tired voice I know as depletion. So I keep quiet. My voice, my demands, my needs, my helpless female, my not wanting to pay a repairman can push him over the brink. He can have a fit of violence, not hurting anyone (yet) but exploding so we all look embarrassed. I fear his temper. But I risk it to save money.

Vapor pours from the freezer into the kitchen. A winter in there. The chill sticks to my legs in tights as I stand behind Alex, still on the floor with his work boots splayed. I see once again what I don't want to see, and I have to know, once again what I don't want to know: the unit that makes the freezer work. It is an ugly complicated thing with a blue silver tube, a network of copper piping, little splatterings of metallic and matt finished spots and bumps and pieces. Like the ganglia of the brain joining the spinal column. Alex picks up his oil can. He points the long thin nozzle at one place or another and the parakeet chirping stops. I marvel. At that moment I really admire Alex. Almost a sensual feel to it. A man who can fix things. And I have so much that needs fixing. I say, "Thank god." Alex sighs. He's rescued me one more time. I've appealed to his pride in knowing what is wrong once again. I begin to cut the lemon meringue pie, and, of course, the ice cream is already out, and melting fast. He gets up off the floor, puts away his tools, and takes his rightful place on the other side of the counter. The panel is screwed back in place. Now my work begins. As Alex forks in heaps of pie, I put everything back into the freezer. Except for the ice cream. He finishes it off.

Sea Birds and Water Fowl

Rain coming down. My bare feet in slip-on shoes, cold, wet. Hairs on my thighs rising against the inside of my musty pant legs. Some jeans that I thought I'd washed but hadn't. Or washed them with Flynn's clothes, so they smell, not fresh. I search the resource room for something to teach. Instead I leave the school. Too dim-lighted and under-heated. Those rooms. I seek a coffee shop (forbidden during the week, allowed only on Saturdays). I try to have Saturday on Monday. I need it, the heat, having my way. The muffin. My tongue waits for the taste of that soggy part, the center, where the oil is. Soy oil now. I try to find the weekend comfort and joy on a weekday, a bleak day. The school leaks. The smell of mold has made the librarian ill. She's out sick. Tarps and pans are all around. The ceiling is stained yellow in places. I looked for any audiovisual aids today so I can sit back. It is too cold to take thirty kids on.

And I've already done a lesson on what keeps a bird dry. It was with a bilingual class. I drew the sideways raindrop shape of a waterbird's body on the board. And all the different kinds of beaks, legs, feet. Showed them where the oil gland is. I've already told them how farmers kill sparrows, spraying detergent by plane on the trees at night, so it washes off the oil from the birds' feathers, so the birds take the dampness and freeze to death. How glad the farmer is to see their little bodies all over the ground the next day. Thirty sets of brown eyes are open wide as they listen. Thirty individual pictures of this. One per head. Better than television. They thought "cruelty" wasn't allowed. That big people knew better. They are learning about the exceptions... I can see questions in their eyes that they have no words to ask with yet. "How come someone doesn't stop the farmers?... the "bad" boy in class asks. Everyone stops him all day long. He wants to know for the wrong reason. They learn all grown-ups are connected in some way so that inevitably and continually "evil" as they understood it, is not only allowed, but accepted as the way to do things. When I leave that class they each have simple line drawings of birds with different lengths of necks, legs, and beaks. And claws. And the oil gland is represented with a dot, I praise them. It is the first time they have ever drawn a bird. I see they are delighted to discover this bird was in them all along. The bad boy's birds have an airplane flying over them. I laugh. It's this discovery that keeps me coming back to the classroom. But it always requires a horror story to get their attention before they are receptive to learning about the beauty of a thing. How birds can *die* first, and then how they actually *live*.

I drive away where I can hug a hot cup. And feel lonely for a man I used to know who no longer exists. Even though I see him every day. I see a retarded couple cross the street, hanging on to eachother, and know they are only a degree different from me and any man I've ever crossed the street with. Only an exaggeration of us. We never knew what we were doing either, and were as innocent believing in everything. I think, "Will a man never rescue me again? Take me down? Make me feel smaller? The men I've known have only made me feel *less*. The retarded man stepping up on the curb now, hangs onto the hand of the one he loves, fearing getting hit by a car, he, no smarter than she. I know I don't want that. I want a man who knows I'm weaker than he, not inferior.

John was a sissy. As a boy, he stayed in the house with the girls to play. Boys were too rough and they got dirty. Except for going down to the lake and masturbating with them. He could handle that. At the coffee shop I read an article in a women's magazine about old female mammals. How, once beyond procreation, they are regarded as wise and knowledgeable. And because of this they become the hub around which the old males, aberrant younger males, young females revolve. Old females are beyond competition, territorialism and possessiveness. Whereas the old males never lose these pugnacious qualities and can't be sought out as company.

After school and the coffee shop, I go home where Flynn and Alex will be listening for the sound of my car to drive up.... Tonight I am surprised. Instead of waiting for me to lead him to the feeding ground, Flynn has taken the bull by the horns. He comes in with a can of ham and a dozen eggs. His mouth is set in a determined line. He pinches off a smile. I tell him we are having steamed carrot. He ignores me and proudly displays his wares, placing them on the counter, setting them out right under my nose. He looks at me. I say. "Oh, ham and eggs." Then, "Do you want me to fry them for you?"

"No," very short and firm. He is quite sure.

"Well, I'll take out a pan. What size?" I hold up one.

A small one, "That one," he says. I stand aside while Flynn goes about preparing for this evening's project of cooking for himself just the food he loves just the way he likes it. It's been months since he's eaten anything that pleases his taste buds. *His kind of food.* Eggs sunnyside up. Ham and eggs. Bacon and eggs. Hash browns. White toast. Butter and jelly. Coffee with cream and sugar. Mama used to laugh that he would turn into a little bantam rooster, the way he loved eggs. And potatoes. His mother always fixed potatoes. Up on the ranch.

"They always had potatoes." I told her he wouldn't eat rice. "No, he says that's for Chinamen," and she laughed like wind chimes.

Flynn moves into my position behind the stove. He tells me he will need a little oil. I ask if he wants olive oil or "regular oil."

He is sure, "Regular oil." Like companions in conspiracy, I aid and abet the naughty meal. Flynn having his way, violating my kitchen with a real American menu. It's been a long time since the smell of meat has risen from the stove. The way he's finally "had it" with all this health food is in his manner. I want to laugh. He's showing the old spunk he used to have. Like John Wayne eating red meat until the end against doctor's orders. No one was going to take away his manhood and put him on fish and chicken. He died in the saddle, after they removed his stomachful of cancer.

Flynn waits 'til the pan is hot, then he cracks two eggs with his left hand into the pan next to the now sizzling ham. My mouth waters. With a svelte left-handed gesture Flynn turns the ham and the eggs without breaking the yolks. He leaves them a split second, just to seal the slime and lifts them onto a plate. He takes his plate back over to his side of the counter and eats like a king.

I can't resist. I ask, "Do you want some carrots?"

"No" It is almost a shout. Then he adds, "I don't want anything *healthy*."

Fifty-Six Hours

One more week chalked off. Another seven planned-out days done. That means I've eaten fourteen grapefruit, seven cups of horsetail tea, three cucumbers, two heads of cauliflower, one tomato, four pieces of sprouted wheat bread, four corn tortillas, two heads of dark green lettuce, two Spanish onions, one red onion, one whole clove of garlic, a half cup of olive oil, a half cup of live apple cider vinegar for enzymes, seven handsful of vitamins, minerals, and supplements. And fourteen scoops of protein powder, and seven tablespoonsful of bee pollen. And a couple of quarts of spring water. I could be a monkey feeding at the zoo.

That means I've lifted weights seven days, thirteen machines, thirty-six reps on each. And lifted my legs backward to make the hamstring work, two hundred times, did five hundred belly crunches on the floor of my room with the television on. That means I've run at least twenty-one miles. At my peak at forty, I did seventy a week.

That means I've curled around Sal seven more times for eight hours a night. That's fifty-six hours of bedtime with this man I never wanted to know, never sought out, or liked on sight.

That means I've done Alex's laundry, ladled out a couple of platesful of food over the fence. That means I've talked long distance to my kids and mother an hour each. That means I've had one cup of coffee and a bran muffin, which is the only thing I really wanted. The only pleasure I allow myself. It's the remnants of a life I used to have where I sought out pleasure and thought I could have what I wanted: John, grease, sugar, salt, caffeine, alcohol, fat, and sex that ruptured my bung. Brutal sex, John's style.

State and A
A Sandbag Affair

Oh, there's State And A. I remember all those times. It was when I was in love with John; and so was the waitress. We'd go for Happy Hour and have half-price drinks. He always ordered.... I can't remember anymore. It had soda with it. I began ordering the same drink. It was light and fizzy but gave you the drunken dullness and lightness you wanted so not to feel any of the bad, just the good. I was a one-drink drinker. If I was feeling so good that I thought I'd feel even better if I had another, I'd get mean after the second drink with my inhibitions down and anguish up. I was in love with John, but he wasn't with me. He never said that, but he watched me suffer when I tried to get it out of him. He wouldn't let me in or out. He held me in a safe position for his use and I let him. We'd meet at State and A and be gay, or act gay, while all the while there was the underlying unrest in my heart and the easy prey caught in his. I drive by and remember even the misery was good compared to what was to come. Being unhappy in love is better, I've come to know, than being dreary all around keeping after all the drudgery at daily life without love. I'm talking about romantic love.

There were my half-grown kids back then. Even after John and I broke up, he'd come walking by and ignore me conspicuously. My eye was faster. I'd see him see me and avert my eye and watch from my peripheral vision as he would startle ever so unnoticeably at seeing me there, drinking the, uh...whatever he drank, and make a big production of turning away as if he really walked looking off to the side. Later, when he tried to get back together again, I told him how ridiculous and obvious it was, this demonstration of his ignoring me; and he looked blank as if he didn't know what I was talking about. I'm sure he didn't. He never could admit his motives. In the five years I knew him and agonized over his not loving me, I saw all kinds of silly antics he played to show how much he didn't care, and when it was pointed out to him by me, he played dumb. I ended up calling him a cement brain. Cement, a friend said, was the additive to the sand which made it hard with the end result being called concrete. I never knew that. It was the next man, Sal, the near mafia sound- and look-alike who knew about cement. It was common knowledge among those who liked to throw people in rivers. Or weight them down with sandbags.

My half grown kids would join me for Happy Hour at State and A. We'd order drinks, nachos, french fries, sometimes burgers or fish burgers. I never ate in those days until I got home. But, I would feed my kids anything they wanted when they joined me. One time we delighted when a whole flock of small birds flew around in a big swoop and settled in one of the trees just outside the State and A patio. We watched them disappear into the foliage and heard their incessant chattering, and one of us said, "That's where they're going to sleep." The sky was ablaze with smears of tangerine clouds. I remember that sunset. The buildings blocked the horizon, but up high the color was brilliant, slanting westward. As a family, single mother and three half-grown kids in their late teens and early twenties, we discovered that a flock of sparrows just went to bed and we were privileged to witness that. It was a high point, and then we gazed at the people going by. The burners came on to keep us warm on that outside patio. If I had it to do over again, I would not have tried to be a family at Happy Hour.

Again

The last Christmas John and I were together he gave me a weedwhacker and a plastic chicken beak mask. Alex gave me a weedwhacker for Mother's Day the last year we were married, and then stole it back during the divorce. When he saw the one John gave me, he laughed out loud. A fourteen ninety-five special that kept snapping its plastic whipping string, so half the time was spent prying off the ill-fitted housing and fishing for the end of the string. I had to call Alex from over the fence to help me find it. He snickered at John's gift. He said he would let me use his, a gasoline engine model. He was proud to display his expensive weedwhacker to me, as superior to anything John could come up with. I'd already heard the noise of it over the fence as Alex went at his field of dry grass. It sounded like a sarcastic Italian at one of Sal's big family parties, going uhuhuhuhuhhhh, So I went around the borders Flynn had missed with his four lawn mowers. Like the cleaning lady who won't do windows, Flynn wouldn't do borders. But when Flynn saw that gasoline engine his eyes lit up...Later he brought one home from Sears announcing that he got a deal on it...

Sal brings flowers. Like the women in the movies, I look for a vase, knowing I don't have one, and find the big gallon jar I used to catch bugs in for the kids, and put the flowers in there, filling it with water. The roses spread out, stems magnified. It's a pleasing sight. (John bragged that he never bought flowers or jewelry for a woman in his life.) Air bubbles stick to the immersed thorns, I turn to Sal half-embarrassed by my vase, and he is smiling, but disgruntlement rides around his head and shoulders. Does he want a girlfriend like my divorced women friends who divorced near-millionaires and spent their twenty years of marriage buying china, crystal, silk, silver, lambswool, and mahogany and cherrywood? And maybe some oak? And calling a vase a vaz. The only thing of value I have is a bird cage that stands to the ceiling. A hundred dollars from Mexico. I don't have to write a will. There's nothing to fight over except the house. And that would have been divided simply in thirds. Now, at age 75, with two deceased children (who died at 41 and 47 years of age), and one left who hates her, Marty will have no heirs to leave her house, The Place, to, that she and Alex worked so hard on maintaining.

Alex came out the front window during the worst part of the divorce with a pillowcase full of any odds and ends he thought of any worth. Not unlike the thief who robbed us once. My best pillowcase was missing along with all the electronic items around the house. Alex makes off with some marble eggs his sister sent from Zaire and a pair of wooden elephant bookends and some copper lids and a silver salad fork. I can leave my house unlocked, while he must stand guard in his field in case anyone breaks into his big shed where all the booty is stored. In his little camper with all the airline passes he can use for the rest of his life, he sits and listens for someone picking his lock....

Flynn comes in silent, intense, eyes steady as a snake approaching a mouse, looking for an ear. I happen to be in the kitchen and a tenant beside me is boiling a sausage. Flynn begins. His words pour like venom, "Boy that jerk, I was doing just fine, but Dan's father was standing at the bus stop, and I was just pulling out. And I had to give him a ride. You can't hardly pass a guy up.... And I keep all my important paper on the seat beside me. My car isn't geared for a passenger. But old Jack gets in and sits on the papers. I had to move them and one fell between the seats and I can't find it. My pocket knife was there too, and he sat on that and now it's nowhere to be seen. Next time, I think I'll take another route."

I can't believe my ears. Flynn's little world never ceases to surprise me. Even though the theme is the same—"Somebody done me wrong"—the fact his head is so full of it always takes me by surprise. I say, "So giving one person a ride upset your entire life." He isn't sure if I'm meaning to be funny or sarcastic.

Then he says, "Is there any of that turkey left, I'm really not hungry but I'd better eat something...." I simmer some.

Next

Alex is down on his knees at my (once our) hearth trying to close the fire screen and glass doors. I hear cursing and then "What idiot put these doors on backward." Of course Flynn did. But Flynn is not around at the moment. He has just gone out the door. Exit Flynn, enter Alex. Alex allows for Flynn's greater age and poor health and remains silent, but exhaling loudly. It could be a Shakespeare play.

§

John once climbed up to the ceiling on a ladder and installed, in a one-handed act above his head, a one-gesture favor, and hooked a paper lantern around a naked light bulb.

Then I climbed up on the roof in the wind to seal my skylights with silicone while he sat below reading on the couch. He never looked up once to acknowledge me. But when I got down he said, "Any other woman would have made the man do it."

Once John helped me dig up a septic pipe and, of course, complained about his lower back into the evening.

(*Years later, when I saw him, he had shrunk and his gums receded, and he was no one to me anymore, when he was at a coffee shop same time I was. He told me his wife left him. I said, "At least you married her for twenty years."*)

§

I sit at a sidewalk cafe with Sal and pretend everything is nice. He is nice. There he is in his white starched and ironed shirt, cotton slacks that fit him just right (He goes to a tailor to be fitted, I learn.). Hair grown out so thick he smiles, the joke between us is that it looks like a coonskin cap. I smile. It is understood that much hair and pure black makes him mistaken for an ethnic. People have already asked him if he could speak English, in Spanish.

§

I know how to pretend. I have pretended all my life. There were only brief times I was not pretending. It was a conscious act. It would come over me, a sense of.... or an absence of resistant.

A certain strain that has always been there lifted. Sal blamed coffee. That annoyed me. Like Mama, everything is rooted in biology with Sal. It used to annoy Flynn. Mama had easy solutions to problems. She saw Flynn's depression as simply too much coffee and too many cigarettes. He would go out the door to some woman he could impress with his depression. His fear of dying, life ending, and his smallness in the scheme of things.

I gave up coffee just in case Sal was right. Instead of a strain came a lethargy. No impact. No passion. And no memory that I had ever felt excited over anything. I knew I had gone mad for five years over John, but the feeling was gone from my nervous system, and the memory of it gone. I wondered over letting myself be tormented by him.

Sal defines any negative human emotion in terms of withdrawal from caffeine, nicotine, sugar, fat, alcohol. We are all caught in one hangover or another after we eat "because the American diet is toxic to the human body. The liver…and he goes on to tell how the body chemistry is the cause of divorce today. "A family loads up on fats and sugars and then tries to sit around together and carry on a conversation and as the blood sugar reaches a high and then descends you have fighting and arguing, etc."

Sal says, "Your father has you in his pocket. He says something and you jump right in there, and he gets you going and brings you around…. Just don't engage in his conversation. Just let him talk and don't answer, You always lose."

"I do not, And I won't ignore him. You insult people by considering their condition…I will honor him by doing battle.

By taking him seriously. I can't see him as just some old man. He's still Flynn... You, the yogi, and Louis...You men. You give nothing personal in dealing with Flynn. You're all business, while the human being he is, sits there being ignored."

"No, we consult the human being. It's the personality we don't get involved with because it's a losing game. He likes to outsmart you, And when you engage in an exchange of words with him, you can't win. He won't let you..."

To calm me, Sal holds my neck and kisses me and says he thinks my neck was made for this...kisses. I shiver, Is he a choker? Will I make him that mad someday? Even Wolfgang yelled once, Larry jerked me around. A guy named Joe threw my car keys once, and John ripped his doors off trying to get me out of his life. And Alex choked me to unconsciousness. Kevin gave me the finger and then shot himself. And Flynn had a nervous breakdown. What will Sal do? The way he fondles my "long stemmed" neck chills me a little. And he talks like the Mafia...

When I tell Sal my fears, that he might be a choker, he says, "That's good. And when I don't choke you, you'll trust me," Finally it comes to a head, Like canning peaches. All the sugary foam you spoon off and wash drown the sink just before closing the lid airtight. All the time I've spent with Sal finally accumulates in my head as waste. All the sugaring in bed, out of bed, at the table, at talks, films. Sickening, finally in its implication. A diversion. Or, I, a stray animal in need, to be fed and petted and belong. Lost from the original owner always there in me. Is that what Flynn did?

The Truth about Sal

After we broke up, people would ask, "Didn't you know what he did for a living?"

I'd say, "He told me he sold health information to insurance companies."

They'd laugh. "And you believed him?"

I'd say, "Well, I'd kid him about knocking someone off because he sounded so much like the Maria, and was raised in New York City."

They'd persist. "Look, he never worked, had lots of money, used your place so he wouldn't have an address, drove your car so he wouldn't have a registration, used your phone, so he couldn't be traced. Come on."

I'd remember that he always had a pocketful of quarters and went off to make phone calls all the time. When I'd ask who he called, he said, "My mothah," dropping the r. I just figured Italian men did that. I'd heard their mothers were like that, expected their sons to call them all the time.

These people who knew Sal through me would sigh and keep their eyes on my face to read if I really was "all there."

I'd say, "Well, as soon as he began hanging around my property, he called the phone company and had them tunnel a cable underground and put a phone in that cabana way back, by the pool where no one could hear him talking when the phone rang."

They'd stare at me. "What? And you still didn't suspect anything?"

I'd feel silly by then, imagining my innocence, my lack of suspicion, my usual trust. I'd say, "Well, he used to call me a California bimbo, or Doris Day, and laugh that I was so naive that he couldn't believe it. He used to tell me that if I'd grown up in New York City, I'd have some savvy and be twenty pounds heavier; that women in ethnic neighborhoods were clued in early to keep a watchful, knowing eye."

By now, these people who knew Sal through me, would walk away shaking their heads and throwing out their arms saying, "I give up; you're too much. How old were you when you met Sal? Fifty? Yee, Gads."

And I'd stand there feeling dumb. I'd list the "red flags." No phone of his own, no car of his own, no address of his own, no computer, of course, just clipping from newspapers about health, kept in an immaculate file box to show people his "profession." And a pocketful of quarters. And, when I happened to pick up the phone in the house when it rang, there'd be this male voice, deadpan, asking for Sal, and I'd ask who was calling, and he'd always say, "The Professor." Ha!

He told me to keep insurance on my car current—and at the end of our friendship, flips it out in front of a Mercedes convertible and gets $10,000 payment from my insurance company.

Sal told me he went to three college libraries to research on his routine trips out of town: Orange County, Palo Alto, and Las Vegas. I stand very still and let it sink in. *Really?* is all that comes up. *Amazing*, is another word. *Unbelievable* is the third word, picturing me with a someone like that. He used to talk a lot about medical maijuana becoming legal someday. Did he think he was the forerunner? He went to the priest a lot to confession. He was a mystery man, indeed. None of us ever really got to know him, when we think back.

A friend finally informed me that Sal was a drug runner, a dealer. And worse than that, a gigolo.

Sal spends money on me—and writes the amount in a ledger for court one day. Like a gigolo, he hopes to get my house. My house was always on his mind. He knew the law. If you spend time regularly at your girlfriend's house for seven years, you can claim half community property in this state on the basis of common law marriage—and then have me buy him out of my own house! His uncle is a lawyer.

On his good side, when I get ovarian cancer at 56, UCLA will save my life because Sal will research the best doctor.

A clue I missed: *Sal says never to say "Sal said..." He says that makes me sound stupid.* No, it announces his presence to other people, which might make it easier to track him down, I realize later.

Flynn at Last

Day to Day

No matter what the circumstances, if someone who hadn't seen us for a long time, came by, they'd think, "Oh, there's Flynn and Marty, typical..." No excuses or extenuating circumstances. It'd look like what it is, in fact: he's still taking up my life, getting me, having me....

Flynn in my car. Such close proximity and without the professional facility for distance, so when he hawks phlegm I try not to swallow as if it is his throat/my throat...needing to separate myself...still... I am taking him for a trial run out to the house. To try out his leg.

I try to get control, to get comfortable. It always has to do with a sense of order and heat. There are the uncomfortable times in a day, getting in the car, a grapefruit too big for my purse, all my hair follicles rising and pressing all over my body as gooseflesh. Shoes always cold and dank. Then the heater begins to warm me as I drive and I sip hot tea.... And I get that feeling that everything is going to be alright, if I can just stay like this....

But I can't and I am in a first grade class with everything in the room at the wrong angle, crooked, dishevelled, even the children needing to be set at right angles and ordered about. I think, "This will pass, I will not get stuck at this point forever. Soon it will be over and I will be getting in my car and driving away.... But not before a Down Syndrome child from another class comes in to use the computer. He picks up the mouse same as John did, and with the same look of intense viewing, uses it the way John did. And John had me convinced he was brilliant to learn to use the mouse when it first came out. I shut the door on that classroom at the end of the day, smarter than when I entered. I have learned one more thing about my need to believe in men. And taught by a Down Syndrome boy. The child, though, has probably learned nothing from me. He taught himself, and knew, that some teachers don't know things.

Wear

When a man gets that weak, a woman can cease to be a woman and her heart may go out to him as it does to a helpless infant or dependent child. I remember when Alex was down. He rolled around in the hospital bed in pain. Helpless. Hurt. Permanently wounded. Struck down. We'd been separated five months. I came back and vowed I'd never leave him again. I could finally love him. He let me for the first time. When he was strong, before his illness, he took my expression of love, any tenderness I tried to show, as babying him. He wouldn't let me pet his hair, tickle his back. It was all too... he never said it. He'd say. "I don't like that." It gave me the upper hand in his mind. Power over him, even if it was only over his flesh. He once said, "As if you think I'm weak and need pampering."

I was kept from loving, touching, fiddling, "diddling and playing with the flesh," as he called it. I couldn't pat or stroke him. Yet he massaged my work-worn back with his massive hands back then as long as I positioned myself conveniently within reach while he watched television. As long as he didn't have to think about it, being stroked meant weakness from his Puritanical, Quaker upbringing. "Leave the flesh alone. It is evil. Put your mind on higher thoughts. Duty..." It was drummed into him... While I had been raised in the flesh. That's all Flynn did was touch me. And he taught me to be a back rubber. I would trade minute for minute with my younger sister. I still owe her thirty minutes. She was four and I was eight. I fell asleep and never paid her back. I was used to and trained in fleshy behavior. Nothing was ever dry or without body odor when I was growing up. It was the organic upbringing the hippies craved and sought later that I had had. When the hippies came along I did not join them. I had had that all along. I played barefooted. I touched the earth. I got dirty. When I took a bath, always in an old clawfoot tub, the water left a ring. When I met Alex he was only dirty inside where you couldn't see it. But I could smell his breath. His lungs and stomach were rotting from cigarettes and canned food.

Alex was protected growing up. He came from a large and rich family that could afford to cover and coat themselves in materials that separated them from touching the earth. No tactile experience. Never using their real fingers for anything. An implement for every movement. He was taught parlor manners from birth. Not to see, hear, say, feel, touch. Especially to keep your hands to yourself. And don't be curious. Quell your monkey impulses and *don't reach out*. It's vulgar. Never grab or elbow... There are stories about the conflicts we had over our differences when we were married, but that's in the past. The attitude Alex carried inside his head was what blew us apart. He was superior. He was better equipped to deal in the world that counted. I simply was not. "Attitude," the kids call it today, in the classroom, "He's got attitude..." Alex had attitude. He believed his ways were right and mine were wrong.. And he knew how to humiliate me. I wonder now why I was so easy to humiliate.

My bare feet, my bold curiosity, my direct approach stimulated him at first, then it began to irritate him. He tried to teach me to be like his sisters, all covered over with cloth from head to toe, curls whacked off up to their ears and pressed down like an obedient cap, any hair out of place a sign of low class, and easing out the right word at the right time. Enunciation more important than content.

When Alex was feeble in the hospital, when all his elitist ways had been exercised to the extreme so that his head exploded (the tumor burst), I could finally love him because he needed me. He let me help him. I equated love with help. Flynn, the helpless, had been my teacher.

As Alex recovered, the equation swung back the other way. Nurturing wasn't needed. I went back from "mothering" him to just that woman who was his wife with all her flaws. In his eyes my role was *duty*. I was, once again, to produce so many yeast rolls a day, blow so many noses, wipe so many asses...

Now Flynn is feeble and I feel the barrier I put up as a female to thwart his maleness lessen, and the mother in me, the one that puts baby birds in the oven in a shoe box at night to keep them warm, comes out. The one that has saved so many stray kittens. The one who picks snails out of the street on my runs so they won't get mashed by cars. The one who dodges butterflies on the freeway in her car. The one who takes potted plants out of the other teacher's wastebaskets and brings them home and gives them a chance in the yard. The one that won't throw a seed into a garbage can, but teaches children, "It's a living thing. Throw it out the door into the soil," That one tries to help Flynn now. That was the one who always tried to help Flynn, even as a child.

When Flynn was strong and arrogant I could battle with him. Now I help him walk, I help him talk. He is forgetting words....

While the nurse bathes Flynn I read the travel section of the *L.A. Times*. The oceanliner cruises require formal dress. The men and women take all those expensive clothes along. I picture it all at the bottom of the ocean and can't see myself dressing in such a precarious situation. I couldn't tiptoe in heels and a gown on top of all that water and all those waiting fish.

I feel my chin. And feel one. And think, *If I never plucked an unwanted hair from my chin I could work at the circus by now as the "bearded lady."* I reach into my purse. I became a tweezer-carrying woman at thirty-five. When I enter Flynn's room again I see his expression, "Is this all I get?" Is this all there is? He looks like a kid watching his snowcone being made and begin to melt. As if he can see his whole life now being over.

In Flynn's new state of recovery I venture to ask him about his childhood. I say, "What exactly *was* wrong with you. Mama said it was spinal meningitis. That you were born with the shakes."

He gestures that aside, "Mama never could get anything straight. They don't know what I was born with, I wasn't born with anything. It came on later, I had a nervous disorder."

"What do you mean, nervous disorder?"

He looks at me as if I might be ridiculing him. He says, "You know, I couldn't stop shaking. They called it 'the St. Vitus Dance' in those days. They didn't know what it was, what caused it."

I ask how old he was and what did his mother do about it.

"I was about five, I couldn't go to school for two years. They kept me out of school and took me to a Chinese herbologist. He gave me some bitter teas to drink. Nothing helped. The Chinese doctor said I wouldn't live past sixteen," He chuckles a bit now, at seventy-seven.

(*My niece's research revealed this: The high fever wiped out the sex part of his brain or damaged it, she said. Brain damage from rheumatic fever was killing kids from 1890 to 1930. Flynn born 1914 and got sick at age 5.*)

I think, *And I got the brunt of your nervous disorder. If you hadn't been nervous and needy I wouldn't have been chosen to hold you together all your life...*

I consider my life without Flynn's needs in it. If I had had *just a father.* I think of my friends, they had normal fathers. And we're still divorced, older... without men, trying to make a life beyond our grown children.... I try to imagine what Flynn did to me in fact... All that emotional turmoil all my life, growing up, in the marriage, even now. The intensity with which I lived, as if everything mattered. That is one difference—my women friends are relaxed. They don't run or work out in the gym or eat "right." Their daily behavior is whatever they want to do. They are not driven. Obsessed. Is that what Flynn did to me? Wired me, made me *survive*, so that there is structure to every detail in my life and nothing simply for pleasure?

Flynn goes on to confirm his illness. "When I was sixteen I had to drive to school. I couldn't take the school bus because I was incontinent...you know, I couldn't hold going to the bathroom...."

Flynn just wants peace and not to have to "put up" with anything anymore. He tells me this on one of my visits to the nursing home. He sits in his wheelchair and I in a plastic guest chair by the sliding glass door. It is in regard to all the fuss

Louis and I are making about vitamin and mineral supplements and the restrictions we've put on him not to go back to his old doctor who will prescribe Valium again. Flynn's well-being, we believe, is due to our insistence on no drugs and all natural nutrients. I am amused by his childlike request to not have to "put up with anything anymore." He explains that he has already done things he had to do all his life, and now at his age he just wants no arguing and pressure to do what other people want. He just wants peace. I move a little in my chair, knowing I have made scenes over his medication. I've made him upset enough to see his false teeth drop out and shut off his words as he tried to defend himself. I listen to him now and decide that he can, indeed, go about his business, that I won't interfere from this point on. That his life is his own. That I will hold my tongue. He breathes a sigh of relief and says that will be nice. Again I can hear my friends' voices, "But why do you care to argue and try to keep him alive, after what he did to you...?"

The sun is setting and it is the chatting time of day. Flynn has had his potatoes and gravy and cobbler and weighed in at ninety-four. He's gained two pounds and rejoices. It is not fluid from his kidneys, or any misfunction of his body this time. It is real weight. Flesh. Flynn is gaining muscle mass. The P.T. and O.T. programs are taking him through his exercises. I ask him about sleeping pills. It has been awhile since he's had a bad depression. He admits that he will not take sleeping pills anymore because he always wakes up scared to death and has a bad day. Or the pain pills. "They made me hallucinate," he confesses.

Reeds

I look at my father, he 77, I, 52. How long can this go on? I see that I am like Flynn in many ways. Physically I am on my way to looking like him. His fat deposits are depleted. The vehicle through which important hormones are carried has been used up. Strip-mined. At his age he has used up his natural resources and long ago dipped into any calcium deposits left of his teeth and bones. His body reabsorbed his teeth ten years ago, so the hollow cadavers of enamel left, fell out or were pulled easily, like plucking Indian corn kernels from the cob. No juice, shallow roots. In fact, the roots had climbed up out of the gums looking for moisture. And the gums had fallen away like the banks of a pond, exposing the pronged root that sat like candles in candle holders, with no real interaction anymore to the bloodstream. He smoked them out like popcorn in a smoke house. His teeth became only reeds in a dried up swamp. Then his skin went. But not his hair. He perches like a loggerhead shrike with a white topknot. In the hospital right after his broken leg surgery he sat in his hospital bed with yet one more I.V. coming from his arm. And I'd wondered how they found a vein. The nurse told me they didn't. They had to use an artery. A photo of his arm could have been put on a medical exam asking: What is this? An arm almost unrecognizable as an arm. The transparent English skin so thin and the muscle so atrophied that only the tendons asserted themselves, stretching and crinkling the flesh. A study in anatomy without autopsy.

A near-absentee father, Flynn. Almost not here in the flesh. I remember seeing pictures of Mahatma Gandhi in his large diaper. In the fifties. Squatting on the earth in India, skin and bone. That popeye jaw and half-lidded eye. I carried his picture from the newspaper in my wallet in high school. I loved him for not eating. For being able to hold out. For his almost non-physical existence. And now here is Flynn. And does he hold out for principle, too?

Flynn's doctor called and said his last blood test shows he's overdosed on the heart meds and could have a heart attack, to rush him to Emergency. From there, they adjust his blood and put him in a Nursing Home until he's balanced. It's what I predicted over drugs.

Back in Emergency

When Flynn's dinner comes it's pureed. Everything has been ground so he doesn't have to chew it. Baby food. A little bowl of what was spinach, a little bowl of what was liver. A dollop of mashed potatoes. A cupped dish of ice cream. Tea. He begins to fidget. Eating is the furthest thing from his mind. Three I.V.s hang above him, tapping into one main one. One is dark red, one clear, and one pink. I read, "blood, saline, and glucose." The basics: Rh Positive, sodium chloride, and electrolytes. Flynn pushes the tri-colored, pre-chewed food around with the top of his fork, hooking up as little as possible and complaining that unless you have an appetite you can't swallow your food because there's no saliva. I tell him to sip water. I push his plastic glass with the crooked straw closer to his reach. He does sip a little and says he will probably strangle to death because they won't let him sit up enough to get his throat at the right angle.

A nurse has come in to raise the head of the bed and fought with him over the angle. She scolded him.

"You cannot sit in an L position," she snapped.

As Flynn worries his food, I tell him I want to see his stitches. An imperceptible reaction goes through him. I know the stillness. And I know what he thinks of this. A morbid streak like my mother's people. His people would *never* ask and *never* look. Mama's people never not looked. Where did Flynn's people learns such manners, quell curiosity, and go without knowing all for the sake of etiquette? Living their lives not to offend. And why should looking at stitchs be offensive. I think of the kids on the playground who will always find out what's under a bandage before the day is over. The child himself will pull it back and show his classmates. Educate his friends.

Flynn says, "I don't want to see them."

I exclaim, "Why not? I took a picture of Mama's stitches. They looked like a red zipper." Mama, a curious child herself, never left a stone unturned. Flynn opens his eyes wide, looks right at me to see if I tell the truth.

"You did?" he asks, learning....

I wanted to say, *I had to see everything you had that I never wanted to know about at one time...remember?*

I have dreams that night of climbing a hill and pulling loose age-old holding places by trying to pull myself up. Still I held and didn't fall as they came loose. And I kept climbing. Vines that had grown and served as ropes for years were being uprooted.

One of Flynn's grandchildren came to visit him in the Home. All of us—Louis, me, and the young adult stand around Flynn in his bed. It's late in the day and he is tired of sitting in his wheelchair. Flynn has always liked an audience. He says, "Well, there's nothing wrong with *pain*, until it hurts." We all shuffle and chuckle.

Afterward, after we leave and go out into the parking lot, the grandchild says, "Ooh, he looks like E.T." Louis says, "He looks like that picture of Great Grandma, remember?" We each react to the horror of old age the way Flynn taught us, with an attempt at humor. This time it's about him.

I say, "He is stripped down to no wallet, no watch, no calendar. No point in time, No I.D. Completely dependent. No familiar food. It's hard on him right now to hold onto an idea of himself. He keeps saying he doesn't know himself like this." I want to bring everyone around to the seriousness of it. I think, *We have maybe twenty years before we're in the same boat? Thirty for the grandchild?* But down deep I vow I'll never get decrepit.

Marty

Kitchen Nook:
Dog Paws and Chicken Claws

Woke up feeling broken, and saw how small I was. Broken
and small. Small legs and arms defined by Sal's size in bed
beside me. And hurt. Broken, small, hurt, and measured by
the man beside me. I began to cry and didn't know why. It
was about yesterday. A delay. The feelings saved until it was
over. The way the day was. My son's graduation day and me
speechless. Following along to the place where it'd be. And all
the people. A campus of thirty-four thousand. Four thousand
graduating from college, four hundred in his class. I tried to
know myself, be myself. But I had no self out here, outside
feeding and running and going on about one thing or another
to do with health. I wanted to push people out of my way
and hurt them with words about themselves. I felt boxed in
and forced to breathe smoke coming from the mouths and
noses of that ignorant and willful generation. Old men and
old women with cigarettes in public. And me with a lungful
of twenty years with Flynn and twenty years with Alex blowing smoke in my face: I was the only one in line who walked
away. All the young women in shorts and suit-tops inhaled,
smiling and smiling. Suit-tops and shorts, a new style, while I
wore my rockstar jacket and tights and was my age.

Suddenly my son's name was called and I wasn't ready.
I tried to click the shutter of the camera in my hand and
fumbled. I missed the moment, got an odd shot. His friends
and father (Alex) cheered. Sal sat poker-faced beside me in
a white shirt, tie, and jacket. His short neck buried so that it
appeared his head sat squarely on his wide shoulders. I cast
around for a connection to something, so habitat-minded I'd
become. Without my house, car, classroom, gym and roadside
wrapped around me I was dazed. My son looked like all the
other young men, big and blonde and buried in his cap and

gown. While Flynn lay abed, ninety-two pounds and ninety-two miles away. My brother and his daughter were suddenly there, out of the crowd, looking foreign. I didn't know them. They were only vaguely familiar.

Without my own identity intact, I couldn't say anything except some relief over having his video camera at my disposal. In all the confusion of greeting and meeting I had no say. Photos were taken, poses posed. Even I participated, but passive, swept away with it. The way it was going to be was still in my head. The preparation for weeks in my mind and now not fitting. I went shy and afraid. The graduation was not close and have-able. Finding it elusive and multi-peopled and not there at all stunned me. I had looked forward to getting away from Flynn's frailty, the tenants, and away from the access to exercise. I pictured a holiday. I saw myself laughing and smiling and being stimulated by every new thing on this weekend away. *Away.*

Getting away was like John. It was out there somewhere and not mine. Only something I thought of all the time. Going to Africa and making love to John. If they both happened at once I would lose myself again, not knowing who I was after all the resignation. Sal was looking at me funny. He put his arm around my shoulders and I shrugged him off. I knew he knew that I had "spaced out." He sometimes called me Doris Day. As if I lived in a fantasy world. I simply told him now, under my breath, "I've stayed too long with responsibility. I haven't been away from all that for so long, I'm without any control over making all this happen...." He nodded, smiling long and tender.

Then we dispersed, found our cars parked far away, stopped, shopped for food and gathered again at the student housing. My son, elusive and unhave-able, too, in my frame of mind. Where did he go, who was he, who was I, when he was right before my eyes. And Alex. Alex's face, always too familiar, striking my senses, And coming in as *glad* to my vision. I'd known him for so long I knew I could count on him if... if worse came to worse.

In preparing for the weekend, Sal had instructed me, "If

Alex gets within three feet of you," and he positioned his body that distance from my face, "I want you to move back and at all times keep that much space between you and him." At this request I had to laugh, while Sal waited with agitated eyes for my promise. I thought how flattered Alex would be to think he was a threat to any man....

I spent the afternoon in the little apartment kitchen nook chopping up vegetables and boiling rice and getting to know myself again. I did not come out to talk, not having anything to say that wouldn't spoil the day. And soon the day was over.

Sal and I went to the hotel where I cried and tried to distract myself with a program about murderers. When Sal began to make love to me I could feel his need to love someone. It was never like that with John. John wanted me to know my own filthy nature. To make me beg for it and moan when he hurt me in one orifice after another. To jab and jab and jab and listen to me cry out in pain which was pleasure to him. He had his needs and it wasn't to express tenderness and love. But to make the woman less.

Sal kisses even my hands, those tendons and veins and knobs and wrinkles, and praises and honors the flesh of them with his lips and words over all they've done.

He wallows in the hotel bed and makes me feel like royalty. How easily I get spoiled. I lie there like John used to, letting him. I feel the rejection of John even as Sal covers me with touches. The memory of John showing me the bad side of myself.

Which was still there, but not with Sal. John didn't make love. He made me apologize and thank him at the same time for letting me touch him. Afterward I would lie back looking at his sleeping face, still longing to please him. With Sal I fall asleep afterward. And he looks at me. I am not left anxious and wanting his approval.

Sal works hard trying to show me my good side. He labors under the covers saying how soft the skin is on my belly, how smooth is the upper thigh. How like the finest chamois that would go for a lot on the black market. I lie there and say,

"What about my calf, is that like a chicken leg?" And, "What about my forearms. Are they like buzzard heads? And my neck is a gizzard…and what about my breasts? Why don't you ever comment on my shoulder blades?" (So used to John's critical eye and honest tongue. "You'll never be sixteen again," was all he ever said.)

John liked to watch a woman take out her money in the morning and pay for his breakfast. And to peer from around his newspaper and see how she looked being ignored. He fed on her willingness to still be there, and her lost look. He needed to be master. And there were always women like me who were willing to be humiliated.

As Sal holds me I feel him needing me to be all that he believes a woman is, smaller, delicate, needing care and protection. And I, so used to protecting myself, resist his loving, warding it off with snide remarks. As Sal tries to fill me up and give me strength I fight him. I take it as an insult, as if he thinks I need help. He lies beside me bewildered, blinking in the shaded room, wondering why I can't or won't accept his tenderness. And I lie there refusing to be an invalid, so ready to hold my own. To "take it," the pain men inflict even when you're in their arms. When I first married Alex, I wanted to pet his face. He'd jerk his head away, saying it made him feel like I thought he was *weak*. And needed care. He had just come from his militant family life and the military. He deprived me of tenderness which I longed to express. Only later with John did I lavish those tender strokes on a male. John was a great mound of flesh, in bed, a heap of a body, and made the sounds of a water buffalo stuck in a mud hole in a drought. His hide would shudder and tremble and quiver like jelled headcheese under my touch. It was love I'd saved all my life, to give.

Seventy-Eighth

I laid out the table with all the birthday things: a big cake with blue roses, a sponge cake with a crate of strawberries beside it, stolen party napkins, real whipped cream, party plates. Forks, a red balloon from Valentine's Day with the words turned toward the table. And went out to take Flynn his white laundry, and found him feeling his own pulse (who else's) and looking up at me in wonder, his eyes saying, *Isn't anyone going to do anything*, but his lips said, "My heart is skipping a beat, feel it." And held out his sun-darkened, bruise-reddened (from all the I.V.'s) English wrist. I reluctantly placed two fingers on it, and sure enough 1 2 3 pause, 1 2 3 pause. I say, "It's strong and keeps the same pattern. I wouldn't worry about it." I wanted to say, *Of course it'll skip if you just sit here in this stink hole of a room with the windows sealed shut and feel it all day and wait for it to skip.*

Later, I say to Sal, "It's skipping because it's his birthday and no one's done or said anything yet." I say to Flynn then, knowing this: that this heart skipping is his infant acting up, having a tantrum, fussing in the crib, *demonstrating*, to get attention, "I've set up your birthday party. I will be home at six o'clock and we'll celebrate...."

He ignored that, saying, "I wish I could get someone to take my blood pressure."

I say, "Go to the clinic and let Finklemetz do it." This is the doctor I have banned for doling out Valium. Flynn lights up, has my permission, lets go of himself (it used to be his penis he held all day, now it's his pulse...) and starts jumping up and down in ever so imperceptible twitches of glee around the head and shoulders.

Death Valley

Sal starts right in as soon as I get in the car. About the tire. What's wrong with it and how to replace it. I feel the break from responsibility ebbing and anger there instead. I can't control it after a mile. I holler, "I don't want to hear about one more thing broken and needing to be fixed. If you can't create an illusion of fantasy that *my* world isn't falling apart on a date, then take me home. I can go out by myself and create it...It's not that I don't know about reality and haven't faced it..." I dwindle down, ashamed, because I can see I've startled Sal into stern silence.

Maybe this is the way Mama felt when she divorced Flynn and married Jolsen. She suddenly had everything Flynn couldn't provide: a nice house, food in the cupboards, a domestic setting to match all the other middle class working people. But no romance. Jolsen spent himself being a provider. There wasn't anything left when he went to bed. They were both forty and into their third marriage. Flynn wouldn't spend on practical things, "only on recreation," Mama yelled all through our childhood. Now she was quiet but discontent. She had her well-stocked kitchen, well-furnished house, steady husband. A tamed man. A trained man. A domesticated one. And she missed Flynn. We all heard about it. How Jolsen was dull. How Flynn never lost his touch for romance. "Even after six kids he'd say, "hop in the car Rosyln. Just leave everything. We'll buy what we need along the way" (although he'd decide they didn't need anything)..." and he'd take her off to Death Valley or Grand Canyon, both singing along the way. There are photos of her in sunsuits wearing wide brimmed hats on the edge of a cliff or under a Joshua tree, smiling her big smile. Her famous smile. She never not smiled when the shutter clicked. Flynn used to joke about it.

Mama would complain about Jolsen's way of going on an

outing. He was president of the Lapidary Society and sought after by the Geology Dept. at the University. "He's a rock-hound," Mama would chortle over the phone. And then go on about how long he took to pack the car. Two ice chests. All the camping gear. "Flynn wouldn't take anything at all. Just himself. A flannel blanket or two. We'd make love all night long. We'd sleep under the stars. Not even any food. After Jolsen gets through unpacking, eating, setting up camp, he's ready to fall asleep. There's *nothing*."

I can see Mama lying awake, wondering what happened to her life. Sal now, kills any chance for romance even though he sets the settings. A full moon. Night. A cliff. An ocean. A Santana wind. Good food. Maybe wine if we go off our strict restriction. (At first I was afraid to stand on a cliff with him at night.…) But it's only him and his quiet control. His own absence of discontent. The men I've known, were always miserable men, fighting themselves, fighting *life*: trying to get the impossible. Wrestling with limitation, angry over their own small lives, And power-minded. Trying to believe their size more than satisfied a woman.

With Sal the race of the blood is anti-yoga. He tries to maintain the calm composure of the Other World. Lives in a state of transcendence. And then what do you know? An erection is suddenly there. But how can I be interested. I'm usually surprised. Can it be over me? How can a dick get hard over nothing evident? What's the arousal? I am certainly not stimulated by all the peacefulness. Then he's all worked up, kissing and carrying on and I'm left out wondering what he is excited about. But my trained animal, the dog of a body, picks up the scent and succumbs in spite of me. A cloistered nun taken against her will. The cloistered nun I am because I can't have John. Or didn't get him. That part went into hiding. Resides in a convent. Acts like sleeping beauty…waiting for her prince. While Sal dashes himself against the solid stone wall of the trying to get to me. Is this how Mama felt when she left Flynn and married Jolsen? Unattainable? Yet, on the outside, went about the business of mating again. Never understanding herself? Mama, the hopeless romantic and ever practical. I've

343

asked Sal, "How can you get a hard-on in the middle of all your spirituality and me, my age," remembering how Flynn hated fifty-year-old women. "I thought you had to conjure worldly images, carnal thoughts, to cause something like that to happen. It's a contradiction, all your beliefs and then suddenly you're hard and wanting in. Where does it come from and how come it doesn't show on you before it happens?"

He just smiles a little uncomfortably, and with some pride. I want to know. To his silence, I demand, "Tell me. What makes you suddenly *there* when all I see and hear are you looking at the stars and talking talk of beauty and brotherly love and humanity?" He never answers. I tell him, "The men I've known, they've always worked themselves up with..." He stops me.

Thought never had to precede stimulation for me with John. And now with Sal I can't get any images to make me feel sexual. "My Men," as people say, "Baggage."

Each man has to find something wrong with the others. Each man, a little god unto himself, thinking he, alone, is right, and all the others are flawed in some important way as to render them no competition. An equalizing mechanism...

Sal instructs, When you wash my pajamas, please don't put the pants in the dryer or the snaps will melt...hand wring them and hang them out to dry." I wonder why I obey when I thought I was finally through doing things for men. Around Sal I feel like the Jews who didn't recognize their king. Sal comes along being and saying everything I've always wanted a man to be and say. He gives me all the pretty words and pretty actions. He gives me all the love I can take. And I don't recognize him as my lover. I thought he'd look like John, my savior would.

§

When Flynn first came to my door to stay I had it out with him. He went to counseling and learned about what he did to me. "A natural aversion" to him was laid down in my nervous system at the time of his violating my flesh when I was

344

a child. Later, when I went back to school, a woman told me she learned the harm of molestation in graduate school. I wondered, "She had to be told? See it in print, read it in a book? Didn't she already feel it in herself?"

Flynn comes in with a big false-toothed smile, holding a postcard from Hawaii and telling me, "The kids wrote from Hawaii." I turn off the vacuum cleaner so I can hear. He repeats it. I take a look. Sure enough. "The kids." That strikes me odd. I'm one of his kids, too. It's my brother and his family he speaks of. And, yes, they wrote, indeed; I look at Flynn's joy as he holds the postcard, turns it to see the picture with palm trees. Like a prize. He's determined to still be the family cat even when the family is over and done with.

The only time John was alert was when a new girl entered the room. He suddenly became interested in picking her brain. Otherwise he is as antsy as a drug addict without his fix. Under the guise that he liked the girl's intelligence, which meant she took to him, he found out all about other men in her life and if there'd be one present when he was about to mount her. Other than that he said people were boring and predictable. He had a kind of "hard on" look in his eye all the time.

Vicious

A vicious session at a free counseling appointment where I felt my face moving involuntarily as the therapist said (after a simple storyline of my life), "You're sick; you're still a victim; you've got to get angry and sell your house, move away, leave the Past, start a life of your own...." She brought out a log and gave me a rolled up newspaper and told me to begin hitting it and saying what I am mad about, to "get it out." I sat, shallow and looking at her, feeling nothing but some awe over her adamancy. I left with one of her perfunctory, weak Christian hugs, where I felt a roll of fat on her waist, even though she's known as tall and skinny.

Just the storyline made the therapist cry out, wring her hands, and get worried for me. She said, with her face contorted, "You're still living their lives. That's being a victim." And she brought out a wood stump that had been sealed in resin so it looked plastic, and a rolled-up newspaper that had been scotchtaped so there were no loose edges. She handed me the rolled newspaper and ordered me to beat the stump and call out, in fact shout, my anger with each beat I have for the abuse I have taken from men. I sat limp. I told her I didn't feel any anger. She wrinkled her face into urgency for me. "That's sick. You're sick if you don't feel anger over all that's happened to you." She attacks me with her angry insistence over my anger-resistance. I sit holding the cudgel and attempt some anger to please her. I inhale and begin, "I'm mad at John for having other women behind my .... " But there is no force behind it, and the slap on the stump falls out of synch with the words. A weak swat.

I had given her all the key words: molestation, nervous breakdown, brain tumor, car wreck, suicide. And heart attack. Each man in turn ending up with one of the above. She says, "You should go a long time without sex. You only know yourself through having sex with a man." My cheeks begin to burn. She has just met me and heard a bare-bones account and draws conclusions. I ask her what it costs—Therapy. She says a two-year package at eighty dollars a session once a week is what she would suggest. I tell her money is my main problem right now. That Flynn will die, Alex is over the fence, so out of my life, that my house is important to me as a kind of homestead. And the only actual problem is Sal. He is the nicest man I have ever known, but I don't want a man in my life right now. And that I still watch for John on the street.

She groans with each statement. And then sums it up, "So you are waiting for things to happen to you again, your father to die, your ex-husband to eventually finish his house and move away, for the nicest guy you've ever met to leave and for the one who abused you the most, a real sleaze who sleeps with his students to come back and rescue you…Oh, oh, oh, I feel so sorry for you…."

I say, "I just don't feel angry today. I gave up coffee so I don't feel that kind of tension anymore…" I am battered by her picture of me. I add, "And I have yelled and screamed at each man in turn. Do you think I have just taken everything without a fight?" Later, I report all this to Sal, except for the part of wanting him out of my life. I have already told him that in the beginning, and then let it go on because his kindness felt good.

"You are a queen bee. A sergeant. A field commander. Maybe as a child you were a victim, but now you have everyone towing the line. You rule, Baby. No one can get away with anything…."

I dream that night that I have two rooms unused and very promising to rent out and make at least nine hundred dollars more a month. I wonder how I could have overlooked them and let them sit so long. A tenant is in one and begins causing a fuss. She does not want to be uprooted. She has not had to pay rent until now, has resided secretly.

Jung said that's your unused mind, your potential waiting for you to tap into.

A second dream: An old broken-down, alcohlic woman

is being held together by me in her shabby suit, a gunny sack of sorts, and awful ruddy complexion and coarse hair. And those good rooms again, appear going to waste.... *Your brain,* the therapist would say.

Contorts

I think about how the therapist contorted her face. The first
session was free. She had recruited all the people who'd
attended her free seminar on "relationships." I went. It was
something to do beside go home and watch Flynn pick at his
food and listen to his false teeth clack. And I missed the subject. My own training in therapy and I had stayed away from
it a few years now. She passed a paper around and we each
signed our name and phone number. The next day she called
and asked me to come for a free session. I think I expected
some recognition for being someone *strong*.

We sat facing eachother and she asked me if I had any
"issues." I gave her a simple storyline, my life up until now,
and with each word she screwed up her face as if I were saying bad words: molestation, nervous breakdown, brain tumor,
suicide, betrayal, deceit, neglect. Her facial expressions com-
miserated with each brief story until the last line, the end of
the story was, "My father lives with me, and my ex-husband
is next door, and I still scan the street for a glimpse of John."
That's when she cried out, "*Oh*, oh, oh, you're still sick," And
pulled out the shellacked wooden stump and Scotchtaped roll
of newspaper and commanded me to beat the stump and get
all my anger out. My mouth twitched. I told her I didn't feel
angry. And I wondered at that point if she had assumed I was
beyond any accumulations? When I walked in, did she believe
I was up in a nice little life, having left everything behind? Is
that what women today *do*?

The way she kept crying out and twisting up her face
and saying over and over, "You don't even feel anger? Oh,
oh, you're sick…" And. "You're still looking for and missing
this man who abused you for five years? And your father's
under the same roof? And your ex-husband lives next door?
And you don't feel anger and won't hit the stump. Oh, oh,

oh, you're still a victim. You're *sick*." Then the time was up. I went out with the rhythm, "And my pig won't go over the stile so I shan't get home tonight," ringing in my ears. An old children's tale!

"You were robbed of your childhood and now of your adulthood. Of your *life!*" Forty-five minutes of her accusations. I leave whacked, beaten, and attacked by her words. The entrance sign says, "Emotional Expression Christian Therapy House." I hadn't noticed when I went in.

I hurry away. My issue was money, in my estimation. And she wanted at least two years at eighty dollars a session, once a week? (over $4,000/year). And Sal. I didn't want him in my life. I simply wanted to be alone. She had glossed over that by telling me that the only decent man I've ever known, I wanted to get rid of. Then the part about not having a sex life. The way she had popped up suddenly with that. "You're used to using sex. It's your only relationship with men." Was she quick to jump to conclusions? Or was I the last to know what was obvious to everyone else?

During the free relationship seminar, she had chosen a few people to work with in a group. One beautiful blonde-California-beachcareer-silk-blouse-leather-briefcase-for-a-purse-thirtyish type talked openly about her incest with her father. She got praise from the therapist for being so "up front" about the subject and for "apparently doing quite well."

I think now that I could have given her another story-line, similar to the beautiful girl's. I got a B.A., M.A., married an airline pilot, travelled the world, bore three beautiful intelligent children. My father was a talented artist who sold over two hundred paintings in his career as a free-lance art-ist.... successful brothers and sisters, a beautiful home, pool, spa, land, savings...etc. But I knew a therapist doesn't want to hear the happy side. Did she think I got my aging skin being indoors nursing on some man's dick all my life? That's the trouble with admitting any problems; your appearance is then interpreted by imagined behavior. Any mole, unwanted hair, wrinkle, worn places. In fact my skin was weathered because of sunning and reading on all the beaches in all the brochures all over the world. Not from debauchery, but from pleasure.

It bothered her that it didn't bother me more. She confessed that she'd been an alcoholic all her life and had been sober only the past ten years. She was fifty-seven. She opened an office, and drummed up business by bringing out the stump and rolled paper and charging eighty dollars for 45 minutes for a two-to-five year package, assisting people to beat out their angers over their "abuses."

I wondered where the Christian part was: forgiveness, understanding, compassion? Or did she use the example of Jesus' righteous anger in the temple where the merchants were selling prayer booths?

Sure: I was probably seething with anger down deep. They call it "floating rage" that alights on any little thing on the surface and is ready to tear it apart. But, as I told her, I'd screamed and yelled at Flynn and Alex and John. Did she really think I'd been a lamb? Just because I couldn't muster a performance in front of her in the first fifteen minutes of a session? I'd broken things. Relished in the sound of crashing and tinkling. At fifty-two, did she think I'd repressed anything?

And did she know anything about Flynn and Alex being right under my nose to "work" through all the "unfinished business," as she called it. If they were off somewhere, they'd remain boogymen. Old memories of mine in their prime that I still feared. I'd never have gotten to witness their weakening and aging and becoming needy. And my own strength up against them. *That was therapeutic.* Educational. I'd have missed that. There were weekend workshops on confronting your perpetrator. Scripts taught, learned, memorized, rehearsed, and practiced until you get the words right when you went to visit an old abuser. I'd seen grown clients shake and cry trying to face an old father in play-acting a confrontation, looking at the therapist and trying to use the words, faltering and flaring up with courage and finally getting them out. The whole thing contrived. Pretend. And then coming back later to report to the group how it really went. And many times chickening out or going about it half-heartedly. Finding the words were the therapists words, not their own. That they simply didn't feel the "betrayal" they were told they were supposed to feel. Coming away feeling like there must be something wrong with them if they didn't feel the hate and anger and rage the therapist told them they should feel. "Studies have been made which show that when a parent does that to you it is the greatest betrayal...," therapists blink, pigheadedly.

No one ever mentioned living with the one who abused you as a cure. Passing time as an adult, no longer being a child and no longer being abused, watching an old abuser grow older and more feeble in the world, and seeing him reach out for help, just like any old parent anywhere.

Therapists are always embarrassed over the subject and afraid of any degree of acceptance. They advocate revenge, throwing the first stone, getting even, cutting off the relationship to punish the aberrant father. I thought, "If I kept leaving everyone who transgressed against me would I be alone?

If I stay and fight, not run, everyone thinks Flynn has "gotten away with it." And that makes the therapist angry. He is still having access to me. She kept telling me to get away, be away, get a new life. A life of my own. A new life without anyone I know in it from my present situation. Leave family?

I told her Alex was like a son. Or a brother. He was a relative now, not an ex-husband. And Flynn was my father. That my life was my own right here. That the men had fallen away like dry corn husks.

"No, no, no, " she protested. "They're still taking from you. You are still putting off your life for them."

I'd said, "Flynn will soon die. He actually died last October but the hospital kept him alive. His health has been bad this year. And Alex will finish his house and sell it and travel."

"No, no, no, You must take an active role in getting rid of them."

I wondered, *Am I passive? Still waiting for everyone who bothers me, extracts my time and energy, to drop dead, move away or grow up so I can be alone?* I can't even tell Sal to go away. I let him stay around. He makes himself useful. They all do.

There was a time I pictured a life of my own. Just after I met John. I'd envisioned a white room, a big window, pastel dishes, a clean and clear place with nothing old in it, a trip to Africa. Me, new, too. Close to my bones and clean inside and out. And seeing, seeing, seeing and understanding. And interested in helping others see and understand. Observation replacing service. Not doing anything that I didn't want to do. Well, wasn't I doing that right here. Money was the only issue. I told the therapist that I would be somewhere else with money. I'd provide everything for everyone. I'd see to everyone's needs with my bank account instead of elbow grease. She frowned on that.

She held onto the popular views: *You can't, absolutely, live with an ex-offender...it is unheard of. You can't simply reduce them down to just any old man.*

I reminded her of the Fright/Fight/Flight response to life. I told her I was the kind to stay and fight. That I never asked for the circumstances to be this way, had imagined them differently, but for the time being my life was this way and I was staying and facing it head on. And that I ran everyday. That was the flight part. That I did both. She saw it as so much cowardice. Instead of taking action.

Alex at Last

Alex's World

I went with him shortly after my mother's funeral just for a distraction and for human contact, I suppose. I wanted comforting, and got into the passenger's seat of his red pickup truck, and put on the seatbelt, maneuvering my feet onto the floor of the car among the debris: paper cups, pinched napkins, gum wrappers, junk and stuff he threw there, thinking he'd clean it up someday. I took one of the napkins and began dusting the dashboard in front of me out of habit. It was an attempt to wipe away his mess, at least the layer of dirt that had accumulated for months, maybe since he'd bought the truck in '97. When I'd first met Alex and took a ride home from campus, I was appalled at the random mess of papers and text books strewn all over the back seat and floor. He had to move a pile just to accommodate my getting into the seat beside him. It was before bucket seats and seatbelts. He drove a Chrysler convertible then; a sea blue, the color of his eyes.

He clears a space for me now, with the same amount of privilege to have my company as he did forty-four years ago. A twenty-eight year marriage, a four-year divorce, and another ten year remarriage hadn't seemed to faze us. He was still himself and I, myself. We were fixed personalities, almost polar points.

The Man Who Could Fix Anything
But Himself (Alex)

Once there was a man who could see inside and outside a thing without even looking. He could see it in his mind's eye and figure out how it worked and fix it. He lay daydreaming at times, picturing the way a house is built, a washing machine works, how the car engine fits all together and makes its sounds and runs. Yet, over the years as he grew tired of fixing things, he began to just sit around. He grew sad and alone and did not know how to fix himself.

The Man Who Loved Magazines
(Alex: could be a children's story)

He got them in the mail. Lots of them. And each time, going to his mailbox, he felt happy. There was the one about flying planes. Ah, yes. What new ideas would he get to read about. There was the one about space travel. Ah, yes. What was the latest news on how to launch a rocket and get way out there away from the earth's atmosphere. And, of course, there was one about gourmet cooking. He didn't cook, but he liked the pictures because he loved to eat. He gave that one to his son, who was a grown man by now and loved to cook. There was one about keeping your home beautiful. He browsed through that one and dreamed of being younger when he could have planted something here and there, laid a stone walkway, or built a garden shed. He was a man who loved new information and found it between the covers of special magazines. And he was a man who lived alone and liked the mailman to deliver him things that made him know someone out there, even if it was just a publishing company, knew his name and address and sent magazines to him. This made him feel special seeing his name on the magazine. Ah, yes, indeed that was himself, after all; when his grown children were busy with their own lives.

The man who loved magazines stacked his magazines in order of their names and dates, and subjects. His mother had been a librarian. The floors of each room in his house were lined with stacks of his magazines. He could not bear to part with these cherished possessions, for each magazine contained oodles and gobs of the latest information, of which he was immensely interested. He gathered the most recent research on science in a tiny periodical called Science News- Briefings on the interiors of the finest scientists of today's minds. In this way, the man felt he was keeping up no matter how old he was getting, or failing in eyesight, hearing, and ability to walk far or sleep well. His mind craved to connect to the greatest minds of the time, to be a part at the great surges of findings in all subjects. He sat for hours, glasses perched on his nose, eyes startlingly crystal blue and focused on print and pictures, studying. This was the man's pleasure.

When the man was interrupted by some necessity such as hunger or thirst or cold, he grumbled to himself and got up, shut the windows, looked in the refrigerator, opened a can, turned on the fire, heated up something to eat, huddled inside his house, putting the magazine aside to be picked up later. As he partook of food and shelter, his mind wandered to dreaming of the contents of the article he'd been reading. Sometimes he'd forget to turn off the stove until he smelled smoke coming from the oven and found his apple pie blackened, or to turn down the heater until he broke out in a sweat. The man who loved his brand new magazines, that came in the mail just to him, for him, with the latest knowledge, was an absentminded man. His mind did not like to think about what he was doing, but daydreamed about ideas which he found printed in magazines. In this way, he belonged to that other world beyond his small home with the daily needs always calling to him to use up his time. He floated and drifted above the mundane world of practicality while reading, reading, reading. The ideas filled up his mind, while the magazines filled up his house. In time, the man who loved magazines was crowded into a small space, surrounded by stacks of magazines.

The Family Man

After twenty-five years of marriage, a nasty divorce when he squandered the children's college fund on two cars so he wouldn't have to share it with her, after saying all the bad things he could think of about her to justify his position of righteousness, he sits in her livingroom in the big easychair he has claimed as his place now and accepts the plates of food she brings to him. Food to clean him out. She administers colon cleansers three times a day, and fiber-rich foods to prevent colon cancer. He is a family man, after all is said and done. He likes a woman bringing him dinner. He likes the sounds of a woman in the kitchen. He likes the sight of a woman in those private moments, brushing her teeth, fixing her hair, putting on make-up, gathering laundry, doing dishes, dusting, vacuuming. He cocks an ear at the vacuum's motor and offers to tighten something. And she succumbs to his ability to fix anything around the house.

Her grown daughters and son have urged her to "take care of Dad, Mom. You're the stronger one. He doesn't know any better. If he's got tingling in his feet, he could die. He could have a stroke. Maybe it's diabetes. You know how he eats...." And so she has complied. He is the new homeless, having given his home to the son whose the age he was when they bought the place. The son with the young energy and belief in the future to carry on, gets ideas for fixing the place up, throwing his back into landscaping. It's better, finally to let the young male handle it, the hardship. There's an exchange of power between young and old men. Nothing is said, it becomes understood by assertion. The old get tired and want to sit. The young get up and get going. Sitting and resting under the guise of reflecting on the past and pondering the next step becomes the activity of choice for the old. "Come on, Dad, let's go. What's taking you so long. Hurry up. I'm

ready. We've been ready for an hour. What are you doing?"
Not much different than when Dad was a young dad with a
teenage son. And now at 70, with his son at 40, it's the same
thing. (The son died of a heart attack at 47.)

He knew she would have a soft spot for him if he gave
his house to their son, and came offering to fix things in her
house. Sure enough, it worked. He did her pool heater, caulked
both tubs, put in a new faucet, one of those fancy kind. She
kept cursing the ones he'd put in when they had the house
together. Said she'd broken her knuckles for years trying to
turn them on and off. It was all her cursing he was trying to
quell with his help, he'd convinced himself after being around
for awhile. Just like when they first met, he tried to still her
emotions, after he'd stirred them up. He knew her so well, but
this new anger she carried around, spewing in every direction
at anyone within range, was new to him. She had it good, if
she'd stop to think about it. Her own home, no debt, teaching
if she felt like it, no pressure there. But, she took everything
too hard, as if it were a life-and-death situation. If she'd just
calm down. He had to walk on eggs, and she kept reminding
him of the marriage and how he'd been. So he made the least
amount of show, coming and going, so not to set her off, fixed
things, and it was a nice exchange. He had the big easy chair,
the daily paper; she'd bring tea and plates of food. He slept in
the daughter's old bedroom. And he was not obligated to do
a damn thing if he didn't want to. He was free to be a family
man now.

Alex Next Door

After all our years together, dreaming of the future turning out; his successes and mine. He's with dementia. Alex beyond failing his dreams. A brain tumor in 1978. Dementia coming on in 2005. He was born in 1933.

Alex wanted to become a millionaire. That was the American dream when he was growing up. His father never made a million; but also dreamed of that as a goal. Alex always feared the system. He was not capable of being, fitting in, blending, doing what needs to be done to succeed by its rules. He fiercely resisted bending to the rules. And resented that he wasn't enough for it.

He was a loner. He fought the phantoms he created in his head, that they were out to get him, to make him fail. I became that demon to Alex all through the marriage. From 1962 until he fell apart in 2006. He called me all the names that he felt he was himself. Poor Alex. Yet he's willing to throw everything away to get even for what he believes was the injustice of the system he suffered, via me. All those thousands of dollars he spent to show me who's boss. Money he needed to succeed. Ironically, he threw away the only property he'd ever have, to lawyers, so that he could put me in my place. This, after seventy years of my giving him all I had in money, time, energy, and love. I cared to help him, feed him, tend him, care to the point of sleepless nights in worry. All silent inside stuff he never saw. And if he did surmise that my efforts saved Alex's property for as long as I could, he'd deny it, needing to see evil personified. Something other than his own limitations had to be the reason for all that's happened to him. That Alex got sick, that one tragedy after another happened. My fault. Sad. Alex is in diapers.

I can hear him next door. Alex hollers for help in his dementia-paranoia.

All those years, before we owned that property next door, Alex and I in this house working on the marriage, trying to do the best we could; my tears over his criticisms. For years, tears and blaming myself, believing all he said about me was really my fault. I was trash, bad, evil, stupid, no good. All those years I took abuse. All those years he needed to put me down. And then, spend his entire estate on trying to destroy me. Smug that he got "Mother." After his lawyers force a sale on his property and pay themselves, he'll realize what he's done. And guess whose fault it will be: "Mother's." Of course she made him do this because she is so evil he had to try to destroy her and it destroyed himself doing so. Like Hitler and the Jews....

Alex

In 1958 I was 19, Alex was 26. I'm 69 in 2008, Alex going on 75 this December. He lives next door because we have never been able to blend or mend as a couple since our marriage in 1962. I go over now to give him his car insurance mail that comes to my mailbox for some reason. His mailbox is next door on the street down the way. He stands there with his hair on end, sheared around the ears and neck the way he likes it, cut by me now for over 45 years. I think that's why he married me: free haircuts and for my pots of spaghetti. He used to come over when he was "courting" me. I'd make a big pot of spaghetti with meatballs, the sauce mixed in, full of chopped onions, garlic, any green vegetables and tomatoes. He was so thin then, in the eastcoast proper white-collar way, vs. the blue-collar need to show muscle and flesh that I was used to in my brothers, that he'd down the spaghetti with lots of melted cheese on top, served up as a big casserole. He loved yeast rolls, too, the way his mother used to make them when he was a kid. I bought heat-and-serve, not good at breadmaking myself. And real butter. I was working my way through college as a beautician then, and spent my hard-earned money on these ingredients for Alex. In trade, he'd lift the hood of my car and check out my engine, change spark plugs, change the oil, etc. Now, he stands there glowering at me as I bring his mail. He, so white without a touch of sun, once-blonde hair turned silver with no balding. People comment on his looking younger than his age, and still good looking. Naturally slender, his pot gut subsiding now that he's lost most of his teeth and can chew only Vons oatmeal soft cookies and canned soup and microwave burritos, drink prune juice and milk and eat the odd fruit he has sitting around getting ripe on his table top. He eyes me with mirth. It's the same mirth he eyed me with on campus back in 1958. A certain knowing, as if I'm a dirty joke. I have taken on a tough exterior to ward off his criticisms still, even though we divorced in the mid-Eighties and remarried in the mid-Nineties for business reasons, and live as neighbors. I would like to show some affection besides bringing plates of healthy home-cooked meals, but know he'd translate that as having a realization that he was, indeed, the right one, I'm the wrong one, and I've come around to grovel at his feet. The light blue eye with the snake-like black pupil has never looked kind or soft or sorry or compassionate. It is a vindictive look leveled like the barrel of a gun scrutiny of my presence that causes me to come and go quickly. He will motion sometimes to sit down, clearing the other of the two chairs in front of the TV so I'll stay awhile and chat. He'll ask me what's going on, if he's in a good mood, full of cookies; and if he has had too much black coffee so that he's turned mean, he'll start accusing me of owing him money. I leave. He follows me out and once told me to lift my shirt so he could check to see if I stole anything while there. I have to make allowances for his pre dementia, as it's due to the cortisone he takes, now since 1978 for a pituitary tumor operation he had. The Alex from campus never came out of that hospital room. He was a different man, one who had to learn to walk and talk again. One that was selfish and mean-spirited, even more than on campus, when he watched me the way a fox watches a hen crossing its path. Forty-six years later, he would devour me, my house, my meager anything that sustains me so that I would not "win" in his mind. As he fails, he talks of having someone do me in. I flee, still his victim in his eyes, but not in mine. He was beaten as a boy and sent out into the world angry.

Alex's Eyes

July 14, 2011

They're awful. At 78 and with dementia and paranoia, they're almost transparent You can see his sorrow of all the beatings he got as a child. Once he said, with tears, "If my father had ever said he loved me, I could have taken all the beatings, but he never said it, even once." Thus his greed to have all that he accumulated in five sheds, a huge workshop. All the tools he never got to have as a kid. His father gave away a tool chest to the neighbor, who gave it to his son, just to spite Alex, who was then named Harold Clement Howard, Jr. On the dance floor in Puerto Rico, full of booze, Alex cried, remembering how cruel his father was for doing that, knowing how much he wanted those tools. And now, next door, Alex eyes his sheds and tool shop, stuffed so full of his childhood longings, that he hasn't gone on a trip with his free airline passes for years. Like a mother hen, he watches for thieves. And like that old man who lived here and feared thieves, Alex let the thief into his house, lawyers to sell off all those tools, one by one, or in great sets. First to go was his welder and generator with all the accessories. While Alex slept, drugged on meds, lawyers sold his cherished possessions off, pocketed the money, liquidating all the contents in the tool chest. While Alex, too feeble to turn the lock and check his tools in his big shop, lies there, peeing in his pants, unable to chew because of his partial dentures coming loose. Losing what Alex holds dear to his heart. The court-appointed conservator thought, *Alex won't need it any more, he's too weak to get out of bed, too weak to stand up and check on his possessions.* The lawyers take the estate Alex and I worked so hard for, and his four thousand dollar a month airline retirement. *We sell Alex's stuff and keep it away from the wife. We call it a "scrivener's mistake."*

Alex's eyes in court, during the trial to get the deed out of the son's name and give it all back to Alex, the half-acre property, were sleepy slits that stared hard and when they fell upon his wife, me, sitting with my lawyers, scrutinized with a look that said, *If I had my .44, I'd shoot you first and then your lawyers, the way I shot at our son and tried to kill him five years before he died of a heart attack. It's all mine, and I'm in court to defend my stuff.*

I've seen eyes like Alex's on a snake. The colorlessness that matches the skin. All camouflage of creatures surviving, blending into the place they sit and gaze out from, waiting for prey. Poor Alex. I remember him on campus. Blue eyes, and with the same pain and rage, that someday he'd get even for all the beatings and no tools of his childhood. I am his mother, father, the hickory stick, his evil sisters, and all the people who made him miserable growing up. I was easy prey, striding across campus with my runner's legs, hair flowing in the breeze. And he, "knowing." I remember that knowing look he had, and the mirth. He'd laugh at me in my smugness that I thought I had a right to myself. He'd have me soon enough. A predator, determined to destroy me; and destroying himself.

Head of the Family

They brought him in in hobbles. Seventy-two now, white hair grown out longer than he liked it, fraying around the neckline, in jail-blue cotton shirt and pants. He'd had enough and had taken out his shotgun and shot at his own life, blasting out the windows of his house. He wanted it over and done with. He saw no future.

The grown son had come home to live to help develop the property when his father seemed to have lost all spine to do anything but sit on the couch and watch television or read his science magazines. At sixty-five, he felt entitled to do just that, even though the plan had been to build the big house up at the front of the property near the street like all the other houses in the neighborhood. After Alex's brain tumor and after the separation, he still had enough juice left in his bloodstream to build a small place at the foot of his half acre in which to live while he was building the big house. The thing he overlooked was that he'd run out of steam and had just enough life in him to get up, take his long hot shower which he'd claimed was the greatest invention of civilization, make up some breakfast, and then aim for the couch, pick up the remote, look at the big guys running America for awhile, talk out loud to them, criticizing them or praising them, encouraging them to go kill our enemies; and then click it off, pick up *Science News*, or *Mechanic Illustrated*, or a tool or clothes catalogue and make out the order form, printing out his credit card number carefully in the boxes. Inside his four storage sheds and inside his dresser drawers, there were unopened packages of items ordered that came in the mail, were never opened, but put away in case he may need them, or because they were too good a deal to turn down. So many shirts for fifty dollars and the company would give you an extra one free. He loved shopping this way, from the couch, with his card, viewing the photographs of the items without having to get up and go looking in stores. He went to stores, too; but on days too dreary to stay home and feel lonely; on days he feared he'd become a shut-in. On those days he'd fire up his fire-engine-red pickup truck and lead foot it to Harbor Freight for tools and machinery, then Walmart and Target, marvelling over all the new gadgetry that'd been invented and available so cheap he couldn't pass it up. And he had a means of carrying any item they sold of any size in the bed of his truck. Behind the driver's seat, if you pushed the lever, it'd pop forward and he'd find his stash of belts with metal adjustable clamps for strapping down any packages he chose to buy. Again the credit card. As the debt grew, his brow furrowed deeper. On the first of the month, when the bills came, he grew livid with rage, caught in a cycle of shopping, the pleasure of empowerment from ownership to the horror of paying dearly for the spree. Overspenders Anonymous he laughed at and brushed aside. He didn't need that: His father died with every camera ever made. That was the way Alex was like his father. Both spenders on what they felt entitled to: Alex with tools, his father, cameras.

Geese Mate for Life

11-17-13

Geese stay together as mates. Yes, that's what I just said. Wolves, too. For life. Lions have a harem. Roosters jump on and off hens all day. They don't pair off unless, like Little Red, our bantam rooster, had no choice. He had his hen and was devoted to her. We had a big weeping willow tree back then in the backyard. Little Red would scratch up a bug and do a little dance with his wing down circling around the find, making a cluck and she'd come running as only hens run, with their heads stretched out and their wings behind and wobbling on those drumstick legs. He'd let her eat the bug. Eventually they had chicks and he pranced around, crowing all day, not only at dawn. At the last he lay down his life for her. It was before I put up a fence. Some neighbor dogs ran through the yard. He stood his ground, little spurs ready; They were the big shepherd dogs from the cul-de-sac. They punctured his lungs. We came running to rescue him and held him as he wheezed his last breath. We found her, his mate, his hen hiding under the car in the driveway. He'd told her to duck for cover and he would protect her. She was fine. He was her man, she his woman. Alex was kind of like that back then. He'd go to the door when there was a bump in the night. I was his wife, he my husband and "head of household," as men were called before all the single parenting took over. Women are now home guarding the kids with an alarm system or 911 in place of the man. A friend of Alex's was near homeless years ago, before it was a term to be used on poor men without a mate or place to lay their head, except on the ground. He killed a gander at the bird refuge and told us, laughing, how the goose cried and cried and tried to get into the garbage can where he was stashed to hide the illegal kill from the police. My dog, once, a big white-and-gray shepherd, always ran the foothill with me. On one run, in the spring, he veered off the shoulder of the road just long enough to snap the neck of a gopher that was pushing dirt up out or his hole. I stopped and yelled and hit the dog. He crouched, shame in place of pride. He was my mate, I his female. He did it for me. It's what a mated wolf would do on a run through the brush. As we went on, Alex and me, we withdrew a part of ourselves from the other. Too much cruelty came from his mouth about how inferior I was to him. I had savage pride, as all humans do, no matter how wretched. Tribal people. Slaves. That pride cannot be stomped on. It is what causes all the conflicts that ever were. Welfare cleaned up its way of distributing their free money and food stamps, to avoid the general public staring and disapproving of them as they went through the grocery store line. A woman with a string of kids, or just her shabby self, peeling off government welfare cash. Now they get their credit card in the mail and no one knows who's needy or not. Savage pride and native intelligence. Alex's words of "lower-class and ignorant," directed toward me for twenty years in the marriage, broke the bond that would have us mate for life like a goose and gander. Imagine a gander pecking at his goose until her feathers were missing all around her neck. That precious part who protected itself, that little human inside of the wife, the social role out front, and the tender one inside. If Alex had only cherished me, told me good things about myself, I would have felt a deep loss when he died. I cried, yes. I cried for the poor Alex who had to be superior to me. After we were divorced, he got down on bended knee and asked me to marry him again. I stupidly did. He'd said all the good things after he lost me. But it was too late to grow a pearl around that grain of irritation for years.

In Memory of Alex

8-20-13

I forgave Alex's violent nature because of his upbringing, "spare the rod and spoil the child," which his father and mother exercised with a certain edge of a cruel streak that went beyond discipline and into a possible sexual arousal of power, same as Hitler. Alex, though, could not forgive me my childhood sexual abuse. Sex is always a bigger thing than plain old physical and psychological abuse. He used it against me and told everyone in his family that he had to put up with a wife who was "sexual." Too bad I wasn't frigid. If I'd been like Alex's mother, who, the father told me was "cold and did not like sex," Alex may have felt sorry for me. He may not have blamed me for my childhood. I never blamed Alex for his parents beating on him; yet he blamed me for getting molested. The difference is that his family liked to "get" something on people, while mine didn't. Alex "had" that on me and passed it down to the one remaining child who looked like me but was the spittin' image of him and his sisters inside. Who carried out the blame, even taking it to court in the form of the book I wrote about it. There it was, bound and printed for all to read. Where was Alex's book about his childhood strappings with his father's belt, and the hickory stick his mother used to whip his bare legs with?

Alex's Obituary

Dec. 3, 1933–April 8, 2012

Alex Howard liked to teach his kids to push back their cuticles; and instruct them in bicycle maintenance. He loved hot yeast rolls with real butter, and spaghetti and meat balls. He loved tools of any kind: woodworking, metal, auto, and marine. He loved to build houses, boats, and repair cars. He had meters that could detect a tiny wire in a heating blanket that shorted out; loved astronomy and taught his kids the wonders of the night sky. He said the greatest invention of mankind was the long hot shower, where he whistled *The Ride Of Valkyries* and sang *The Student Prince*. He was blond, lean, handsome and full of high energy. He flew planes for a living with a major airline; but his true love was invention. He built a two-man scuba submarine and got a patent on it. He could fix anything; and reinvented the wheel each time with his amazing innovative repairs. As a young man, right out of the Air Force, a cadet, before marriage and a real job as a pilot, he started a High Time Repair service. It was a skill he'd use as a homeowner for fifty years. All the above is gone now. Alex had 80 years of self-expression of his talents, intelligence, and his family man heart.

Marty

Flynn's Last Days

Flynn, down to ninety pounds at eighty, makes his way around my property with the neighbor's old red dog walking slowly beside him, knowing the old man needs help. "Red" came up from the neighbor's yard down below and never went home. He was an old red shepherd, medium to large, who loved my yard with all the activity of kids in the pool, me at the stove, and Flynn still young enough to pat him on the head and say hello. That was when Flynn first came to live here. Now, years later, Flynn and Alex have buried Red in a shallow grave in my far back yard. When it rained, Red's fangs were visible under the wet dirt that eroded. It was a morning when I got up early to go teach, patted Red, and noticed that he had a far away look in his eye and was sitting low and hard on the rug. It was the morning of his death. When Flynn was weakened by emphysema, had to walk very slow, he'd say to Red, "Get out of my way, you're going to trip me." The old dog and Flynn were about the same age by then and each feeble, weakened by time and lifestyle. Red had cauliflower ears, and so did Flynn, so to speak, both tough old males who'd done battle, the dog by fang, Flynn by word.

It happened one evening I got a call from Flynn's doctor. He told me he had just read Flynn's blood work and found his digitalis too high. "It can cause a heart attack; rush him to Emergency." Digitalis is a derivative of strychnine. Too much can stop the heart. Just a little can keep the heart ticking. His mother (lived 97 years) and older sister (lived 94) each in turn, had to go on digitalis when their hearts slowed down and allowed fluid to accumulate in the lower legs. When it was Flynn's turn, we all laughed at Flynn's swollen ankles. Flynn had the skinniest legs of anyone, and now they were thick and full with fluid. The doctor put him on digitalis and a diuretic to drain off the fluid, which took the trace minerals with it. He got tinnitus and had to take potassium to replace the mineral that was causing a crinkling sound in his ear. Flynn, who had lived his life without doctors, had now become a guinea pig for their chemical experiments. I reminded the doctor that I'd told him not to wait a month to check Flynn's blood. I told him Flynn was so thin that he needed to check once a week just so this wouldn't happen. Flynn had no flesh on his body. One daughter came to visit and told me that she had never seen tights sag the way they do on Grandpa.

Once in Emergency, they adjusted his medications and put him in Beverly Manor, a nursing home to have the staff nurse continue to monitor him. That nurse was mad. She wondered who could have been so stupid to overdose a ninety-pound weakling. I went to visit daily. I took Flynn tapes of Kipling's poetry from the Braille Institute. Flynn was too tired to read, but he could listen. He resented the big tape recorder on his bedside table and my believing that I was helping him pass the time. He shared a room with a man from Oklahoma who had his leg amputated and played the TV too loud all day and all night. Flynn hated "Okies," as a son of the pioneers. The *Grapes of Wrath* people poured into Californa and took all the jobs and wore their cowboy hats indoors, and were loud and coarse without the proper manners of country people in the west who had established homestead ranches. Now, Flynn was one bed away. He complained about the water pipes that crackled and popped right outside his door where the plumbing and garbage was housed. "Just about the time I get to sleep there's all that noise when some jughead has to take a shower."

There was a beautiful young therapist who would come in and tell Flynn that he had to have all his food coagulated with a starchy mixture, so he wouldn't choke. Flynn usually liked pretty women, but this one he resented. She sugared him, came right up close, and checked his swallowing responses and told him his swallowing mechanism was off just a tad and he couldn't have water, milk, soup, or coffee or he'd choke, thus the thickening stuff they put in his food. He had a downright hateful look on his face each time she was appointed to check in on him. He asked once why she was doing all this to him, and when she said it was because she cared about him, he slung pure hate at her hypocrisy, saying she did it because she got paid for it, or else wouldn't be in his room at all, and to cut with the love and care talk. I remember she drew her face back as if he'd slapped her; and after that was all business with him and no sweet talk.

I kept telling Flynn I'd bring him home right then and there if he wanted to come home. He'd say, each time, that he wasn't ready yet until he could get his, uh, well, uh, under control. I guess it was the bathrooming activities. The last time he sat around the house without taking a bath, I insisted that he undress and let me turn the shower on him. That he could sit on that shower chair. He was so weak getting undressed that I had to help him, and then help him into the shower. It was embarrassing for him. And now, he must be remembering that day. And so, he never came home again. I got the call from Beverly Manor to come in, that my father's heart was beating hard and maybe he was having a heart attack, and to go right to Emergency. I did. It was one of the hottest days of the year, in June, the month of his birthday. They told me to wait just outside his cubicle where they were performing "heroic measures," which is what Flynn had chosen in his health papers. He had to ask what that meant when the doctor was filling them out, and when he was told it was to keep him alive, he said, "Yes, why wouldn't anyone want to be kept alive." When they called me in, Flynn was dead. I was mad. I told them I had wanted to stand by his bedside and hold his hand the way he had told me he'd done with his own father. If he could just have known family was there, that I was there, that we cared to be there…. The sound of my voice could have revived him more than the jump start he got with the medical equipment to his heart. And then I could have waved them away the way he did with his own dad and let him go. But, no. I entered and they said he was "gone." I held his hand just in case he was still hovering around. And then I went to call my brother, Louis, who lived forty minutes away. I sat with Flynn, felt the top of his head where they say heat escapes. By the time Louis got there, careening over the mountain pass on his motorcycle to save gas, I'd had a long talk with Flynn. He lay, red as a rooster as when alive, with no heart beat. I felt his chest, put my ear there. Both sad and curious. As Flynn said of his own father, "Before my father died, I didn't think fathers could die."

Louis called a mortician under the name of Crockett; and like a little kid, explained to the guy that we had Davy Crockett in our lineage is why. Flynn had left enough money tucked away in his bank account and in his little "shack" as he called it, at my place to pay for his funeral. Louis didn't want to look money hungry, so did not go to Flynn's bank to close the account. By the time he did, there was no money. Social Security had taken it back. Between Flynn, me, and Louis, we buried Flynn in that beautiful hilltop cemetery overlooking the whole Pacific Ocean where he had pulled us water-skiing in his racing hull and outboard motor with the propeller he'd invented for speed. The funeral was at the mortuary. Flynn had been attending Bible study at the Church of Christ. It was the church of his childhood, the church that had scared him about fire and damnation should he sin. At the last few years of his life, he feared going to Hell for what he did to me. He had men come to the house, go to his room with him and study the Bible. One man commissioned him to paint Jesus on the beach. He paid Flynn to do the painting in oil on canvas. When he came to pick up the painting, he asked where Jesus was. Flynn pointed to the palm tree in the foreground and told him he was standing behind it. No one told Flynn what and how to paint. The guy was okay with the painting after the laughter and realization of being wrong for the request.

My little sister drove down, the hippy. The Church of Christ was black in this town. When Flynn was growing up, it was all white. Now the black sat on one side and the whites sat on the other; and my sister asked if it was a segregated funeral. We all all smirked. I told her that everyone sat where they wanted, it just happened that way. The preacher was about four hundred pounds and had a hard time pronouncing Flynn's name, first and last. The family tried not to snicker at his dialect. The singers sang without music, the hymns Flynn had sung in church all his life. It was beautiful. And Flynn sang at his own funeral. I'd brought the tapes he'd made playing and singing with old Ernie when they played at senior dances and before that in Las Vegas. My brothers looked at each other when the tape had recorded Flynn's famous cigarette cough. We all filed up and took a look. Yes, indeed, that was Flynn, our father. Louis, the self-assigned poet of the family, got up and read a poem he'd written just for Flynn that included, "some people may not have liked him, had been mad at him for things he did, but…" essentially ended with *what the hell, he was my dad…* When the service was over and the men who worked there came in and everyone filed out and the hearse waited curbside out front, and they carried Flynn out in his casket (We'd asked for a simple pine box, and Crockett said they weren't cheap anymore, so we ordered an upholstered material that would decompose soon enough), I panicked a little. They were taking him. Why did I not know they would take him? I followed the hearse with the rest of the clan. We chose a plot by a lone pine tree. Flynn had sung a song about the Lonesome Pine. And so it was. I ran to the store and bought a dozen roses for everyone to throw in. It cost me twenty dollars and when they began to lower Flynn down, and all the roses were tossed in, I turned to go back to my spot with tears in my eyes. My little sister scrutinized my face and asked if I was okay. I said, no, I'd just thrown tweny dollars down a hole, and we laughed. Everyone was worried how I'd take our father's death. It was like everything else. He was eighty. I'd done all I could and now it was over. I felt that it was the way it was supposed to be. What more could I have done? I never hated him. I'd always understood he was a sick man and had to lean on someone and Valium from the disease he was born with. I'd held up under it all because I thought

I had to. And now I came out the other end of it. Everyone came out to the house. My uncle, Flynn's youngest brother, stripped down and dove in the pool. His big sister sat and ate, the way she had said she'd just come the "one time," meaning, after Flynn was dead. Funerals are fun. You get to sit and eat and visit with people you haven't seen for awhile. The only person missing is the dead.

Once Was Willow

On my side of the fence, the family willow tree blew over the March before last. It hit me hard, not the tree itself, but the fact that I couldn't save it, had overlooked its need. The trunk, where it lay on its side, could be closely inspected, as could the roots that stuck up in the air. It had starved to death, dried out and drowned in one. Mushrooms grew around it in the grass, meaning that the ground was too wet. Yet, the trunk was pithy and already dead. Dead wood still standing, roots letting go. And where was I? Flitting around the place oblivious of what was happening to my tree, a tree as old as me. When we moved in, that weeping willow was as young as we were, in its twenties; when the wind blew it over, it was in its sixties. Alex and I used to be proud of that tree, climb it as young marrieds and have sex standing in its branches. We'd hear our own woodpecker riveting into its bark after insects, just outside our bedroom window, and smile. Later, Al built a playhouse for our toddlers. When they eventually grew out of it, he built them a tree fort. Still later, our teenage son built a platform way up high in its branches, trusting the strength of those massive, fissured growths, and took his girlfriends up there, one by one, to make out up there. What did I know. In my forties, the tree in its forties, we were both battle worn and hanging on. I remember buying a package of those spears of bull piss fertilizer sticks and hammering them into the ground all around the root system, to care for my tree. To feed and nurture it. And then I never did that again, neglecting it the way I neglected myself in the line of duty and survival. I counted on the tree to take care of itself the way I did; to get by, make do, go without, eke out a living, live on a subsistence diet. It was in the ground after all. I figured it knew how to suck up what it needed.

In place of the air space it took up, where it came back

each season, hanging its greenery gracefully, like lace, waving in the spring and summer breezes, there now stands bamboo, which they say is simply giant grass. I let the tree lay dead and blown over for two years, unable to cut it up for firewood. Such a sadness to lose such a beautiful big live thing like that. I had plans: I'd hire someone to saw it into stepping stones, so to speak. I'd honor and respect it as a walkway into the far backyard. I'd create a path with its magnificent trunk, sliced into six-inch rounds and have it in the yard forever. I'd never burn it or give it away. The awareness of the tree knowing it was gone was there in its hulk lying on the grass. And still, at its topmost place, it sent out new life last spring. One sapling of a new thin branch growing as if it had a chance, like the willow post fences in Mexico growing. Willow sensing water. That woman who came down the field once to snap a switch from the tree and go willow witching on her acre across the street, looking for moisture, for a place to dig a well. The magic of willow and water, the seemingly dead trunk sprouting greenery, two years later. The insult that one year, having the chainsaw massacre take off the ends of some mighty threatening branches that could have broken and gone through my bedroom window in the next wind storm. I video taped it as if it were the first trip to the barbershop of my son. And, of course, the severing of any of its branches that dared to reach over the fence and into the yard of Alex. He gleefully performed his rights as my neighbor, to now cut and trim any growth from my yard to his. Off came those branches.

This spring, I had the trunk cut up for firewood, but it fell apart as mere dust.

A Scene I'd Like

I am standing on a cool breeze-wafted veranda on the tundra facing Mr. Kilimanjaro. I have just dressed in fresh khaki cotton shorts and shirt, the baggy men's kind. My thin tan arms and legs extend out, as strong and muscular as the black guides' who squat around the periphery waiting for the safari to begin. I have my camera ready. I am working as a freelance photo-journalist. A man sits at a wicker table and a steaming pot of coffee, in a clear pyrex pot, has been laid out with several cups. The pyrex pot sends out a bright star, reflecting the lion country glare. It is a lodge, and there are several lodgers not yet seen. Perhaps interesting or mysterious strangers. The man looks up at me as I step onto the veranda in my freshly starched and ironed army-colored cottons. I see that he admires me. His eyes are blue as the sky beyond him and I see that he is vulnerable to everything. That he is a man of feeling but control; he smiles as I near the table.... The coffee is perfect: strong, like espresso and the aroma fills my nostrils as I pour pure thick white cream into my fresh steaming porcelain cup. The cream sinks and curls and I let it seek its own place without stirring it. I am thin, so flat and thin. Everything I am is present. All my flesh is present. There is nothing from the past. No deposits of fat or bulkage that I accumulated, even a week before. What I am is *now*. I need only to carry a toothbrush. I eat and immediately use up what I eat. I store nothing. In an emergency I would be in trouble, except for what I know. My spirit would keep my thin empty body going until there was food again. I gaze at the plains and see myself surviving there. I sip the coffee while his blue eyes watch me. I warm him. My presence is exquisite to him. There is no one else who could be more perfect for the moment for him but me. If Jackie O. appeared, I would still be exquisite. I would not fade in the light of a jet setter. I am here, a photographer, a writer, an understander of nature, animals, men, myself. He sees my self-possession, he watches my simple pleasure over Hemingway-perfect coffee....

The sheets are still tossed and open and disheveled in my bed on the west wing from love making. He took a long time and every moment was magnified like music from an electric piano. His leanness against mine. His male torso with crisp lemon-scented hairs against my smooth hairless almond-scented femaleness. There was no effort. Our knee-caps seeking safe places among the tangle of our legs.... And afterward, lying back, pushing the pillows under our heads watching the orangy curtains move with the warm breeze.... Dampness inside my thigh drying in the African air, as we lie back and measure our fingers together to compare the size of our hands. Mine always being as big as his. A special pride I take. Loving the hairs on the back of his tan outdoors hands. His square man's fingernails. Pink with blood. We are not in love. We simply love being together right now.

We knew each other because we are alike. We have been on earth the same length of time or close to it and have carried about and wanted the same thing: to tread lightly and respect things. To let things be. And to observe. Not to go tramping through making changes or knowing answers, but to tread softly and be curious. Asking what is this thing called *life*? And because of being alike that way, we knew each other when we met on the boat coming up the river to here, glancing eyes catching glimpses over the chug of the old engines, and the smell of diesel fuel. He stood watching me. And then he took courage and approached. He made me laugh. It was over an alligator. We both laughed. A real laugh, that ended in a sad sigh. Ah, yes. There it all is: we are all that alligator. We knew. There was no getting acquainted. We had always been acquainted. We're here in Africa, travelling upstream in this old boat, because we were acquainted. We're searching for the same thing at the same time and place. Both blue-eyed and recent fleshed, and knowing the same thing about the alligator.

It's the smell of the freshly starched and ironed cotton.

The way the sleeves and pant legs fit so loose around my thin tan arms and legs. The scent of wicker, and the blast of glare beyond the shade of the veranda of the lion inhabited plains. The dryness of the air. The pending threat of heat. It is early. The air is still light. It is not bearing down. The foreboding of how hot it is going to be when we are all out there this afternoon working, wearing our hard army-colored safari hats, contrasts with the cool sweatlessness of the early morning veranda.

I am at peace. I have arrived. I am here, a place I pictured all my life. Lions are out there. I am here to do honorable work to record lions faces on film. To present these faces to school children. To observe, capture, pass on what I've found out. I am not here on a less honorable venture. I am not depraved. I am not a nymphomaniac. I am an infomaniac. I am not an alcoholic. I an not here because a man is paying for me. I have earned my own way by taking pictures at home and working hard. I am not full of cancer. I am light and clean and healthy like a brand new clean pullet chicken. All by conscious effort. And because of these things there is a beautiful man's face across the table from me. Lions beyond him, perfect coffee on the table, and a well-supplied photographic unit on the floor beside me. Various lenses, filters, rolls of film in black tight, light-protected cartridges. My life has come together, even after all the chances I took dashing out on emotional binges, trying to find what I needed in the wrong (or strange) places before I understood what it was I wanted.... Notebooks, filled with my handwriting. Notes on cat behavior. Cats of all kinds. From domestic, man-made varieties without fur or tails, fangs or claws. To the best nature can offer: a testicled, maned, never-been-touched-by-man male beast, now sunning himself in his pride beyond those bushes which float on the horizon heat. Out there, in a mirage. There, because he is the biggest and strongest and made it. No help from science or the 20th century. This is my enlightenment to kids. This malleable cat material in all forms. My favorite photo being a house-trained ocelot sniffing the head of a mountain lion rug...thrown over the back of a couch. In the classroom

I would stimulate children's imaginations with this, one of many antithesis. The tangle we make of the material we have on earth to work with. Always trying to make the lion lay down with the lamb and getting a kick out of it. Mixing and matching ingredients. My daughter's childhood experiment once being to make the pet sparrow land on the cat. And I taking a picture of it, trying to catch that idea.

We make conversation over breakfast. There is a pair of binoculars beside his cup and saucer. He is a biologist. His mind has been on such pure and decent subjects as the flora and fauna Every word now, floats into the perfumed air and works as an emollient between us. After love-making, then a nice breakfast. A purple-black guide comes with a tray steaming with scrambled African peahen eggs, boar (or is it slices of dik-dik), rough-grained toast, thick jam with apricot peels still in it, or a strawberry stem, ice cold squares of goat butter. The guide wears a white twist of rag around his long lean loins and I turn and look at his beautiful animal hindquarters. The muscles of his buttocks, face level as I sit and he is so long-legged, move like currents on the thick alligator infested river. Above us, a black soaring bird twists and turns as he serves the perfect food. An arousal goes through my groin as I envision his glistening purple-black, slick male part between my lips. The tight and hairy scrotum as he is ready to ejaculate in waves and waves of muscular spasms. The frothy whiteness of his sperm. I could use it as cream in my second cup of coffee. The man with the blue eyes knows what I am thinking. He smiles. His teeth are white, not perfectly straight, but healthy. He has a very clean and fresh mouth, His tongue us as pink as a baby's. One of my pubic hairs is probably lodged at the back of his throat and he is washing it down with the freshly squeezed orange juice (or is it kumquat juice).

As we eat, the other lodgers appear. They are a long and lanky woman with a hank of hair tied back by a zebra striped rag. And an Esquire man. She is older but raw-boned and attractive because of the sunbaked quality about her. She appears to be game for anything, and now finds herself here, in jodhpurs and boots. I like her on sight and also am a bit afraid of her. She is like me. A hungry woman prowling, and there is room for only one restless female in the house. She eyes me and I eye her. Her man eyes me too, and his eyes linger. I am his wife, but younger.... He likes my type.

Married it. Then he eyes the man I am with, knowing what he is getting. Envious. This eyeing goes on all behind what we do. We nod. They nod, They take a table. The man is ruddy-faced, of course. With white hair that has slipped back from his forehead. The kind who takes a stiff whiskey when he comes in from a day on the trail. Looks like a hunter, but it can't be so. This is a reserve. The animals here cannot be killed. They are served champagne in sparkling goblets. He mops his forehead. I look at his earlobe to see if it has a line across it. A fold on the earlobe means heart attack, I remember reading. They make familiar sounds to eachother, so used to places like this, good service, champagne with Eggs Benedict. Wealth exudes from their overheated pores. She fans herself with the linen napkin and asks for the overhead fan to be turned on. A black two-bladed propeller slices silently through the ceilinged air. An arid tsetse fly, or is it a long-waisted male mosquito lands on the old man's damp and shiny forehead. He brushes it away, lifting a solid furred arm from his grey barrel chest, rustling a silk hand-painted sport shirt. The movement is done with effort and confusion. It is over a need to protect himself here, in these safe quarters. We are not out there yet. His blue eyes narrow down as he gazes beyond his wife, who sits with her back to the plains. The glare. The threat of pending heat. The blast of glare from the furnace beyond the veranda. And his high blood pressure. This could be his last trek, I am thinking. I see her ordering the guides to carry him back. His large round rib cage higher than any part of his old carcass as he lies on the canvas stretcher. An old specimen. A dying breed. The old American Safari hunter almost extinct. Her precise instruction in having his body shipped back to the U.S. Probably Chicago or Ohio. He has that air of a midwestern adventurer. An old newspaperman. And she is his third wife. In his study back home, trophies line the panelled walls, hardwood teak floors, table tops. The enrichment of his life from my imagination (and love of Hemingway) draws me to him. His tough pink hide with the bristled white hair. An old boar. With tusks. A long time away from being a milk drinker. His flesh soused with booze. Booze calming him down or keying him up. Booze being his medium. They are obviously a couple of alcoholics. And their money allows them this respectable style. They choose exotic settings in which to drink. They go from the South of France to the plains of Mt. Kilimanjaro to perhaps Southern California. Wherever it appears people are taking a vacation from the important matters in their lives: writing novels, selling properties, owning companies, painting famous canvases. I cannot guess what these two are vacationing away from. What are they resting from. The man with the blue eyes across the table from me has turned around to survey the plains. I gaze at his shoulders and the twist they make beneath his cotton shirt.

Already dampness has appeared at the armpits. When he turns I see that his pupils are pinpoints from gazing at the fluid horizon. The guide clears the table, pours a last cup of coffee for us. Four-wheel-drive Over-Rover jeeps are parked in the shade under a banyan tree which also harbors buzzards. When he turns his eyes back to me I see that the work he has to do is on his mind. The foliage. He is gathering specimens. There is a certain hybrid growth. A 1991 version of an age-old plant that has evolved because of insecticides and the imbalance of herbivore population. He has explained it briefly and I saw the way his lips moved and hands gestured, and the way he was involved with his subject. I saw his dedication, his excitement. The reason he was so far away from home. I missed the content altogether, fascinated over his fascination.

It is time now. To go. We must be on with what we are here for. I gather my camera equipment. Our movements are cues to the movement of black bodies resting on the grounds, in the shade. One guide approaches a jeep. We part with a simple nod. A smile. Distracted. Our work calls. The interlude is over.

Postscript

The African safari happens after I recover from ovarian cancer at age 56 (1995). Chemo—I lose my hair. Mama breaks her hip; her husband dies. I bring her to my home and take care of her for ten years, where she spends that last decade in a wheelchair.

It is 1997. Flynn died in 1992 of nothing at all, just old age, the way they do in that family. He was 80 and only 90 pounds. He lived eleven years under my roof with both heaters on, keeping his bones warm even in warm weather. All he predicted came to pass. I got old!

At 60, I go with the San Diego Zoo with a vanful of teachers to Nairobi, Kenya and Tanzania, and bounce along dirt roads in "the bush" for a month. It's not like Hemingway at all. The females inside the van are catty and not as well-mannered as the lionesses out there that we view, who hunt while the great maned males wait for her to bring them their dinner. What else is new!